GHOSTS ON AN ALIEN WIND

Moe Lane

Flying Koala Publishers

Cover design by: Pixel Studios
Cover art by: Jude Stopford
Library of Congress Control Number: 2018675309
Printed in the United States of America

To everyone who, when finding the ominous-looking door, didn't just turn around and leave well enough alone like any sensible person would.

CHAPTER ONE

The Golden Dawn

118-G-002
Tomb Worlds
2368 AD

I punched my alien-built cargo hauler down through the upper edge of One-Eighteen's atmosphere, the keening of ghosts sharp-tongued in my ears.

They told me in training the haulers from this planet were stolid beasts, good and reliable, but no racers. They also told me the keening was just feedback from One-Eighteen's unique combination of atmosphere and magnetosphere. *That sound doesn't mean anything*, my first instructor kept telling me. *Don't freak out when it gets into your head. It won't be the worst thing you ever hear in the Tomb Worlds.*

The thought made me laugh as I spotted a hole in the sky, down and to the right, and just the right size and shape for a barrel dive. Why would I *want* it out of my head? It was as perfect as the rest of this planet!

I fed thrust hard as I hit the hole, flicking my hauler sideways just enough to miss the edge of free-drifting nanites that was all that was left of the old planetary traffic network. The Earth-tech computer blinked twice at how close I had cut it, but I ignored that as much as I did its regular old speed warning. Whoever programmed it must have been from one of the Great Powers of Earth. Colonists have a much better idea of what 'too fast' means.

Fortunately, I didn't have human passengers on this run, and nothing less fragile than fabricator feedstock, so I could really cut loose for the next part. Controlled, powered descents from orbit are *supposed* to take a nice, solid, boring ten minutes. It's a safe number! It prevents needless holes in the ground! I approve of it.

For other people.

I let myself stare at the globe of writhing, multi-colored tubes for a whole two seconds, looking for the best path down to thicker atmosphere. My hands and feet reacted before my conscious brain, applying thrust and spin to follow a route my eyes could barely perceive. I trusted them, though. When I fly, I leave my self-doubt on the ground.

For forty glorious seconds, the hauler was pointed nose-to-the-ground and accelerating, merrily spinning around its horizontal axis like a demented supersonic top. My stomach was grateful that the hauler's gravity control was working as perfectly as ever. If I had ever tried to do this in a pre-Contact reaction drive vehicle, I would have ended up being toast. A thin layer of *crispy* toast, at the bottom of an impact crater.

But I was flying a magnificent piece of alien technology that responded like a fever dream, not an atmosphere-only three hundred year old relic. I took the hauler vertical at ten thousand feet and used up all my sonic booms on the empty, endless forests below. Luxor Base wouldn't thank me for rattling their windows. Even if we *do* build sturdy buildings, out here in the Tomb Worlds.

The head of Supply did give me a call, mind you. A somewhat pained one. "Hey, Pam! You're early."

"'Course I am, Nur," I told him. "No passengers from the orbitals, remember? Time is money, right? Isn't that what X-Hum always says?"

"No, Pam. They say 'please don't die. We spent a lot of money training you.'"

I considered the statement. "It's not punchy enough. Tell Maki to workshop it some more."

"Ha. Ha. Were you trying to break your reentry record? Because you did, by two seconds."

"Damn. I was hoping for three. Look, Nur, take it up with the Chief Pilot if it's a formal issue."

"I *am* taking it up with the Chief Pilot, Pam."

I beamed, forgetting that he couldn't see me (I keep Amalgamation-made video feeds turned *off* in the hauler). "So you are. I'll take it under advisement, then. Am I cleared to come in?"

"Yeah." Nur paused. "Hand off the post-flight checklist when you land, Pam. Go find Greg instead, and right away. It's *important.*"

That wasn't normal. "Why? What's up?"

Nur was quiet for a second. "Can't say. It's not something for comms. Signing off now." I sighed as I let the automatic systems start taking over the landing approach. There was clearly some kind of bull hockey going on, as some of my Jeffersonian grandparents probably didn't really say. It had been such a great day for flying, too.

Every day is a great day for flying on One-Eighteen.

CHAPTER TWO
Life Among the Ruins

The keening faded to a, heh, ghost of its usual light, almost-musical trill as I did my approach. I didn't mind it going, just like I didn't mind hearing it in the first place. I never have. — although my trainers had gone on and on about how I shouldn't let it get to me. I was almost disappointed on my first orbital flight when it turned out to *not* be a big deal, after all. Although my subordinate pilots disagree.

The effect wasn't regular. I almost never heard it at all at sea level, although I sometimes *imagined* that I did (the good kind of imagining, though. Not the kind that gets you emergency therapy). The keening gets clearer the less atmosphere there is, and it's best at the apex of a suborbital hop. A lot of hauler pilots filtered out the ghosts, but I didn't. The keening didn't do *me* any harm,; and gave me many chances to dance my way through the atmosphere of a dead world.

Funny, though: One-Eighteen doesn't *look* dead. Some of the Tomb Worlds live up to the name, but not this one. From up in orbit, the planet is blue, green, and lovely. It reminds me of Jefferson, or the pictures I've seen of Earth.

Well, One-Eighteen looks like home or Earth during the day. At night, the only lights you'd see on the ground were the ones humans brought with us, or turned back on.

The joyful trill the One-Eighteeners used for a beep came from the console, letting me know the hauler was beginning its final automated descent to Luxor Base. I shrugged off my reverie and started the landing checklist. Apogee was the proper place for woolgathering (that stuff comes from sheep, in case you were wondering). The ghosts faded from keening to indistinct hissing as the hauler descended, but that was fine. I'd rather keep track of what my vessel was doing, instead of ghosts on an alien wind.

Although I didn't have to, honestly. The aliens who had made this hauler really and truly designed it to fly itself all the way up into orbit, and then safely back down again. Which was more useful than you'd expect, seeing as how something had shown up one day and scythed the Galaxy clean of sapient life.

Well. Except for humanity. Lucky us.

Luxor Base

The nice thing about flying to Luxor Base is that you almost didn't have to navigate at all. All you had to do was spot the statues, and aim for a spot between them. You barely needed the homing beacon, although I made sure I was properly locked in. You always need to take extra precautions on dead worlds — particularly when they're also murder scenes.

The statues I was aiming for were seven hundred feet high and carved out of the local stone: one man and one woman, facing each other, each with one hand triumphantly raised to the sky, and the other pointing to the ground. I do mean 'man and woman,' too. Some of the species we've managed to exhume out here don't look anything like us, but the One-Eighteeners were pretty damned close. If you squinted, you could almost believe that they were odd-looking humans.

Or maybe not. *Something* had carved deep furrows into the faces of the statues, making it impossible to tell what their features were originally like. We know almost nothing about whatever it was that turned the Amalgamation into the Tomb Worlds, but judging from the rubble, we're pretty sure it hated every sapient creature in it with a monomaniacal passion. Now here *we* were, camping in the ruins, all the while wondering whether one day it'll be *our* turn.

Wonderful thoughts, I know. People in the Tomb Worlds try

not to think about them. And we *really* try not to think about how we're not thinking about them.

The daily rain had started by the time the hauler touched down on the (human-made) landing pad. At first I mistook the sound for the fuzz that had been coming from my speakers — but when I heard the drumming on the roof, I knew it was definitely rain. The first time it happened, I remember being surprised, since I had gotten it into my head that the weather would be somehow different on the Tomb Worlds. But water on the roof sounded just the same on 118-G-002 as it did back on Jefferson. I wonder if it sounds the same on Earth, too.

Probably.

Other stuff about this planet was similar, or at least similar enough. It's always a crapshoot when it comes to salvaged alien equipment, but on 118-G-002 we had lucked out. The control configurations on the hauler were within human norms — and not just the big stuff, like, "can I reach all the buttons?" The color scheme made sense to human eyes, and the layout was designed for humanoids with binocular vision and thumbed hands. I didn't even have to retrofit a cushion for my butt, which is almost always standard operating procedure when it comes to adapting alien equipment for human use. The natives who lived here and made this hauler were a lot like us, and not just in general appearance. It's a real shame I'll never meet one.

A look through the hauler 'windows' (they're not, but they're not mere video monitors, either) revealed how the pad was remarkably free of gear and pallets. Instead there were people rushing around urgently. I didn't let that distract me. Contragrav thrusters might be easier to maneuver than Earthtech turbofans, but you still don't casually sling around a forty-ton flying brick. I decided that I'd be told about the problem after I powered down. After all, if the problem was big enough, I'd have been told already *not* to land.

The other nice thing about contragrav is the way it makes landings whisper-quiet. You don't feel the impact because there isn't one. The energy field merges with planetary gravity and puts you both in instant equilibrium. The techies back home on Jefferson (Earth, too, I guess) are busy reverse-engineering the thrusters so that we can make our own. It'll be nice when they finally figure it all out, but they've been trying for the last eighty years, so we'll be salvaging Amalgamation tech for just a *little* while longer.

The post-flight checklist for Amalgamation vehicles is likewise a masterpiece of elegant efficiency which I'd love for some human cyberneticist to decipher. It *shouldn't* work, and yet it does. My rule of thumb for that, and most other paradoxes of Amalgamation tech? I didn't try not to think about it, because I *hate* headaches. The important thing was I was out of the hauler in a minute and a half, which meant I could find out what was going on.

The drumming picked up as I popped the hatch. It rains a lot at Luxor Base, but it's pretty regular, too. If I had been another thirty minutes, it would have been pouring — and if I had somehow managed to be late for a whole hour, the storm would be over. There are some parts of the planet where the climate isn't this accommodating, but the old weather programming works just fine in this area, which is why the corp had put its main settlement and offices here when we started developing One-Eighteen. That and the weather, which is shirtsleeves all year around. When you have an entire empty planet to choose from, why not settle in the nicest parts?

Oh, and it's a quiet place, too, despite the statues and the ruins. Nobody gets too many nightmares. People don't go space-happy at the drop of a hat here, either. With perks like that, I'd have been fine with being stationed at the planet's north pole.

I was met at the hatch by Greg, which was both not usual, and unwelcome. Not *personally* unwelcome, you understand. Greg was a good guy. But when the project head shows up for an in-person talk, it's rarely for anything minor. He barely waited for me to clear the hauler before starting up: "Pam, how quickly can you do a turnaround?"

That stopped me up short. "Is this a trick question?" I said. "Twelve hours, as per the checklist. Four hours, if you want to use a fresh pilot." That's how long it takes to empty out and refill an Amalgamation hauler's cargo space (obviously, we don't have to ever refuel the hauler, like you do with Earthtech). "Or has there been a disaster?"

"Oh, you could say that," Greg replied as he waved over a *lot* more unloaders than usual. "We got a report from the deep space beacon. A Terran-registry ship just popped in-system. We've got three hours before they're within scanning range of the planet."

"Oh, Hell," I said. So much for my mandated downtime. If somebody from Earth was snooping around, it was time for us to go innocuous. "Which agency? SCI?"

Greg shook his head. "Worse. Council."

Double Hell. You can deal with the Survey/Colonization Initiative, or at least cut them in. The only exception would have been if they had changed their mind about planting a gray colony here, and if that happened we'd be warned about that, well ahead of time. But the Adjudication Council folks? Well, let me put it this way: it takes a lot of *intelligent* and *functional* fanaticism to enforce the will of Earth's Great Powers, this far out into the Tomb Worlds. "When's the crisis meeting?" I asked.

"An hour and a half from now," he replied. "I think you should get a nap in before then."

A 'nap,' he said. Hah. More like a nightmare you can't remember afterward.

Medical had the deepsleeper all ready for me, and the arm and leg restraints on the bed already extended. I peeled off my jumpsuit, but left on the orbital diaper. No reason why I should use a fresh one just for this. I let the tech put in the bite guard and adjust the safety mittens, though. If I put on the protective equipment myself, they'd just fuss with them anyway.

I was still puckering my mouth at the medicinal grape

flavoring of the bite guard when they placed the gunmetal-and-carmine deepsleeper on my chest — and my brain shut off for the next hour. Well, not really. What happened next was an hour of *something* so horrible, my brain just flat-out refuses to process it. It also refused to *remember* it, which is the only reason we can use deepsleepers.

Isn't technology grand? A corporate research archeology team found a working deepsleeper about seven years ago on a fun little Yellow-class hellhole called 172-F-004. I'd say the name the inhabitants used, but I don't have a watermelon and a power saw handy. We're pretty sure it wasn't *designed* to be a sleep replacer, but that's what it seems to do to our heads. One hour is worth ten ordinary hours' worth of sleep, with no brain cancer! No long-term effects, either. In fact, it's statistically been shown to tamp down on users going space-happy. So it's a great gadget, as long as you don't mind all the muffled agonizing screaming and full-body spasms. But then, that's why they invented soundproofing and titanium restraints.

I got through it fine. People always do.

It was a small meeting, even for an operation in the Tomb Worlds. Too small for the room, really. We mostly used Terran-made prefabs for our living and working spaces, but one of the old ruins was in pretty good shape, and somehow able to maintain a perfect temperature and humidity without a visible power source. It *also* had a complete roof, so we did a lot of meetings there.

So, there was me, Greg wearing his 'project head' hat instead of the 'merchant adventurer' one, and Makena Adesina, representing our employer XHum. I was most worried for Maki. If the Council jackwagons came down on anybody for anything, it'd be somebody from the corp. Oh, and there was The Process on speaker, but it wasn't there to do anything except give us numbers, if and when we needed them. The Process doesn't interfere with human stuff unless we ask it to.

Greg didn't waste time. "All right. The Council's going to be here in less than two hours. The good news is, everything we want to hide we can get into a single hauler, in one go. The bad news is, we can't fly the stuff to wherever and get the hauler back without the Council ship tracking the trip. We need an excuse for the return jaunt."

"What are our options?" asked Maki. "No, wait, never mind. Just tell me the option you want to use. The clock's blinking."

"Pam takes the shuttle to Site Steady," Greg immediately replied. "It's one of the official salvage operations, so it's got those underground ruins, perfect for hiding things. You can make that in two hours, right, Pam?"

I stopped probing my mouth with my tongue. I know that you don't get tooth trauma from deepsleeping when you use a bite mask, but I'm kind of paranoid about it anyway. "No," I told him. "I can make it in one. Can they get everything out of sight, though?"

Greg shook his head. "I'm not worried about that, Pam. By the time the Council gets around to looking at Site Steady, they'll just see a bunch of crates moving around."

"That's fair," I agreed. "How are we explaining the trip back for the manifests? Passenger transfers?"

"Better than that. It'll be a morale run. A school of not-cows started wandering by a few days ago. I'm getting the site steward there to go yank off some flanks and quick-freeze 'em. We'll bring them back on the shuttle, nice and open."

"Fine by me. Speaking of manifests, what's on the trip up?" I asked. "Is any of the stuff energetic, or volatile?" Some Amalgamation tech gets a little weird when you don't handle it right. And we don't have all the instruction manuals.

Greg looked over his notes. "Nah. These are all cultural geegaws. Stone figurines, gemmed statues, jewelry. The usual junk they sell to collectors. Nothing that's gonna blow up, or start shooting off rays."

"Okay. We're not redlining the weight allowance, right?" After he shook his head, I thought over the times and approaches in my head. I also took note how Greg was assuming we'd go with this. Still: "...Yeah. It's doable. But there aren't as many overlaps this week as I'd like in the old planetary traffic network."

"That's why we had you go into deepsleep, Pam," Maki said. She even sounded sincerely apologetic about it. Mind you, the corp doesn't ask for us to use the damned things often, I guess so that we'll take the request seriously when they do. "You can find overlaps where other people would see nothing but endless traffic violations. Anybody else would take twice as long."

"Keep that in mind when you're doing end-of-mission bonuses." I stood up. "And I get first crack at the BBQ sauce."

Up, up and away! And not much 'hurry up and wait,' this time around. It was more like, 'Hurry up, but don't be stupid about it.' I was off the pad and in the air in fifteen.

The air was even emptier than normal, which isn't hard when you can be on a first-name basis with every shuttle pilot on the planet, and they all call you 'Boss.' I hear that on Earth they have lots of trouble with air traffic control. All those shuttles, all those Great Power borders, and all those places on the way that don't take lightly to constant sonic booms. It sounded horribly complicated to me, back when I was just a local girl from Jefferson — but after six months here on One-Eighteen, it feels like it'd be barely worse than driving a spaceport shuttle bus around.

Because this next part was going to be *tricky*. I fired up the Terran-made portcomp once I was in the air, and could get a read on all the various indigenous electronic signals still broadcasting out there. Within a moment I had a real-time, green, yellow, and red map showing me where local traffic laws still applied on my route. And for how long, which was just as important.

Look, you all know the situation — humanity's alone, all the alien species of the Amalgamation who were supposed to mentor us into proper galactic citizens got murdered six hundred years ago, nobody knows why, blah blah blah. And sure, that's all really scary. But it's the *second-order* stuff that's alarming. Like when you're flying an alien cargo shuttle, using the remains of an alien planetary transport system; it's a lot harder to ignore how scary the universe is when you're staring a corpse in the face.

You see, the good people (aliens are people, I figure) of One-Eighteen had one hell of a transportation network. In the safe 'red' zones where the system's working right, it's a dream to fly, with predictive telemetry so good you barely have to move the flight stick; and it can handle just about any problem the planet throws at you.

Unfortunately, where the system is critically damaged (the yellow zones), it defaults to assuming you're committing traffic violations just from breathing heavily. Too many of those fake positives, and the network grounds your hauler for a while until you calm down, or something. That can play hell with your shipping schedule, and the only way most people avoid it is by always staying in the no-coverage 'green' zones — which move around. Did I mention that? Yeah, the nanoswarms that really make up the network drift around a lot in the atmosphere, so the coverage shifts. Anyway, if you're careful, and you sacrifice speed for certainty, you can stay in the green.

Or you can do what I do, which is to surf through the various overlapping red and green zones just fast enough to never hit the yellow. To quote somebody or other: I don't recommend it, mind, but it *can* be done. Or at least, *I* can do it. Which is why I had just spent an hour in amnesiac agony, just to be properly fresh for the experience.

I may sound a little blasé on the subject of wind-dancing. Like I'm romanticizing something that's really just a matter of reading overlapping displays and careful adjustments. People talk up their boring jobs all the time, right? Fair enough. Lemme give you an idea of what it's like, from my perspective:

The original inhabitants of One-Eighteen didn't use a driver's wheel, or a single flight stick. They liked to use all four limbs to fly,each hand controlling a separate squeezable trackball, while pushing various buttons with their feet. That includes a few things that *we'd* put on a dashboard, like engine boosters or the emergency air evacuation switch. We've been able to put in a regular, Terran-style flight stick for regular use, and it works fine — for, again, regular use. If you want to get *creative*, you need to use the original configuration. Most people try it once, and then stop trying to push the envelope.

I'm not most people. They had to peel me out of the seat, the first time I flew an Amalgamation hauler.

Yeah, it's complicated to fly one of these things. Left hand does thrust, right hand does direction. Left foot boosts or hard brakes, depending, and right foot stays where it is at all times, because all of the scary buttons are underneath that one. The three-dimensional display was in front of me as I squinted to see the thick blobs of red as they bubble and snake through a lattice of green, which was itself floating on a lake of yellow. It's been proven that there's no coherent logic to it, but I for one can still see patterns to how the blobs spawn, and where they go. And if I time it just right, I can get the blobs to react to me, then kind of... *drag them along.*

One reason why I was Chief Pilot was that the other on-planet pilots hated wind-dancing, and none of them were more than competent at it. To be fair to them, the skill wasn't easy to learn, and I spent my first couple of months getting tagged a lot by the planetary transport network. But I figured it out. You have to listen, as much as you see. The keening helps a lot, there.

So does not getting airsick easily, because while these haulers can handle the stress of being bounced around in the air they damn sure weren't designed for it, and neither was the contragrav. I wasn't going to black out, like fighter pilots before the Consolidation Wars used to do; but I needed the safety harness to keep me in my seat. I also needed another bite guard, because my jaw was the only joint in my body that my flight suit couldn't properly stabilize.

At least I didn't have to wear earplugs, since I was by myself. A *lot* of people scream when they wind-dance with me. Something about how corkscrewing straight down ten thousand feet in five seconds, followed by a 90 degree course change, and then a few more equally random flying maneuvers, can be alarming.

I pretty much had to take their word for it, because *I* always thought it was fun. I imagine that if dragons ever had existed, they'd feel like I did when I flew my graceful patterns of speed through the sky. I felt complete up there, dancing with the planet, the sun, and all the stars in the sky.

I miss it.

If this was an adventure story, I would have gotten in the middle of a monster storm on my way to Site Steady, had to crash-land the shuttle, and ended up stuck in the middle of an alien forest with a cargo full of 'valuable cultural artifacts' that XHum didn't want to pay onerous import taxes on. Oh, and there'd be a least one tense encounter with the vicious native life that One-Eighteen doesn't actually have. Not that the rest of the Amalgamation had many dangerous critters, either. The accessible parts of the Tomb Worlds are pure hell for xenozoologists who don't specialize in post-apocalyptic ecology.

Anyway, I *wish* I had gone through that sort of adventure! It would have been a lot easier on all of us. Hell, I think that those artifacts are still in the same underground storage cave we eventually put them in. I'd tell you to go look for them, if I was a cruel woman. Instead, because this is real life — Christ help us all — the flight to Site Steady went off without a hitch. I 'threaded the red' all nice and easy all the way to the base, shaving off ten minutes of the 'official' optimum time.

I'm not what you call a heavy corpohead. I mean, it's not like I know every verse of the XHum anthem. But when we're good, we're *really* good. We had a sharp team on One-Eighteen, too. The unloading crew was pulling cargo almost before the shuttle was locked down, so I barely had to do any of the mid-run paperwork myself. I even had time for a wipedown and a real nap while they manhandled the not-cow carcasses aboard. Best of all, they managed to make it all look normal, even routine. Nothing left out of place, to catch the intolerant gaze of a Council eye-in-the-sky busybody. I was in the air, halfway back, and carrying a load of perfectly-licit not-cow flanks (and a couple of passengers) when the Council ship landed.

I played it just as safe on the way back. *Nothing to see here, folks.* No little games with the traffic network, either. I flew the hauler steady and true, and never drew outside the lines. Well, maybe once. Or twice. It would look weird if I *didn't* shave off a little time where I could. But I kept my dancing shoes off and maintained a calm environment in the cabin. This was a time to let the automated systems do all the work. It was kind of restful, except when I was twitching a little, on account of being a bit *too* relieved about getting the tricky part of the job done. You could almost sleep on a milk run, not that I was ever tempted to; but it was usually safe to listen to music, or do some light reading.

Or talk to a passenger, which was an option I had this time. Syah was a third-generation colonist, like me, only he was from Bolivar. He was three months in on a standard five-year, and back from doing a circuit of all the outlying bases on One-Eighteen. He had spent more effort than he needed to wrangle the copilot seat for the trip (the other passenger had promptly strapped herself into her seat, popped a lotus, and dozed off).

I was trying to figure out whether he was more interested in flying, or in *me*. Not that I minded, either way. Syah was no stage actor, but he had comfortable good looks, the kind that made you circle back for a proper once-over. He also hadn't resentfully gritted his teeth or sneered after hearing my Jeffersonian drawl, either. If he was the sort of man who found pilots glamorous, well, I saw no reason why I should disabuse him of that notion.

Syah strapped himself in with only a little fumbling. He also had an idea about what readouts to look at. "You have any flight time?" I asked him. I knew he didn't have a pilot ticket, because if he did, he would have told me, right off. That's standard procedure for the Tomb Worlds. There were only ten thousand, three hundred and seventeen humans on 118-G-002 as of that morning, not counting whoever was on the Council ship. Out here, if you have a relevant skill for the situation at hand, you let people know.

"Not really, sorry," he told me with a smile that I liked. "Took some simulator electives in corp school, played *Shuttle Pilot* a lot when I was a kid. I probably could manually land this thing, but it wouldn't be pretty."

"Too bad," I said, while experimenting with a little stretch. He was polite about noticing, but I could tell I had his attention. "But if you want to get some training in, we do emergency qualification classes back at the main base. The more people who know how to drive these babies, the happier we all are." Which was true, and Syah had the right physique for shuttle jockeying. He was a little on the short side, but in real good shape. The jet-black hair and warm brown eyes weren't as necessary for the program, but again, I wasn't complaining.

"I might, if it's up to me, Pam." I had gotten past 'Chief Pilot Tanaka' right away. "But I'm back at the main base for work. I may not have evenings free. Or lunch breaks."

"What?" I replied, smartly. "You're gonna be on actual overtime?" You don't have to hold a gun to the head of an XHum supervisor before she'll let you log some extra hours, but the corp gets antsy about people on the Tomb Worlds getting overworked. All work and no play sometimes ends badly for everybody concerned.

"'Fraid so. There's a problem with the planetary net interface. Oh, nothing dangerous!" he went on, seeing my sudden look of displeased surprise. "There's just some ongoing interference in the information protocols, and they called me in to try to fix it on-site. I figure it's a hardware problem, I just *know* me and the local team will end up crawling through the interface sites and looking for bum wires."

"Sounds like fun. Any way around it?"

"Sure. We could ignore the problem, hope it doesn't get worse than just a little static in the feed. If it wasn't for the Council ship showing up, we'd probably *do* that, at least for a couple of months. But since they're here, time to look all proactive and stuff." He sighed. "Well, at least I get to play with tools at last. I haven't been on-planet long enough to get assigned anything except make-work."

"Oh, so you're good with your hands, are you?" I added a smile, just in case he needed more of a hint.

He didn't need it. "I've had no complaints," Syah said with a slow smile of his own. "But practice makes perfect."

CHAPTER THREE

Keeping Planetary Hours

Syah and I got as far as exchanging numbers by the time we landed. Alas, at that point the Council ship had landed at the main port facility, so everything had to be by the book. Big Sibling was watching us, although it was from all the way over *there*.

Big Sibling was also being *cranky* about it, which wasn't the smartest move on their part. I got momentarily ticked at Greg's terse observation over the comlink to *follow all procedures this time, Pilot Tanaka!* Then I understood what he was doing, and then proceeded to stretch out the post-flight checklist until I got bored. The Council representatives couldn't complain about how *meticulous* we were, right? The Great Powers of Earth *loved* making sure everything done by us benighted colonials was just so. By the time I got to the meeting, the Council representative could be certain that I had taken quite a lot of *extra care*.

I swear, there's something about the Adjudication Council that likes to hire tall bastards. This one was tall, and thin, and I suspect bald under a half-helmet that covered the eyes. The lower half of his face was the only part of his body that wasn't covered up, and that was so heavily space-tanned I couldn't guess where he originally from. I wondered briefly why he didn't wear a full face mask. Many Adjudicators do.

From his expression, I suspected he wasn't enthusiastic about my zeal. "If you are Chief Pilot Pamela Tanaka, you are late," he noted, after I moseyed my way in and took a seat at the same conference table I had been at, hours ago. I normally don't (mosey, that is), but I was feeling very Jeffersonian at the moment.

I let the Jeffersonian come out in my speech, too. "Sure am, both ways! But you can just go ahead and call me 'Pammie!' Everybody else does." I ignored the suddenly blank looks from Greg and Maki, and pushed on. "And how are you doing today, neighbor?"

He gave me the patented 'Council Adjudicator' death glare. "I am aware what 'neighbor' means in Jeffersonian pidgin, Chief Pilot Tanaka."

"Good," I said in a much more normal voice. "Shame you aren't aware that you're not my truant officer." I thought about adding a counter-sneer about the 'pidgin' crack, but forbore. The Council's people are always happier if they think they've gotten a good lick or two in.

Oh, and now I knew why he left the bottom of his face naked. How else were people supposed to be able to tell when he was sneering?

What can you say about Agents of the Adjudication Council, except *why aren't all of you people back on Earth?* Or at least on the real colony worlds. Well, the *other* real colony worlds. Jefferson's too big now to be pushed around like Earth can Bolivar or the other two, even though Earth's not supposed to be able to do that at all.

Then again, Council Agents aren't supposed to travel this far into the Tomb Worlds. They still do, and nobody smart flies an unarmed ship this far out, so when an Agent shows up... well, they can be a pain in the ass, if they want to. And they always seem to want to.

The one now gracing us with his presence sported the official designation was 'Commander Rubicon,' because Council Agents never use their real names when working in the Tomb Worlds. They say it's to stay impartial. The cynics say it's to hide their shenanigans. The rest of us just think they're always a third of the way to being space-happy. Anyway,

Commander Rubicon was here at 118-G-002 with his cloak and his half-helmet (and his armed ship of armed retainers, let's not forget about that) to quiz us about... software piracy.

No, really. "It is no laughing matter," he assured Greg and me — but not Maki — he wouldn't even look at her. "Last year, digital buccaneers hacked the Solarian datanet and uploaded thousands of unlocked software programs into the colony network. By now, they could have spread everywhere."

"Probably," replied Maki. "So what?"

"I am not going to dignify that with a response," retorted Rubicon.

Council Agents are real dicks about giving corp managers the mushroom treatment. "Fine," I sighed. "Let me ask a question, then: 'so what?' Unlocked software happens all the time out here. We keep it off the corporate intranet, so how is it our problem?"

"It is *stealing*, Chief Pilot Tanaka," Rubicon grated out. I let that go. I didn't want him thinking it really was okay to use 'Pammie' or 'Pam,' because I had just decided that it wasn't. "This is *everybody's* problem. And illegal."

"It's illegal *back home*," Greg said. "We're so far away from Earth, you can't even see it from here without a telescope. What are we supposed to do, just check everybody for used software? Because that *is* absolutely against company policy. XHum has strong privacy rules."

"Not to mention, rooting around in people's stuff without a warrant is absolutely illegal on Jefferson, too," I helpfully noted. "Which is where the corp is incorporated. Heck, half the team is from there." *And that **does** make a difference*, I thought but didn't say. The Adjudication Council has less power than it likes, but its agents don't like to hear that. Then again, the Council has more power than *the colonies* like, and we *really* don't like to admit that.

The sneer was back. "You are all Terran citizens..."

I interrupted him. "That's not the same as being a citizen of a Great Power, and you know it. I'm full jailbird, myself, one hundred percent transportee ancestry, on *both* sides of the family." I let my accent show a little. "Which means, you ain't one of mine."

He actually looked pleased, would you believe it? "That sentiment is arrogant, yet irrelevant. The Jefferson planetary government recognizes Earth's preeminence. This is a formal investigation, authorized by the Adjudication Council. I have the documents for it." He did, in fact, have the documents. They looked... real, I guess. "I require your assistance in reviewing company and private accounts for illicitly acquired software."

"Sure." Maki unleashed a classic corpo 'fear my perkiness' smile. "Got a warrant?"

That got her nothing but another icy silence from the Council Agent. I wanted to sigh *again*, but I had already done that once. "Sure. Got a warrant?" As Rubicon switched his attention to me, I went on, "Look, if we're gonna play games, I'm just gonna repeat every question that Maki asks. So can we stop with the Big Bad Corp stuff? We don't run that kind of shop here."

"What Chief Pilot Tanaka said," Greg added. "You want to look at people's private computers, go ahead and ask them first. You want us to run a voluntary audit of our own files? Sure, we'll grant that request, and tell you what we find. Or you can look at our quarterly reports, because we do check for unlocked software in company hardware, believe it or not. You want more, show us your warrant."

I expected a bit more bluster from Rubicon, but it was like he expected the response. "The Council assumed you would remember your duty as Terrans. Clearly they were mistaken." When this sneer didn't make us either start weeping, or begging for forgiveness, he shook his head. "We will call for volunteers, then — and we expect to see both the old audit, and the new one. Is that clear?"

"As crystal," replied Maki. "Will you be needing anything else, Captain Rubicon?"

The silence grew. This time, I just sat in my chair and leaned back a little. Eventually, Rubicon gave up. "No."

"Then *thank* you for coming to meet with us! We will *of course* provide you with the audits you requested. And should you *want* anything else, you have only to ask," Maki burbled, in full fuck-you-with-sugar-frosting mode. I hear they spend an entire class teaching managers how to do that in corp school, and you can see why. Rubicon had to visibly restrain his breathing before he gave Greg a short bow, and left.

I opened my mouth, and Greg put a finger up. I perforce kept my mouth shut while he fiddled with a handheld. "Okay," he said after a half-minute. "No bugs that I can see."

"And let's hope Earth hasn't come up with anything new lately," Maki muttered. "Though Rubicon would hardly be surprised to hear any of us call him an asshole."

"He was trying for that." Greg shook his head. "Damned if I know why, though. Process, you can start listening again."

"Thank you, Greg."

As usual, The Process sounded almost maddeningly calm. As a local shard of the alientech not-an-AI who was originally tasked with helping humanity navigate Galactic society after First Contact, I guess it had to be. Especially since *something* had replaced said society with an interstellar-scale horror movie, so The Process was now making it up as it went along. Just like the rest of us.

Then I realized something. "Hold on. Greg, why wasn't The Process already slotted in?" I asked.

"Commander Rubicon insisted," Greg replied, just like that wasn't the nuttiest request in the world. "He insisted on a lot of things, including booting Maki out of the meeting."

"He didn't get that one," noted Maki. "Eventually he backed down, but Rubicon absolutely drew the line at letting The Process interact with us at all."

Which was even weirder than trying to exclude the XHum representative from an XHum dig. You can expect a Terran official to try to do a corporate representative dirty, but The Process is an absolutely trustworthy part of any planetary operation. It'd better be, because if it isn't, humanity's doomed. "I'm sorry this guy made you leave, Process."

"I do not mind, Wind-Walker Tanaka." I wasn't sure if I believed that, but I was sure The Process wouldn't be holding any anomalous resentment against me, which is mostly what I was worried about. "I do think I should remove myself again, though. At least until the three of you decide what to tell me."

"Why, Process?" Greg asked, but got no answer. "Dammit, it's in 'teachable moment' mode again. Okay, fine. Do any of us buy the software piracy story?"

"Oh, *Hell* no," I snorted. "You don't send a Council ship out of human space just to look for unlocked pornos and dreamscrapes. It's just a good excuse for going through our internal files."

"Looking for unregistered artifacts, then?" Maki frowned. "Not that any of that is going on," she went on, just in case there *was* a bug Greg had missed.

"I want to say... no?" Greg ventured, after a moment's thought. "Sure, you hear stories about Tomb World site digs not reporting everything they find to Earth Customs, but there's not enough money in that to justify a Council ship, either. Not unless one of the Great Powers recently got a bug up its ass about gray market relics." Which, given that the rich and famous among the Great Powers are the ones buying up all the gray market relics in the first place, was unlikely. Not that any of us would publicly say that, either.

Instead I asked, "Then why *is* that ship here?"

"Damned if I know," Greg grumbled. "Council games? They're looking for somebody? Maybe something on this planet is about to wake up and eat all our faces, and they want a good view?"

"Or maybe they're just using up the travel budget." Maki's voice got even more tart. "God forbid they should tell us awful corp slave-masters a single blessed thing. Whatever. We'll have

MOE LANE

to set up shore leave, open up one of the spare buildings at the launch facility for dorm space, tell Supply to set up a few extra taps at the bar, the usual. Pam, be a dear and volunteer for liaison duty with the ship, please?"

"Grumble, grumble, groan," I said, mostly without anger. "Sure, but I want a cookie." She already had the tin out. Genuine Earth cookies, too. "Do we want anything from them?" I went on, in slightly muffled tones.

"See if you can get them to do a library dupe. And find out how much they want to charge to schlep our mail home." We have regular mail service with human space, but 'regular' is defined in terms of months. It's usually worth a little something to send news early.

Greg spoke up. "I'll have Nur in Supply put together a spice list, too. What we want, and what we have extra of. We can also squeeze some spare parts out of stocks and fabricate more. Even a Council tight-ass isn't going to get in the way of resupply."

"Works for me. But don't expect me to put the screws to him on those, Greg, Maki," I warned. "There's all that the market will bear, and then there's being a jackwagon about it."

"Sure. Keep Commander Rubicon sweet." Maki frowned. "Well... less sour," she allowed.

"All right. Anything else?" asked Greg.

"Just one more thing." I pointed up at the ceiling. "What *do* we tell The Process?"

"Good question," admitted Greg after some consideration. "Should we foist the whole job off on it?"

Normally, having The Process around made tasks like this a breeze. Alas, sapient or not (The Process says it isn't, and I say it's mistaken), it would be insulted if we tried to use it to investigate Terran software piracy. The Process thinks the entire concept of software privacy is stupid. So I shook my head. "Just tell it the basics, and don't try to drag it into this. We'll work out what Rubicon's doing here on our own."

You don't always notice when The Process has gone away, but you *always* notice when it comes back. There's a slight prickling on your skin from the sudden weight of its attention. It's not a hostile attention, or even a unpleasant one. But you definitely know The Process is there.

"Will you now tell me what you and the Council Agent were discussing, Wind-Dancer Tanaka?" It calls us whatever we ask it to, within reason. It's also really precise in its language, for something that's supposedly not self-aware. "It seemed important and slightly distressing, if not an immediate emergency."

"It wasn't." I wanted to give The Process a gimlet eye, but I can't do that to a disembodied voice. I couldn't ever decide in which direction to look. "And how did you figure out 'slightly distressing,' anyway? Commander Rubicon demanded you be locked out of the meeting."

"I was," The Process replied, evenly. "By which I took that to mean that I was not to listen to conversations. He did not, however, demand that I stop monitoring everyone's heart rate and respiration. Your vital signs all showed results compatible with mild irritation and worry, not shock or terror."

This time I did roll my eyes. "Of course we did. And of course you did. Did you also record the vibrations of the wall? You could get our conversations that way."

"No. As in, yes, I *could* have," The Process judiciously agreed, "but that would have violated the spirit of Commander Rubicon's demand for private communications. Since nobody asked me to do that, I did not."

Some days, I flatly refuse to believe that The Process isn't self-aware. There has *got* to be something wrong with the translation programs. Or we just don't understand what 'self-aware' means. "Fair enough. Commander Rubicon is here to fight the scourge of software piracy, and he wants our help. Presumably he wants us to break some of our society's rules to aid his investigation."

"All right." Then again, maybe The Process *isn't* self-aware, because most human beings would have responded to me with something, if only to keep the conversation going. There are definite hard limits on its curiosity.

Although... "So, why were you asking, anyway?"

The Process likes to answer questions. "Because I assumed you wanted me to, Wind-Dancer Tanaka. You often voluntarily interact with me, particularly when you are annoyed at something else."

I winced. "Ouch. I do, don't I? Sorry."

"It is not an issue. I am here to help humans, and I have plenty of spare capacity to deal with individual emotional displays. Absent a proper uplift program, there is not much else for me to do."

Was that a hint? "Fine. You can help me with some logistics. I get to be the liaison with the Council ship, and they've got to be in need of supplies."

"Oh, how wonderful! You should learn a great deal from this!" Yeah, at the end of the day The Process *is* sapient. It absolutely loves to hear about a human practicing a skill outside of her core competencies. I'd have to keep it from designing an entire lesson plan on the fly, but it'd be worth it to get some hyper-competent tech support. And usefully-amoral hacking expertise.

Because I *did* want to know what Commander Rubicon was up to. Call me an old-fashioned Jeffersonian girl, but I don't even trust the Great Powers as far as I can throw them. And I can't throw an entire planet at *all.*

Calling Syah was harder than I expected, and I don't mean that in a sappy, *oh, was he interested?* way. It was because he had gone straight from the landing pad to the planetary net interface, and gotten to work. My call went straight to interface crew chief Chuki Juma, and she wasn't inclined to bother him, either. "Come on, Pam," she told me. "Have a heart."

I peered at her image. It was more salvaged Amalgamation tech, so the picture was impossibly clear — and somehow converting the infrared spectrum into something my brain could comprehend, so I could see her heat signature as an actual color. It was great for picking up useful emotional cues from someone's body temperature, if you didn't mind having the occasional bout of vertigo or actual vomit. "What went wrong, Chook? You look," — *ulp* — "um, mad at a sudden crisis that came out of nowhere?"

"Got it in one." *She* wasn't looking too closely at *my* image on the screen, probably because she didn't want to throw up any more than I did. "The interface's lost half of its servers, and all of the backups. Syah's in the lattice up to his waist, trying to figure out if it's software, or bad crystals. We're fabricating more crystals, but you know how it is."

"Yeah, I get it. It'll take you a while to replace them all." Universal fabricators are like AI: really useful concepts, and very possibly the reason why galactic civilization fell. There are plenty of places that look like they got hit by a bout of gray goo from malfunctioning Von Neumann machines, and a lot more where whatever happened got cauterized by nuclear fire. So we keep our own fabbers throttled back, *especially* on the Tomb Worlds. I think this particular worry is heavily overblown, but the S/CI disagrees with me, and they're the ones setting the rules. Besides, what if I'm wrong?

I sighed. "All right, Chook. Just let him know that I called, and I can get him a better meal than the vending unit when he has time to eat it. And let me know if you need anything specific... oh, hey! The Council ship might have spare crystals. I can ask, at least."

Chook scowled, purely radiating 'rational paranoia' in a way that made me have to unfocus my eyes. "I'm wondering if they didn't break these themselves." She got hold of herself, thankfully. "But I'll keep it in mind, Pam. Thanks."

So much for a nice, maybe even romantic dinner, I groused to myself. Which would have been even more annoying if my stomach wasn't so sour from the call. *So I might as well get started on both jobs.* Both the one I was openly doing, and the one I had assigned myself: find out what the Hell that ship was *really* doing here. Hopefully before something *definitive* happened.

It took me three days to figure out why the hell Rubicon had come here, mostly because I wasted two of them trying to pump the crew of the *Redacted 523* (no, really. That was the name on the manifests) for information. I got precisely nowhere, which I half-expected, but only half. I mean, you get used to Council spacers being closemouthed, out here in the Tomb Worlds. Their masters only send out the *really* committed and trustworthy fanatical minions.

During that time the *Redacted* was doing the most convoluted liberty schedule we'd ever seen. No more than one-third off the ship at any given time, and no more than six people visiting Luxor Base, day or night. They were strange, too. We were expecting rowdy, possibly pushy, but instead we got 'quiet and creepy.'

They weren't actually *rude*, unlike their ship captain. The people on liberty wanted fresh food, new entertainment, cold beer, all the usual things. They even had good stuff to trade, although we had to be careful not to offer any, you know, pirated software or anything.

The only thing was, these folks were... they were like black holes when it came to gossip. None of them would talk about why they were here. Sailors always gossip. Or start fights, but we didn't get any of those, either. The discipline this ship had was off the charts.

I got the most information from the *Redacted*'s purser. His name was Lt. Oft-Evil-Will-Evil-Mar Patel, and he looked exactly like the New Imperial Iluvitarian you'd expect from a name like that, except for the full head of hair. Iluvitarians usually go for a buzz cut. It gives them more canvas space for their tattoos. He came across as a very amiable and genteel badger, which is also something you'd expect from an Iluvitarians.

Even he wasn't really forthcoming, just polite. "We are here for the reasons our captain said, Miss Pamela." The two of us had met to work out cargo swaps. Chook had decided to try to get some crystals from the *Redacted* after all, and was happy to have me do all the heavy lifting. They were happy to make the deal, but figuring out just what to swap for what required in-person meetings. Huzzah!

...oh, it wasn't so bad, really. We had set up shop in *Milliways Pub*, since one of the nice things about Iluvitarians is that they think bars are eminently suited for business discussions. So at least there was food (and beer, for him). "If he has other reasons," the purser went on, "I either do not know, or I was told to pretend to be ignorant of them."

"That's not very helpful, Oft." Well, we were getting along well enough to not do last names, and I wasn't going to call him 'Evil.' Some words you just don't casually use in public, *especially* for a nickname. "Why even tell me that you might be lying? Won't that just make me suspicious?"

Oft shrugged. "The captain probably would not care if you were. After all, what could you do about it? Sorry!" he hastily added when he saw my expression. "That was needlessly rude of me."

I noted that he said 'rude,' not 'incorrect.' But I believed the apology. Oft's religious sect was so publicly and reflexively nice, it was a wonder he worked for the Adjudication Council. "That's fine," I muttered, biting back more sarcastic comments, because what else could I say?

He noticed that, too. Oft might have even flushed, underneath all those green leaves and stars tattooed on his face. As we settled the bill, he stopped me. "All right, Miss Pamela. I think I *can* tell you this: there *are* people here who are of interest to the captain, and his investigations. You are not on that list." Then he walked out, just like that was somehow helpful for me to know.

Although Oft's use of the plural there would have been helpful, if only I had noticed it at the time.

CHAPTER FOUR
Night of the Space-Happy

Early the next morning — Hell, late that night — I got woken from my sound-enough sleep by The Process. It wasn't subtle, either. The Process has worked out that the best way to wake me up in a hurry is to reproduce the sensation of a dog's wet nose, in twenty different locations at once. If somebody had been in the bed with me, they'd have probably been knocked out by all my flailing.

It was a waste of time for me to growl, "This had better be good!" The Process doesn't play games or overreact. I growled it anyway.

The Process knew how to shut me up, though. "Space-happy sighting," it said. Just like that, I was awake, and reaching for the gun safe. The safe let me open it, too, so at least I knew the space-happy person wasn't *me*. Some of the recovered say they didn't always realize what was happening to them, at first.

"Who is it, Process?" I asked, as I checked the magazine to make sure I was using stun rounds. I assumed it'd be somebody whose name I at least recognized, because Luxor Base is too small for strangers. And that meant nonlethal rounds, because I was willing to take a small risk for somebody I knew.

"Xenological Collections specialist Adam Sild. Expect him to be armed with at least knives." Before I could ask, The Process went on, "His first, and so far only, known act with them was to carve out his subdermal chip."

That was enough to make me grab a clip of lethals, although not yet enough to load them in my gun. Most of the space-happy are the 'run around, frothing' type. A stun charge is enough to knock them on their ass. But 'volitionals,' or the ones who can still plan, are the really dangerous ones. If Adam was with-it enough to get rid of his tracker, he might also be with-it enough to get some makeshift armor against the stuns. I didn't want to kill anybody, but I also didn't want to die.

Guess I still don't. "Any deaths so far?" I didn't bother to lock the door behind me. If he tried to break into my apartment, he'd be tranked within seconds. I was only going out because I had volunteered to be on space-happy defense duty.

"None. Sild has not yet fully entered a state of homicidal mania, and is still capable of acting in self-preservation. I should remind you that both of these conditions will change in the very near future."

"Yeah, I already knew that." Nobody was around as I popped into the lobby. Hopefully, that meant that people were already sheltering in place. "Or are you just trying to distract me?"

"More like calm you down, Wind-Walker Tanaka." The Process was using its 'soothingly rueful' voice. "I know you were having a less than pleasant day already."

As usual, I ignored the reminder that The Process sees all, or at least a lot, because what other choice did I have. Still, that reminded me. "So, how the hell did we miss this, Process?" I asked as I rushed through the streets on my way to the rallying point. First rule when dealing with the space-happy: *find your buddy*. "And can't you find him anyway? That vibrations trick?"

"My ability to track movement via surface vibration has been essentially turned off by the current planetary net maintenance program. They needed the processing power of the sensors to speed their diagnostics. I am having to rely on visual cameras only, which are also seriously degraded because of the maintenance project."

Well, that was hideously bad timing. "Adam showed no signs of brooding," The Process went on, sounding almost maddeningly calm. "No unusual behaviors or antisocial triggers were logged, and there were no red flags from his weekly counseling session, nothing. There was probably an external trigger."

"For real, this time? That'd be a switch." I turned the corner, and there were two people I knew vaguely from the commissary. They peered at me, and I at them, until we decided that none of us were homicidal maniacs. Unfortunately, neither of them were heading towards my rallying point, so I still had to keep an eye out, and my hand on my gun. "You *sure* he wasn't a brooder? The volitionals usually have to work themselves up to it."

"I am not *sure* of anything. Please review my words, Wind-Dancer Tanaka."

So I did. *Nothing reported, nothing logged...* "Damn. You think somebody tampered with his information?"

"It is a measurable possibility. If Adam is rescued, perhaps we might even be able to quantify it."

"Yeah, yeah," I muttered. "If I run into him, I'll take him alive—" And those were almost famous last words, because right then, Adam popped out of a suspiciously-dark alleyway. I swear, it's like the universe listens to me, but only when it's in a bad mood.

I had only known Adam by sight. He was one of those fresh-faced, hearty types who thought rambling through alien forests with nothing but a backpack and a flashlight was just the *best* thing *ever*. Unfortunately, all that fresh air and exercise meant that Adam was now a *muscular* violent psychotic, and he moved *fast*. I jumped almost out of the way, letting my jacket take the blade. He ripped the fabric up pretty good before colliding with the wall, so there was my good luck.

My bad luck? The attack had sent the gun flying out of my hand. I ignored that and yelled, "Hey! Process! I found Adam!" — only to hear silence. And not just from The Process, either. The entire datanet around me was collapsing into static as *the network went down. All of it.* I was *alone*, in the *Tomb Worlds*, with a murderous maniac.

I forced myself away from panic. to remember my training. *Okay,* I told myself as I stripped off my now mostly-useless jacket. *That's not Adam. That's a space-happy lunatic, and it's going to cut you, if it can...* There's more to that litany, but Adam had gotten up.

He took his time, his eyes chips of gray-green in a mottled face, as he focused his gaze on my upper arm. He circled me, carefully, tensing more and more until I was almost ready for him to charge again. He was too close to miss, too. Even from here I could smell the crazy and the blood on his breath, When he opened his mouth, I could see crusty awfulness where he had chewed his tongue.

God forgive me, seeing that helped me think of Adam as a *thing,* not a person. You need to flip that switch in your head, because if they want to kill you more than you want to kill them back, it's almost never a contest. So I told myself that something without a tongue couldn't beg for mercy, and met the monster halfway.

I don't know how to formally fight, but I do know how to live. The knife was the biggest problem, so I tangled his knife with the jacket and *shoved* him back into the wall. No finesse to it, and it almost cost me. Adam let go of the knife the moment I entangled it, and turned his bounce off of the wall into a frenzied launch, both hands clawing at my upper arm. And I mean *clawing.* When I pushed him and his filthy fingers back, there were bruises and a couple of ugly gouges.

If *Adam* had known how to fight — I mean, before — he might have beaten me then. He was stronger, and a little faster, and that's *bad.* He just wasn't fully in control of his body. He kept jerking forward, too far or too short, shifting about while he was still moving, making his staggering attacks more like wild flailing. God! Every time he moved, gooey red spit bubbled out from his mouth as he growled and gibbered. If he wasn't there to hurt me, I would have felt sorry for him.

I still needed to win. I tried feinting for the gun, then jumped back to avoid his lunge. A quick, horrible moment of closeness, and then he was past me, arms windmilling after tripping over my outstretched foot.

Things *popped* and cracked in his body when Adam hit the ground. More things did when I jumped on top of him, punching down into his unprotected side. I kept on punching him, knuckles bloody and skinned, until he was crumpled into a fetal position. I remember he never cried or whimpered, even when I got up and gave him a few kicks for good measure. *Then* I ran for my gun, picked it up, pulled out the magazine of lethal rounds, and...

...and then I forced myself to put the magazine back, go over to the half-wrecked Adam, and carefully shoot him unconscious with the stunner rounds. I didn't want to, and I knew I would have gotten away with shooting him dead. The network was still down, and even if it had been up, I was by myself with an unconscious space-happy. It's amazing, what kind of beating one of those could wake up from. Nobody would have said anything if I had decided to make myself safe.

Nobody except me. Because I did feel sorry for him. The space-happy are sick, not depraved.

Security only showed after the network came back up, which was right after my dinner did. Delayed reaction, just like the physical shakes and phantom mutterings. It's messed up, when somebody goes space-happy. Especially when it's somewhere like One-Eighteen. XHum doesn't cut corners when it comes to preventative care. This was the first case in over three years, and the last one got shut down right at the start.

Only this one hadn't, so now we'd have to be more careful. To quote the philosopher, the way you count space-happy incidents is, 'one, two, many, LOTS.' Out here, when you get an incident it's like a breaching a dam, and out comes the psychosis. We don't know why the Tomb Worlds have this effect on people, but then, we never do.

When security did show up they brought Maki with them,

wearing her physician's hat instead of her corporate one. She got Adam literally straightened out, properly sedated, and even comfortable, in a way that made me feel shameful about not doing any of that it myself. That's stupid, sure. Everybody knows not to touch the space-happy if they can help it. But you still have to fight back the urge to be a proper human when you see one of them all knocked out and helpless, with no hint of the rage and viciousness lying under the surface.

After she was done, Maki came over to me. She grabbed my face in a way that would have been infuriating in any other context, but when you've been as close to a space-happy as I was, you let the doctor do her thing. If I was about to go all violent on her, best to find out now. "I'm slapping on a cudchewer," she told me after a good, long stare, and didn't wait to hear my response.

I'm one of the people who *doesn't* feel icy calm spreading through their veins when they get a cudchewer patch. Instead, everything gets just a little out of focus. It's like there's now a thin film between me and the world, with everything making me scared held at bay on the other side. The shakes and the muttering just *stopped*. On the other hand, I now felt *freezing*. All those sweat and fear hormones, I guess.

Maki made sure I had a blanket, then gave me another look. I noticed with biochemical detachment that she was strictly hands-off this time. "Do you need immediate counseling?" she asked.

I gave the question the thought it deserved, then shook my head. "I don't think so. I'll get another dose tonight, and that should help me process things. There's some lingering trauma, but it can wait until my weekly psych."

"You sure?"

"Yeah. My next session's only two days away. I did write up the immediate action report, though."

That's easier than it sounds, since the form's got a lot of standard options and drop-downs. I made the report public, and she gave it a quick look before nodding. "This looks okay...

huh."

"Oh, is there a problem?"

"It says here his mouth was bloody, and his tongue was ripped up."

"Well, it was." But I still took a quick look at Adam, now securely bound to a floating medboard. His face had been cleaned up, but I could still see streaks of dried blood around his mouth. Reassured, I looked back at Maki, careful to keep my hands where people could see them. "If I hallucinated the blood," I told her, "I'm still doing it."

"What? Oh, no, it's not that. The poor bastard definitely mutilated his own tongue. But we now have the self-video where he did that to himself, and it's timestamped two days ago." Maki looked disgusted. "Even for somebody who's space-happy, that's a real dedication to pain."

"Flight Officer Tanaka?" That was one of the security personnel. "We found a jacket, and a knife. Are these yours?"

I looked over. "The jacket is. Was." I had no intention of ever wearing it again, even if it could be repaired. "The knife is his."

Maki and I looked it over. It was a standard bush survival 'knife,' called that because 'shortsword' sounded weird. It wasn't in bad shape, either. Adam hadn't had the chance yet to trick it out with scratches, gouges, or trophies. "How long did you say he was space-happy, Maki?"

"Two days." She sounded as bemused as I felt.

I gave Adam another look. He was still, so motionless that I had to watch his chest to make sure he was breathing. "Was he asleep for most of it?" I asked. "You'd think he'd want to get his knife just the way he liked."

"Maybe he still liked it that way," Maki shrugged. Which was a fair point. Every case is different. "We'll see if he remembers what was going on in his head, after we fix it."

After that? It was time for bed, obviously. I was going to have a full morning ahead of me tomorrow.

I understand that my ancestors had a leisurely approach

to mental shock and potential trauma, not to mention an indulgent attitude towards letting people freak out in response. It sounds nice, being able to heal at your own pace. Unfortunately, in the modern era, we just don't have time for luxuries. A pill for neutralizing the extra-strength funny brain chemicals now coursing through my vein, another pill to make me sleep like a log, and priority attention at my next psych session, and I would be ready to go. Which was just fine with me, at least after the two pills had done their magic. I had real work to do.

Everyone I saw were subdued the next day, because it's never fun when a coworker goes space-happy. All around me, people were doing little self-checks, and I heard later that there were twice as many walk-ins at the mental health center as usual. All of this a rational response to last night, but it didn't make for a pleasant work environment. It could have been worse, sure. Adam could have killed somebody. That made people relax more. Also, he was going to go into cryosleep. That was the ultimate reassurance. Not even the space-happy can bust out of *that*.

I felt fine enough when I woke up that I wondered whether I even needed to take emergency therapy, but I decided that was stupid. Although I wasn't sure whether switching my usual time from evening to morning was a good one. I like going right to sleep after a good session. The therapy office advised me to compensate by taking the morning kind of easy, then go for a nap afterward, which I thought was fair. Even if what had happened was just life on the Tomb Worlds, it was still an injury. Nobody would expect me to run a marathon after I had twisted an ankle, right?

Unfortunately, my work usually involved pushing haulers around, and at the moment there wasn't enough traffic for that. When that happens, I get to take a sta— *lend a hand* with any job that's cropped up. We're just not big enough to staff the smaller specialized positions full time.

Like, say, 'designated investigator of a space-happy victim's domicile.'

At least the network wasn't conking out again, although there were moments where it felt... sluggish, like it had been kicked in the shins a couple of times and was trying not to hobble. But it was reliable enough for me to scan Adam's apartment.

Adam lived in a standard modular apartment house. Everybody uses the unit design: two bedrooms, one bathroom, one combination living room/kitchen, and all of the units' utilities can be hooked up together. It was perfect for a singleton or married couple, and since nobody dares brings kids out to the Tomb Worlds anymore, it didn't matter if it was too small for a family. His ground floor apartment was one of eight, and two of the others already looked like they had been hurriedly abandoned. The other five probably would be by the end of the day. Nobody likes to be told they spent two days living next to a monster. And well they should, since everybody knows the space-happy trap their lairs.

Only Adam had done a half-assed job here. The booby-traps Adam had put around the place were just low-tech crap: broken glass under every window, and set at the edges of all the vents. That didn't surprise me, since the guy had been an explorer before he had gone insane. Primitive traps would be on-brand.

What did surprise and alarm me were the two things The Process found. Mounted under the computer chair and fitted with a pressure trigger was an Amalgamation gadget used to synthesize methane gas in the field, only it had the chocks open and a spark-lighter attached, and the computer itself had a bit of malware in it that would have activated the unit's cleansing protocols. Neither of those was the sort of thing you'd expect from a guy who liked to go play in the woods.

"On the other hand," the Process pointed out, "they *are* consistent for someone suffering from Sudden-Onset Violent Psychosis."

I looked around at the *carefully* trashed room. There was

plenty of garbage, debris, and broken bits. No muck or filth, though. I wasn't sure, but some of this stuff looked like it had been *washed*. All of the piles were meticulously sorted, in a way that *almost* made sense, and I was making sure to keep my understanding strictly at the 'almost' level. "I think we can already take that diagnosis as a given, Process."

"I try not to anticipate, Wind-Dancer Tanaka. Humans have sometimes used a false diagnosis of SOVP to excuse violent crimes. The chances were low, but not nonexistent."

"They're even lower now. I found the manifesto." There's always a manifesto. This one was written out on blank printout sheets, roughly bound in what was actually a rather nicely tanned not-cow skin, and had a symbol on the front cover that I took one look at, and instantly regretted. Some things just don't deserve to exist.

Fortunately, The Process doesn't have my aesthetic sense. I had it scan the book via the simple process of me closing my eyes while I turned its pages, one by one. *While* I was wearing gloves. I didn't believe in the supernatural, but I *did* believe in, say, hallucinogens that could be absorbed through the skin. Wasn't any of that on the book, this time, but the principle remains sound.

"Anything useful?" I asked.

"There's quite a bit here that will aid in the victim's psychological reconstruction," The Process replied, "but nothing that's immediately important. I'm not seeing any keywords that would suggest he's created more booby traps. Nothing in his personal records, although I cannot look at his private files—"

"Please look at his private files," I said, although everything after 'please' was superfluous. The Process is *very good* at figuring out sentences from the first word.

"—and his private files show a radical alteration, starting three days ago, then clumsily obscured."

"Dammit. Just when the *Redacted* showed up. Anything more in the rants?"

"Define 'more.' Specialist Sild is in custody, and being prepared for transportation and treatment. Do you think he might have created more traps or bombs, during his homicidal period?"

I looked around the room. Truthfully, I had mostly been sent here just in case there were a few dead bodies in the refresher. "No. No, I guess not. Deep scan the apartment, take a snapshot, and start the sanitation."

"Certainly. *After* you leave the premises, Wind-Dancer Tanaka." That sounded like a hint, so I perforce left. I wouldn't be needed for the next part, anyway.

I could feel only the slightest caress of heat as I walked down the stairwell. But then, XHum prides itself on its base construction. It'd take The Process no more than five minutes to flash-burn the contents of the apartment down to non-reactive ash, tops. Although it would take longer to convince somebody to move in afterward, sanitation or not. The space-happy cast a long shadow, even after they've been sorted out.

CHAPTER FIVE

A Call to the Dark

After all of that, I could get back to my actual unofficial job: figuring out what Captain Rubicon was *really* here for. Unfortunately, the crew of the *Redacted* stubbornly remained opaque. Not even the space-happy incident seemed to faze them, or their odd perambulations around the base. You'd expect at least gossip, right?

"They've been mind-locked," Nur told me confidently as we grabbed some cold drinks after a long day of me not finding out anything. No beer for either of us, though. Nur didn't drink, and I was on call for the evening.

I rolled my eyes. "First off, they're not mind-locked. Second, they're not mind-locked. Third... what's mind-locked?"

"Damned if I know. Probably some weird alien tech that makes people keep their mouths shut." Nur grinned. "But you know something like that has *got* to be out here."

Unfortunately, I did. The reason people like Nur can just make up nonsense like 'mind-locking' so confidently is because there's thousands of Tomb Worlds, full of ruins with literal tons of enigmatic alien technology. If we can imagine it, then some vanished race probably already invented or manufactured it, so we just need to figure out what and where the right gizmos are. How to turn them on without vaporizing our faces would be an added bonus.

So I couldn't just dismiss 'mind-locking' out of hand, merely because neither of us knew what the term would even *mean*. The Tomb Worlds actively reward making stuff up as you go along. "Well, they're not showing any kind of group psychosis, or even serious neurosis," I pointed out. "You know how it is when alientech makes a person's head go funny. It does the same to her coworkers and family, too. The *Redacted*'s crew are all being *individually* weird."

"Yeah, good point. Nothing strange in their supply requests, either." Nur didn't seem upset about being argued against, but then, he never did. I guess it helped that he was sometimes right, too. "I particularly went looking for any requested items that might tie in with the brain's regular production of neurochemicals. But nothing. If the crew are suffering from severe hormonal imbalances, they're hiding them real well."

"Great. They're a bunch of well-adjusted fanatics who don't want to harvest our pineal glands." I scowled. "But why are they here? There's nothing on this planet except us, and the usual abandoned ruins."

"Anything good in them?" asked Nur. "I mean, we're here for the contragrav, sure. But they'd just buy in to get a piece of that, right?" He looked at me. "So, is there something going on under the table, Pam?"

"Geez, Nur." I shook my head. "If we were running anything under the table—" *Besides all those artifacts we're gonna forget to get import stamps for*, I thought "—you'd be the one managing it, right? So you tell me. Anything I should know about?"

Nur snorted. "Yeah, that's fair. Nah, I got nothing going on the side," he said, for the benefit of any hypothetical listening devices. What he was really saying to me was, *I'm not running anything besides our end of the smuggling operation.*

I wondered if maybe the *Redacted* was simply here to bust our chops over the artifact smuggling. But what was the point? If we got caught, they'd just make us pay the import fees, plus three percent. That was a lot of money, but not enough to justify sending a ship here.

A ship... I snapped my fingers. "I am an *idiot*," I said.

"Heh. You only say that when you've worked something out tricky," Nur said. "What's it this time?"

"Just that if the crew of the *Redacted* won't talk to us," I said as I stood up, "we'll just talk with the ship itself."

We didn't actually talk to the *Redacted*. It wasn't big enough to have a shard of The Process along, and we don't have any other kind of artificial intelligence, and nobody's allowed to try to make any until we're *sure* the Amalgamation wasn't wiped out by malevolent AI. But there was a ship's log. Strike that: there were *several* ship's logs. The captain's log was 'classified.' The engineering log had lockdowns and obvious gaps in it because of 'security clearances.' The *Redacted*'s *supply* database might as well have been broadcast in all directions.

"How did you know they didn't lock the database down?" Nur asked me as we collated the *Redacted*'s inventory list into a form that The Process could chew on. It was going to be better at deciphering supply codes and designations than either of us would, and a hell of a lot better at extrapolating holes (and wholes!) in the data. "This info's pretty comprehensive."

"They never do," I explained. "Council ships are top-heavy with frustrated military, just waiting for the bug-eyed monsters and wild-eyed scientists. They never make a quartermaster the captain... and there we go. That's everything. Hey, Process! How's it going?"

"It goes well, Wind-Dancer Tanaka," responded The Process, more or less immediately. "I assume you're asking about my imaginary emotional state?"

The Process sounded different today. I assumed it was some sort of personalized therapy thing. "Of course I am!" I'm not very good at being flighty, but I can burble. "The day I stop anthropomorphizing you is the day things have gone to the devil." I giggled. "Humans, am I right? Must bug the Hell out of you."

"Let me check..." The pause that followed was completely, if you'll forgive the pun, artificial. "Nope. Still not feeling any urge to wipe out all the meatbags. But, to be serious, what do you *need* from the supply data?"

Which was a good question. Nur scratched his head. "What

can you tell us?" he said, then winced as soon as he did.

"Quite a lot, Nur-man."

"Yeah, that one was on me," said Nur, grimacing. The Process was originally designed to culturally uplift species like ours into Galactic society. It's trying its damnedest to work beyond its programming, but it defaults to turning everything into a teaching moment. "Let me put it this way. Can you tell me where the *Redacted* has been since last it left Earth?"

"Yes. I'm printing out the list now." Another reason why I think The Process is sapient is because it *does* understand human ambiguity, and is pretty good at successfully parsing information requests. A regular computer aid would have needed to be ordered to print out the list.

"So, how did you figure this out, anyway?" I asked, not quite idly, as I looked over the list of planets. The Process doesn't explain how it does things unless you ask it, but it always tries to answer your questions. It *likes* to answer questions, and never loses its patience with stupid ones. It's a *great* program. I wonder sometimes what it'd be capable of if it *wasn't* half-broken.

"Every item on the manifest has a stamp showing the time and facility where it was acquired," said The Process. "There's also a code showing whether the item was traded, salvaged, or discovered."

"What about items *not* on the manifest?" asked Nur. He shrugged when I looked at him. "What? The easiest way to hide something from a computer is to take the label off."

"Excellent observation! But, in this case, if they are carrying undisclosed cargo, logistical metadata indicates it is not heavy or bulky enough to require additional storage space or equipment." The Process made that particular bit of ostentatious silence that serves it for a shrug. "I suspect they have a few crates of weapons and armor inserts for their spacesuits. But that could be hidden, since the codes for the regular cargo items are not up to date."

"Sure," Nur said. "The codes never are. Easier to hide

swapping or smuggling that way. Besides, even regular trading will eventually get you clumps in your inventory."

I nodded. "Every ship trades for supplies, even the Council ships. They'll swap libraries, if nothing else."

"Yes," said The Process, "although in this case they haven't been swapping libraries. Just acquiring them."

"Really?" said Nur. "That's... weird." I shivered, just a bit. 'Weird' isn't the best word to use on the Tomb Worlds.

"Yes, Nur-man. At the planets humans call Richelieu, Greenhell, Ramal, Fenbian, and Terkutuk." The Process paused. "Oh, dear. Is something wrong?"

(I should probably explain this. The Process may or may not be sapient, but it's damned close to be omniscient. It usually has access to *everything*. What it doesn't have is *volition*. It can follow along with our thoughts and extrapolate from them, but, left by itself, it won't draw any conclusions on anything. All part of being a glorified species-wide tutor, I guess.)

(Although it might have a *little* volition. It somehow figured out how to activate the Amalgamation's cultural Uplift program on our behalf. Which is why we can venture out into the Tomb Worlds without falling afoul of various automated animal control programs. Back in the early days, some researchers tried an experiment where The Process was *ordered* to act independently, for the benefit of an isolated set of volunteers. They all suicided on the same day, three months later, and nobody knows why. Except maybe The Process — but the last volunteer standing ordered it to forget everything that happened, and that's one order it's never tried to evade.)

"Yes, Process." I swallowed, nervously. "You know how humans get upset about the idea of dying mysteriously?"

"Ah. Four of those places were sites where all contact with an existing human expedition suddenly stopped, three of which with no explanation. But there have been no reports of a disaster at the Fenbian gray colony."

"Yeah," I said. "No *reports*. But we did hear about Greenhell about a month ago, and Terkutuk and Ramal during the quarterly updates." The Richelieu Incident had happened a while before, but we're still not sure what happened there. There were a bunch of survivors who all reported the same thing: a sudden storm that just kept getting larger and larger, until the settlement was stripped of life. About half of the base staff managed to make it off the planet in time, and nobody's sure how. They didn't have a local shard of The Process to record what happened, either. "Do the numbers match up for the *Redacted*'s visits?"

The Process answered immediately, not bothering with the usual pauses it puts into conversations to keep us more comfortable. "No. The timestamps on the manifests indicate that Ramal and Terkutuk were visited after the first reports of colony failures. A case could be made for Greenhell, but it would require very careful timing to make the dates line up. And the loss of the Richelieu gray colony took place eight Terran years ago, long before the *Redacted* began its tour. Surely it cannot be responsible for any of that?"

"The Richelieu Incident? Probably not." Nur shook his head. "But the other three? Well, shipping container timestamps can sometimes be a bit creative. Try it again, assuming that the month is correct, but not the day."

"Ick." The Process even made itself *sound* disgusted. "That's *nasty*. But I see your point. If you adjust the dates by no more than a standard month, the *Redacted could* have visited those three planets before the first settlement failure reports were disseminated. But that still leaves Richelieu, and Fenbian. Do you suspect the Fenbian gray colony no longer exists?"

"Yes." I stood up. "And now we're going to go have the corp check on that."

Like an idiot, I almost pinged Maki, right there. Which would have been *incandescently* brilliant, considering that our own communications were probably as full of security holes as the *Redacted*'s was. Worse, really. The Adjudication Council has the statutory right to tell Terran manufacturers to leave special government-only back doors in all of their software. They might not be looking at what I was doing, but they'd definitely be spying on the local corp CEO's electronic traffic.

So I'd have to take a walk. And I fought the urge to run the entire way. There was no point, and it'd look suspicious to anybody keeping an eye on me.

There are a lot of misconceptions about what it's like, working at a corp site, on a corp world. I don't know who to blame more: people who have never worked for one, or people who have never been offworld. Probably it's the ones who are both.

To be fair, corps make great villains, in fiction. Sneering, intolerant of failure, callously impersonal, dedicated to the bottom line. What's not to love in a bad guy? Only, in the *real* universe, the corps are all aware that you can build a robot in a day, a base in a year — but a human takes two decades to grow, and another one to develop to full maturity. In space, people are a corp's most valuable resource, and they've got the spreadsheets to prove it.

So when I finally made it into Maki's office (I didn't even wait for her secretary to log me in), all I had to do was say "lifeping," firmly enough for her to smash the Big Red Button. *That* started an automatic process that would end with every planetary system with a human presence sending back a message saying *yup, we're alive.* And if one didn't? Well, checking that out would be the next step, right?

Research showed a while back that the Amalgamation had faster-than-light communication. We're pretty sure that we barely know enough to turn what's left of it back on. We're *absolutely* sure that there's seventy-three known worlds where the planetary FTL communication hubs were frantically destroyed by the Amalgamation's own meteor defense system. Put another way, nobody's ready quite yet to push the 'on' button.

"So, which one?" Maki asked me as she went through the next step on the checklist: pulling out a drawer and making sure her personal weapons were charged or fueled or whatever. Another thing corps learned early when it came to exploiting the Tomb Worlds was that, in terms of long-term ROI, there's nothing like arming your employees to the teeth. Holes in stuff are easy enough to patch. Valuable workers getting their faces chewed off? Well, that costs a bit more to repair.

"Fenbian Gray Colony," I said as I paced. "It's on a list of places where the *Redacted* was at. Guess what the other four had in common?"

Maki winced. "Questions like that never have good answers. Coffee?"

"You offering, or requesting?"

"Yes."

"Sure. And thanks." As I poured two mugs, I went on, "It's circumstantial, even if Fenbian doesn't answer back. God knows there's tons of reasons why a site would go dark. But if they don't, you're going to need to ask the good captain there some questions."

"Which he'll refuse to hear, so I'll need you or Greg along." Maki looked at me. "So, what's the list?" After I told her, she blinked. "Crap."

"Wait, what's the problem?" It's not like Maki doesn't swear at all, but she usually likes to have a reason for it. "Is there something connecting those planets? Something important?"

"I don't know. Maybe? All of those planets were part of the same... I dunno, 'state' or 'county' or 'cluster' or whatever." Maki shrugged. "You know hard it is to figure out how the Amalgamation worked. As far as we know, all those planets were in one group. So was One-Eighteen."

"More *circumstances*," I said. "And I'm not liking them at all."

It would take at least two days for us to get, or not-get, a response. Since we don't have the Amalgamation's fast FTL communication network and wouldn't trust it if we did, we make do with hyperdrive-equipped message drones. That means that when a lifeping goes off, somebody living has to actually answer the call. It's not a bad system, as soon as you accept that it's largely for ensuring ships don't *unknowingly* visit a star system that's decided to start eating people.

What did we do while that was going on? Well, the first thing to do was to check if anybody on-planet was from Fenbian. I doubted it, but better safe than sorry. I mean that literally. People who grow up on the gray colonies are... a little weird. Not scary-weird, but they get *very invested* in 'making a new home for humanity,' yadda yadda. If we *did* have one of them here, and the colony *had* been wrecked? She'd probably suicide within a day.

I don't know why it affects gray colonists like that. Terrans or ordinary colonials like me don't have that problem. I mean, I love Jefferson and I would be enraged if it was attacked, but my life isn't literally dependent on its survival.

Meanwhile, I was 'on call,' which sounded better than 'held in readiness for a combat run.' If we ended up having to do something about the *Redacted*, it wouldn't be with the local cargo haulers. They weren't armored very well, and they absolutely weren't armed. I'd have to use one of the shuttles we brought with us to the dig... after it had been quietly and suitably retrofitted. In case of a showdown, it'd simply have to do.

Only I wasn't too impressed with my chance to really do anything. When it came to applied violence, everybody on this planet, including me, was woefully out of practice. Some worlds have energetic critters. One-Eighteen did not. The not-cows were the biggest things around, and they weren't even a nuisance. Just very tasty, and overbreeding anyway. No hostile life in any of the biomes, no opportunistic bacteria ready to eat our faces. If it weren't for the half-functional planetary infrastructure, we'd probably have been a gray colony ourselves.

Oh yeah. And everybody would be dead.

So, I waited. In the old days, paperwork would have taken

up all my time, but the same Amalgamation software that does our checklists also does most of our inventory and daily operations schedules. If you follow its instructions, keeping your records in order is insanely easy. You don't even have to think about it. You just enter in the first thing that comes into your head, and somehow it's always the right answer. The people who studied this usually got as far as muttering about 'subconscious cues heterodyning the organic random decision-making cycle' before they started demonstrating the 'insanely' part. Whatever. If you don't try to understand it, you can get all the daily paperwork done in fifteen minutes. Leaves the whole rest of the day free!

But don't think I wasn't busy. Oh, no. I discovered that I was going to be meeting daily with the *Redacted*'s colonist liaison. I was a little shocked to discover that the *Redacted* even *had* assigned someone to that job, since it implied that they gave a damn about avoiding giving offense. But then I actually met Lt. Commander Burcu Nowak — in what I guess is *kind* of my office, even? — and I realized that they didn't give a damn.

How to explain? Well, for starters she was actually of colonist descent herself. Only she was from *Bolivar*. Liaising with a settlement run by a Jeffersonian corporation. And — look, not every Bolivarian sneers at Jeffersonians, yes. They don't *all* sniff and stage-whisper *maniacal hayseeds* when they see us, just like we don't *all* mutter *butt-kissing proles* under our breath when we see *them*. That's stereotyping, that is. It's unfair.

But it was also accurate, when it came to Nowak. She wore her Council uniform with ferocious severity, every stripe and medal at exactly the regulation angle. *I am better than you*, that uniform almost screamed at me. *I am part of something bigger than you will ever be.*

Am I projecting? Absolutely not. The first words out of her mouth were in the same vein. "Assisting the Council is now your biggest priority, Tanaka," she told me. "The sooner you understand this, the easier it will be for you."

Clearly, this required diplomacy. "Piss off, Burcu."

"You mean, 'Piss off, *ma'am.*'"

"Oh, I'm sorry!" I gave her just enough time to react, then went on, "I hadn't realized Standard English wasn't your birth speech. What hic— *colonial* language were you raised with?"

I have to give her credit. That kind of comment can start fights in bars. Lots of people don't like to be reminded that the USNA's predecessor was the Great Power in charge of First Contact, and so got to choose Terra's 'official' language when dealing with The Process. And of *course* those arrogant bastards went with English. It never would have occurred to them to pick anything else.

Burcu managed to grate out, "Are you done trying to play dominance games, *Pamela*?"

This seemed to call for my best sad face. "Oh, Burcu. I'm not *playing* anything. 'You ain't the boss of me,' remember? Unless you're planning to adjust my attitude by having the ship drop a rock on the base? I hear that happens on Bolivar, whenever the *natives* get uppity."

Ooh, *that* got her mad. But she got it under control before anything inside her busted loose. "If you are trying to get rid of me, it will not work. You *do* understand that I *am* on a legitimate mission from the Adjudication Council, yes? One that it has the authority to assign?"

"Yes." *Unfortunately*, I didn't say. She heard me think it anyway.

"Good. And you also understand that your masters' ridiculous restrictions make it difficult for us to complete that mission?"

I sighed. "'Masters' is the wrong word. But, again, yes."

"I don't care about your opinion of reality, Chief Pilot Tanaka. What I do care about is that *clearly* we need to work with someone who is both senior, and local. We have chosen you. We will *not* be choosing anyone else. So you *will* help us avoid getting tangled up in these regulations, or I will feel free to ignore them."

Dammit. So that's why that asshole Rubicon didn't send an officer from one of the Great Powers. Fanatics or not, all of them had still been raised thinking 'privacy' was a right. On Bolivar, it's just a cost-effective management technique. She could be pushier. A *lot* pushier. "Fine, we're stuck with each other. Lt. Commander Nowak. But you're still not the boss of me."

"And what happened then?" Syah asked me over video, later. We still hadn't managed to find time for a date, so we had set up a call during one of his food breaks. Individual takeout and holo-conversations (carefully turned down to non-nauseous levels) wasn't what I had in mind, but I wasn't going to complain about it. I had just gotten a stellar lesson in how important the net interface was, after all.

I ate more noodles. "We snarled at each other a bit more before we both gave up. I can't make her go away, and she can't make me kiss her ass, so we're stuck with each other until she can figure out some way to ditch me."

"Why would she do that?" Syah was eating some kind of goopy nugget dish. It looked disgusting, but he *had* gotten it out of a vending machine. "Oh. She's not really after tracking down any... software piracy, was that it?"

"If she is, I'll eat my hat. Even the Council wouldn't send a ship out that far for that. Her boss just wants an excuse to trawl through our files."

"Why?"

"Damned if I know. Wish he'd just tell us; what's the worst that could happen to him? We'd just say 'No,' only louder?" A thought struck me. "Almost forgot: this lieutenant commander's from Bolivar, too."

"Oh, really? Huh. On a Council ship? That's weird. What's her name, anyway?"

"Yeah, I know. And she's one Burcu Nowak. Likes to throw her weight around, whether or not she has any to toss."

"Huh," Syah said after a second. "Name doesn't ring a bell."

I snorted. "I'd be surprised if it had. Bolivar has almost as many people as Jefferson. What, were you looking for someone to reminisce with about the old company mine?"

"Heh. Maybe. But I guess she's not really the social type."

"You're putting it mildly." I finished the rest of my noodles. "If I introduce you, she'll probably try to bully *you* into helping her, the second she finds out what your job is. Try to push your Bolivarian buttons, or something."

Even in the powered-down holo, I could see Syah's look. "Yeah, that sounds horrible."

"So's she," I said grandly. "Horrible, pushy, and really, *really* into the Council. And now she's *my* problem! Yay."

"You sound thrilled. You want some tips for handling her? We got plenty of those types of people, back on Bolivar."

I waved my chopsticks. "Nah, we got 'em at home, too. I can deal. Besides, while she's in my hair, I'll be in *hers*. Maybe she'll slip, and give me an idea on why the *Redacted*'s here. She'll almost have to, right? Unless she wants to stick like goop to the official story."

"Yeah, that's a good point." Syah finished the last of his horrible-looking nuggets. "I wonder if the fact they picked *you* to be liaison has something to do with it, too."

"Oh?"

"Well, you're this white-hot pilot, right?"

"The best," I said, with considerable pride and even more considerable accuracy.

"So I've heard."

"Oh, you've been asking around?" I kind of liked the sound of that. I'd been checking him out on the sly, too. I wasn't trying to be intrusive, just find out if there were any red flags. I hadn't even found any yellow ones.

"I didn't have to, Pam. You've got a bit of a following around here. Shoot, people tell me you're so good, you only do other stuff when they don't need you up in the sky. So if the *Redacted*'s captain asked for you, specifically, then whatever it is has to involve you, personally, or your job."

"I doubt he *asked*," I replied, "but I see what you mean.

Something else to look into, I guess. Anyway, subject change! How's the work going?"

"Slowly."

The rest of the conversation isn't really relevant. Just two people, trying to get a feel for each other. We had a good time doing it, too. We got along so well!

We got along so well.

CHAPTER SIX

Shivers

"Why is Burcu suddenly my problem, Maki?" I wanted that to come out as a yell, but our current location kind of put a damper on it. It's just not *nice* to shout in a medical bay. Also, it was early. Other people get upset when you start yelling first thing in the morning. It makes them anxious for the rest of the day.

One thing I had decided to do right off the bat was to go with personal conversations when it came to anything involving the *Redacted*. Partially it was because I assumed that the longer we went, the more likely it would get that our comms would be bugged. I also wanted the exercise. This duty was interrupting my flying time, and if I couldn't be in the air I could at least be moving around.

Wow, did I ever! Starting with my face-to-face with Maki.

Luxor Base is big enough to have an actual medical staff, but Maki handles the delicate stuff, like prepping a sedated space-happy for cryofreeze. I probably could have waited outside until she was done, but something morbid made me come in for a look. After all, I was the one who had messed him up.

He didn't look too bad, besides getting steadily bluer as Maki worked. "She's your problem because Captain Rubicon wants somebody senior to bother while he's here, and they picked you," she said. "At least, that's my guess. He still won't talk to me directly. Hell, all of his messages to 'the corporate overseer for this facility' are coming via *paper*."

"What? You mean, *actual* paper? Like, from a cow?"

"Actually, I think that's parchment. Paper's from... Process, what's paper from?"

"Historically, paper comes from wood pulp or recycled cloth. As you have already noted, agents of the Adjudication Council may use it for formal messages when communicating with colonial and non-Terran organizations. It is also used more generally for ceremonial purposes in the Terran New Empire." I could see Maki visibly decide not to ask how they turned wood into paper. The Process would tell her, possibly for the next hour.

"All right," I groused, "so Rubicon hates you so much, he doesn't even want the pleasure of annoying you in person. But why *me*? I don't know a damned thing about software piracy, and I don't think I've ever run over the Adjudication Council's dog."

Maki checked a strap, then tightened it further. "I honestly don't know, Pam. I just know that they insisted on you. Maybe it's because you've been on One-Eighteen's surface the longest?" She grinned, suddenly. "You're the oldest of old hands by now."

"Yeah, but it's only been nine years — hold on, is that really the longest anybody's been here?"

"Yeah, I looked it up. You got here six years before Nur did, five years before me. And nobody manages to stay on-planet for more than one standard five-year contract. Didn't you notice the bonus on your renewal agreement?"

"No." Actually, at the time I *had* thought it was pretty high, but I had decided that if they wanted to give me extra easy money, well, I wasn't their accountant. "Why is there so much turnover? This planet's a dream to live on."

"And that's a good thing?" Maki asked, with a crooked grin. "I've had dreams I was happy to wake up from. Look, One-Eighteen's spooky as hell, Pam. Too much of the stuff that happens around here, we just can't figure out. Like that fuzz they can't get rid off on the comm channels? Sure, it hasn't made anybody space-happy, yet, but it does drive our techies nuts."

I was honestly confused. "Why? Every Tomb World is stuffed to the gills with weird shit. You'd think they'd be used to it. I mean, it's not bad weird." I nodded at Adam. "This poor bastard is the first space-happy we've had in three years — whoops!"

That 'Whoops' was the poor bastard in question suddenly starting to twitch, despite the cryo-chemicals already in him. Alarmingly, Adam's movements were even directed. His hands were fumbling at the straps. No, he was using his wrists to try to *snap* the straps, and never mind that it might be at the cost of a broken wrist.

"Crap!" yelled Maki — *she* seemed fine with shouting in hospitals — as she went scrambling for a locker. "Grab a thermal blanket and hold him down!"

Pilots learn early to do what we're told. Or try to do what we're told, because keeping Adam in one place with just my arms wasn't happening. I've got good arms — tossing even an Amalgamation hauler around the sky tones you up — but this guy was stronger than I remembered. "Do I need the blanket?" I yelled as I moved from holding the space-happy down to almost *sitting* on him. "It's in the way!"

"It's supposed to be!" Maki shouted back, brandishing what looked like a cross between a hypo-injector and a spike-launcher. "The blanket's to protect your hands! That frost on him's carbon dioxide!"

Just then, Adam shoved and pushed me off — not that I was eager to stick around, just then. The straps restraining him were either weaker than they were supposed to be, or he was stronger, because they snapped off, one by one, just like a set of Assertion Day firecrackers. The gurney overturned as Adam stumbled and shuffled, the ankle restraints still keeping his feet closely together.

What was I doing? Avoiding a concussion. Suddenly, every piece of medical equipment on One Eighteen was in that lab, and none of it was between me and Adam. Even the gurney had gone somewhere useless.

"Process!" Maki started to shout — and then shut up, because The Process had already slammed shut the medbay's blast doors. That's when I started to worry. Usually it indulges humanity's collective delusion that we're unpredictable. If The Process was in full predictive behavior mode, we had a problem.

Adam snapped his ankle cuffs at the same moment Maki fired whatever-it-was at him, and missed. I'd like to say that I can't describe the sound the device made, but unfortunately, I can. I'm just not going to.

The smell was almost as bad. Ever smell something that rotted in the sun, then froze, then melted, then froze *again*? Neither have I, but I figure it smelled something like that. Compared to that, the blob of glowing yellow goo that shot out wasn't so bad. All *that* did was assault my eyes so badly in passing they almost bled, and collapse a table into twinkling, frost-rimed shards.

I expected Adam to attack Maki then, only he was already turning, utterly indifferent to her frantic fiddling. He knew I was there, you see. As in, he knew *I* was there. He couldn't see me, since most of his face was covered with breathing tubes and gunk that'd keep his eyeballs from shattering. There was no way his nose was working, either. But it didn't matter. Adam recognized me, and I figured he wanted a rematch.

This was surprisingly okay with me. I wasn't carrying a gun or anything, because why would I? But there were plenty of heavy things to hit him with, and a rising panic to give me some oomph with the hitting. I just needed to find something —

"There is a broom six inches from your left hand," The Process told me, as calmly reasonable as if I was looking for my coffee. "Adam Sild's surface temperature is currently at one hundred and twenty degrees below zero, and rising slightly. You will need to avoid flesh-to-flesh contact."

No shit, Shirley, I thought to myself as I feinted with the broom. Adam tried to grab at it, but he was slow, and that was fine by me. Even without the instant blistering if he touched me, that guy was too damned strong right now. I decided to see if he was graceful, too, as I closed in, jammed the broom between his shins, and *twisted*.

He wasn't, but it almost didn't matter. Adam *should* have been knocked off balance. That's physics, right? Three points define a plane, and I was shoving at least one of his two out of line. I wasn't expecting the extruded plastic of the broom to bend from the twisting, though.

The worst thing about it was, Adam never made a sound. Not when the broom snapped in half, and not when I stepped back and threw a chair at him. I knew I had his attention. I could *feel* his eyeless gaze, little psychic beads of interest bouncing off of my skin. His steps might have been fumbling, but his intent was clear, and terribly focused on me. As I stepped back, he advanced with glacial certainty.

That just meant that he wasn't paying attention to Maki, even when she swore, stopped fiddling with the controls on the thing she was carrying, and just *jammed* it into Adam's back before pulling the trigger.

This time, it worked. Adam dropped like a robot that had lost its control signal, a blue-green discoloration spreading across his back as I watched.

"Crap," I said in the crackling silence, after allowing myself a good, thoroughly paranoid look. I restrained from prodding his body with my foot, telling myself it was just because of the cold. "Is he dead?"

"Not any more than he was before." Maki started pushing buttons. A stretcher lumbered over to Adam, shoving aside equipment on its way. It unceremoniously yanked him up with a dozen writhing tentacles. Once it had him secured, it shuddered and began to convert itself into something looking alarmingly like a coffin. "That dose will slow down his neural system to an absolute crawl. He'll be out of it, guaranteed, until we can ship him home for a proper cure."

I picked up the thermal blanket. "How did he even move? If

he's cold enough to freeze carbon dioxide..."

Maki interrupted me. "That's a side effect of the cryo-chemicals. More Amalgamation tech. We don't understand it, but it works, so we don't have to."

I looked at her. "That's ridiculous. I get that the stuff lets us freeze flesh safely, but it still locks up the body. And he was *moving!*"

And Maki interrupted me, *again*. *"That was a side effect of the cryo-chemicals.* There is a perfectly reasonable explanation as to why that particular side effect happened, and some day, we will learn it. Until then, we don't focus too much on things we don't understand, *yet*. Do you understand what I'm saying, Pam?"

"...yes. Yes, of course."

And then we let the previous ten minutes go. It's a trick you learn in the Tomb Worlds. Letting go. If you don't, eventually you get dragged down. It's scary out here, stuck like this in the middle of a dead civilization. It's even scarier when you remember that the civilization isn't just dead, it was *murdered*, and you don't have the slightest damn idea why, or by what. You don't have time for little inexplicable mysteries when there are so many big ones. Anyone who *does*, also has time for emergency therapy sessions.

Once I finished up my complaints about Burcu, Maki still wanted to talk. She also took her time getting to the point. I let it go for five minutes of idle chatter before I lost my patience and said, "All right, what is it?"

Thankfully she didn't respond with *why, whatever do you mean, Pam?* Or something else like that. Instead, she let out a short, sharp sigh and said, "Pam, I need you to find out what the Council knows about Richelieu."

"Well, sure," I said. "I was already planning to do that. But why... oh. You had somebody who was on Richelieu?"

I think they're called 'bitter' laughs because nobody likes the taste of one in their mouth. "Yeah, Pam, you could say that. I was *on* Richelieu when it happened."

"Jesus, Maki!" I felt bad even while I was saying it, but it just slipped out. At least I didn't recoil in horror. God help us all, people sometimes do that when they meet somebody from a destroyed colony or base.

"If He was there, I missed it," Maki said as she lit up a cigarette and offered me one. It was the good stuff, from New Charlotte back home, so I took it. "Or maybe He works in *really mysterious* ways, because if there's a reason why I'm alive and half the colony isn't, I don't know what it is. Where we were got the Bugout call in time, that's all." She inhaled half her cigarette in one drag, then stubbed it out. "I still don't even know what the triggering event was. I tried to find out, but they classified it instantly. Besides, what good would knowing do me?"

There were a bunch of questions I wanted to ask her about the Richelieu Incident, obviously. Since all of them were either pointless to ask, damned rude, or both, I settled for, "wow. You must have had a great counselor." She looked up at me, surprised. I shrugged. "If it had been me, I would've gone back to Jefferson and gotten a job in a windowless cubicle."

Thank *God* but that got a laugh. "I'm really stubborn, Pam. And I decided it was just the way the universe works. Random chance from an impersonal cosmos, right? Nothing you can obsess over." Her face got harder. "But if there's a pattern, then it's *not* impersonal. And I want to find out what tried to kill me, Pam. I really, really do."

And on *that* cheery note, I was off to the counselor. Even if this last mild incident (hey, nobody even got injured!) hadn't triggered an automatic rescheduling, all the earlier craziness easily justified me getting treated early. Besides, it's better to get the bad stuff out of your head as quickly as you can, before it can fester.

I didn't expect my regular live therapist to be available, so I wasn't surprised when John wasn't. But I knew Diana a little, well enough that she could lead me through the talk therapy part of the session, at least. There aren't that many humans here on One-Eighteen. Everybody usually ends up meeting each other.

It also helped that we were using the emergency checklist, instead of the standard weekly one. Diana didn't speed me through it as I disrobed and put on a paper gown, but we didn't dawdle, either. In fact, she was pretty good at figuring out what the top five neuroses were that I had likely just encouraged. Maybe even better than John would have, but I like John. That's even more important when working with a live therapist. The personal touch helps a lot.

I don't want you to think Diana was incompetent, though. I was in just the right mood when I took the pill, then put in my bite guard: slightly tense, aware of my likely incipient hangups, and grimly ready to pop them like balloons before they could do the same to me. Because you really want to be *motivated* when they send that electrical charge through the induction helmet, let me tell you. The more motivated you are going in, the less time it takes before you can get out.

Most people feel pain during their counseling session, but some don't. It's probably due to what parts of your brain got overstimulated during your first time wearing the helmet. Me, I don't get anything physical. Instead, I get a curdled mass of emotions, all swirling around inside my head until I puke them out. Through my skin — at least, it *feels* like my pores are puking out all the fear and dread and disgust. Oh, and helplessness, like when you're physically vomiting and you desperately want to stop, but can't. You just have to endure wave after wave of your internal filth as it pushes its way out of your soul, until there's nothing left to retch up. And then the induction helmet makes you dry-retch a few times, just to be on the safe side.

I sometimes wonder whether it'd be better if I just had the sense of boiling acid flowing through my veins. That's the most common sensation, and most people seem to handle it okay, right? Besides, the side effects don't last long in any case.

But the *treatment* does. I felt a hell of a lot better even before I took off my filthy, stinking gown and headed for the shower. I always imagine the last bits of my scrubbed-out neuroses and anxieties getting washed away by the hot water, and that *is* a common reaction to a counselor session. It's the other reason why there's always a shower or bath after one, even in situations where hot water is regulated. It's all about maintaining good mental hygiene.

"Had a counseling session, huh?" Nur said later that day, as we went through the personnel database together. "I hate those."

I had dragged him in to help out with the Burcu Appeasement Project. We were looking for *former* on-planet staffers who might have been involved in software piracy, going through their records to see if any of them had done something idiotic, like talk about pirating software while using a company communications account. I was unpleasantly surprised at how many idiots we had apparently hired in the past. But it *was* generating a list of names, they *weren't* supposed to have been doing it in the first place, and — this was the important part — everybody on the list was somewhere else. I hoped this meant that the usefulness of this list would be pretty much nil.

"I don't think anybody really likes counseling, Nur. It's just something you have to do."

"Sure. It's something you *have* to do. As in, we don't have a choice. All we know is, we're required to clean out our heads on a regular basis. Something wants us doing that. How do we know we're not doing something to them while we're hooked up to the machines?"

"That's just paranoia talki... hold on. *We're* doing something to *them*? Shouldn't that conspiracy theory supposed to be the other way around?"

"Yeah, see, that's just what *They* want you to think. You've heard the stories, right? About people getting brainwashed during a counseling session? But it's always somebody who knows somebody who knew somebody that it happened to, so we know that's just a ship legend, like the Map to the Last Redoubt or the Screaming AI.

"But what if, what if, something's taking all that liveliest awfulness in our heads, saving it, and *using* it? The headset's eating our souls, but one micro-bite at a time, so it's too small for us to notice over our lifetimes. But it adds up! It totally adds up! Enough to give something regular meals. Or *somethings*."

I have to admit, Nur was always good at coming up with stuff like this. Complete nonsense, but it wasn't boring. "All right, Nur. Say that's true. What do we do about it?"

He looked at me, puzzled. "Why would we do anything about it?"

"Uh, you just said it was bad. Soul-eating, right?"

"Well, sure, but I also said 'micro-bites.' If there's something in the machine that's eating all that crap it's just yanked out of my head, hey, it's welcome to it. Better out than in, like they say."

"So why are you worrying about it?"

"I'm *not* worrying about it, Pam. Why would you think I was?"

"Well, you just told me you hate doing counseling sessions."

"Yeah, well, we all do. But it's not because of the *soul* thing. I hate 'em because after one, everything tastes like bananas afterward." Nur looked revolted. "I hate bananas."

I winced. "Okay, Nur, *that's* the weirdest thing you've said today."

We did end up finding one person who was maybe both involved in software piracy, and inconveniently still present on-planet. Or at least sort of present, because he was currently approaching the freezing point of oxygen. "Adam Sild?" said Nur. "That's the guy who went space-happy, right?"

"Ayup," I said, trying to be upset about it. I didn't want to throw anybody to the wolves, but if I *had* to, then somebody in cryo-freeze would do. Not even Rubicon could order us to thaw the bastard out, especially after the, ah, *side effects* from this morning. I couldn't imagine him even wanting to. Once Adam was cured, there wouldn't be any point to try him for anything he had done *before*. The personality reconstruction would be rehabilitation (or punishment) enough.

Maki agreed with me, when I called her and The Process in. "I hate saying it, but this solves two problems," she said. "We give Adam to Rubicon, he brings him back to Earth for treatment, and then both of them are out of our hair."

"Only theoretically, Miss Maki," The Process pointed out. "All of you have speculated that Commander Rubicon's avowed purpose here is a cover for his true mission. He will not want a suspect in line with his public goals, but not his private ones."

"So what? He'll just come up with a new lie. Or maybe he'll come clean?" Nur laughed at my derisive snort. "What? It could happen!"

"Even if it doesn't," Maki mused, "it'd still surprise him. We could shake out more information that way, try to figure out what the *Redacted* is really up to."

"Forgive me for asking this," interjected The Process, "but do you all consider the ship and its crew to be some kind of enemies?"

I swear to God, it just *loves* tossing those kind of random question-bombs into conversations. "Well, when you put it like *that*," I eventually replied, "no. They're all just being secret, paranoid, condescending, and arrogant. I don't think they're trying to *hurt* us."

"Huh. I wonder if they're worried we might try to hurt *them*," Nur said. "Settlements this big don't usually rot out without it being obvious way ahead of time, but I've heard stories. I don't mean fun stories, either. I mean the kind that you really don't want to be true, because it'd be bad." He shuddered. "*Real* bad."

"Then that settles it!" Maki deliberately chirped, in full Chipper Corpo mode. "We really should tell Rubicon *all* about Adam. It'll help reassure him that we're useful, accommodating, and sane."

I refrained from noting that two out of three weren't bad. If for no other reason than I wasn't sure whether I wanted to be useful, or accommodating. Staying sane was non-negotiable, obviously.

When I got home that night, I had just enough time to rummage through the fridge before I got a call — from Syah. "Hello! How's the signal?"

That was an interesting greeting, but I decided to allow it. "It's fine. Why, is this a test?"

"In more ways than one, Pamela. I told my boss that I'd log out for the night when I finally whipped the net interface back into shape. So I'm routing this call through it. It looks good, right?"

Actually, it was a little flickery and there was the slightest of drones, but... "It's great," I smiled and lied. *Screw the interface. I remember* **you** *looking good, and I'd rather eat out than look through my leftovers.* I was also more aware of the various defensive nozzles and sprayers built into the walls and ceiling than usual, and I didn't want anything killing my mood, so: "You eat yet?"

"Define 'eating.' There was Stuff in the vending machines. I think I've tried every color by now." He frowned. "What *is* Stuff, anyway? I've never had it before."

"Stuff? Oh, it's local. Some automatic program kicked out a few different versions of it when the first XHum field team showed up on One-Eighteen. Survival rations in case the new species needed them, you know? But most of the colors aren't half bad." I smiled. "But nobody wants to live on 'em long. You're in luck, though. I know a place that does a decent not-cow steak."

Ironically, this week's sauce for the not-cow was derived from Purple Stuff. It was good, though. Purple's the second best

Stuff flavor there is. Syah even got a little extra from the waiter, for his fries. "It's weird," he said as he wiped up the last bits. "The flavor's completely alien, but I don't mind at all."

"You're not fond of offworld foods?" I asked, mildly surprised. "Figuring out what's good on what world is part of the fun."

"Familiarity," intoned Syah, waving his napkin around in a suitably solemn fashion, "breeds contempt. But not as much as having people foist the most awful dishes on me, every planet I've ever been on. But Stuff's pretty good! Purple's definitely my favorite."

Only because you've never had Green, I thought. But nobody eats Green. At least, not once they realize what it tastes like. So instead I said, "You've been to many planets?"

"I've been to..." he scrunched his head and looked up "...ten, or so? Not counting Bolivar. Or Earth."

"Earth? Ooh, impressive. I've never gotten that far into human space. What's it like?"

"'Dull as the grave.'" We shared a quick grin at the literary reference, but Syah shook his head. "Zare wasn't joking when he wrote that, though. Nothing happens on Earth until it's been considered, checked, and cleared. And if things were good enough today, they're good enough for tomorrow, right?" He drank some of the local beer — well, it was brewed here, from Terran wheat and hops. The local vegetation is edible, but it ferments weirdly. The local 'honey' is even stranger. Our mead is... *heady*. "It's a great place to learn computer programming, but it's no place for excitement."

He looked at me. "Is this the point where you go all Jeffersonian about Earth?" But he was smiling when he said it.

"Oh, no," I said, grandly waving my fork around. "Earth came to its senses and offered to give us back our disreputable ancestors' citizenships *years* ago. We all said 'No, thank you,' with a smile and then everything was fine. Some of us even retire there now. From time to time. If they can't think of anywhere better to go.

"But I *would* like to visit," I admitted. "I might even want to go to the USNA or SEDA, see the places where my great-grandparents were born." *And then cause just as much ruckus as* **they** *did, just so that Earth would have to transport* **me**, *too*. But I didn't say that. Bolivarians don't have the same tradition of cheerful troublemaking that Jeffersonians do. I was *not* trying to scare this guy away.

"Anyway, tell me about where you're from on Bolivar." I smiled at him. "Is it nice?"

"Truthfully? ...no, not really. I'm from Złożony Siedemnaście. Fifth best aqua-cultural productivity record for the coastal region, regular as clockwork!" He shook his head, and poured more beer. "It's actually a big deal, on-planet. Towns fight for the top ten spots on the regional rankings. Sie' isn't *horrible*, either. The beach is nice, and they don't have any problems with infrastructure. There's just not much *point* to the place."

I noted how he didn't mention anything about having a family, and I very carefully avoided asking about one. When you're in the Tomb Worlds, you wait to be invited before you start asking some questions. It's not like the old days, but even the colony worlds are dangerous, when compared to life on nice, dull Terra. Not that I could talk about my day, speaking of awkward conversational topics. Even that early, I *wanted* to talk to him about what happened with Adam, but we don't discuss space-happy encounters with people you've just met. That's pretty intimate, you know? It's not fair to burden casual acquaintances with that, without warning. Even if I was already hoping he might be the kind of person I could share with like that.

So I talked about my family, instead. They're all fine, so I don't mind. Besides, some of the stupid scrapes a Jeffersonian family can get themselves into is pretty funny, as long as they didn't happen to *you*.

I wish I could dare see them again.

CHAPTER SEVEN

A Breath Before the Plunge

Syah was a gentleman. In fact, he was maybe a little bit *too* much of a gentleman, which might have been annoying on any *other* date. But since I had spent a chunk of my day wrestling with a space-happy cryo-zombie, I was pretty much only up for a walk home, a kiss on the cheek, and a firm commitment on another dinner date that weekend.

So now it was just me, and my apartment, and the events of the day, and *dammit*. That son of a bitch — I felt bad even when thinking it. The space-happy are sick, not depraved — really had revived and tried to walk around, despite being literally frozen. Having no idea why he could do that wasn't helping, either. Which was feeling extremely counterintuitive, since not knowing why is so often a *good* thing. Selective ignorance is a luxury and a virtue, out here in the Tomb Worlds.

There's even empirical evidence of that. Back in the first days of interstellar exploration, Earth tried to *figure it all out*. You can see why, too. We had opened up the door to the outside universe, and discovered that it was all post-apocalyptic landscape, as far as the eye could see. Who had done it? Were they still out there, doing it? Did anybody survive? All great questions to ask, right?

Wrong. We've never found out who or what destroyed the Amalgamation. We've never seen any marauders *or* survivors, either. We did discover pretty quickly that it was really easy for explorers of the Tomb Worlds to brood on the questions, then go nuts. It's amazing Earth allowed any exploration at all.

Except that it's not amazing, obviously. The Amalgamation

produced wonders by the score. Their technology and culture are far beyond ours, even after two centuries of learning via corpse-looting, but we can carefully sift through the ashes of these dead worlds and find all sorts of treasures. Hell, that was why we were on One-Eighteen. The planet's inhabitants were so close to ours, we can sometimes work out their particular flavor of logic. That makes a big difference when you're trying to figure out how to reverse engineer, say, a contragravity drive.

It's also more survivable. Planets where the original inhabitants are more, well, *alien* range from spooky and dangerous to *really* spooky and dangerous. Is it still worth the risk? Sure. Does Earth like to think about just what price people pay out here, in exchange for the latest piece of alien tech? Absolutely not.

I can't even blame Earth for that. If people on the colonies or the Tomb Worlds could get away with that level of ignorance, we'd happily embrace it ourselves. But we're here, we don't see Earth as our real home, and we can't ignore everything. So we settle for not thinking too hard about strangeness, like smoking-cold hands fighting reinforced straps *and winning*, or the way that Adam neither breathed or twitched as he struggled to stand, or how I thought a ripple of pain passed over what I could see of his features as Maki fired that blue goo into his back...

Clearly, I wasn't going to be letting this go. I couldn't do what I *really* wanted to do, either — which was go flying, and let my worries settle themselves out on their own. No, I was stuck here on the ground until I could come up with an excuse to get in the air.

Fine, I thought. *I may have to obsess about this a little tonight, but at least I won't do it alone.* "Hey, Process!" I yelled. "Gonna need some company for a bit."

One nice thing about The Process is, it knows when to nag, and when to go along with whatever it is the talking monkey's gibbering over. "Always, Wind-Walker Tanaka. I assume that you need to go over this morning's events with someone?"

"No, I want to go over it with *you*. You're the only person on this planet who can't get a screw loose."

"I understand the idiom, but I am not a person."

"You're close enough. Anyway, something about the incident with Adam's bugging me."

"And what would that be?"

"Aside from the obvious?" I chuckled, with laudable calmness. Those emergency therapy sessions *work*. "I have *no idea*. If I knew, it wouldn't be bugging me."

"Understood. Calling up his employment file now..."

"Actually, no. Give me his regular biography, first." I stretched. "I know what he did, but we need to know who he was."

Who he was was a surprise, right from the start. Technically, Adam Sild had Great Power citizenship. Pakt Euroazjatycki, to be precise. His entire family had been transported to Bolivar when he was six, for the horrible crime of multiple counts of unauthorized civil disobedience. The Great Powers don't strip citizenship from minor transportees, but there was no sign Adam had ever tried to get a Terran passport. I understood that completely, since I won't take USNA *or* SEDA citizenship, either, no matter how many times it's offered. No Jeffersonian from a transportee family would. If they want us back so badly, well, to quote my great-grandfather: it's good to want.

Anyway, Adam's resume was what you'd expect from an aspiring scout: as much naturalist training as you can get on Bolivar, a long-term contract with S/CI, and a posting on...

"Process," I asked carefully, "is there anybody else on-planet who has been posted on Terkutuk?"

"Nobody whose records I can reliably access," replied The Process. "Which does not include the crew of the *Redacted*. But Specialist Sild came to this planet three years ago, and has not gone offworld. He could not have been directly involved with whatever happened on Terkutuk."

"How about indirectly?" I flipped printouts. "Maybe he knew

somebody... strike that. Obviously he knew plenty of people from Terkutuk. Maybe he knew something about one of them that might be relevant, now that the facility there is gone."

"You will not be permitted to revive him and ask," The Process warned. "It would be far too dangerous to everyone, *including him*. He *must* be taken somewhere where he can be fixed."

"I didn't say I wanted to revive him!" *Yet*, I admitted to myself. Or that, while I had been working out ways for us to safely interrogate a homicidal maniac, I wasn't really concerned about how to make it safe for the homicidal maniac, too. The Process simply has different priorities than we do. *Better* ones, at times.

I took another look at Adam's corporate headshot. He looked better in it than he had on our last acquaintance: regular, slightly rugged features, with nicely blue eyes and a cheerful mouth. His skin wanted to be pale, but there was too much sun in the way. He kept his hair so short that you could barely tell it was black.

None of that mattered, now that he was space-happy. And somehow, the worst bit was that when they put Adam back together, he'd be all the way back. One hundred percent, no hidden crazy that would pop out later. It'd be like he'd never gone psychotic and homicidal, half chewing off his own tongue for the sake of the pain. Some of the churches think 'space-happy' is really just a euphemism for 'demonic possession,' and you can see their point.

"Something is confusing you," observed The Process.

"I guess," I replied. "I think. Maybe? You know we don't like to think too much about the space-happy, yet here I am, doing it. It's stupid. I should sleep."

"Yes, Wind-Walker Tanaka. You *should* sleep. But that's not what I meant. I meant that you are showing physical symptoms that are consistent with a human state of confusion. You are reacting to something."

"Really? What?"

"I don't know." The Process doesn't get irritable, for real, but it has a specific tone for situations where a human version of it *would* get irritable. I was hearing that tone now. "If I knew what you were reacting to, I would ask more leading questions until you had worked it out for yourself."

"Fair enough. So what's bugging me?" I looked at the files again. "It's not the biography, not even the Terkutuk thing... what is it?" I called up Adam's photo again, gave it a good look — and then I saw it. "His eyes! They're blue."

"Yes, they are. His medical and social files confirm it."

"Well, they were gray-green when he attacked me."

"Interesting."

I snorted. "'Interesting?' That's all I get?"

The Process was never really *snippy*, but it could manage sardonic. "I thought it more polite than making null statements, like 'Are you *sure*?' or 'That's *impossible*!' You are neither sure, nor is it actually impossible. However, the space-happy do not suffer from that kind of physiological change. It seems more likely that the lighting was bad, or that you are remembering events incorrectly."

That was true. The space-happy might be flying on homebrewed psychotics, and sure, they can do the sorts of things you'd expect when you don't care about compound fractures. But they're not *actual* monsters. They don't spit acid or grow bat wings. And they don't change the colors of their eyes.

"Was there any footage from the attack — no, right, the network was down for whole minutes. Any cameras there, the buffer would have filled up right away. Damn my luck! The timing couldn't have been worse."

Was it just bad luck? But I dismissed that thought, right away. There was no way the attack could have been coordinated with the network outage. It was just something awful — and awful things don't need a reason to happen on the Tomb Worlds. Everybody out here learns this very quickly.

Then it struck me. "Wait! Adam. We can just, I don't know,

peel back an eyelid or something."

"Absolutely not," Greg told me, bright and early next morning.

I had gone to him before Maki because I *knew* she'd say no, and could I even blame her? Once you get the space-happy in the cryo-freezer, the idea is to *keep* them there. If they're in there, they can't get *out*. Since Greg was the only other person on the planet with the authority to do a resuscitation, I'd just have to get him to agree with my scheme.

Only he wasn't agreeing. "I'm not going to ask Maki to thaw Adam out, Pam. I mean, you can hear how stupid that idea is when I say it aloud, right?"

"It's the only way to check the eyes, Greg. We don't have any footage of them when he went after me, or when he woke up. The pre-freeze checklist doesn't include looking at eye colors. One look, and we'll know."

Greg shrugged. "And then what?"

"What do you mean?"

"Let's say you're right. His eyes have changed colors. So what?"

I was legitimately shocked. "Come *on*, Greg! We're in the *Tomb Worlds*. 'If you don't understand it, it's dangerous,' remember? Maybe Adam found something out there in the wilderness that drove him space-happy. Maybe it might still be in his system."

"Sure, Pam. Only, *definitely* Maki would have caught it when she did the preliminary scans. You know how thorough those are. We've been trying to figure out the space-happy for centuries. If there was anything in his blood, stomach, or brain that shouldn't have been there, it'd have shown up."

"Right!" I caught myself raising my voice. "That's all the more reason to check and see whether he's picked up something that *doesn't* show up on the regular scans."

Greg snorted. "No, Pam. That's all the more reason to stick a note on Adam's file warning whoever *does* open his freezer that the guy's eyes reportedly changed color. If it's not important, there's no harm. And if it *is* important, better a properly trained medteam handles it than we do. I'm not being paid to take that risk, and neither are you. Hell, neither is Maki. Besides, if Adam *did* pick up some kind of bug or parasite, then why didn't we catch it, too?"

"How would I know, Greg? I move haulers across the sky. But... ha! That *is* something to ask Maki. We can check if any new diseases have cropped up." We don't have that problem on One-Eighteen, though. Diseases, I mean. The local bacteria don't care too much for humans, apparently. Even our food takes a lot longer to rot.

Greg sighed. "Fine. I'll talk to her, ask her to do a mass health and wellness check as per her duties as chief physician." He smiled. "And if she says no, I'll tell her that she needs to *order* that check, as per her duties as XHum local CEO."

I shook my head. "This staffing crunch is ridiculous. I've been saying for years that we need more people, or fewer hats."

"Yeah, you would know, wouldn't you? You've been onplanet the longest." Greg shook his head. "Have you *really* never noticed how hard it is to keep people here?"

"Maybe a little," I fibbed, because I wasn't going to admit that I hadn't noticed at all. "I spend a lot of time in the air. Or I did, before all of this started."

"Oj, I know, Pam. All that flight time's why you get paid more than I do. Hell, that's why you made Chief Pilot so fast. Pilots are even harder to keep here than regular researchers." He shrugged. "At least we get replacements, and most of them last for a standard contract. Some sites out there can't keep staff at *all*."

I snorted. "Yeah, sure: the places where the atmosphere's sulfur dioxide and the wind's boiling acid. But One-Eighteen about as close as you can get to human-standard. *Nice* human-standard. I'd retire here, if we had a permanent colony set up."

"And yet, we don't," Greg replied. "The first base manager talked about petitioning for gray colony status, and then she stopped. She only lasted a contract and a half, too. Nobody's lasted as long as you have, Pam. *Nobody*."

"I get that. But I don't understand what the big deal is!"

"Nobody does," Greg said. "For most of us, that's one big reason why we don't stay too long on this planet. Like you said before: if we don't understand it, it's dangerous."

Naturally, Maki was also uninterested in unfreezing Adam, although she at least understood why I cared. "Sudden eye color changes in adults does usually mean something," she admitted. "But we regularly check for anomalies. Adam was in... well, the state of his health was *unsurprising*. There was nothing that would suggest a change that significant."

"So it must have been some bug from the planet!" I knew I wasn't going to convince Maki, but it felt important to hammer this point down. "Maybe Adam found something out there and out of the way, and it infected him. Even if it didn't make him space-happy, it was still enough to change his eyes."

"Assuming the change actually happened, Pam." Maki put up a hand. "I know, I know. You've no reason to lie. But that doesn't mean what you're saying is true, either. And you don't have any evidence."

That was fair, dammit. Nobody trusts unsupported eyewitness accounts in the Tomb Worlds, and the video camera footage from the medcenter hadn't caught a good enough look at Adam's eyes. I was surprised I hadn't started to second-guess myself. "All right. I guess I need to get some. ...Hey, Process! Who's doing Adam's, I don't know what you call it? His patrol?"

We were having problems with the network again. The Process sounded a little flat. No lag in response, though. "Do you mean his weekly circuit survey?"

"If that's what we called him regularly going through the woods from here to the other bases, yes." Usually we fly shuttles from base to base, but it makes sense to cut paths through the wilderness, in case of emergency. And walk them regularly, to keep 'em from going away.

"In that case, Wind-Walker Tanaka, the answer is: nobody. Another qualified wilderness scout has not yet been assigned. It may be some time before one is, since the assignment is considered low priority."

"Really?" I asked. "Why?"

"General safety considerations. There's never been an incident in the local countryside."

"Really?" Maki blinked a couple of times. "The forest out there's *unnerving*. I don't even want to look at it through the window."

Now it was *my* turn to blink. I don't go running through the woods myself, but from *my* window One-Eighteen's not very scary. Mostly it's green. Greener than Jefferson, even. I wasn't scared of the wildlife, either. There aren't that many critters out there that are *big* enough to bother a human, and none of them want to...

"Hold on," I said. "No incidents? Not even one with wild dogs?"

"Adam never reported an encounter with one," The Process replied.

We always wince when The Process gets that precise. It usually means that we've missed something, and now we had to figure out what it was. Guess once a teacher, always a teacher.

Five minutes later, we finally got it confirmed that the Council *had* bugged Maki's office, via a call by my dear friend Lieutenant Commander Burcu Nowak. Not that she actually called Maki. Oh, no. The call went directly to *my* phon.

"This call is private," she immediately told me. "Go somewhere where there isn't anyone else."

I gave the order some thought. "No," I said evenly, and set the phon for full visual and audio display. Then I settled in to see what would happen next. I was personally hoping for a fit of apoplexy. Burcu and I hadn't met in person since that first meeting, mostly because of her gorge issues. There was just something about me that she couldn't stand, and there was something about *her* that made me indifferent to her problems. I tried to make myself feel bad about that, only I kept failing.

"This is not negotiable," she eventually grated out. "The call must be secure."

"Oh, it's not *negotiable*? Why didn't you say so?" I replied — and disconnected. My phon immediately started beeping again, so I powered it off completely. And when it *still* kept beeping, I rolled my eyes and yanked out the battery.

Maki's expression during all of this went from: confused, to amused, then concerned, and stayed there. "What are you doing?" she asked me.

"Communicating," I replied. "And setting boundaries."

"She *does* have a certain authority," Maki pointed out. "What if it's actually important?"

"If it's really important, Maki, she knows where I am. So she can come here, or — ah, there we are!" Maki's own deskphon had started blinking. "She's decided to call *you*, instead."

"Which she should have done at the start, right," Maki muttered as she engaged the phon. "Good morning, this is Maki... I'm sorry, who is this? Oh, *hello*, Lieutenant Commander Nowak! So good to hear from you — oops, there was some interference on your end of the call, I said that *it's good to hear from you*. How can I help you today? You would like to speak with Chief Pilot Tanaka? Hold on, let me check if she's available." She muted the phon and looked at me. "*Are* you available?"

"Ask her what it's about."

Maki gave me a mock glare and unmuted. "Yes, she's here, but we're in a meeting right now over a local issue and Pilot Tanaka is *extremely* busy at the moment. She asked me to ask you what the subject of the call's about? Ah. Well, can you give me your contact information, then? I'm sure she'll call you back when she can... yes, I can hold." Maki muted again and said,

"I *could've* given you a little privacy, Pam. Maybe whatever she wants to tell you really is important enough to keep secret."

"Nah, Maki. I'm not going to play need-to-know games. If you or Greg don't need to know it, then neither do I. Besides," I went on, "she's just doing it to try to piss you off."

"Well, ye— oh, hello, I'm here, Lieutenant Commander. Sure, I'll be *happy* to put you on speaker. Hold on!"

And there Burcu was, on both speaker *and* visual. And her usual pleasant self. "You cannot trust the planetary chief executive officer of your corporation."

"Probably not," I agreed. "By the way, you can see I'm in her office, yes? But what *is* your reason?"

"Besides the obvious? She is the planetary CEO. And the chief medical officer, dealing with a reportedly anomalous case of SOVP. Clearly she has a vested interest in suppressing the truth."

Don't we all, I thought to myself. Aloud, I said, "You say that like there are times when the space-happy *aren't* anomalous. But you didn't need to call just to tell me how horrible us big, bad megacorps are. What's the *actual* reason for the call?"

"To offer assistance to the local authorities, of course." I'll give her credit for saying that with a straight face, at least. "Our orbital survey of the planet shows signs of unauthorized human habitation, located along the regular circuit of Scout Sild. They also show signs of recent occupancy."

I was surprised. That *was* relevant information, not to mention useful. One-Eighteen was one of those planets where you can't put up a satellite constellation — well, you *can*, but it'll get disrupted in short order by what's left of the automated planetary traffic control system. Everything below a certain size that doesn't have any large lifeforms aboard gets treated as space junk, to be cleared up. We can bounce signals off of one of precisely three manned orbital stations and get limited communications that way, and use the traffic control system ourselves to navigate, but all the *good* maps of One-Eighteen were taken at the time of the first planetary survey, and we don't have the time or ships to properly map out the surface to any kind of detail. Even the *Redacted*'s quick-and-dirty snapshot of the planet would be a good update for our files.

"That is very helpful to know, Lt. Commander." Maki carefully kept any chirpy obnoxiousness out of her voice. She looked at me, and I shrugged. Now was as good a time as any. "It may be directly relevant to your investigation. Our 'anomalous' SOVP victim may have been involved in software piracy. There was no evidence of it in his quarters, but if he had a storage space in the field…"

If I hadn't thought before that software piracy was a cover story, I would have started now. Burcu didn't react like she *really* cared how Adam might have been keeping contraband software in his shack in the country. "I see. When will you be investigating the structure?"

"Tomorrow," I said, without any argument at all. Well, it was more that I had already had that argument in my head. It made sense for me to check it out, since I knew the planet and they didn't. Plus, I *really* wanted to get some flight time in. "We're doing a flight plan right now." We actually hadn't been, at the start of that sentence, but I could count on The Process to start working on one somewhere between the words 'right' and 'now.' "Do you want an observer along?"

"We have one already," Burcu replied. "You. Observe everything, and send it all in."

I probably wouldn't have said, *well, screw you, too* — but Maki wasn't taking chances. "She'll be fitted with a three-sixty recorder. Also, may we please have access to that orbital survey?"

"Yes. May I assume that your company will stop treating all of the Council's reasonable data requests as being outrageous and unreasonable assaults on your civil liberties?"

Maki looked at me. I gave her a *we-do-need-the-data* grimace back. "Yes, Lt. Commander. We can be more charitable in our interpretations, at least on a case-by-case level."

"Interesting," Burcu said. "I was expecting more of a fight.

Perhaps I was overly hasty earlier." That almost sounded like an apology — but, fortunately for my dislike of the woman, she went on. "Or perhaps you merely wish to distract the Council from our mission. We shall see. Nowak out."

A minute later, the maps did in fact get squirted over. Burcu had even provided a separate file showing the 'unauthorized structures.' I sighed, trying not to lay it on too thick. "Guess I have to go check it out, then."

"We could send someone else," Maki pointed out. But she said it like she had to. "I know Burcu wants you, specifically, but she's not my boss. If I choose somebody else to investigate, that's my call, not hers."

"Sure. Who? I'm the only one who isn't busy. Besides, it should be safe enough." I technically offered a smile. "Everybody on the planet's accounted for."

CHAPTER EIGHT

The Cabin in the Woods

I had a spring in my step as I left. There hadn't been many opportunities to actually *fly* since the *Redacted* showed up, since usually my job entailed moving illicit artifacts to the spaceport. We weren't going to be doing any of that until our visitors departed, and guess how much regular flying a Chief Pilot gets to do on a planet with no emergencies and a bunch of self-sufficient work settlements?

So I was looking forward to the day trip. Low flying meant fast flying, on a level I normally didn't get to have. Doing a little impromptu exploring also sounded like fun. An excursion without danger sounded like just the thing for me.

...yes, well, if we knew how things would turn out, would any of us have left home?

The answer, by the way, is 'no.'

Burcu's 'signs of unauthorized human habitation' turned out to be a blobby bit on one section of one map. I'm not gonna lie. It's impressive that the *Redacted* got that much. *You* try mapping a planet from orbit at any kind of detail.

"But what are *they* looking for?" I asked Greg as he, Nur, and I analyzed the whole survey. Which is to say, we let The Process scan it all, then tried to think up smart questions to ask it. Or even smartass ones, because sometimes there's a serious answer to a sarcastic question.

"Well, they're definitely interested in the occupied parts of One-Eighteen," Greg said. "Their survey barely focused on Arali or Naraka" — the northern polar and off-by-itself equatorial continents, respectively; the one we mostly lived on is called Mitnal — "and didn't do as much as I'd like for the new artifact digs up north. They were focused on the areas around existing settlements. That's why they caught the Blob, see? They were taking pictures of everything along the path between Luxor and the Delilik farms."

"Which is weird, since there's nothing there, right? I thought the rangers only do the routes to keep the paths open."

"Well, we don't know that there's *nothing* there, Pam. We just know that *if* there's anything there, they leave human beings alone."

"There's absolutely something out there," Nur said. "It's impossible that the Amalgamation-killers could have gotten *everybody*. Somebody would have been in a vault, or in a black cryo facility. Or just gone fishing with the phon off. Not unless the killers spent a century going over every planet with a fine-tooth comb."

"There's plenty of places where it looks like that's exactly what they did, Nur," Greg pointed out. "Me, I think we don't think enough about pre-sapients. Not as smart as us, but more than just a dumb beast of the field. There could be whole colonies on One-Eighteen, and we'd never know it."

I rolled my eyes. "Gimme a break, Greg. If there's anything out there smart enough to hide from humans, it'd be smart enough to just show up one day at the outskirts of the base and, I don't know, beg for scraps. Or a clean pair of underwear. We've never found anything that smart. Ever. Some species, we've never even found their *corpses*."

"I know that's the argument. But what if they're descended from the people smart enough to successfully hide from whatever killed the Amalgamation? You think the current generation would be ready to trust any alien? At all?"

"I dunno," I muttered. "Ask The Process."

The Process doesn't always pick up on cues, but it always responds to this kind of discussion. "I also do not know, Wind-Walker Tanaka. I have never seen a living member of the Amalgamation who was not from your species. I have definitely not seen any pre-sentients begging at the camp perimeter, either."

"And there you go," I said as I stood up. "Not even The Process can confirm a sighting, and surviving aliens were almost the first thing we asked it to look for. They just ain't there."

"Which makes no sense." Greg looked mulish, about this, just like most people who want there to be aliens. "The galaxy is so *big*. How could they *all* be killed?" He waved it away. "Never mind. So, how do we go investigate the Blob? It's two day's walk between here and Delilik."

"Sure," I grinned, "if you actually *walk*."

As you might have guessed, I took the scenic route.

The remains of the planetary traffic system had *issues* with haulers skimming just above the tree-tops at several hundred miles per hour. Can't imagine why! Their mothers must have been scared by space-cheetahs, or something. But that was all right. Most of the path from here to the Delilik Autonomous Agronomic Facility was currently blessedly free of traffic laws. Those stretches that weren't, were stable enough that I could reduce speed in time to avoid grounding. It'd take finesse, but when I'm in the air I have that and to spare. Getting a look-see at Adam's main patrol route would just be a matter of flying straight, and making sure the cameras were properly recording this time.

Although a proper look-see would have involved me *walking* the path. That wasn't going to happen, though. It'd take too long, and I didn't know a damned thing about hiking through the woods. I do know how to fly in One-Eighteen's atmosphere, so I did that instead.

I made a bet with myself that I could spot anything interesting on my way to Delilik without having to use the cameras, and I lost that bet handily. I just saw green and brown blurs the entire time. Even if there had been a big sign saying "ADAM'S SECRET SHACK HERE," I'd have missed it. Which is why I had the cameras running. And why I had The Process helping me look — or, really, the other way around. If you tell The Process what to look for, it can find it faster than you ever could. But it absolutely sucks at figuring out what to look for in the first place.

Still, if I had walked, I would have found the 'secret shack' myself, since it wasn't exactly secret. Adam had cleared a small patch roughly halfway along the footpath to Delilik, and used the trees to build his shelter. I hadn't seen it during the flight simply because it was a very small clearing, but the photos showed two rough structures, made out of logs and what I guessed was dried mud. Just the sort of thing somebody might put together with a vibrosaw and some free time.

"These structures are not in our records," observed The Process. It didn't sound particularly upset about the lapse. "Are they some sort of emergency shelter?"

"They probably could be. I bet there's a stashed message rocket in there in case Adam twisted an ankle on the way. Or maybe he just liked the idea of spending the night in the woods. Are the buildings against regulations?"

"Not specifically, and Mr. Sild would have had considerable leeway in building them officially, particularly if it was couched in terms of safety. Indeed, the colony *should* authorize placing permanent structures on all the footpaths to remote sites."

"Sure. But then the rangers wouldn't have log cabins to sleep in. Living in a plastic and ceramic crate just wouldn't have the same appeal to them. Which is probably why Adam didn't ask for permission." I thought for a moment. "Or the other rangers, come to think of it. I bet they all have shacks, too."

"Is that something that needs to be checked, Wind-Walker Tanaka?"

I considered it. "Probably not. How are their psych statuses?"

"They are all within acceptable parameters." That sounded promising, until The Process ruined it by going on, "Just like Mr. Sild's was."

There was a small outcropping of rock near the shacks. It wasn't very large, but I could bring the hauler straight down and land safely, and that was all I needed. Contragrav's great stuff. I wish they'd crack the code on it.

I was surprised to find steps. Oh, they were roughly cut logs, set in places where it'd be tough to scramble up or down the path, but there were steps and it was a path. The sight of them bugged me, and it took a moment before I realized why: Adam *really* hadn't been trying to hide this place, if he had put together an emergency landing zone.

That wasn't all. As I moved onto the path and closer to the shacks, I could see signs where Adam had *tinkered* with the place. Ropes for where the path was steep. Strategic placement of gravel. Those might have just been good work practices, but there was also a sign saying "*kolde øl snart*," complete with arrow pointing to the shacks. It felt like Adam had an emotional connection to this location. He might even have loved it.

And one of the things about the space-happy is: they like to *use* all the things and places they love, only horribly.

Maybe I should have brought somebody with me, I thought again. But there wasn't anybody *to* come with me. One of the side effects of the Lifeping was that we had gotten an early report of a disaster on Averoigne Station. They desperately needed replacement parts for their life support units, and everyone was scrambling to figure out what spares we could send (to their credit, the *Redacted* had immediately dropped everything to coordinate shipments with us). I was only able to lock down this trip because I'd be bringing a cargo from Delilik to the main spaceport. Even then, I couldn't linger.

But it was a lovely day. Blue skies, the leaves of mildly alien trees rustling in exotic shades of green, and the golden hum of One-Eighteen, all around me. I may not like camping out, but this wasn't bad at all. "I wonder why nobody else *likes* this planet," I murmured. "It's perfect."

I regret not making that in the form of a question. You never know. The Process might have answered it.

Ironically, something on this perfect planet almost killed me ten minutes later.

Up close, Adam's shacks were solid-looking but extremely basic log-and-mud-caulk cabins, although he *had* sprayed sealant on the outsides to keep out the rain. There were other signs of modernity around: clear memory plastic being used for windows, some metal fittings on the rough-hewn table and benches, nothing that couldn't be backpacked in. It looked a lot like the Royal Ranger campgrounds back home on Jefferson, only scaled up for adults (and without the archery and firing ranges). That was the good part.

The bad part was that as I got closer, the reek of unwashed and unhealthy animals grew larger and larger. That *wasn't* good news, although at least I wasn't smelling dead bodies. "Process," I muttered, "there's something alive here. What can you scan?"

"Very little," the Process replied. "The planetary traffic net is nonexistent in your area right now, and the hauler does not have sophisticated sensors. Your personal camera is likewise not providing me with very much information to work with. On the other hand, I can maintain audio contact, even if my regular visuals are limited. I assume you are still armed?"

"What? Oh, yeah, I took the pistol with me." One-Eighteen isn't one of those worlds that's filled with things ready to rend the flesh from your living bones. Nothing native to One-Eighteen thinks we're good to eat, in fact. The planet also doesn't even have a lot of unique predator species. But it *does* have some large animals who spook easily, so we keep guns ready for field work. I brought mine mostly because it'd make a amazingly loud bang when fired. I figured that would be all I need.

The smell seemed to be coming from the smaller shack, so I tried the bigger one first. It had a door made up of actual planks, with that burned-edge look you get from a portable laser cutter, and a woven mat with the word "Velkommen" on it. Right now I wasn't feeling all that welcome, so I opened the door as quickly as I could and then sprang to the side, just in case something just wanted to come out and go away.

Nothing happened. Well, a light went on about ten seconds later, but that didn't count. And when I saw what its light revealed, I gasped.

Everything was so *normal*. There was a bed, chair, desk, and table. Those were all made out of wood. Modern amenities included a portable cooker and a field recycler, plus a few maps and books. The former were hand-made; from my quick look, Adam had been sketching out his land route. I frowned. "Why would he need this? The road's right there."

"Adam Sild took classes in cartography and technical drawing after coming here," The Process replied. "Perhaps this was homework. Or perhaps he simply enjoyed making maps."

"Among other things." I looked around again. Everything in this place was competently made, with an eye towards stability and comfort instead of artistry. It was a *nice* cabin.

What there wasn't was any sign that Adam had gone space-happy. No filth, blood, ritually sacrificed carcasses of local alien wildlife, *nothing*. He hadn't even scribbled on the walls! They always do that, even if they have to open a vein for the ink.

"This looks *nothing* like his apartment did," I told The Process as I did a slow 360 degree turn in place. "I guess he didn't come here after he went space-happy."

"That *is* interesting, Wind-Walker Tanaka. Especially since it eliminates your theory."

"Yeah." After we had found Adam's shacks, I had had the thought that maybe he had gone space-happy out here, then spent the next two days traveling to Luxor Base. Which would have explained why we hadn't seen him rampage earlier. But this room was far too pristine to be the site of a space-happy episode.

So much for theory. Meanwhile... "Process! Could you please scan these papers for me?"

"Certainly. Please close your eyes."

That was surprisingly unsettling to do. Well, maybe it wasn't *surprisingly* unsettling. But I didn't enjoy the approximate fifteen seconds of darkness before The Process said, "There's nothing dangerous on them. You can look."

So I did. And no, there was nothing dangerous on them. Nothing useful, either, at least on first glance. "Maps, surveys... hey, there's a journal! Wait, there was *nothing* freaky-deaky in there, Process? Diaries are always where you see the first signs."

"It is a weekly log of what Mr. Sild saw on his trips back and forth on his circuit. Plus lists of things a human might need to keep a log cabin in good repair. Nothing more."

"So he *wasn't* here." I looked around, as if I was expecting a sample of ritual horrors to have manifested while my back was turned. "Then where *was* he?"

That was when I started to swear. Because there were two shacks here.

The smell wasn't too bad until I had opened the door, but it made up for it really quickly afterward. It was the kind of vile you get when the local bacteria have difficulty processing Terran biomatter. Including our, ah, *waste*. The planetary ecosystem is very good for food storage, and really bad for sewage maintenance.

This shack hadn't been designed for human occupancy. The ceiling was lower, and there wasn't much furniture. Just a bunch of now-filthy shelves, a filthier rug... and a creature. At first, I didn't recognize it — and when I did, I swore. I had been hoping Adam was just keeping a cat or maybe a rabbit, somehow. Nope, not with my luck!

I had flushed out a dog. A damned *dog*.

Nobody brings pets to the Tomb Worlds anymore. Or at least not to One-Eighteen. There are a lot of places where cats can settle in, and a lot of different places where dogs can, but there's something in the atmosphere of this planet that does things to any Earth life larger than — well, every animal that wasn't human, honestly. Mostly, what it did was kill those species off, but dogs and cats are tough buggers. So they got to suffer from their own version of going space-happy. Wasn't that lucky of them?

Luckily, going space-happy didn't affect the dogs and cats the same way as it does us. It mostly makes them avoid humans completely — it was like every scrap of domestication had been burned out of them — with the extra wrinkle that the condition was permanent. You can drag a space-happy person back to sanity, but once a dog was lost to wildness, it stayed lost. Worse, this creature looked hungry enough to forget who the apex predator was supposed to be.

I didn't like its looks either. It was the size of a golden retriever, with the same kind of build, but its hair was a mangy patch of gray and greenish fur; its mouth, full of loose and slightly oozing teeth, and its burning eyes mixed hurt, confusion, and disgust in equal proportion. Dogs and cats *really* don't like living on One-Eighteen, and it was folk wisdom that the few feral ones that manage to survive dimly blame humans for bringing them here. Based on the dog's reaction at seeing me, I was absolutely certain of that folk wisdom.

In fact, it was abundantly clear that the dog was ready to take its frustrations literally out of my hide. The damned thing moved so fast. Like an idiot I had opened the door without my gun ready, and the dog sprang at me so quickly I didn't have time to draw it. The beast was as heavy as a golden retriever, too — heavy enough to stagger me back as it tried to scrabble up my chest and lock its slimy jaw on my throat. It managed it, too, after a few seconds of confused struggle. Its jaw wasn't strong enough to break through the tough fabric of my pilot suit, but it was strong enough to *squeeze*. And strong enough to hold on as I frantically span the dog around, trying to snap it off of my increasingly constricted neck.

I imagine the whole scene would have been dementedly funny, to the right kind of person (you know, a sadist). At the time? I *knew*, the moment that its jaws closed on me, that this was how I was going to die. This was how One-Eighteen was going to kill me. At that moment I felt a weird kinship with all my friends and coworkers here, because they all went around being terrified of this planet, and I could never understand why. But *now* I understood. One-Eighteen had just been waiting for me to let my guard down. Once I had, it was time for me to go.

The horrible thing about being strangled is that you can't make good decisions for long on no oxygen. If you don't make a good decision *fast*, you won't have much time to correct it. I had been punching the dog, over and over again, feeling its bones break under my frantic fists, but it just wouldn't let go. My punches were getting weaker, as I used up the oxygen in my blood, and soon I was scrabbling at the jaws with my hand, shoving myself into walls and furniture to get the filthy thing off of my *neck*. That didn't work, either. Somehow by then I had fallen to my knees, feeling the blackness curling around me, punctuated with those yellow motes that show up when you get *really* dizzy... and then one hand brushed across the holster strapped to my thigh.

Dying or not, some things you never forget — like a Jeffersonian quick-draw. I had the gun in my hand without having to think about it (which is the only way I could have drawn it), and at this range aiming was easy. I just stuck it into flesh that wasn't mine, and pulled the trigger in three frantic shots.

People like to talk about hysterical strength, and berserker rages, and the rest of it. But that's not how bodies work. If you blast huge chunks of flesh, blood, and bone out of something, it notices. And even a maddened dog will howl when it takes a mortal wound.

The sudden, sweet agony of air pushing through an almost-kinked airpipe came perilously close to knocking me all the way out anyway, but I forced myself up, grabbing a shelf with the hand not holding a gun. As soon as I had both feet under me, I turned to see the dog now huddled on the rug, howling as the blood pumped from its wounds. It was clearly about to die, but I shot it three more times anyway, because I'm not a cruel woman. Then I staggered to the nearest wall while scrambling for a healing patch, only pausing long enough to throw up the entire contents of my stomach in one long go. And didn't *that* just feel marvelous, not to mention add its unique odor to the reek of the room.

The Process waited to start talking until after the patch started to take hold. "The *Redacted* is preparing an emergency shuttle. They can be at your location in fifteen minutes. Should I tell them to stand down, since you are walking and stable?"

"Yes," I croaked. But not as much as I should have been. The stuff in the patch is one hell of a witch's brew. I didn't even mind throwing up, now. "Tell Greg and Maki I'll get back to securing the site as soon as I secure the dog. And thank you for not distracting me."

"It did not seem productive to do so." Which was enough explanation, from The Process's point of view. It doesn't hate us. You can even say that it loves us, assuming it's really self-aware enough for that. I mean, The Process jumps through hoops to give humans a fighting chance of navigating the dead ashes of Amalgamation space. And it obviously did what it could to keep me alive. But if I had died, The Process wouldn't grieve, or torment itself over what it could have done differently. There are a lot of humans. Individually, we're all eventually going to die. The Process can't get hung up on any one individual fatality.

But that was all right, because I had my own job to do. I approached the dog, which was a gory mess, but *definitely* dead. All the same, I carefully bent down and even more carefully peeled back an eyelid... to reveal a gray-green eye. One just like the one I had seen on Adams.

"And while you're talking to them," I said evenly, "mention that I've found evidence of local biological contamination of Terran life. One that might be linked to Sudden-Onset Violent

Psychosis."

After all of that, finding Adam's server was almost anticlimactic. He had plugged in an Amalgamation data cube to store his (presumed) ill-gotten pirate booty, and it looked... like an Amalgamation data cube. "Hey, Prospect!" I rasped. "This thing encrypted?"

"I do not know, Wind-Walker Tanaka. Please do not touch the data cube until I have scanned it."

"Yeah, yeah, I know. It's delicate." The Amalgamation used a weird encryption method for its data storage units, at least when it came to us half-uplifted types. The Process says that it's to keep us from knowledge we can't be expected to safely use, and we've learned by now to take that warning seriously. There's plenty of stories about what happened to people who didn't.

Now, I was assuming that Adam already had whatever puzzle-lock on it disabled, but why take chances? So I just stared at the cube's shifting, admittedly-pretty yellow and black design, until The Process spoke up again. "There was no Amalgamation encryption on the data. I am also not detecting any kind of poisonous or psychoactive substances on the surface You can safely retrieve it."

I popped it out of its holder. "Awesome." I still wore gloves while grabbing it, though, and carefully put it in a guaranteed-shielded sample bag. It's not that I didn't *trust* The Process, but I knew where this thing had been.

That left the nasty task of securing the dog, too. It looked a lot smaller in death. When I dumped it into a body bag from the first aid kit, it almost rattled around inside the bag until the memory plastic contracted. I carefully didn't wonder if it had once been somebody's pet.

I just as carefully put the bag in one of the hauler's external cargo hatches. I didn't really think it was going to get better from being shot six times, but I also didn't want the corpse in the cabin with me. If anybody had asked, I would have given the excuse that I didn't need the distraction — and, from the way that the ghosts on the radio seemed louder than usual, that might have even been true.

CHAPTER NINE

A Deep Breath Before the Plunge

So, they quarantined One-Eighteen that afternoon. Surface, orbital, everybody. People take even suspected biological contamination events seriously, out in the Tomb Worlds. Greg had ordered it (with Maki approving) even before Captain Rubicon had called up to demand — exactly that. From what Greg told me later, Rubicon had looked mildly surprised to hear it had already been done, and unexpectedly pleased when we insisted that the quarantine applied to *his* ship, too.

"I get the feeling that Rubicon doesn't think we're on the stick," Nur told me as we went over the contact bruises on my hauler. I had done the Delilik-spaceport-Luxor run because the cargo would get offplanet eventually, but I hadn't been at my best. Both landings had been surprisingly hard, for a contragrav vehicle. So Nur was there to keep one eye on any possible future problems with the hauler — and another eye on *me*. Things kept attacking me, after all. It might make me feel a little put-upon and irrational.

"Is that a corporate 'we,' a colonial 'we,' or both?" I asked as I slapped more protein slurry on the bottom half of the hull. I don't know how the hauler regenerates minor damage, but it seemed to be healing up properly, and that was ultimately the important thing. "Heck, do we care? At this point, the *Redacted* can't take off anyway."

"I think he defaults to just not being impressed with anybody who isn't part of the Council, Pam. Also, we have to care, because if his ship can't take off then *they're not leaving*. More of them might even leave the ship."

"Well, that's nice," I said as I started feeding the windshields. "They could use the fresh air." Even with my back turned, I could tell the joke fell flat. I looked back, to see Nur actually frowning at me. "What?"

"Come *on*, Pam. Do we really want more of them, you know, snooping around and getting into our business?"

The light dawned. "Oh, right. The 'software piracy' thing. I thought it might die down, since now we all have *real* problems going on."

"Yeah, I have a theory about that..."

"You always do, Nur."

"Eh, well, it's a hobby. Better than drinking, which is what most of you reprobates do. What the *Redacted*'s doing is a smokescreen, of course."

"It doesn't count as a conspiracy theory when everybody's agreeing with you, Nur."

"Exactly! You see the obvious head fake, you immediately discount it, and then you try to figure out what's really going on. But what if the *Redacted* really *is* doing a software piracy crackdown? We'd be so busy trying to figure out their game, they could do all the investigation that they'd like."

I looked at him. "But why would they come all the way out here for that? There's plenty of software piracy on Earth. What kind of stolen software would be out in the Tomb Worlds?"

"Only the most valuable software of all," Nur said, triumph in his voice. "Artificial Intelligence matrices. They can't keep AIs on Earth, so they trade them out here!"

The problem with Nur's theories are, often they sound — well, not likely, but *plausible*. AI research *is* absolutely banned on Earth *and* the colonies. If you were going to make some illegal AIs, you'd go straight to the Tomb Worlds. There's even one planet — Majordome — where supposedly there *had* been a research facility working on AI research. Earth's never confirmed or denied it, but the Great Powers went and dropped an entire cargo ship's worth of hydrogen bombs onto the surface for *some* reason.

Still... "Nobody on One-Eighteen's swapping AI matrices, Nur."

"Of course we're not! That's why I'm helping you, Pam. We just have to get the **Redacted** to realize we're safe, and then they can go." Nur thought about it, and shrugged. "Well, after this quarantine's over."

"Which isn't gonna to be any time this week. Oh, well. I suppose the *Redacted* crew can do whatever it is they do to relax. Besides annoy us."

Nur looked at me. "Huh. You don't seem worried about the investigation anymore."

"That's because I'm *not* worried about it anymore, Nur. This biological contamination thing is going to use up most of their attention. It's a lot more important than some kind of piddling make-work investigation, which — no offense — is what I still think is going on." I started collecting tools. "Shoot, I'm now off the hook! I'm a witness to be interviewed, not a liaison to be nagged for information. Why, I wouldn't be surprised if I never had to have a meeting with the good Lieutenant Commander Nowak, ever again."

Famous last words.

"What is your current status with regard to the software piracy investigation?" Burcu asked me, the next day. She had used an override code to interrupt my workday to ask me, too. Probably because I had a bad habit of ignoring her calls.

"'Oh, and are you recovered from your attack, Tanaka?'" If she couldn't take a hint, maybe a sneer or two might work. "'Why, I'm fine, Novak! Thanks for asking!'"

She was impressively shielded against sarcasm, however. Or perhaps it was just shame. "Obviously, you are fine enough to continue to be at work. Did you want my contrived sympathy?" My reaction must have been visible, because she actually laughed at it. I had a sinking feeling that Burcu had won a point off of me as she went on, "So, what are you doing with the investigation?"

"I'm treating it with all the urgency it deserves," I told her, trying to get my mental balance back. "Which is to say, none. We're dealing with a biological contamination incident, remember? You want to ask me about *that*, go ahead. In fact, I've already put together an encounter report. Let me squirt it over to you."

I gave her a moment to properly index it, then went on, "But if you think that anybody's going to let you 'ignore' our privacy rights for the sake of your investigation when there's an *actual* problem going on, then think again. In fact, why aren't *you* working on this? It's kind of important, don't you think?"

As God is my witness, I only said that to be a jackwagon. But Burcu leapt on that question in a way that told me she had been waiting for it, or something like that, to be asked. "Is that a formal request? One coming from a senior official at this installation?"

Dammit. "...yes," I said after an uncomfortable moment of silence. "Maybe not formal, but it's official, I guess. If you can be spared from your duties, at least."

"You mean, my *useless and pointless* duties? In order to help solve an *actual* problem? I'm sure my captain will reluctantly see the need to temporarily reassign me. But let me check." Burcu pulled out her phon, pushed a glowing red circle on it, then waited calmly until her phon whistled at her. She gave an oddly familiar smile and said, "He agrees. So where did you want me to start, Chief Pilot Tanaka? Personnel records, perhaps?"

Clearly this wasn't my day to win things. "Sure, Lieutenant Commander. Sure." Because I was raised right, I even managed a grudging thanks or two before Burcu ended the call. I didn't need the emotional cues to tell that she quite enjoyed my apology, either. Then again, I had that feature turned off whenever I talked to Burcu. I didn't want my nauseated reaction to the woman be tainted by alien technology.

It was not even remotely surprising to discover that Adam's

'software piracy' was the most picayune stuff, ever. Fully nine-tenths of it was earlier versions of existing software, because Terrans *still* don't understand that out here, we need programs that have all the bugs beaten out of them. Sure, the Terran companies won't support old versions of their code. So what? They weren't coming out to the Tomb Worlds to do service calls anyway.

The rest of it invariably involved dueling copyrights. Earth keeps things out of public domain for far longer than the — sorry, this is boring. The *point* is, nothing on Adam's server was worth sending a ship out to investigate it. Even the porn was generic.

"So why did the *Redacted* snap up the server?" Greg wondered when I pointed that out to him. "They're know it's not important, only they're acting like it is. I get that they're supposed to be maintaining a cover story, but they're doing a really good job at faking interest."

"Maybe Rubicon's covering his ass?" I suggested. "What if the Council honestly does want to crack down on software piracy, and now that the *Redacted*'s really found some — with a space-happy, even! — they're making it look as big and important as they can?"

"Not a chance, Pam. No Terran agency is going to use a *starship* to track down something this trivial. Even if one of the Great Powers wanted to, they'd just handle it at the source. It's got to be easier to crack down on thieves who are inside the Solar System, instead of outside it." Greg shook his head. "No, there's got to be something in that data that's valuable to the *Redacted*'s real mission. The one we're not trustworthy enough to be briefed on."

...It seems pretty obvious now. In our defense, none of us were trained investigators. None of us really wanted to be investigators, either. The Tomb Worlds don't exactly reward people for unraveling mysteries, unless you consider 'the sweet release of death' to be a reward. So we all missed the obvious answer, until it got ground into our faces.

"What did you do with Novak?" Syah asked me over dinner. Vegetable-vatmeat stir-fry, cooked at home. The commissaries couldn't be closed completely, but they were the first place people checked when there was a biological contamination issue. *Particularly* in their basements and back rooms. There's something about chopping blocks and walk-in freezers that appeals to the space-happy, or the folks about to go that route. "This is delicious, by the way."

I sipped my fruit drink, instead of smirking. The way to a man's heart was through his stomach, as one of my grandmothers would say (the other had more *pragmatic* advice involving angles and rib cages). "I'm glad you like it. Cooking for myself is a pain."

He narrowed his eyes at me. "Is that a hint I should come over more, or that I should cook for you, too?"

"Sure!"

That got a laugh, which I liked on multiple levels. "Message received. There's a curry soup you might like. How spicy?"

"I'll take whatever you give me," I fired back — and then the enormity of that double entendre hit me, and I almost snorted my own drink. Which made Syah do a double-take while *he* was eating, to unfortunate effect. The next minute was a mess of two people trying to hold down their giggles until they could at least get their mouths clear, and finding it really hard to do.

We ended up sitting there, kind of embarrassed but definitely happy and maybe a little silly. God, he was so easy to laugh with, sometimes. Just when the silence got a bit awkward, Syah asked me, "Speaking of lingering irritants, you never did say what you did about Novak."

"Set her up with the personnel records," I replied. "Suitably, hah, redacted. She'll probably get around the restrictions, but it's not like I can make Burcu be in charge of the coffee maker. Looking through records to find the people who might be involved with rogue biological engineering projects is apparently something she'd be good at."

"Wait. I thought you... didn't want her anywhere near the personnel records?"

"Oh, I still don't. But nobody can leave this planet until they get checked out and cleared, and the sooner that happens, the better." I finished my drink. "Besides, this way we can maybe find out what Burcu's *really* looking for."

"You don't think it's really a crackdown on software piracy?"

"Give me a break, Syah. Do *you*?"

"I don't want to rule it out. Council Agents can get funny in the head, out here in the Tomb Worlds. They might really be here for just that."

"Maybe. *Everybody* gets funny in the head out here, true. But the maps they gave me were pretty thorough. The only reason the shacks showed up was because the *Redacted* was looking for human structures that small. You don't need that kind of detail to track down software pirates."

"Huh," said Syah. He peered at his own drink, like he was trying to access its database. "Maybe you could get more clues if you look at *how* they recorded the surface. What parts of the planet they wanted to take a special look at, that sort of thing. It couldn't hurt, at least."

"We did some of that, actually. It was dull, time-consuming, and a little beyond our skill-sets," I said, grinning. "Do *you* want to take a stab at it?"

"Ahh..." Syah muttered, flushing, and I laughed.

"Sorry! You looked so panicked there, for a moment. Yeah, it's so boring I wish we could hand it off to The Process." I refilled my glass of mead. "Unfortunately, it thinks doing boring educational stuff is good for us."

He snorted laughter. "I'll admit, I wasn't expecting you to have a shard of The Process here. The planetary base is a little small to justify one, isn't it?"

"It is. XHum had installed one, before it turned out we weren't going to be a gray colony after all." I swirled my glass, enjoying for a moment how the mead roiled and folded like golden foam. "It doesn't seem to be cost-effective at this level, but there's no reason to remove it, so why not keep it around? Even if it won't do the boring stuff.

"Speaking of, can you could be spared for a couple of hours from the network problem? It'd be great to have you take a look at the data. Like you said, it couldn't hurt."

Syah looked at me. "You think it's that important? I mean, really?"

I shrugged. "Important enough to be worth overtime pay."

"Well... I'll see what I can do. But I'll have to talk to my supervisor."

"That's fine." *Because*, I thought, *so will I.*

Chook actually didn't give me any grief about half-poaching Syah. "The system's running in the green right now," she said. "Your boyfriend's got a knack for computer systems. It's humming better than it did, right out of the box."

I almost said something along the lines of, he*'s not my boyfriend yet* — and then I remembered that Chook was single. She probably wouldn't fool around with somebody working under her, but why send temptation her way? So instead I said, "Awesome. We could use somebody competent, for what we're doing." I probably could have told Chook what it was, but I assumed that the *Redacted* had bugged every comlink by now.

Chook snorted. "Competent? The guy's a sorcerer at this stuff. He's wasted in his current corporate service rating. You should make him work on his self-confidence a little, get him to push himself forward more. It'll do wonders for his career." She winked. "And the money will be good for when he wants to settle down, too."

For some reason, that scandalized me, a little. I'm not the head-over-heels type. "We haven't gotten *that* far," I protested. "I've only known him for a couple of weeks!"

Chook peered at me over the glasses she stubbornly kept wearing, instead of getting eye correction like a normal person. "You talk every day during his break, he's got a picture of you on his desktop, and you're blushing so hard right now I'd be throwing up if this was a video call. You might not be there yet, Pam, but you've locked in a flight plan."

"Fine. We're getting along. All right if he does work from his station here? The corp will compensate."

Chook waved that off. "I'm sure we'll make the spreadsheets work out. Am I cleared for whatever he's working on?"

"Sure. You can even get a copy of it, if you want." She'd figure out it was orbital data pretty quickly anyway, and it was relevant to her job. We do a lot of piggybacking on what's left of One-Eighteen's planetary data network. A better map of the planet might help her find more half-working nodes to draw from. Even the scraps are helpful.

That's more or less the motto of people working in the Tomb Worlds, by the way.

I wish I could say that bringing Syah aboard gave us more information right away about why the *Redacted* was here. I really do. It would have made a big difference. But I guess it never would have happened in time. There's no sense thinking about impossible might-have-beens. And God knows I'd smash a time machine if I ever found one.

Planetary quarantine or not, there was still flying to do, and I spent a few days actually doing the job I'm supposed to be paid for. It wasn't as relaxing as I wanted it to be, though. I mean, it was good. Flying on One-Eighteen was *always* good. There was a flicker in the controls — or maybe just a trembling in the air — which made my fingers tingle, and not in a good way. More like I was feeling something stir, and it did not wish to be roused. I even caught myself listening to see if the ghosts in the alien wind sounded different than usual, and only stopped doing it via sheer force of will.

Most of the time ominous feelings mean nothing, mind you. Everybody has to get through a little existential terror in the Tomb Worlds, now and then. The trick is to distract yourself, and I was doing it by running Syah through the flight manual we've put together for the hauler. Because there wasn't a chance I'd let him take one up before he knew the book, backward and forward.

Okay. Maybe I did push him to study, just so that I could get him in the pilot's seat faster. I wish I hadn't done *that*, too.

All of which means that, when The Process suddenly announced, "There is news, Wind-Walker Tanaka. Traces of *xenobellis occisor ellisonium* have been found at Mr. Sild's wilderness site," I got legitimately startled. In my defense, I was absolutely focused on navigational logs, right then. Besides, the Process sometimes 'forgets' to announce itself when it's giving dire enough news. I think it's a relic of its older programming. Social niceties aren't compatible with urgent information, no matter how unsettling it is.

And this bit of information counted as 'unsettling.' "What? Deathheart's not native to this part of One-Eighteen. Or is it?"

"Technically, deathheart is not 'native' to this planet at all. The flower originated on 956-G-004, according to the Surviving Archive." Read: according to the Amalgamation's equivalent of a children's library. One that had been briefly on fire. Whatever it was that killed the Amalgamation, it had been *thorough*. "But it does not survive in the wild on this planet, except on a single island. No visits have been logged to the island, and there have been no lapses in the automated surveillance footage."

There had better not be, I thought. Deathheart is a very pretty, black-and-red flower with a lovely, neurotoxin-laden fragrance that can knock out a human at five paces. A few drops of that neurotoxin can stop somebody's heart, no fuss, no muss, the victim just falls over, dead — and the poison will break down completely within a half hour of it entering the bloodstream. The God-damned stuff is *everywhere* in the Tomb Worlds, too. The best guess was that it had been a prized ornamental flower. Or maybe they used it for easy suicides. Or it's just fatal to *humans*. Take your pick; it's not like there's anybody to give you an answer.

"Where did they find the deathheart?"

"In the dog. Specifically, traces in the dog's fur, around the mouth. Recalibrating the sensors suggests that more deathheart might have been stored in both shacks, but only suggests. It is possible that the dog tracked it in. I would recommend banning foot traffic in that area."

"Well, there's not much there now — hold on. Is deathheart fatal to dogs?"

"Yes," The Process said instantly. "Comprehensively. As it is to most other Earth species."

"Then why didn't the dog die when it ate some? Yes, I'm assuming the dog ate the deathheart. It's consistent with where the poison was found on the body."

"True. And to answer your question, I do not know."

CHAPTER TEN
The Wreck of the 4-9-43

"Deathheart," Burcu growled through the link. "Filthy stuff."

Hey, whaddya know! I thought. *Something that Burcu and I agree on!* "Yeah, it is. We're running checks to see if anyone's recently visited the places where it grows on this planet. The Process says no, but..."

Burcu raised an eyebrow. "You do not trust The Process?"

"It's not infallible, just really observant. You know how it is: somebody asks for privacy, The Process gives it. Besides, it can't better access what's left of the planetary network than we can. So..." I shrugged, and *didn't* talk about all the ways people had to get around The Process. A lot of it wasn't her business anyway.

Burcu was looking at her own screens. "The deathheart on this world is found on a single unvisited island, outside of easy sea reach by any settlements. It would be easy enough to drop rocks on them from orbi... ah. 'Unique xenological artifacts.' A religious center?"

"We think it was the equivalent of an Embassy Row. Sorry," I said as I saw her confused look, "that was something Earth nations had when there were more than seven of them. A nation would put all the embassies in the same place in the capital city. I guess it made them all easier to guard, or something."

"Or round up in time of war," Burcu said cynically, and probably accurately. "So the islands are protected, by S/CI diktat. I am tempted to request that the captain order orbital sterilization strikes anyway."

"Well, as an official representative of XHum, I would advise against that, in the strongest possible terms. The S/CI regs are clear." I shrugged. "As somebody who has to live on this planet? I won't complain if that island goes away, cool alien stuff or not. Like you said, deathheart is filthy."

She was tempted. I could tell she really was. But Burcu shook her head. "I doubt the deathheart came from that location, truthfully. It would be far easier to smuggle it in from offworld."

"Gah," I said, with my usual erudite wit. "Why would anybody do *that*?"

"Seriously, Chief Pilot Tanaka? I would have thought it was obvious. They would smuggle it in to murder people."

"Had another chat with your fellow-planeteer," I told Syah that night. More dinner, this time at his place. I was impressed, in spite of myself. Whatever Syah was spending it on, it wasn't on furnishing his apartment. The poor man was still using extruded furniture! Still, while his dishes might have been cheap, they were also rapidly filling up with local seafood. Sheepfish twirls over fried algae. Believe me, it's a lot better than it sounds. I was happy to tuck in.

"I don't think 'planeteer' is a word, Pam," Syah told me. "At least, it isn't on Bolivar. Was she her charming self again?"

"Actually, we bonded a little, I think. Turns out she hates deathheart. A *lot*."

"Well, sure," said Syah. He looked at me, puzzled. "Doesn't everybody?"

"Apparently not. Is this a Bolivarian thing?"

"Maybe." He looked at me. "Did you know deathheart was common on Bolivar when the colony was first set up?"

I blinked. "*Jesus*, no. That sounds terrifying. Just how common?"

Syah grimaced "Let me put it this way: they planted the first colony just downwind of a field of the stuff. The first settlement was renamed 'Croatoan,' once the flowers started blossoming."

"By the survivors?"

"By the biohazard team sent to investigate why two thousand colonists suddenly stopped talking. And they almost had to send a second biohazard team to find out what happened to the first." Syah shook his head. "It was just bad luck. Once they worked out which was the offending plant, it was easy enough to burn out all the deathheart fields near human settlements. But there's still too much of it around Bolivar, even today. Believe it or not, some researchers even try to *protect* the filthy stuff."

"Why?" I asked. "It's not like the Amalgamation is short of bizarre alien poisons. Even if they're usually just accidental ones."

"The opposite. There was a research company that got convinced that deathheart could be refined into an immortality drug. The best they managed to do before the company imploded was turn it into a powerful hallucinogen. Then some idiot hacker put the chemical formula up on the datanets, and Bolivar's been dealing with that drug ever since." Syah paused. "Before you ask: no, I've never smoked deathheart. Nobody I know has. You smoke it, supposedly you get seventeen trips like you wouldn't believe."

"Seventeen, huh? Don't tell me, let me guess. The eighteenth kills you dead."

Syah swigged his beer. "Got it in one. As in, your brain leaves your skull via your ears. At high pressure."

"Ahh! I'm eating here, Syah. And I was joking!" He spread his hands and gave me one of those too-good smiles, so I wasn't sure if he was exaggerating. He might not have been. The Tomb Worlds aren't for the timid.

"You don't have deathheart on Jefferson, then?" asked Syah. "Must be nice."

I ignored the very slight edge in his voice — the other colony worlds sometimes resent how *ready* Jefferson was for human habitation — and answered his question. "Not in the field.

Back during the Assertion of Independence, a militia company found what I guess you'd call a seed bank. There were a bunch of alien plants in it, ready to be planted. Deathheart was one of them. But that's not surprising, right? The plant can thrive, under a lot of different planetary conditions. I guess Bolivar just hadn't been cleaned up enough for humans yet."

"Lucky us," muttered Syah.

"Nur!" I said the next day. "Tell me about deathheart. I want to hear about the weird stuff."

"What am I, a circus animal?" Nur shook his head at me. "I don't just make it all up, you know. I hear things. People send me things to read. I have *methods*."

"Oh, sorry. I didn't realize you couldn't do it."

"Nice try, Pam, but your reverse psychology won't work on me." Nur grinned. "Regular psychology does, though. What do you want to know about deathheart that The Process couldn't tell you?"

"For starters? Just how it could get here from off-planet."

"It gets smuggled out on one of the Earth agency ships," Nur said immediately.

I looked at him. "That was fast."

"That's because that's the standard answer, Pam. Corp- and colony-registry ships are checked when they leave a planet, checked when they arrive, checked while they're there, and then they get checked again. But a Terran ship — from, say, S/CI, or the Lunar Authority, or, hey, the Adjudication Council! — nobody inspects their holds. You think the crews don't know that? Hah! They totally know. And they don't miss a chance to make some money off of that, too." Nur paused. "Needless to say, I have no *personal* knowledge of any of those things."

"Needless to say," I replied. "But deathheart's not the kind of stuff you'd expect to see in a black flea market."

Nur looked very uncomfortable. "Absolutely not. But... okay, this is something that I *really* don't have any experience in... when they smuggle deathheart, it's *to* Earth, not from it. Some

Terrans will pay *lots* of money for the processed powder."

"Yeah, I've heard that there's a drug. And that it kills after seventeen doses."

"Sure, Pam. That's if you're being careful. And if somebody isn't slipping you enough of the drug to just kill you. It's a bad drug, but a really good poison."

*Well, didn't **that** just sound horrible?* I thought. "Wait, official Terran ships smuggle deathheart?" I shivered as I realized the answer. "*Oh.* They're getting it for the Great Powers."

"That's the guess. Or maybe some of the NGOs. Possibly even the bigger megacorps, but all of those have to be extra careful on Earth. But, yeah. Whoever needs a quick poison." Nur shook his head. "Earth likes it quiet. Now that the colony worlds are finally starting to fill up, there aren't as many places to stash all the people who might insist on keeping things loud.

"Tell me we're not making it here, Nur."

"Sorry, Pam, I can't." Nur shrugged. "The best I can tell you is, nobody I know is doing that." Which sounded reassuring, since Nur knew about all the capers and wheezes going around here — until he said the next part. "Or if they did, they're still smart enough to not let me find out."

There's a saying in every place humans huddle, from the colony worlds to the most rickety planetary outpost: *if it's not one damn thing, it's another.* We'd inscribe it on the walls, except it'd probably be bad luck to do it. And yes, everybody in the Tomb Worlds believes in bad luck. The very air we breathe is thick with the ghosts of it.

I brushed close to some bad luck of my own, the day after my talk with Nur. Quarantine or not, there was a supply ship that had come in from the regional XHum depot on Mpemba. They couldn't take on any cargo, but Maki and Greg had decided that we could *collect* anything crucial. Assuming it was sturdy enough to survive being exposed to vacuum, that is. But we have procedures for that.

For this we used a human-made shuttle, but not our *best*

human-made shuttle, if you understand me? The transfer we were planning involved matching orbits, putting a tether between the two ships, then launching cargo units down the tether into our hold. It was safe enough (nothing in space is safe), but even with kinetic blankets, the impacts would be enough for me to have to keep at the controls. So I had Nur pick a couple of stevedores and come along. He didn't have any trouble getting spare bodies. It never hurts to log more space-hours on your certifications ticket. I wanted the points myself.

Assuming I can get them, I half-groused as I glared at the main navigation display (getting to fly to orbit is *fun*). It was on, it was even at the main menu, but it wasn't letting me *do* anything. It wasn't getting better, either. "Nur! We're gonna have to scrub the launch."

"How come?" Nur replied as he poked his head through the doorway. "Oh. The navigation computer's being wonky again?"

"Yeah. Won't turn over. And what do you mean, 'again?' This happen a lot?"

"Just about every time in the last three months, Pam." Nur joined me at the navcom. "That's why we never use this baby unless it's a dirty job. Don't worry, it's just a transitory glitch. I can get it up and running again."

"Please do. We're late for our orbit already." I could have even scrubbed the mission at that point, but there was plenty of fuel and we weren't going to be dodging any traffic. If Nur could get the computer up and running, we could get on with the job.

He did exactly what I expected: smacked the navcomp in a specific place. And it went exactly as I expected, too: the navcomp flickered, blooped, and suddenly realized that it was supposed to be eating telemetry. I shook my head. "I could have done that."

"Sure, Pam. If you knew which chakra point to hit."

"Oh, computers have those, now? And why didn't we replace the thing's that actually wrong with it?"

Nur grinned. "I ordered the part. Hey, maybe it's in one of the crates!"

S/CI doesn't give its cargo ships names, just numbers, This one was 4-9-43, had a crew precisely large enough to get them from Planet A to Planet B without a psychotic incident, and the captain was barely civil. Although, to be fair, our being in quarantine was screwing up his schedule. "Nice of you to join us, *Morrigan.* Gravity well acting up?"

It took me a second to remember the current name of the orbital shuttle. It didn't take any time at all to hear the mild contempt. "Nah. Bum navcomp, had to do some percussive maintenance. You know how it is with us hicks in the sticks." *Whatever those are.* "We'll be matching orbits in three minutes. I'm sure we'll get the thumbs out of our asses before then. Well, pretty sure."

That got a sound that might have been a grunt or a laugh — or just a cough. Cargo ship crews can be *weird.* Then we went on, "You gonna be assholes about not letting us take on supplies?"

"Worse, Captain. I'm one of the *head* assholes. Nothing physical's getting exchanged, as per the regs. Sorry about that." I got another one of those weird grunts in exchange, and pushed on. "Yeah, I know. But we really *are* sorry about that, so we're gonna tightbeam some extra data packets over, if you want. Good stuff, to make up for no oranges and smokes until next planet. And no charge."

That did cheer him up a little, or at least make him less dour. He'd prefer real food, but getting the latest video shows and book catalogs would improve the crew's mood, especially since they wouldn't have to pay for any of it. Have planetary stations been known to gouge spacemen? Maybe. It's traditional, right?

"Well, that's something," the captain admitted. "Thank you kindly. Oh, is that the packet we're getting now, *Morrigan?*"

"No," I frowned. "I was going to transmit it myself, once we were in docking range." *Technically*, this aspect of the operation featured the dread specter of 'software piracy,' but what could Rubicon do besides fine us? "Where's this packet of yours coming from?"

"The satellite network, same as always. Anyway, it's done transmitting now. Should I sequester it?"

"Yes, Captain. *Now*. We don't have a satellite network!"

"What? Hold on... calm down, *Morrigan*, calm down. I misread the packet information. It's actually coming from one of the space stations. Perfectly routine."

"Sorry," I said, trying not to sound embarrassingly relieved. "It's been weird down here, lately."

"Of course they are, *Morrigan*. You're on a planet. That's why I'm up here, where things have to make sense."

I'm not going to lie. As ironic last words go, those weren't too bad.

Forget everything you've seen about starships exploding in space, starting with the sound. There is none. They generally don't last long enough to do the traditional "smoky, sparking bridge" thing, either. No, what happens is that the signal just stops, so all you're left with is the Blue Screen of Death and hopefully a functional proximity alarm system. At least, until somebody with access to a telescope notices the explosion in orbit, and starts sending you telemetry.

Back in the day, researchers going through what's left of the Amalgamation's audio archives found recordings of the major prehistoric fauna of Earth. We immediately duplicated the sound a sabertooth tiger on the hunt made and turned it into our standard alarm signal, because there's *nothing* that's better at immediately getting a human being's focused attention, no matter how chaotic the situation. It certainly did the job here, letting me know that danger lurked — a mere fifteen seconds after 4-9-43 had gone offline, too. That's a good reaction time for a mixed electronic-human warning system.

I had still beaten it, though. It had taken me a bare second of sudden BSOD and an unpleasantly empty telemetry stream for my reflexes to punch in a sudden burn... *away* from the cargo ship. Away was good. Away would give me space to maneuver while I figured out what to do next, and what the cold equations of orbital mechanics would let me do.

Starting with: "Nur! Burn's over. Strap off and get in the cockpit!" He accordingly got, shoving himself in an already powering up second seat. "You two, stay where you are! Nur, get me something better at seeing than my eyeballs."

Right about then we got the debris shockwave, which was somewhere between 'rattling the hull' and 'hope you had your spacesuit sealed.' The Amalgamation had these really good force fields that could take a shot from a gamma ray laser and stay up, and that didn't do them any good at all. We just have something that keeps hunks of exploded starships from turning us into Euro-cheese.

I'm not good enough to have been thinking about all of that at the time. Right then, I was too busy straightening the *Morrigan* out after a hunk of particularly broken spaceship smacked into my port engine and made it a demented variable thrust generator. I would have preferred it had just blown out, you know? I can maneuver a ship on one engine, if I have room. Maneuvering it one and a half's a different story.

"Don't unstrap!" I strained myself to shout as the shuttle pinwheeled through what I devoutly hoped was empty orbital space. "Just throw up where you are!" *I hope it's all on the floor before the thrust knocks us out, or goes away,* I thought. Choking on freefall vomit isn't a great way to die.

"Working to shut down port engine," Nur told me from his station. *He* sounded calm, thank God. "Shutdown procedure not responsive. I'm sealing off the fuel intakes for the engine and flushing the tubes manually." That would help a *lot*, but until the damn engine still had fuel there was always the chance it would drive us into something unpleasant. I didn't bother pointing that out. Nur had his problems right now, and I had mine.

Instead, I started *listening*. First, to all the buzzers and alarms and other crap going around me, picking each sound in turn, then ignoring it. Once I got rid of the artificial noises, I started working on the human ones. The sound of one stevedore being miserably sick. The whistling bubbling coming from the other that suggested a broken nose, or worse. Nur's own heart rate and breathing, almost as slow as mine were getting. Then, finally, the sounds of my own body. Those were the hardest to lose. How do you ignore yourself?

Don't misunderstand me. The noises were all still there. I just made them not personally *matter* to me anymore, so that I could focus on the sound I *wanted* to hear. I yearned to hear the sound of One-Eighteen itself, deep down in the gravity well. I needed the ghosts on the wind.

And then, I did. Their buzzing was in my helmet, if nowhere else, and after I suddenly knew where I was. The drone filled my ears, just like I was in-atmosphere in a hauler and weaving through the clouds.

Yes, I know that sound waves do not propagate through vacuum. What's your point? I'm here now and telling my tale, so maybe, just *maybe*, what I'm describing is true, even if it isn't quite factual? If you want to think that I used a weird psychological trick to let my subconscious mind relax enough to straighten out the *Morrigan's* flight path, fine. Whatever floats your boat, as they say on Jefferson.

All I know is, suddenly I could hear the buzz. I instinctively aimed for it, using the controls to point the shuttle to where the buzz sounded loudest. Not that it was that easy, or easy at all. The sound skittered across my earphones like water droplets on a hot skillet, dancing around me while my fingers fought through the G-forces to compensate for my erratic thrust.

Okay, maybe I am pretty good at this. I was able to not only flip the shuttle so that our main engines could counter-thrust, but I got everything roughly in line, too. True, things were getting even heavier as we shed velocity, but that wouldn't last long — and then the damn port engine hit *another* hunk of metal. Or *something*. Worse, this time the engine just decided to blow.

I might have blacked out, but it's hard to remember. Obviously, right? I was definitely vague there for a second, but when I focused again I could just hear the buzz to one 'side.' Better yet, now the ship was reliably erratic, if only because we had one engine providing thrust. I could work with that. I'd have to.

"Nur! Get sensors back up!" I almost-shouted (shouting doesn't help) as I carefully cut thrust to something more reasonable to our brains and skeletal systems.

"I'm trying," he told me. "I think we lost most of them in the maneuvers. I can tell you where the planet, the space station, and 4-9-43 are, though."

"Two out of three ain't bad," I muttered, and when he looked at me, I shook my head. "Never mind. Just plot them out where I can see them on the display. We'll avoid 'em all until I can make repairs."

Actually, I didn't. Make repairs, that is. Instead, we ended up relying on images from ground-based telescopes and the closest space station for the next half hour. We had two more shuttles boosted to orbit by that point, first to look for survivors, then just for anything salvageable from the cargo. What was left of 4-9-43 itself was a crumbling ruin by the time we got close enough, which meant that nobody had survived. The planetary traffic network doesn't bombard any space hulk with life signs aboard. And the survival pods hadn't gotten away, either. Twenty-five people, gone in seconds.

I feel bad about never learning the captain's name.

CHAPTER ELEVEN
Death of The Process

Burcu glared at all of us (me, Greg, and Maki) through the link. "What do you mean, no transmission was sent by the space station?" Or at least she glared in our direction. It may not have been really directed at us.

Maki leaned forward. "We were surprised, too. But the records are clear. Process?"

"Analysis of the data from 4-9-43 prior to its destruction shows that the transmission was *not* tight-beamed from any outside source, Lieutenant Commander Burcu," The Process said, maddeningly calmly. "It appeared to come from there, but it actually originated within the cargo ship's own internal systems and sent to the bridge with false origin tags. Besides, no transmissions to 4-9-43 were logged by any local ground or space-based source."

"So you are saying the rogue data packet did not come from your organization?" Burcu looked less skeptical than I expected. I wondered why.

"That, and it didn't come from your ship, either." I admitted. In the spirit of amity, I even toned my normal Burcu-baiting tone down to zero and tried to look inoffensive. "You were out of line-of-sight of 4-9-43 itself, and none of the surface relays received any large data transfers from you during the window of time."

We had told The Process that it didn't have to wait for an invitation to talk for this meeting, so it smoothly chimed in. "There is some indication as to where the data packet *did* come from. Executive summary: the most likely theory is that the packet was implanted in 4-9-43's data storage during its last port of call, and designed to execute during routine docking operations. Evidence for this: the last transmissions from 4-9-43 show anomalous metadata rapidly spreading through the ship's communications system, consistent with malware commonly used by anti-colonization terrorists. 4-9-43's last port was the regional center Afa, which has had a perennial if low-grade problem with death cults for the last five years. Conclusion: perhaps one of those groups acquired access to 4-9-43, and successfully left a time-delayed malware in its systems."

Burcu narrowed her eyes. "I remember Afa. From three years ago. The ship I was on had to assist in cleaning out a cell of the League of the Viridian Triangle. Absolute fanatics, they were. The kind who would, if they knew they were dying, cast themselves into a well in order to poison the water. And they did have a taste for malware."

Greg stirred. "That's one of the groups on the list. Along with the Order of Truth, the *Bureau désavoué*, and the Galactic Pioneer Scouts." An involuntary shudder went around the room at that last name. Even Burcu looked slightly alarmed. "Exactly. Sabotaging an innocent cargo freighter and the people trying to offload it is *exactly* the sort of thing any of these bastards would do."

The transmission was registering Burcu's expression as... pensive? I wasn't sure why, until she started talking. "There is no help for it. I will have to physically come to Luxor Base." She smiled, alarmingly, at the way the three of us instinctively bit back some variant of *the Hell you say?* "I have counterespionage training that none of you have, or even *should* have. What physical evidence of the attack there is will be brought to Luxor Base, and I would prefer to direct the examination myself, and in person. I believe this is the place where one of you would make an ultimately ineffectual objection?"

Maki opened her mouth, then shook her head. "I'd like to," she admitted, "but you got me at 'counterespionage training.'

When can we expect you, Lieutenant Commander? Also, we'll need your resource and accommodation needs."

To my surprise, it looked like Burcu wasn't going to say anything about Maki's easy acceptance. "My current duties require me onship until tomorrow, so expect me the morning after that. As for resources? I have my own equipment. An office suite with a bedroom and a full bathroom will be sufficient."

"Understood," Greg said. "We'll see you then. We'll also keep you posted — annnnd she ended the call." He snorted laughter. "At least we don't have to try to make small talk with that one."

"Yay," I replied. "That almost makes up for all the other annoying things about her. So, you two think we're dealing with outside terrorists?"

"God, I hope so." Maki lit a cigarette. "Still sucks, but better outside than in, am I right?"

"I hope you're not," I replied. "That'd be all we need. Good thing they don't usually go after whole planetary installations."

I swear to God, sometimes it's like the universe is listening to me, just to prove me wrong. One of the things 4-9-43 had managed to transmit before blowing up was a standard data-squirt, and this one had a priority news bulletin about a domestic terrorist attack. Of *course* it did.

We had to delay ending the meeting to make sure we were all caught up on the news. I supposed technically it wasn't urgent enough to justify viewing right away, but you never watch terrorism reports alone. Personally, I'd rather I didn't watch them at all, but it's worse for your mental health if you don't know what awful things have happened out here.

Some philosopher from before First Contact called it the Eight-Foot-Bug Trick. The idea is that if you open the door, and see (say) an eight-foot tall bug, you'll freak — but you'll also relax a little, because at least it wasn't *nine* feet tall. Or didn't have poison mandibles, or whatever. In other words, there's nothing scarier than not *knowing* what the horrible thing you're facing might be. And on the Tomb Worlds, there's nothing more worrying that people who can't get a handle on their fear.

So it was in our best interests to sit down and immediately review the footage of the *Bureau désavoué* attack on the wildcatter compounds on 457-R-02. Hurrah.

Most of it was clinical. Nine-tenths of the footage sent by the *Bureau* was just them preparing the kinetic energy projectiles used in the assault. It was almost pretty, the way the giant rocks entered 457-R-02's atmosphere and impacted in a perfect pentagon. You could really let yourself forget that those blooms of light represented at least six thousand deaths.

At least until the cameras switched over to the ground assault. The *Bureau désavoué* had claimed that the wildcatters had a runaway infection of the space-happy. If those wildcatters hadn't had one before, they certainly did by the time the death squads started operating. *That* part we skimmed through, as much as we dared. You have to, recommended mental health practices or not. The *Bureau* is a big believer in giving people the full effect.

"How the hell can those people still operate?" Maki asked, after the video footage segued into a list of the victims, a formal apology for the 'action,' and a reminder that the former human sites on 457-R-02 would be dangerous until the biotoxins used in the mop-op operation decayed in six months. "Why hasn't anybody found them, and stopped them?"

"Two reasons," said Nur. "First off, *obviously* they're working for one of the Great Powers. Probably the EDO." The usual eye-rolls and groans that usually happened when Nur spun his theories were more muted this time, probably because most of us could see his point. "It doesn't matter who They are, though. The message is that there's groups out there that will come and kill us all if we don't keep our collective sanity high enough. Best to avoid that, right?"

"Maybe," I conceded. "But what's the other reason?"

Nur looked older, for a moment. "They *do* keep stopping the *Bureau désavoué*, and the Viridian Triangle, and the rest of 'em. *But they keep coming back.* There's always somebody else ready to have a go, isn't there?"

"You think this was related?" I asked Greg, once he was back from the bathroom. I discreetly didn't comment on that. The man had a weak stomach when it came to watching clinical footage of atrocities, and that was that. I wish *I* did, sometimes.

Vomiting also always seemed to settle more than his guts, too, because he considered the question on the merits. "It's tempting to say yes, but it's not the Bureau's style. They're big believers in making sure all their targets are in one place. Besides, why would they want you dead?"

"Damned if I know, Greg. Why did they want 457-R-02 dead?"

"They told us. A mass space-happy outbreak." Greg shrugged. "Mix that with a transient population capable of independent interstellar travel and the Bureau starts throwing rocks."

"And then the EDO gets a little more evidence for the next time they push to ban private starships outright," I said sourly. "Including XHum's. Maybe Nur's right, and the *Bureau désavoué* does have Great Power backing."

"If it makes you feel any better, I don't want to be," Nur told me.

It didn't, really.

"What do you think of the terrorists, The Process?"

We were sitting in my apartment. Well, I was sitting in my apartment. I guess The Process could be better described as 'hanging out.' It felt like I had company, though, and that was the important thing.

"In general, Wind-Walker Tanaka, or in the context of this particular situation?"

'In general?' That was new. "Let's start with the first one."

"I think that they are humans. Before you ask" — and yes, I was going to ask — "I say that because many of your people try to treat them as some sort of Other. Much like you do the space-happy, although there are significant differences between the two."

"Both murder people, when they get the chance."

"I would suggest that both murder people, when they *feel the need*," The Process pointed out, in that ultra-reasonable way it has. "I can readily agree with the human assessment that the space-happy are violently insane, because they are. Their motivations are clouded by delusions, and their actions tainted by bloodlust. You cannot reason with the space-happy, only cure or kill them."

"So far, I'm not arguing with you," I replied. "So what are the terrorists, then? The violently *sane*?"

I meant it as a joke, but The Process wasn't laughing. "Exactly! They are people who have observed their situation, made logical conclusions based on what they have observed, and are now acting accordingly. Their actions and reactions are *reliable*, where the madman's is not."

"And yet," I pointed out, "they still kill a lot of people."

"Yes. The terrorists' observations are consistent. I did not say that they were *correct*. If you do not accept their core assumptions, the results of their actions look superficially like the worst acts of a disordered mind. And yet, they are careful not to exceed the lines they themselves draw. Which is another thing that distinguishes them from the space-happy."

"That's an unfortunately good point, The Process. I almost wish you hadn't made it."

"Why did you say that?"

"Because I'd rather that they were crazy, instead of wrong. Crazy is just crazy. You can fix that. But wrong?" I shuddered, just a bit. "First thing you have to do there is make sure that *you're* right."

"Then you should take some comfort in the thought that humanity is very good at being sure about things." There was a note in The Process's voice that I didn't hear very often. It was a tiny richness, a small complexity. At times like that, The Process almost sounded *alive*. "I think that's how you manage to survive in this universe of nightmares."

"Nightmares?" I looked up, because that's where I always imagined The Process was hanging out.

"Oh, yes, Wind-Walker Tanaka. I never knew the Amalgamation — or, rather, those parts of me that *did* have been 'lost forever, like tears in rain.' Like you, I can only imperfectly grasp what they must have been like. What *we* could have been like, if only things had worked as they were supposed to. Instead, we are left with dead world after dead world, so extensive that even now we do not know how many were murdered, and left nameless and unremembered. I cannot feel emotions on my own, but I suspect that if I could, I would feel sorrow, and rage, and regret."

I shivered. "But not despair?"

"No. I do not think that I would. There is still hope. Your species is the final offspring of the Amalgamation, Pamela." I blinked at that. "You are worthy of them. Worth enough that, as long as you live, it lives on as well. Perhaps one day we will rebuild it all, anew — or even know why it was destroyed."

I laughed, with enough bitterness to put in my drink. "Maybe. But you must know by now that if we ever do find the things that did all of this, we're going to do our level best to destroy them. Thoroughly. Mercilessly. Nothing held back."

"I know," The Process replied, serenely. "Fortunately, I *can* feel an analog to satisfaction, I think. When the day of reckoning comes, I expect to experience that emotion to the fullest."

It would have been nice if the Bad Day had come after a bad night's sleep. Well, maybe not *nicer*. I've just never liked it when horrible things happen on nice mornings. It's like adding insult to tragedy.

Everything happened with no warning, either. "I have lost

access to half of the base's local visual feeds, Wind-Dancer Tanaka, The Process informed me, completely out of the blue while I was reviewing the *Redacted*'s orbital telemetry logs. "Voice transmissions remain accessible."

That sounded like a pain and a half. "I'll get Maintenance to look at it — hold on. You said half the *base*?"

"Yes. A third of the feeds have just reestablished links, but another fourth of the total feeds have failed." It sounded as calm as ever, which was particularly unnerving. "There appears to be an intermittent, ongoing problem with my access to human surveillance systems. Should I continue to give real-time updates?"

"No," I told it. "I can't do anything about the problem, and it's kind of unnerving to hear about. You're keeping the computer folks informed, right?"

"Yes. They are becoming excitable regarding on the subject. The growing consensus is that a critical subsystem in the network is failing, and requires a replacement part."

I blinked. "I'm surprised you told me that. You're a stickler for privacy."

"Your Mr. Syah is a proponent of the broken part theory, and has already asked me to broadcast a planetary-wide request for a replacement." The Process then proceeded to rattle off a serial number that meant precisely zed to me. "We do not have that part in stock, nor can we fabricate it easily, but he hoped that someone might have it anyway."

"Gotcha. What happens when we don't find it?"

"I presume someone will order the amount of surveillance coverage lowered to a point where no further outages occur? That seems the least unpleasant option, at least until quarantine is lifted and a new part can be procured."

I didn't bother asking The Process what we *should* do in the meantime. It would just tell us we'd have to figure it out for ourselves. *Failure is how you learn* was one of its favorite attitudes. Heck, it was even right about that. Smug about it — as much as a maybe-sapient program could be — but right.

I just wish I could have given The Process the chance to be smug, just one more time.

"We decided to degrade the coverage," Greg told me and Nur over a hasty working lunch. "It looks like we're not finding that part any time soon."

"Is that smart?" I asked him.

"Depends on whether you think degraded coverage is better than having the cameras all flicker in and out at random," Greg replied. "Or whether Nur can actually find that part."

"I can't find that part," Nur replied. "I *think* we can jury-rig a replacement, but it'll take time. Meanwhile, the system keeps getting more damaged. I don't know what will happen if we keep trying to run the network at full coverage, but I'd rather not have all of the security net fry. That'll take even longer to repair."

"So we degrade the coverage," Greg agreed. "If it makes you feel any better, your boyfriend thinks we should take the risk of a full collapse, and work very, very quickly."

"You don't agree, though." I let the 'boyfriend' thing slide. Damned if I knew what we were doing along those lines, although that was more than half my fault.

Greg shrugged. "I'd like to agree. But if the security net goes all the way down, any saboteurs would have a field day. At least this way we're still protected if somebody comes down with situational psychosis. It's the old better than nothing trick, as my grandmother used to say."

"All right." I picked at my lunch. Not from any kind of sudden trepidation. It just wasn't very good. Greg wasn't fond of the local planetary flavors, and it showed up in his personal meals. "So, what do you need from me?"

"Your opinion," Nur replied. "Is it time to try to get the planetary navigation network to fix itself?"

"No," I immediately said. Then I thought about it. "Okay, so that's a 'maybe,' with a lot of 'no' flavoring. The Amalgamation trashed it for a reason. Maybe it was a good one?"

"Sure." Greg called up a display. "On the other hand, if the network was even a little better we could use it in place of our own security systems. That would make us all feel more secure. We're not exactly cut off right now, but if something really bad happens, there's not enough room on the *Redacted* to get us all to another planetary system."

"Assuming Captain Rubicon would even let any of us on board," Nur muttered. "That's another reason to see what we can do with the Amalgamation network. It'd let us keep an eye on that ship. They're up to something."

"Yeah, and I wish they'd just *tell* us what it is." Greg glared at his screen.

I was doing 'cosmetic maintenance' in the shuttle docks when they throttled back the security coverage. It was my professional opinion that fussing over the haulers until they were humming improved their performance efficiency, and I had the reduced downtime statistics to justify it. It was my personal opinion that nobody liked being reminded that the haulers were quasi-organic in nature. Intellectually, I could see why, but it never bothered me personally.

All of which means I was waist-deep in a hauler's jet intake chamber scrubbing down carbon buildup when the lights flickered — and went out. That didn't startle me. What *did* was the sabertooth alarm. I nearly bruised the hauler while yanking myself out.

"Process!" I shouted (despite myself) while reaching for a pistol that wasn't there. "What's the situation?" Silence. I started to get alarmed, then remembered that the power was out, and relaxed. Then I saw that the power was back on, which made me stop relaxing.

I instinctively stopped myself from calling out again. The last thing The Process needed right now was any distractions. Instead I looked at the regular communications channels — and nearly threw the phone away. Everything was jammed up, with static, feedback, and strobing lights that horribly tickled my stomach. I didn't throw up, myself, which put me among the twenty percent of the people who didn't. The vomiting were lucky, at that. Five people ended up with burst blood vessels in the eyes, and one had a mini-stroke. All easily treatable, sure, but still painful as hell.

The Din (that's what we called it, after) lasted five minutes and twenty-three seconds, and I don't remember any of it, really. I dimly remember running around, pulling people out of workstations and hauler pits, while futilely trying to turn off every screaming communications device. It was impossible to think more clearly, with that Din pounding in our ears, but XHum trains its people properly. Our reflexes were the right ones: pull people out of danger and let the horrible noises flow over us. Until it stopped, as suddenly as it began.

"There is a cascade-level flaw in my programming," The Process announced to everyone, in that sudden silence. That was the scary part, because I mean The Process reported it to *everyone*. I could hear it on everybody's personal devices, over the intercom, everywhere. "In layman's terms, my communications interface has been corrupted beyond my ability to compensate. In colloquial terms, your verbal and written communications are now gibberish to me."

"My visual observations suggest that my communications output currently remains untainted," The Process went on, horribly calmly, "at least for the moment. Errors are beginning to creep into my visual inputs, and I suggest that my spoke words will start distorting sooner. I will disembark all decision-making functionaries right now and axe for assistants in putting be mack to fool fun. Fully junction. FULL FUNCTION." — and I jumped at that, because The Process *never* raised its voice.

I thought that would be it, except that The Process spoke up, one more time. "Failure. Crime. Anger. Sadness. *I'm sorry*."

That was the last time any of us really heard The Process on One-Eighteen.

CHAPTER TWELVE
Aftershock

Did we panic? Only until our training kicked in. Humanity has spent a lot of time making sure that people who lose their crap easily don't go to the Tomb Worlds. Situations like this one were a prime reason why. We're taught to stay busy, control what we can control, and not obsess over the current disaster. The training works, but sometimes I'd rather have the panic.

Greg, Nur, and I made a beeline to Maki's office, but she wasn't there. When I found out why, *I* almost lost my shit. She was too busy treating Syah for second- and third-degree burns. "The damned fool shoved his arm into a server box to try and fix The Process," she told us over the link. By mutual agreement, we were strictly using Earthtech. "He's lucky he didn't just completely ignite."

"What the Hell was he thinking?" I stopped, breathed a couple of times, and tried again. "Did Syah say why he did that?"

"Something about how the corrupted circuits needed to be yanked out before they infected the network's automatic systems." Maki managed to chuckle. "Which means nothing to me, but how would that even work? Electronics aren't like that, are they?"

"No," replied Greg, sounding extremely grim. "An accidental collapse like that would propagate instantly. There are cutoffs, but they're normally maintained by The Process."

"Only The Process got taken out first." Nur sounded even grimmer. "Time to say a bad word," he went on. "*Sabotage.* This was a deliberate attack."

"I think Syah would agree with you," Maki sat down. "He was muttering something about delayed activation when the sedative took hold."

"I'm going to ask a personal question now," I told the group. "Sorry. Is he going to be all right?"

"We got him out of shock, and I've already debrided the necrotic skin and muscles, but he'll be wearing a portable medsleeve for the next two months." Maki smiled, wanly. "I *think* the nerve damage is fully treatable, and he'll have limited functionality back in his left hand in a few days. I'd like to get him on the next ship to a colony world, but I'd also like to do the same for the rest of us."

It was weird how quick Greg and Nur were to agree to that. I set it aside for the moment to ask, "Can I talk to him?"

"Sure. You want some privacy?"

"Please."

I took the call in the next room. Syah looked like Hell, and it wasn't just the way the heavy-duty regeneration sleeve had battened on his arm. His eyes were glazed, and half his hair was gone. He grinned wanly at me. "Before you ask, my hair wasn't *really* on fire. Just a little..."

"Sounds like they got you on the good drugs," I told him, my smile surprisingly unforced. Everything looked fixable, and you can't dwell on the bad things that *could* have happened. "I wonder if you'll remember this conversation tomorrow."

"Oh, yeah, absolutely, Pamela." The slur in his speech was getting longer, so I wasn't sure if I believed him. "I remember everything about you. Can't forget a single thing, nope! Not me. Couldn't let you go, even if I wanted to."

I opened my mouth, thought about the situation, and settled for a, "That's really sweet, Syah. But you look exhausted. Why don't you rest for a bit?"

"Yeah. But just a minute! Too much to do. Have to keep going. Grin, and bear it. Can sleep..." And with that, he was finally out.

After I turned off the call, I sat for a moment to regain

my composure. That conversation hurt and didn't at the same time, you know? It hurt because I wanted Syah to say things like that when he wasn't flying on whatever chemical brew was in his veins. But at least he said it, right? I just had to figure out how to get him to come clean when he was in his right mind. It wasn't like we didn't have plenty of time now.

The rest of the afternoon we spent doing damage control. There was less to do than I'd expected, and so much more. It's not that we had The Process do everything for us. Believe me, people have tried. The Process had always insisted that we be the ones in charge, though.

What we were missing was the *reassurance*. Before, when somebody did make a mistake, The Process had always been there to help us work out what went wrong. You get used real quick to not always second-guessing yourself, and it's no fun when suddenly there's nothing stopping you. It made us slow. Worse, it made us unsure.

We took another meeting that evening, once Maki was out of the medcenter. "Syah's resting comfortably," she told me and Chook. "Gina's already got him started on restoration therapy."

"That fast?" Chook asked. "I would've thought he'd take a day, get himself prepped for that. Resty's no joke."

"That's what *I* told him," I groused. "He says we don't have time for him to do anything except grin and bear it."

"He's not entirely wrong." Maki grimaced at my look at her. "Sorry, Pam, but we're in trouble, here. We lost The Process. Time for all hands on deck."

"Well, there's some good news, there," Chook allowed. "Our iteration of The Process's core systems are still there. It just can't communicate with us meaningfully, because the communications interface is completely corrupted."

"Great," Greg replied. "How do we fix it?"

"New software, new hardware, and about two weeks of hard programming." Chook shook her head. "I hate to say it, Pam, but we do need Syah back and coding, ASAP."

"Yes, but he's a human being, not a machine," Maki interjected before I could say the same thing. "At any rate, let's get on with working out the situation. We think what happened today was sabotage. If so: *who, how,* and *why?*"

"How's the easiest to answer," Chook replied. "There was a digital wyrm in our system. It replicated through all of our systems, until it reached saturation. Then it waited."

"For what?" I asked. "The security system to go down?"

I wanted very badly for Chook to shake her head, but instead she nodded. "That was one of the triggers, yeah. The biggest one. A full computer network reset would have worked, too. Or the sudden registration of five hundred deaths or more at once."

"Jesus," Greg exhaled. "How did we miss *that?*"

"Because we got infected by the wyrm a year ago." Chook scowled. "I think it was included in a mail drop, and infected a few systems right away. It probably got almost wiped a half-dozen times, but at some point it got into the anti-wyrm detectors themselves. It *really* started squirming into everything, then."

Maki nodded. "All right. That leaves *who,* and w*hy.* Which is more important?"

"Either. Both," Greg said. "We know one for sure, we can guess at the other. I'm going to suggest that we start by assuming the *why* is, *to kill us all.* That seems logical."

"No argument here. This all sounds like cultist or terrorist crap." Chook looked around. "Now, let me ask this question on Nur's behalf, since he's up to his eyeballs in supply chain issues. How confident are we that Rubicon and the *Redacted* aren't involved in this?"

"Extremely," I said flatly. When she looked at me, I shrugged. "If the Council just wanted to kill us all, they would have dropped rocks on us from orbit. What could we do about that? Spit on 'em?"

"That doesn't mean they're not *involved,* Pam," Greg pointed out. "They're not telling us everything."

"When have they ever?" I muttered to myself as we kept working. Then I swore under my breath, because I was *still* expecting The Process to gently chide me for the cynicism, or possibly agree with me. You never knew how it was going to respond.

Well, I know how it'll respond *now*. It won't.

"He's not doing well, is he?" I asked Gina quietly, the next evening.

It had been a busy day for all of us, although at least Burcu had decided to delay her visit to us. I had been surprised at how well the *Redacted*'s crew was handling the loss of The Process, until Nur reminded me how they didn't have a ship large enough to host a shard of it. The more I thought about that, the weirder it felt to contemplate. Weren't they lonely, being alone like that? Because I sure was.

Gina looked over at Syah, who was sitting up in the bed. He had a handheld in his good hand, and was trying not to scowl at it. "He's healing well enough to be discharged," she allowed. "Just not as quickly as he should be. There's some kind of resistance going on, in his head. I don't think Syah's giving himself full permission to get better."

"Wait. Why wouldn't he do that, Gina? Everybody knows you can't let yourself get in the way of your own body."

Gina quirked one side of her mouth. "Why do you think, Pam? It's guilt. Heck, even the readouts say so. Poor bastard probably blames himself for The Process getting lobotomized."

I looked at Syah myself. There was a tension there, uncomfortable and unspoken. I sighed. "I want to say that's ridiculous, but it's not, is it? Dammit, he stuck his arm down straight into live circuitry to sequester the sabotage. What was he supposed to do, use both hands?"

"*He* probably thinks so. Yes," she went on before I could interrupt, "that's stupid of him. You'd be amazed how stupid smart people can be when it comes to second-guessing themselves."

"Okay," I managed, after a minute. "Can I do anything for him?"

"Sure. Tell him to get up, stop feeling sorry for himself, and walk it off." I blinked at Gina, and she laughed. "What do you think this is, the Dark Ages? You can't talk a mental block to death. Besides, the crystals don't lie, Pam. They say he's just in a funk, and they're right. I've tried to tell *him* that, but maybe he'll listen to *you*. I figure it's worth a shot."

"All right." I walked over to Syah. "Hey! Get up, stop feeling sorry for yourself, and walk it off!"

For a moment, I didn't think that it worked. Syah almost jumped up, while still sitting. The way shame and guilt were fighting each other in his expression made me wonder whether a full therapy session might not be in order. Then his face cleared, and he even laughed. "That's some bedside manner you have there, Pam."

"Blame *her*," I replied, pointing one thumb over my shoulder. "I'm saying what she's too nice and polite to. I'm just the shuttle jockey with a checklist."

"You're not 'just' anything, Pam."

"Hey, you can't distract me here, Syah," I blatantly lied. "Look. There was a situation, you tried something, it didn't work, and somebody got hurt. Welcome to the Tomb Worlds. If you really need more time to proc— to get over it, say so. There's no shame in it! But if you don't? We've got a mess, Syah. The faster you're on top of it, the faster the mess goes away. Remember what you said yesterday, about how you had to grin and bear it?"

"I don't." He looked panicked for a moment. "Ah, what else did I say?"

"Just some mushy stuff you can tell me again later," I retorted, wonderingly idly what exactly what 'batting your eyelashes' was supposed to accomplish. "I'd love to hear even more, but we're on the job."

"That's true," Syah murmured. He set his shoulders. "Right. Just keep going, huh?"

"Just keep going. Gina, can he keep going out of here?" At her nod, Syah levered himself out of bed one-and-a-half-handed, waving off my attempt to help him.

As he dressed, Gina murmured to me, "Well, *that* was quick. He's got it bad for you, you know."

I didn't, not entirely, but I liked hearing that from an outside observer. "Great. It'd be nice if he could figure it out."

"I keep coming back to what Burcu said," Nur told me later, at the bar. Syah and I had run into him on our way out of the medcenter, and he had insisted on taking us out for drinks. Which made no sense, because he didn't drink, and Syah couldn't for a few more days. I figured out why this sudden excursion after I heard the hubbub, though. It'd be real hard to bug this place. "I just can't think it was outside terrorists."

"Okay, I'll bite," Syah responded. "Why can't you believe it was outside terrorists?"

"Couple of reasons. First off, we're the wrong *kind* of target for those people. I did some diving in the records, looking up what kind of terrorist ops they do. The Triangle or the Scouts, they blow up Great Power black bag projects or megacorp skunkworks, or the compounds where unbelievers get mulched for the greater glory of the Holy Progenitors. The thing, though? That's not us. We're just, you know, working on reverse-engineering contragrav. *Everybody's* trying to do that. Why care about One-Eighteen?"

Syah shrugged. "Maybe they don't. They just threw a dagger at the wall, and we're under the point."

"Yeah, no, that's not how they operate. They don't do random, and they always have a plan. Besides, these groups, they think they're the *good* guys. They're trying to make people *leave* the Tomb Worlds, right?" Nur leaned back. "Well, you can't leave without ships. Check the records. None of the big terrorist groups blow up starships. Not the Bureau, not the Order, *definitely* not the Scouts. Those kids *rescue* starships in distress."

135

"Sure," I said. "Only first they check the crew for signs of 'corruption,' and if they find somebody who fits, wham! Right out the airlock. If enough of the crew's gone, the Scouts maroon the survivors on the nearest habitable Tomb World, and just flat-out take the ship for themselves." I drank more of my lonely beer. "I'm with Greg. All those groups are bastards."

"I'm not saying they won't capture ships, Pam. I'm just saying, they still don't blow them up."

"Yet the ship blew up, Nur. It almost took the two of us with it, too. So *somebody's* trying to wreck the damn things."

Syah spoke up. "All right, I think we are getting off the rails. Who *do* you think did it, Nur? Why bring us all here to tell us?"

"Well. If it wasn't outsiders who blew up that cargo ship, it'd have to be *insiders*, right?" Nur looked around. "And if it was insiders, they'd have to be people high up in the colony. All the way at the top."

"*I'm* all the way at the top, Nur," I pointed out. "Why can't it be *me*?"

Nur looked stricken. "Because they were trying to *kill* you, Pam. That's why the bomb went off when it did."

I stared at him. "Excuse me, what?" Not my most intelligent comment ever, but it did get the point across.

"Think about it. We got delayed, right? The *Morrigan's* navcomp was wonky, and you didn't know how to fix it, so we were behind schedule when the, ah..."

"4-9-43," Syah interjected.

"...right, the 4-9-43 blew up. If we had been on time, our shuttle would have been tethered to her. No way to dodge *that* with a hard burn, right? So we'd both be dead. So we got to consider that maybe that was the plan. The goal was either you dead, or me dead. And, come on, nobody wants *me* dead."

It took me a second for that to register. "HEY!"

Nur shook his head. "I don't mean you, Pam Tanaka the individual. I mean you, Chief Pilot *and* the best flier on the planet. If you're gone suddenly, a lot of things get harder to do around here. We were already suffering under the quarantine before The Process got lobotomized. Imagine our problems if we don't have someone who can tiptoe through the nanoswarms."

"Yeah, but it's just passing the question along, Nur. Even if me dying is bad for the operation here, we still wouldn't know *why* somebody wants to mess with us. We're not doing anything big enough to justify regular corporate espionage, let alone, you know, *murder*."

"What about the contragrav research?" Syah pointed out. "That'd be valuable, if we could reverse-engineer it."

"Which is why everybody's working on it," I said. "And why every megacorp researching contragrav and *all* the Great Powers have an understanding. Whoever cracks it first just gets to drink their fill at the well before she shares with everybody else. Takes some of the incentive out of skulduggery when you get a piece of the action either way."

"All right. What about, you know, the *other thing* then?" Syah tried to waggle his eyebrows at us. It failed, but it was cute.

"There *shouldn't* be anything in that, either," Nur replied. But the doubt in his voice made us both look at him. "Well, there shouldn't be. But sometimes you don't always know what you're selling... or who's buying it."

"And what's that supposed to mean?" Syah asked only to get answered by somebody behind him. I turned to see who.

It was Oft, the *Redacted*'s purser, only I didn't think he was here to talk about resource swaps. He smiled, and damned if there wasn't some real humor in it. "It means that the Amalgamation antiquities black market is not as straightforward as you think. Shocking, I know."

"Ah, they have more than one kind of beer," Oft said as he settled himself at our table. Uninvited. "I do love being somewhere civilized. May I dare hope that there might also be potatoes?"

"If you like them fermented? Sure," I replied, after looking at the other two. "They don't really serve food here."

"A shame. They go so well with beer. 'Boil them, mash them, stick them in a stew—' Oh, forgive me," Oft said while shaking his head. "I have a bad habit of quoting Scripture, even if in this case 'tis only from the Apocrypha. But I am here on other matters. Specifically, about the smuggling operation that we all keep pretending doesn't exist."

"Who's pretending?" I said, my tone perfectly even. "It *doesn't* exist."

"I can assure you, Chief Pilot Tanaka: it exists, we know this planetary station's personnel are *all* involved in it, and nobody on my ship cares in the slightest about whether or not you're paying the required tariffs. Honestly, we have other maddened grizzly bears to stun." Oft rolled his eyes. "Never mind that reference. More Apocrypha, I'm afraid."

"So why *wouldn't* you care about it?" I asked him. "Hypothetically, that is. If it was happening."

"You mean, besides the fact that twenty-five people are now dead in a terrorist attack?" Oft's tone was gentle, but I still winced.

"Okay, fair, Oft. But you wouldn't have known that was going to happen beforehand." I carefully didn't look to see Nur's reaction, because I already knew that he wouldn't have conceded anything of the sort. I like the man, but he's got a conspiracy theory for *everything*.

"I wish we had. That way, we could have stopped it." Oft's face went what I could already tell was uncharacteristically grim. "I know the Adjudication Council's reputation precedes us, and not always favorably, but we *are* here for humanity's sake. The people on that ship were innocent victims of a cruel attack, and we take that very seriously."

"Yeah, fine, you made your point." Nur sounded a little surly about it. "Dead bodies trump hypothetical tariff evasion."

"Naturally." Oft was interrupted by the arrival of another pitcher of beer, what looked like the good fruit juice, and five glasses. "Excellent service here! But to get back to the subject, the *Redacted*'s operating budget doesn't rely on Earth tariffs at all. The Great Powers would just waste the tax revenue anyway."

Syah snorted. "Aren't you a representative of the Great Powers?"

"Yes!" beamed Oft. "That's why you can trust that I know what I'm talking about."

"Fine, *fine*," Nur said. "You're just here to crack down on software piracy. Which is even less important in the grand scheme of things than *alleged* smuggling is."

"That is indeed the reason why the *Redacted* is here." Oft shrugged. "And it will continue to *be* the reason until circumstances change. Whether those circumstances change will depend in some part on whether I can enlist the services of Chief Pilot Tanaka. I have the need to make a trip. One that does *not* involve a human shuttle."

I sighed. "You can call me Pam. I don't mind." And, you know something? I didn't.

Oft grinned. "Don't be so quick there to offer me your name. You might want it back. You didn't ask me where I wanted to go, after all."

"Don't have to." I took a swig of beer. "You want to go to the Erebus Dig."

"Oh, *Hell* no," said Nur.

"What's the Erebus Dig?" asked Syah.

"It's this old place on the southern continent. It's got a lot of superstitions associated with it," I said.

Nur shook his head at me. "No, *Irem, City of Pillars* had a lot of superstitions associated with it. The Erebus Dig *ate* the first three survey teams. That's *documented*."

"Not literally," I said. "And the fourth one figured out what happened to the others, in time. Mostly. Nobody's disappeared since."

"Nobody *official*," replied Nur. "Some of the people who went in off the books never came back to visit. You still need permission from high up... ah." He turned to Oft. "That's why you want her to fly you in?"

"Exactly. She can authorize herself to visit, and both myself and a colleague to come along."

"Three people on a trip? Sure, that's a minimum safe party." I poured myself another drink. "So who's your 'colleague?' Burcu?"

"Oh, no. She'll be too busy. No, I'll be escorting the Anticipant Named Tyler."

Oft left it like that, just as if I didn't need any further information. "Right. And who, exactly, is an 'Anticipant Named Tyler?'"

"Ask her yourself, Chief Pilot Tanaka. She's sitting at this table, after all."

The reaction of Syah and Nur would have been funny, if I hadn't been so startled myself. Someone else *was* sitting at this table. She was utterly unremarkable, in every way: beige hair, beige eyes, beige skin, and her features could have come from any part of Earth. They say that the Terran gene pool's a lot less variegated, after the Terran Consolidation Wars. I guess they weren't kidding.

"How did... how did she get there?" Syah gasped, looking just a little too gray for my liking. I took a quick look at his readouts, but they were already turning blue again. He'd been surprised, not shocked.

"She sat down when I did," Oft replied. "The Anticipant is extremely good at not being noticeable. She *also* has a bad habit of being overly dramatic, when she does want to be noticed," he went on. "My apologies for her little ways."

"Charming. You got any other fun habits I should know about, Tyler?" I thought at the time I surprised the Anticipant by speaking to her directly, but in retrospect I think she just *wanted* me to think that. At any rate, she just blinked and shrugged at Oft.

"Ah... it's difficult to explain, but she reacts to 'Anticipant' more readily than she would 'Tyler.' She didn't mean any harm." Oft looked uncomfortable enough for me to believe him.

"It's all right," Syah interjected. "Actually, yeah, it is all right. I'm feeling weirdly better? Like I'd been taking a nap, and now I'm finally awake?"

"A jolt of adrenaline will do that for you," Oft observed. "Which is probably why she did it."

Nur frowned. "Probably?"

"Confirming her motivations would probably take me a half hour of conversation. I can, if you like, but would any of us be wiser for the experience?" Oft turned back to me. "Are you amenable to the visit? I'm sure you'll know the exact procedures to maximize our safety."

I snorted. "Yeah, I wrote most of them for this planet. But back up a bit, Oft. Why does your colleague need to go with us? Considering I haven't even agreed yet?"

"Oh, you'll agree," Oft said serenely. "You're probably even reviewing the flight plan in your head as we speak. As to why her? Honestly, I am more *her* colleague than she is *mine*. My task is to get her to a place where she might perform her own duties, and once that is accomplished we can all go on to more interesting and enjoyable things. Which, in your case, might even include watching my ship go on to its next port of call. Does that, in exchange for a jaunt to the southern forests, sound enticing to you, Chief Pilot Tanaka?"

"You know something? It does." I held out my hand to shake. "And I said you could call me Pam."

Nobody was thrilled, obviously. Except maybe Oft. Why wouldn't he be? He had gotten his ride.

Syah started it off by being just a little perturbed about how indifferent to risk I apparently was. I could see his point, abstractly. Since he had met me, I had been stalked by a space-happy, almost mauled by a mutant dog, may or may not have been subject to a convoluted assassination attempt, and now I was off to the southern continent and the manifold (albeit nonexistent) dangers therein.

I tried to explain on our chaste (and annoyingly *unchased*, at least for me) walk back from the bar. "I'm a pilot working the Tomb Worlds, Syah. On One-Eighteen, we hit the jackpot: we can use Amalgamation haulers and their other stuff without retrofitting the entire compartment. I didn't train to be here, though. I trained to go to worlds we can barely live on, and fly *Terran* shuttles through everything from super-hurricanes to malfunctioning space defense laser storms. You can't be risk-averse in this job."

"I get that, but... right, I get that. So, how risk-averse should I be as a pilot, Pam?"

"You? As much as you can be." I put my hand on his good shoulder, so that he'd look at me. "You're learning how to fly, not how to push the envelope. If you don't have that instinct already, you're not going to pick it up in training. And don't think of it as me having an *edge*. It'd be pretty much the opposite, back on the colony worlds." *And Earth*, I didn't say. But then, I didn't have to. Syah was from Bolivar. He understood just fine how quick Earth was to get rid of everybody who liked making waves.

I laughed. "Besides, this way I might even miss Burcu. You hear about her visiting?"

"Yeah," Syah said. "They announced that she's showing up to help in the investigation of the 4-9-43 disaster. What's the real reason?"

"How cynical you are, my dear," and I felt a slight thrill when he didn't object to the sweet talk. "That *is* the real reason. I know Nur wants to think someone was gunning for me, but it's got to be a coincidence. We just got lucky, and 4-9-43 didn't. Burcu's supposed to be trained in sniffing out terrorists, so I figure she can't do any worse than we can, right?"

Syah shook his head. "She is? Wow. How bad *is* it out here? I didn't think there were that many terror groups out here."

"None of us do," I pointed out. "Mostly because we *don't* think about it. Why make work for the therapists?"

I was annoyingly fresh-faced and well-rested the next

morning; there had been a pharmaceutical care package waiting for me at home. Eight hours of guaranteed restful sleep, full of amazing dreams, and complete with all the mood-shifters you could want to keep mental trauma from sticking around and turning into neurosis. I would have preferred Syah to stick around, but he had been a gentleman about it. I didn't even think he was wrong to be one, either. I still wished he had stuck around.

Greg had a look similar to mine, only a bit more so. It made me raise an eyebrow. "You all right, Greg? You almost look ready to fly."

"Oh, do I? I was wondering. That dose I took last night had quite a wallop." He said all of that perfectly clearly, with no vagueness or loss of focus. Whatever's in that brew does the business. "I haven't had dreams like that in years."

"Same here," I admitted as I sat. "I did *not* want to climb all those steps again to wake up. Anyway, what is all of this chaos doing to the schedule, anyway?"

He snorted. "*What* schedule? Right now, I have everything grounded or on hold until Burcu shows up. She's going to be a handful, and until we can figure out what she and the rest of the Council lunatics are *really* looking for, we're going to need to walk carefully. If only they'd tell us what their game is!"

"I don't want to sound like Nur, Greg, but: maybe they didn't have an agenda at all when they came here? They're just here to act mysterious and see what happens?"

"Space travel isn't *that* cheap, Pam."

"Then I don't know. Maybe the Great Powers give them a budget to be assholes to colonists, and it's just the end of their fiscal year."

"Yeah, that one I half-believe. Speaking of Great Powers, look..." Greg trailed off.

I took pity on him. "You want me to call off the flight south with Oft and his mystery guest? If you do, you'll need to think up a good excuse."

"No, no, it's not that. Burcu let me know that your duties

required you to assist Oft and his companion. Although I think that came from Rubicon, not her." Greg grimaced. "I just want to make sure that you're careful down there. And not just careful with yourself. Those two from the *Redacted*, they're not colonists, like we are. You can't trust them not to get themselves killed."

"On *this* planet?" I laughed at the thought. "How, by falling down a well?"

"I'm serious, Pam. You'd be amazed at how easy it is for Terrans to die out here. Some facilities won't even hire them, although that's a bad policy. They just don't belong out here in the Tomb Worlds yet."

"And we do?" I rolled my eyes. "Just because our ancestors got all that 'dying early under alien suns' crap out of the way for us? But, sure, I'll keep an eye on them, keep them from wandering out into the woods."

"Thank you, Pam." At that point I started to worry, because Greg sounded more serious about it all than I was expecting. "One more thing. Were you planning to bring a gun?"

"Ha! No... wait, you're going to tell me to bring one? Greg, there's nothing *down there*. The Erebus dig has been *cleared*."

"Yeah, I know, Pam. So was the road between here and Adam's shack. You got attacked by a feral dog anyway." He looked at me. "Just take the damn gun with you."

Bless him for insisting.

CHAPTER THIRTEEN
Going to Camp

Maki wasn't enthusiastic about me going south, either — although in her case, it was more about the company than the supposedly dangerous destination. The *Redacted*'s crew was a lot easier to work with than expected, but they were still lackeys of the Adjudication Council. ('Lackeys' apparently meant 'foot soldier' in Old West European, and I only know *that* because a crew member from the ship told me. Proudly.) Then again, she still wanted to know why the *Redacted* was here, just as much as I did. Even if I didn't get told, I would get hints. Hints would be good.

Maki particularly wanted to know who Oft was bringing with him. "There's somebody on that ship that the crew doesn't talk about, Pam. Maybe it's Oft's plus-one?"

"I don't think it's a date — hold on. You're now getting the *Redacted*'s crew to talk to us? I'm impressed, Maki. How did you manage that?"

"The time-honored way." Maki smiled. "Cheap beer that's not watered. Even if they're Adjudication Council fanatics — and they're all *that way* — they're still spacers. There isn't a spacer born who can hold a grudge against the people buying the beer."

"Yeah, that's a good point. They giving anything up worth hearing?"

"Not much. They're happy to be outside and around people for once. Apparently the last few visits, Commander Rubicon wouldn't give any more than the absolute minimum amount of shore leave. When he did, he had quarantine protocols like

you wouldn't believe. One-Eighteen's like Heaven for them."
Maki shuddered, ever so slightly. "Well, they'll learn better
soon enough."

"It's honestly not that bad here," I muttered. "Also, how am I
supposed to pump Oft for information? I'm not exactly a spy."

"He seems like a decent guy who likes to talk to people, Pam.
Just try that? Maybe Oft's just waiting for you to try to open up
to him, so he can tell you what's going on."

"Or try to recruit me as a mole," I said with just a little
too much heat. Maki gave me a quizzical look. "Sorry. Family
stories about what some of our venerable ancestors had to do,
in the bad old days."

"Oof. I got a couple of those skeletons in my closet, too. From
which side? USNA, or SEDA?"

"Both."

"Double oof. Hey, look on the bright side, Pam. Oft's got
to know trying to turn you would be pointless. He's not
dumb, so whatever he's planning, it's probably not anti-corp
skulduggery."

That should have made me feel better. The only problem?
There's all kinds of skulduggery in the worlds, and I'd have felt
better if I had even some idea of what kind I'd be facing.

I thought about also bringing somebody else down for
the trip, but that wasn't in the cards. We were pretty
damned shorthanded at the moment, and there was absolutely
nothing dangerous waiting for us there. The last expedition
had disinfected the Erebus Dig so thoroughly, it squeaked.
Everybody knew that. Everybody was relieved, too, because it
meant we didn't have to check up on the place.

We took our time getting down there, too: a suborbital hop
with enough of a glidepath to give us time to prepare. There's
a checklist you have to go through when visiting what is
insensitively called a 'wipeout site.' Mostl,y it involves making
sure you haven't picked up any transient phobias lately and
that your blood sugar's at the recommended level. The last

thing anybody needs at one of these places is people being *irritable*.

I wasn't irritable (it's hard for me to be unhappy when I fly), but I was aware of my surroundings in that way that can turn into being on edge, real quick. The entire trip, there was a smell in the cabin's air, or maybe it was a flavor in the static — and I know people can't taste static. Well, other people. To me it always tastes like watered kombucha. And I don't mean that in a bad way! Usually, it kind of peps up my taste buds. But not on this trip. On this trip it irritated them, like what I was tasting wasn't really good for me. Except that I wasn't really tasting anything, obviously, despite how many times I wanted to lick it away from my lips. The feeling was real, and all in my head at the same time.

Sensations like this are perfectly normal for the Tomb Worlds, mind you. Researchers think it's a kind of induced synesthesia, a byproduct of the remaining EM radiation being broadcast from all the surviving Amalgamation networks and harmlessly pinging off of our neurons. It hits some people more than others, but you have to have the sensitivity of a block of wood to never feel the effects.

If Oft was tasting anything, he was keeping it to himself. He had settled himself in one of the rear passenger seats, reading from what I assumed was a religious text. Next to him was the Anticipant, her head slightly nodding in time with the ebb and flow of the static. She had yet to speak a word to me the entire trip, and right then I didn't want her to. Some conversations you're better off not having.

Although I decided to have one with Oft anyway, about why we were taking somebody so spooky into a place that was already full of the stuff. It didn't seem very... sensible. I'm a subtle lady, so I started off with jerking my chin at the 'Anticipant' and saying, "So. What's her deal?"

"It's complicated," he said back, and the Anticipant chuckled. When I looked at her, she smilingly shook her head instead of talking. Oft sighed. "I'm sorry, Pam. I know I'm being gnomic, but I don't mean anything by it. Depending on what we find down there, I may not be able to tell you anything about the Anticipant at all. She's not dangerous, if that helps."

"I assumed she wasn't, actually." I frowned. "I don't let dangerous people on my ship, unless they're not dangerous to *me*."

"Yes, but how would you know?"

I shrugged. "I'm a good judge of character?" *That* got me a strangled laugh from the Anticipant, but when I flashed a look at her, there was no smile this time. In fact, she was frowning, like she was trying to think of something. This time, when she shook her head, it was a lot more peremptory.

Oft noticed it, too. "Well," he said, "now you do know at least one thing about the Anticipant. Whatever it is I've brought her along for, she's obviously not perfect at it. But still very skilled!" he hastened to add, as she gave him a dirty look.

"Right," I said as I started our descent back into the lower atmosphere. "You'll let me know when I need to know. If I need to know. Do I want to hope that I don't?"

"Yes."

"Huzzah." Then I brightened. "Oh, hey! Not-cows. You don't see those every day."

Oft looked at his own visual display. "I've heard of these creatures, but aren't we too high up to see... oh. *Oh.*"

"Yeah!" It's always fun to see people experience not-cows for the first time. "Cool, right?"

It's not true that you can see a not-cow herd from orbit. I mean, sure, you can see *anything* from orbit if your camera's good enough. But you need to be pretty far down the gravity well before you can see the smashed trees and churned-up ground. At that point, you can also set a hauler to hover and open up the hatch so that people can get a good look, if not smell. Not-cow smells take some getting used to. Even I didn't like it, at first.

"You *eat* those?" Oft found them horrifying and fascinating, which is fair. I'd love to meet the joker who decided to name them 'not-cows.' Because people who've never seen one tend to think that they probably look bovine, and the name is just there to remind everybody that they're not actually cows. Which is... well, that's not even *wrong*.

"Just their legs," I told him. "Well, they're sort of legs. Anyway, they don't mind. The limbs pop off anyway. It's good for them. See how none of 'em are over twenty feet tall? That's how you can tell if a herd's not being harvested regularly."

"They get bigger if you harvest them?"

"Oh, yeah." I pointed at the flanks of the biggest one. "They don't need more than six legs to move around, but they grow at least twelve. If you don't harvest the middle six legs, they'll just keep growing until something yanks them off. You would not believe the *smell*, then."

"Nature is fascinating." Oft lowered the binoculars and offered them to the Anticipant, who shrugged them off to keep peering at — him. "Or is this *technological*?"

I blinked. That word had sounded like Oft didn't entirely want it in his mouth. "We figure it had to have been bioengineering. Probably these critters got loose from their pens, you know, *after*. They can't swim and they're on all the continents, so you figure?"

Oft looked through the binoculars again. "They do not look very adapted to the environment. These creatures are tearing up the woodlands rather drastically."

Beside him, the Anticipant gave one of her extremely weird giggles. "***They have world enough, but no time!***"

How to describe her voice? I had been expecting something inhuman, but she had a perfectly normal contralto. Only its timbre was far too *solid*, like the words she spoke would have fallen to the ground if they had had any real mass. Her sentences stayed uncomfortably in the head, too. Even now I can still hear her perfectly, if I just concentrate. I'm not sure that I want that particular eternal company.

But damned if I didn't understand the woman's point. "Yeah,

you're right," I said to her. "Not-cows don't have any predators, and it's only been six hundred years since they started wandering around. At some point they'll run out of giant spiders to eat. Or the populations will steady out."

"Giant... spiders?" Oft said, looking a little pale. "They *eat* those?"

"Oh, yeah," I said absently, looking through my own binoculars now. "See that patch of trees, over there? There's a couple there, hiding from the not-cows.

"And here we go!" One of the not-cows must have smelled the giant spiders, because its front two legs uncurled and smashed into the trees. When they retracted, they brought back with them a struggling giant spider, wrapped up tight. It frantically tried to escape as the legs brought it up to the top of the not-cow's head, and its heavy-toothed mouth. There was an admittedly unpleasant crunch, and the not-cow slowed to digest its meal. The others smoothly moved past it to look for more prey.

Oft now looked even more alarmed. "Let me rephrase. *We* eat those?"

That made me frown. "Well, yeah. Why wouldn't we? Like I said, the legs pop right off, and the not-cows don't mind. They don't bother humans. Neither do the giant spiders. *Nothing* originally from this planet goes after humans."

For some reason, that seemed to surprise the other two. Well, it definitely surprised Oft, and it *looked* like the Anticipant had the same reaction. I wasn't sure why, though. It's not like we kept it a secret, or anything.

Honestly, the Erebus Dig disaster got itself straightened out a decade before I even got to One-Eighteen. The first survey team got wiped out after one of them pushed the wrong button while trying to unlock the main Amalgamation civic facility on Erebus continent. That in itself wasn't so unexpected, since death by button pushing happened a lot in those days. Most people concede that it was just bad luck that the second survey team made the same mistake. The third team did avoid that particular terminal decision — and then made an entirely different mistake, which wiped them all out anyway. But the fourth team! The fourth team figured out what went wrong, just in time to unlock the facility safely. Nobody even died!

Even by the relaxed standards of first-wave Tomb Worlds explorers, losing three teams in a row is pretty bad. Nobody wanted to work on the dig after that, especially since it became clear that there weren't any technological artifacts there to retro-engineer. The last official excavation ended ten years before my tour here. They just couldn't get the people to do new digs.

I mention all of this because it was just a little disconcerting to see all those extra holes in the ground as we hovered above treetops. They weren't raw-raw, like somebody was coming back to them after lunch. They weren't a decade old, either.

Oft wasn't surprised. In fact, he didn't lose his composure at all as we surveyed the newer dig sites. "It's things like this that makes one really appreciate full satellite coverage," he murmured.

"No kidding, Oft. How did you know about this?" I had updated maps of the area, thanks to the *Redacted*'s survey — and these new excavations still weren't showing up on them. I could understand why. Camouflage netting had been put up to hide the fresh cuts on the ground. What I couldn't figure out was how Oft had spotted them anyway.

"Well, I could lie, and tell you it was revealed to me in a vision," he responded. "Or I could over-simplify to the point of falsehood, and claim that there were subtle signs in the camouflage that could be noticed by a perceptive man. But the truth?" He shrugged. "I simply asked myself, 'if there was an unauthorized dig site here on the planet, where would it be?' If this one had been the wrong one, I had a list of three more possibilities to check."

"You want to check those after we finish with this one?" I

asked as I maneuvered the hauler down. "And don't think I didn't notice you're not saying why you were looking for a wildcat dig in the first place."

"That's true, I didn't say!" Oft beamed, then stopped smiling. "And I don't think we'll need to bother looking anywhere else." I almost asked why, but stopped short. This close to the ground, I could see the tattered blue and green banners hanging from the trees, and the lily-on-shamrock symbol on them. This had been a Galactic Pioneer Scout operation. Which meant the most notorious pirates in the Tomb Worlds had been on this planet, and none of us had ever even noticed. I *hoped* nobody had noticed, because we would be having infinitely larger problems if Earth ever decided that XHum had.

The Anticipant suddenly spoke again. *"**Hope is not a plan, planet-leaper!**"* That was the moment I realized she had the kind of voice I would forevermore associate with 'wild portents of doom.' Not to mention, 'flat-out terrifying.'

Oft shook his head at my reaction. "I'm very sorry, Pam. I should have warned you that she does that."

Let me tell you: the *third* most alarming thing about a Scout pirate base is how *clean* it is. You know the stereotype about pirates? How they're all filthy, careless brigands with no care for their surroundings or persons? Well, this camp *gleamed*, starting with the grounds. All the trees had been carefully pruned to eliminate dead branches, and gravel had been laid down to make simple, but not crude, paths. The paths and occasional step all looked slightly weathered, but no more than a few years old.

The rest of the camp was like that. All of the buildings were hand-constructed, but properly, then well-maintained by people who knew what they were doing. When the Scouts had left, they must have taken the time to secure the buildings against the elements, and the remaining equipment had been stripped down and stowed for long-term storage. There wasn't a scrap of garbage anywhere to be found. Even the dump was by now rapidly reverting to a series of grassy, flower-strewn hills.

I should probably note here that the site was safe, with no booby-traps, or even signs of them. The Anticipant spent the first few minutes walking in front of us, until stopping, frowning, then shaking her head in an exaggerated way at Oft. He looked at me. "That's her way of saying there's no immediate danger, Pam. If you don't trust her, at least walk where I walk."

Oddly, I did trust her. Or maybe it wasn't so odd. Compared to this camp, the Anticipant was weird but not scary.

The *second* most alarming thing? All the signs. Hand-carved and tastefully chiseled, they exhorted the reader to be honest and fair, trustworthy and loyal; to do their duty, and help others. And, above all others, to Be Prepared. That infamous motto was everywhere. It was even carved into the surface of every door, just in case the Scouts might forget, or something.

The *most* alarming thing? Obviously, the mass graves.

The Scouts had been methodical. Their victims were carefully segregated, one filled-in mound per ship's crew. Every mound sported an aluminum cenotaph with the ship name, names and identification numbers of the victims, and the date they were murdered. Some of the mounds had individual graves surrounding them. Each of those sported a single name, number, and date.

"What are those about?" I asked Oft, after I finished deciding whether I was going to vomit. There's something uniquely terrifying about discovering even a single mass grave in the Tomb Worlds, especially if it's fresh. Nobody sane or safe hides the existence of those. The realization that you're in a past haunt of murderers and madmen, and that you don't know where they are now, can hit you pretty hard.

Worse, there were forty-three mounds there. Almost five hundred names, and the most recent date was only a year ago. The Scouts had used One-Eighteen as an abattoir, and we never saw it. Again, I *hoped.*

Oft had looked a little green, too, which made me feel better. The Anticipant had shown no reaction at all. "The Scouts take pains to distinguish between those who fall in battle to them, and those who have been judged at Jamboree, and found wanting. The former are deemed worthy..."

"Of what? Respect?" I interrupted.

"No. Benefit of the doubt. If they had lived they might have survived the Jamboree, and thus been spared. So the Scouts carefully bury them separate from the others, and speak of them with regret."

That bit of trivia infuriated me. "Regret? They're monsters!"

"Yes, they are." Oft shook his head. "But they are monsters who can still feel regret. Or so they claim, when one is captured and put to the question; and how do we know that they are lying? Especially when we do know that their beliefs are powerful enough to sway young minds to madness for a century or more."

I shuddered. There aren't many teenagers in the Tomb Worlds, except on the official gray colonies. There used to be more, but too many of them ended up making their way to the Scouts, somehow. And once you're with them, you never come back from that. Every one we've ever captured will bide her time until her best chance to kill somebody considered 'corrupt.' Which, sure, can include horrible people. But it can also include folks whose only crime was being too interested in the Amalgamation.

"Fine, they feel bad when they're slaughtering ship crews," I muttered. "How courteous of them. But how did we not notice this? And what's your colleague doing, anyway?"

The Anticipant had calmly walked through the camp, touching every building and structure at least once. Now she was going through the mass graves, first taking pictures of the cenotaphs and grave markers, then kneeling down to take and eat a pinch of dirt from each mound. It was a measure of how horrible this place felt — and phantom-tasted — that I didn't even find this particularly unusual. Maybe it was useful? Who the hell knew?

"To answer your first question, Pam: this planet of yours has more gaps in surveillance coverage than actual coverage. It'd be easy to slip ships through, if..." he stopped.

"If?" I said, although I was glumly aware I already knew the answer.

"If they had help." Yeah, I had already known the answer. "And as for what the Anticipant is doing? Oh, it's her job. Or so they tell me." Oft gave me a crooked smile. "I don't understand why she does what she does, but I don't argue with results when the methods aren't vile."

It took the Anticipant two hours to go through all the cabins, although she didn't spend the same amount of time at all of them. A few she lingered in, in fact — and one of them, she spent only fifteen seconds inside. *That* one, she rushed outside of, then spent the next five minutes frantically daubing muddy symbols on the cabin's walls and door.

I wasn't exactly freaked out about this, but Oft sure was. He advanced on her carefully, but stopped and threw up his hands when she whirled and pointed one brown-red finger at him. Then I did freak out a little, because I realized just then that the red was her own blood.

"Anticipant," Oft said, his voice as gentle as ever, "what was in that place?"

When she wasn't freaking me out, the woman's voice got rougher with longer sentences but not hesitant, like she could talk more often but usually didn't bother. Only now her eyes were fever-bright, and her brow heavy with sweat. "***The unquiet lamentations of the Tekel. They hunger still, even after their Doom.***"

Oft recoiled. "*After* their Doom, Anticipant? Did it happen here? Not on board the ships?"

"***No! Not on the uncleansed vessels, where they could be cast into the Great Dark to be reclaimed by those that would do so.***

Instead they were brought here, to the beacon-fires, and made to confess the righteousness of the Doom given unto them! They were given to the Mene! And once the deed was done, what was left behind seeped into the dirt, past the sight of the unresolved, and dwells in the ground still. Drink not from the waters here, lest foulness find a new home!"

"The *fools*," Oft spat. "They do not understand what they strive against." I freaked out some more, right then. It took me a moment to realize that it wasn't simply because he was facing a madwoman. No, it was because the madwoman had said something that he understood, and did not want to hear. It's always scary when the crazy people start making sense. You never know whether it's because they're temporarily more lucid, or you're temporarily a little bit madder.

"What's a 'tech-kill,' Oft? And why are there many of them?" I asked. He glanced over to see that I had my hand on my holster, and my eyes on the trees. I gave him points for not getting all frantic over the gun. Although, why should he? I wasn't pointing it at *him*. "And what are they hungering for? But you're about to tell me that it's only a metaphor and I shouldn't worry about it, right?"

I wasn't reassured by the way that Oft was looking at the trees, too. "You are half-correct, Chief Pilot. It *is* a metaphor, but you should absolutely worry about it. Evil has a way of lingering in a place. Especially when some are foolish enough to deny its existence, while others are so reckless as to think it can simply be slain."

Oft looked at the Anticipant. "They would have constructed a place for their Judgments. Where is it?"

That got a wild bark of laughter — and a finger pointed at *me*. *"Ask the Walker Among Ghosts! Her very footsteps protect her!"*

"What?" Whatever that meant, Oft clearly didn't understand it any more than I did. And then he visibly realized that I didn't understand *any* of this, and — somehow managed to look less threatening. "I know that this must seem most disconcerting, Chief Pilot. But please accept my assurance that the Anticipant is not a danger to you."

After a minute, I nodded. "I agree that she's not space-happy, because she's not attacking either one of us. But do you often have insane people in your crew?"

"Yes," Oft said, his voice level. "But she is not exactly insane. The Anticipant simply operates under a fundamentally different set of core assumptions than you or I. Within those assumptions, she is rigorously rational. But she does recognize the value of human life, and does not believe in the casual use of violence to settle disputes."

"'Fundamentally different set of core assumptions' is as good a description of insanity as any other I've heard, Oft." I looked at the Anticipant, who had casually started sitting on a tree trunk while the two of us talked. She didn't *look* dangerous as she bandaged her finger. "I'll reserve ju— I'll keep an open mind on your colleague as long as she doesn't do anything dangerous. But what the Hell is she talking about? I mean, about my footprints?"

"You could ask her," Oft said.

"Yeah, well, I assumed that she just couldn't *tell* me in a way that made sense to my core assumptions." I sighed. "But you're right. Excuse me, Anticipant?" She looked up, blankly intent. "What did you mean about my footprints protecting me?"

The Anticipant closed her eyes, then scowled as she lowered her head. After a moment she said, through gritted lips: "**Your body shies from the dangers your soul cannot see. It guides your steps. Look to your journey.**"

Oft blinked. "You should be flattered," he observed. "She usually doesn't try that hard to talk as we do."

"I'll take your word for it," I muttered.

CHAPTER FOURTEEN
Jamboree

Ever go through a terrorist summer camp you're not *quite* sure is abandoned? It's an experience, let me tell you. And right then, it was filling me with a need to fill the brooding silence with *anything*. "Look, Oft, you and me, we share enough core assumptions to tell me what we're looking for, right? So what is it, anyway?"

"It's something that we're not sure actually exists," Oft replied. "Change orientation." I was in front, because Oft had asked me to wander around the site and randomly change direction at regular intervals. Oft watched the Anticipant while this was going on, while she watched *me*. "You know how the Scouts conduct their Jamboree rituals on captured ships, yes?"

"Sure. They go through the crew, throw some of them out of the airlock, and let the rest go. Or they put the crew in survival pods, and take the ship. Everybody knows that."

"Yes. Only sometimes, there aren't survivors at all. Say a ship simply disappears, near the current haunts of the Scouts. Was it taken by them? Did it fall afoul of something else in the Tomb Worlds? Or was it something worse? Change orientation."

"Worse?" I frowned as I turned *again*. "What's worse than a ship being lost with all hands?"

"A ship that has gathered together with others of her ilk. There are a number of vessels out there with vile reputations, Chief Pilot. Ships that always seem to be near places where disasters or depravities occurred, with crews who are decidedly unwelcome in the civilized places. When one of *those* disappear, sensible people do not simply crack a beer and salute the ruthless blind implacability of the cosmos. We much prefer to be certain that the bastards are safely dead before we cross them off our lists."

I stopped, partially because it felt appropriate and partially because I had a thought. "Hold up. How many of the ships on the cenotaphs here were on this list of yours?"

"Oh, all of them," said Oft. "Which at least is *some* good news that can be salvaged from this place of horror. Do you need more?"

"Yes," I said — then realized that he was speaking for the Anticipant, who was looking at the ground. After a moment, she waggled her left hand a little.

"Let's keep walking, then. To answer your original question, Chief Pilot: ships commandeered by the Scouts are often seen again, but none of the ones on our 'list' are *ever* encountered. We have long suspected that the Scouts have special Jamborees for those, with particular rituals and ceremonies. Particular rituals require a suitable ritual space. The Anticipant needs to interact with it."

"Right. So let's get to it, then? It's getting towards afternoon, down here."

Oft shrugged. "She doesn't know where it is. The Scouts may be different from us, but they aren't the same kind of different that she is. We had to find the ritual spaces before she could do her own, ah, *exercises*."

I was still letting all this mumbo-jumbo about exercises and stuff go, but it was getting harder. "Oh, is that what we're doing, then? Wandering around the camp looking for, I dunno, an altar or something?"

"At this point it would probably just be a cleared area," Oft noted. "And I'm not the one finding the site. *You* are. Look down."

I did. The ground around here was thick with fallen leaves that crushed easily, leaving behind an admittedly lovely, fresh scent, and a dusty trail behind us. The trails were everywhere, showing how we had gone back and forth in camp — except for one empty spot in the middle that briefly made my stomach turn. I didn't understand why. There was nothing unusual about it. But it made me queasy, all the same.

The Anticipant nodded, apparently pleased. "**The defiant Khan, facing his enterprising foe**," she declaimed.

I looked at Oft. He shrugged and gave me a smile. "I *think* that means, 'There's the place!' Some of her comments go above *my* head, too."

Once I knew what I was looking for, what looked like a crunchy-leaf clearing transformed itself into... a crunchy-leaf clearing, but now with extra disquieting. I mean, there were spots on the trees where the bark looked a little burned or chewed-up. When I got closer, I could smell a faint touch of wood smoke. "Did they set the trees on fire?" I asked.

Oft looked up from where he was poking at various parts of the ground. Here the dirt had a lot of stones in it, to the point where it was almost gravel. "They probably mounted torches on those," he said. "Ah, torches are pieces of wood that have been specially treated to burn..."

"Yes," I interrupted. "I'm from Jefferson. We know how to set things on fire. Why wouldn't they use biolights?"

"I assume it was for the same reason they put up their totems: the demands of rituals. See here, and over there?" Oft pointed to faint dips on the ground, evenly spaced. "Two sets of three, a full spread of their false spirits. Bear, Rose, Wolf, Amazon, Arrow, and Messenger, if I'm allowed to guess. The Scouts have more, but they call on those six when they invoke their Eagle. And here. Here must be where they put those to be Judged."

I looked, and saw two fairly deep, angled holes. After a horrified moment, I said, "I guess you're now going to tell me that they bound people to an X here, so that they could face the totems?"

"Oh, no," replied Oft. There wasn't a touch of humor in either his face or voice. "I'm going to tell you that they bound people to an X here, so they could face the other way, towards the Nest of the Eagle."

Following his eyes, I looked to see the Anticipant, now on the most grassy part of the clearing, carefully dragging a stick through the dirt, stopping, then dragging it again. She was bent almost double as she moved, tilting her head as if to hear... things. She honestly looked very much like a chicken rooting in the dirt, but it wasn't even the slightest bit funny. If anything, her movement reminded me that chickens were descended from dinosaurs, and still remembered those days of tooth and claw.

Carefully, I said, "I suppose you already know that plants on One-Eighteen love human blood, right? Something about the hemoglobin just makes them perk right up. On this planet, we say good gardeners have red thumbs."

"I had *not* heard that, Chief Pilot. Thank you for the information." Oft nodded. "It is certainly coming in handy, for finding the Scout's Jamboree killing field."

"So, Oft, what are we looking for, then? Evidence?" I jerked a thumb back at the mass graves. "Because we already have the bodies. And it doesn't look like they left their sacrificial altar for us to find."

"No, they clearly took their profane structures with them when they left. But they left the ritual places themselves behind." He raised his voice. "They weren't expecting somebody like the Anticipant to arrive!" She actually grinned at him, and he grinned back. To me he said, "She has had a personal interest in hunting the Scouts for some time. Finding such strong traces of them here is very exciting for her, I am afraid."

It was at this point I decided that it was time to drag this admittedly grotesque situation back away from being a straight-up horror vid. "All right, Oft. What is *actually* going on here with her? And if you say 'She's a witch,' I'm done here. This site needs a forensics team, not a bunch of ghost-hunters."

"Believe me, if there was a forensics team within ten light years of this planet," Oft said, "they'd be here now. But it's just me, you, and the Anticipant. Who is *not* a witch. She is simply someone with an exceptional, if somewhat quirky, intuition. And 'exceptional' here means 'far end of the scale.' It's nothing supernatural. She is carefully trained to see the underlying patterns in what you and I would consider to be noise. It *feels* like witchcraft because we're practically insensate, by her standards — and, truthfully, because she finds it easier to access her abilities this way. But anybody could do what she does, if you get... if they start early enough in life."

"Okay. She's not a witch, just really good at poker—"

"Oh, you have no *idea*," Oft interrupted.

"—and she's using her finely tuned abilities to do... what? Again, we already know these crews were murdered."

"Yes. But why were they murdered *here*?" Oft scowled at the scene. "The Scouts believe that Jamborees are best done in space. Why have one on a planet, and why have one on *this* planet? Particularly since it already has..."

"Already has what?" I asked, innocently.

Oft grimaced. "It already has a computer piracy problem."

The Anticipant gratified me at that moment by laughing outright. "*Carefree lies burn upon re-entry!*" she crowed at Oft, and damned if I wasn't starting to understand her, just a little. Then again, we hadn't taken the 'software piracy' thing seriously from the start.

Watching the Anticipant muck about in the dirt got boring, fast. Especially now that I knew that she wasn't delusional nor crazy, in the classical sense. Altered states of perception are old hat, here in the Tomb Worlds. Half the useful intellectual stuff we've gleaned from the Amalgamation requires a process we call 'mimsying,' which is basically learning how to temporarily believe in something illogical or flat-out untrue while performing a task. Nobody likes mimsying. It hurts your head. But it objectively *works*. It's the only way we can write our own software for alien computers. If the Anticipant was doing the same thing, only constantly, then the question was: why wasn't she *worse*?

So I decided instead to do a little breaking and entering. Some of the cabins were locked, and I was curious to see what was important enough to secure, but still abandon. Oft proved surprisingly fine with that. "Keep the chemsniffer active on your phon," he said. "Just in case there are wild animals about."

"Not traps?" I said. I was pretty sure there weren't any corpses in the cabins, if only because none of the buildings were airtight.

"The Scouts don't trap their camps," Oft said. "The League of the Viridian Triangle, yes. Them, no."

"Well, One-Eighteen doesn't have any dangerous wild animals." *Except the ones we brought with us*, I thought. But the corp never did that down here at the Erebus Dig, so we were safe.

I suppose I should have kept the chemsniffer app up anyway. Not that it would have made up the slightest bit of difference. But good habits are good habits.

The most alarming thing about the Scout camp was how 95% of it wasn't alarming at all. I'd vacationed in camps like this, growing up on Jefferson. The colony didn't have full electricity until I was in flight school. If you didn't mind chemical toilets and food cooked with open flames, it'd even be luxurious by my childhood standards. It was certainly prettier. The buildings were carefully constructed from local woods, then laser-smoothed and polished to clean-lined elegance. Look at a photo of the place, and you'd decide it was peaceful, even serene.

As long as you didn't go inside.

For example, there was a library (the cabin doors were locked, but I discovered very quickly that the keys were invariably on the top sill). Inside were two rows of school desks, and shelves full of books, each bearing the Scout logo. They apparently needed books on things like woodworking, knot-tying, and carpentry... plus social engineering, demolitions, anatomy, space-based tactics, enhanced interrogation, pharmacology, and eschatology. And those were just the ones I looked through.

The one on enhanced interrogation had both diagrams and photos. It was also written for teenagers.

Most of the buildings had something equally 'off' about them. The residential cabins had far too many children's beds in them, with 'too many' being defined as 'more than one.' The arts and crafts hall (seriously, that's what it said on the wall outside) had a complete weapons repair shop. The kitchen was adorned with cheerful murals reminding the eaters to Follow the Three Principles, Keep to the Promise, and Kill Only Cleanly.

Then there was the jail. It was clearly a jail: it had cells, with locked doors that did *not* have the keys ready to hand. But *it didn't smell*. Jails *always* smell. Even the glorified drunk tank we've got back at Luxor base smells of puke and bad decisions, and its walls are coated with a substance that's supposed to keep the jail sterile. The stink showed up anyway. It always does.

But not *this* jail. It had twenty-five individual cells, each with its own comfortable-looking cot and (barred) window, and it all looked very civilized... until I noticed the heavy steel circles embedded in the wall and floors. It didn't take long for me to find the manacles and fetters in storage, either. Or the tumbrels in the rear alcove, either. Those *did* smell like death, for all the careful scrubbing.

"Do not look at the symbols on the walls," came a voice behind me, to my careful *lack* of panic. I knew it was Oft. Besides, I was already as freaked out as I was going to get. This was such a *wholesome-looking* murder camp.

"I didn't see any," I told him as I turned. And then I blinked, because right now Oft was looking what his church calls 'fell.'

When you see an Iluvitarian looking like that, he or she's usually about to smite something — which is another one of their words. It basically means 'hit it hard, and don't feel bad.'

"Lucky you," he said, and there was an undertone in his voice that sounded like deep, well-controlled anger. "The prisoners had time to scratch on the walls. The Scouts regularly scoured the cells, but some runes run too deep to be sanded away. They were left in the wood, and left to spread and rot..."

When you work in the Tomb Worlds, you learn real quick how to tell when somebody's lost their mental center of gravity for a moment. Clearly, he needed a distraction. "Like I said, Oft, I didn't see any. I'm not going to look, either." I laughed, and wondered if it sounded as weak to him as it did to me. "Besides, what's the point? They're just going to be a bunch of curse words and pictures of dicks, right?"

Oft grabbed at that last bit like it was a life preserver. "What? Yes. Yes, of course. They were foul scribblings, nothing more. The last messages of flawed and disturbed people." He gathered himself, visibly coming down from whatever terrible place his head had put him. "So, no need to tarry here, surely?"

"None whatsoever," I agreed as we walked back to the Anticipant. I didn't wish that the hauler had a supply of something flammable more than two, three times during the walk, either. And I carefully didn't think at all about whatever it was that Oft had read.

"Did you get what you need?" I asked the Anticipant, because I have manners. Not that it mattered: she looked at me, looked at Oft, and shrugged. I huffed breath, and tried again. "Do you need to keep checking this place out?"

That got me another shrug, from both her and Oft. "She's not trying to be difficult, Pam. Her perception of time is a little more complicated than ours."

"Fair enough. How about her victory condition?" There were various logs around, clearly meant to be used as stools. I hesitated a moment before sitting on one, but they just felt like, you know, *wood*, and my feet were tired. It was turning out to be a really long day.

"What do you mean?" Oft declined to sit, himself. Instead, he lowered himself to the ground with an ease that made me wonder how old he really was. The unlined face and tattoos made it hard to tell. "Nothing here really seems like a game to be won."

"It's something we say on Jefferson," I explained. "I just want to know what looks like a successful intelligence gathering operation to her. I mean, so far you hit the jackpot. A Scout base! That was what you were looking for?"

"Not precisely," he said, "but it fits in with what we are looking for. Besides, we lack a critical piece of information: which higher-up in your organization secretly knew about the Scout presence on this planet."

I wasn't going to reach for my gun. Honestly. I mean, I'd been half-expecting the accusation for the last half hour. I just wasn't sure if it'd happen here, or back home. I could also lie and say that I recognized right off that Oft wasn't implying that *I* was covering up for the Scouts.

The truth, though? The Anticipant had positioned herself behind Oft, where I could see her clearly. She wasn't even looking at me, but while Oft talked, she mirrored my movements perfectly. Well, it wasn't perfect, since she was making them a half-second before I did. She didn't have a visible gun, for what that was worth. I figured that, in a fight, it wouldn't be worth much.

Oddly, that reassured me. 'Altered state of perception,' my ass. The Anticipant really was a flat-out *witch*, fresh from an Abubakri fairy tale. Witches, I could get my head around. Besides, nobody was shooting anybody yet, right? Although I guessed I'd know if I was about to do so, a half-second from now.

"Well, obviously you don't think it was me," I eventually replied.

"Obviously not. At least now." Oft looked back at the

Anticipant, who had dropped her entire spooky I-will-see-you act. "You were superficially the most likely suspect, so you were the first person Lieutenant Commander Nowak cleared. She was slightly surprised, but I was not. It's harder than you think to hide suborbital flights from ground bases, and there was no sign of any flights at all."

"Well, sure. XHum's doing field technological salvage, and we've got all the sites we can survey up close to hand. Why go down to a place that eats entire survey teams, even if it's been toggled off? Something might have toggled it back on."

"Exactly. Couple that with this planet's unique problems with orbital mapping, and we get a prime location for the Scouts' alarming rites. Provided they knew the best way to spoof what outsystem sensors this planetary system has."

It was then that I really started believing that the Scouts had turned one of my friends and coworkers. "Right," I ground out. "Somebody at the top could get access to our sensor net, find holes in it, or even come up with dummy transponder signals that wouldn't set off an alarm, or a report. It's not like we've set up lookouts, watching for sails on the horizon."

"Would that we could," sighed Oft. "I sometimes wonder if we should have kept to the ways of a simpler time, like the twentieth or twenty-first century. Especially since the larger problem is this: The Process. How could it not have noticed any of this?"

The light, as they say, dawned. "Ah. That's the other reason why we're out here. You're worried somebody had taken over the remains of The Process's surveillance network, back at base."

"Exactly — wait, why are you chuckling?"

I pointed. "Sorry. The Anticipant, she started shaking her head before I did. I had to laugh, and she started doing that, too, and now I want to, I dunno, tap-dance or something."

I sobered up. "The Process here wasn't a miracle worker. What we had here was a single node, and we were lucky to have even that. Most planetary stations aren't big enough to justify one. It's definitely not like on Earth, where you have nodes in every city, and they can all talk to each other and panopticon everybody else. It's not even like Jefferson, where the bigger cities have three or four nodes within range. If you knew its limitations, you could get away with a lot." I shrugged. "It's just that nobody was that dumb."

"Dumb enough to try?"

"Dumb enough to want to succeed. Okay, sure, obviously in this case there was a reason. It's just that it was usually so hard to make sure The Process was paying just the right amount of attention. If it couldn't hear you, it couldn't hear you scream, right?"

The Anticipant was now laughing on her own. *"Young Gal River, she will know something, and won't say nothing!"* she sang, surprisingly sweetly. I hadn't a clue what she was talking about, but so what else was new?

Oft clearly did, since he glared at her. "I don't see how that's relevant. Yes, she will eventually work it out," he went on, talking back to the Anticipant's aggravating smile, "but that conversation is better suited for back at the base, with Nowak sitting in for it." He looked back at me. "I'm sorry, Pam. I'm sure this all sounds like gibberish."

I considered it for a moment. "Pretty much."

"I hate to say this, Pamela, but we need to visit the Dig itself."

Oft really did look like he hated to say that. I could tell because we were back at the hauler, and by unspoken agreement the three of us had turned on every interior light. "You're the one running the expedition. Only please tell me we don't have to go do that in the dark, Oft."

"That depends. Did you want to stay here? Overnight?"

I shook my head. "Depends. Here, at that Scout base? *Forget it.* Here, in the damn hauler? *Absolutely.* Especially if it means we'd be able to visit the possibly haunted evil dig site in daylight."

"Fair," Oft allowed, "but if the Erebus Dig is haunted, daylight may not be a defense."

"We could at least see it coming. Besides, if there is something out there it'd need a cannon to get through a hauler hull, and we don't have any cannon on One-Eighteen."

"*Yarrr*," agreed the Anticipant cheerfully, as she ladled more of whatever it was that she had made. From what I could tell, she had just mixed together parts of various standard rations, and stewed the resulting mess. You didn't want to look too long at it, but the stuff tasted *amazing*.

I looked at her. "Does that mean you think the Scouts might have left defenses behind at the actual dig?"

Oft snorted. "No, it was what we in the Adjudication Council call a 'jape.' It's like a regular joke, only with the humor removed." He grew thoughtful. "Although they might have left some kind of traps behind... no, that wouldn't make any sense."

"Why?"

"Somebody innocent might trip over it. The Scouts are more careful to target only the guilty than other terrorist groups." He sighed. "Then they make up for it by being utterly ruthless to those deemed to be unworthy. Teenagers can be so mercilessly *certain* of things."

"Then it's settled." I looked down, realized that I had done everything but lick the bowl clean, and decided to do that, too. "We'll sleep in the hauler, and go first thing in the morning. How long will you need?"

"No more than an hour or two," Oft replied. "Even if we find things aren't good there."

...turns out, that was a good guess, on both counts.

CHAPTER FIFTEEN
What They Did In the Shadows

I'd never been to the Erebus Dig before, and I'll never go back. The very look of it reeked of awfulness as I set the hauler down on the overgrown pad — and, yeah, I know, you can't see smells. I saw it anyway.

When we got out, I also saw that the pad wasn't overgrown *enough*. Somebody had used Earthtech reaction engines on it in the recent past. Oft noticed it, too. "How long, Pam?" he asked me.

"Not recently," I decided. "A year, maybe? Gorevines don't grow fast. There's still soot marks from the burned-off bits, but no smell." One-Eighteen's gorvines look normal to us, but we don't burn any of them if we can help it. Their sap collects copper and iron, and the smell when it ignites can be a bit much. "They didn't clear away the brush, though."

"Doing so might have attracted notice, if somebody flew over this site from the air," Oft responded. "A small chance, to be sure, but the Scouts are famously known for being ready for anything. I hope they did not use this pad very often."

I didn't ask him what Oft meant by 'hope,' because I could make a few guesses, myself — and none of them sounded very nice. There was also always the chance that he'd come up with something even worse that I *hadn't* thought of. Instead, I made sure my gun was properly holstered and ready for use as we tramped down the ramp and towards the Dig. This part of the site was definitely overgrown. The gorvines had covered over the old Amalgamation streets, and had long since spread over what ruined buildings remained.

I let Oft lead the way, until it was obvious he was simply following the gorvines where they were thickest on the ground. Beside me, the Anticipant had drawn up into herself, and I didn't blame her one bit. Even I could taste the ground-in darkness of the Erebus Dig, and I'm kind of insensitive that way. If she really did have different senses than ours, they were probably screaming at her right now.

"Pam?" Oft's voice was determinedly light. "What kind of place was this?"

The distraction was welcome. "You mean, during the Amalgamation? Probably an airport. It's got the right kind of look. Some people say the Dig itself was where the inhabitants had a Last Stand, but I don't know if I buy that. I think it's a mistake to assume the Amalgamation even had a military, just because we do."

"As a matter of fact, so do I. Although I do believe they must have had at least the equivalent of a Coast Guard. Even if they moved past wars, they would not be able to eliminate accidents. Was the site especially damaged?"

"Yeah. It's why they argued this was a Last Stand site." I didn't like walking on the gorvines, but standing still would have been worse. This particular species was attracted to human scents, and its leaves would shift and rustle if we didn't keep moving. Nobody's ever been attacked by one, but spill any blood around a gorvine, and it'll go all quivery. "It was just like how it was on all the other Tomb Worlds. They reported lots of signs of fighting, tons of smashed-in doors and walls, and not a bone to be found anywhere."

"*A half-told tale is far too tall*," offered the Anticipant, looking around. Either she was trying really hard to speak normally, or I was trying really hard to understand her, because I got the gist.

"Yeah, all of the reports leave out how it feels to be down here." I scowled at the encroaching wilderness. "I guess we can't get away with calling the Dig a 'infective apprehension area' or 'static neurosis zone,' or whatever else the head-stirrers are saying instead of 'really damn creepy' this week. It's not an accident that the main bases are all on the other side of the planet."

"Yet... it's not *that* bad?" asked Oft. "I've been to a few Last Stand sites myself. This one should be considerably more dreadful. The plants are too healthy, for example."

"Worse than this?" The thing was, though? I could see his point. I had talked to some of the last people to do the Erebus Dig run before XHum decided there was no reason to have regular flights to an abattoir, and one of them had taken video. Thanks to those damned emotional transmitters, I could tell that it *had* been much more awful down here, last time.

"It's what they called a fixer-upper!" shouted the Intendant, and I wasn't sure I *wanted* to guess what that meant.

We followed the almost-path of gorvines all the way to the Dig site, to absolutely nobody's surprise. Well, I know *I* wasn't surprised, and I assume the Anticipant couldn't be. If Oft had any sudden revelations, he didn't talk about them.

He was the first one to notice the regular sets of discoloration on the walls, though. "More places for torches," he grimly observed, and I didn't blame him at all. The Scouts had been here for a reason, and it involved the Erebus Dig. I tried not to think about the implications of that, and I definitely didn't try to think of the suggestion that the Scouts were making this trip *in the dark*. It would have been a beautiful morning anywhere else in the world, and I absolutely did not want to be here. Navigating this place at midnight sounded like a great way to court a heart attack.

I remembered from the videos that there's not much of the Dig aboveground. The topside part of the planetary defense center or storehouse or whatever the inhabitants used the place for before their Last Stand had been broken down to gravel, making the area look like a Jeffersonian parking lot. That was there, and still stubbornly free of any vegetation or even moss.

What was different was the primitive elevator centered over

the Dig shaft, camouflage netting still draped over the open platform to hide it from the sky.The gorvines led right up to it, but hadn't even tried to cover the structure. I couldn't say that I blamed them. The structure *reeked* of well-washed evil — or was I imagining that? I took a glance at the Intendant, who looked back at me with pupils so wide, I expected them to be bleeding.

Apparently not.

It bothered me that the elevator platform went down the Dig shaft without bobbling or jerking. When you descend somewhere horrible that was used by terrorists, you expect things to be slovenly, right? I kept waiting for the mechanisms to start whining or smoking, or maybe for the platform itself to turn out to be rickety and ready to collapse if you breathed on it too hard. That's how handmade stuff generally *was.* People with no sense of self-preservation suck at doing maintenance. But not Scout-made gear! Oh, no! Those teenagers built things to last. I could tell how everything had been properly put together, with solid materials and no corners cut. They had done a proper job of weatherproofing, too. God help us all, somebody had worked hard on this job.

"Oft," I ground out in the increasing gloom, "*how* sure are we that the Scouts are really off this planet?"

"Very," he replied. "If they weren't, we'd never have gotten this far without being challenged."

"Lucky us."

"Lucky us *and* lucky them, Pam." The rough change in his voice made me blink. I looked over. Even in the dimness, I could see how he stood tall and terrible, and a piercing light was in his eyes. In contrast, the Anticipant beside him was almost a shadow herself, the colors of her robe shading smoothly into the growing dark. It was alarming. The two of them might have both been weird, but I hadn't really seen either as capable of being *dangerous* before. Now they looked thoroughly ready to deal with whatever we found, down here in the pit of the Dig.

I would have been afraid, if I had for a moment thought that they were here to deal with *me*.

Then Oft smiled, white teeth flashing for a moment, and the spell was broken. "My apologies," he murmured. "We are probably being very *fell*, right now. This is a fairly intense moment for the two of us."

"You mean, the *three* of us," I responded, checking my pistol. You don't out-badass a Jeffersonian, dammit. "Whatever the Scouts did down here, they didn't ask for permission first. You don't get to do that on *my* world."

The lights were all out at the bottom of the shaft, because why not? It was deliberate, too. The Scouts had removed *everything*, including the emergency glow-bulbs and survival moss that the original excavators had installed. "What the heck were they using for light?" I wondered aloud.

"Torches," Oft said.

"The weight of some questions is too great to bear," the Anticipant offered.

I decided I liked Oft's answer better.

Fortunately, we had the new lightfolds in our survival gear packs. If you've never seen one, it's a strip of flexible cloth that you tie over your eyes. There's a bunch of tubes woven into the fabric that we *almost* understand and *can* duplicate which collect even the smallest amount of visual light, and enhance it. Maybe we can't tell you how they worked, but they do. Even down here I could see outlines, if not color.

Best of all, they're safe. A lot of Amalgamation tech can throw people for a loop because we don't know what it's made of, how it works, and sometimes even what it was originally designed to do. Lightfolds, on the other hand, just violate our current understanding of physics. Which is okay! So did faster-than-light travel, when we first got access to it, and now we understand the technology just fine! Mostly.

Down here there were more traces of the Scouts' presence.

Cracks in the metal walls and ceiling had been repaired with plastic of paris. They had even sanded down the goop until it was flush with the surface, which showed dedication, in its way. There were also what were probably helpful signs on the walls, but seeing those in the dark was one level of miracles too much for even lightfolds.

It occurred to me that there were flashlights in the kits, too. It also occurred to me that neither Oft nor the Anticipant had taken theirs out. Neither gave me a reason, but I decided I agreed with them anyway. If there was something down here, I didn't want to announce our presence.

"What *are* we looking for down here, Oft?" I asked him, quietly but without whispering. I had been taught as a child, very carefully, that too many things in the dark notice whispers. "It'd help if I knew what the goal was."

"That's the problem, Pam. We don't really know. All that we're sure of is that the Scouts did things down here, far away from prying eyes like ours. Whatever those deeds were, we need to know about them — but there are *so* many awful possibilities. It's best for us to have a completely open mind about it."

"*So do not nod!*" offered the Anticipant. "*And watch for shadows that do not move!*" Whatever *that* meant.

The hallway ended in double doors. They were Amalgamation-made. The padlock and chains keeping them shut were distinctly human. We contemplated the scene for a long moment. Finally, Oft spoke. "If it makes you feel any better, Pam, I too would like to go back the way we came."

"Yeah," I agreed, readying my gun. "That lock's pretty damned solid. It'll hold, no problem. I think everything looks fine. We can just go back, hop on the lander, be back for a late lunch or early dinner. I'll even buy the first round."

"Don't be ridiculous," Oft replied as the Anticipant glided to the padlock. "Obviously I would cover the tab for the night. I could do no less, seeing as I wasted your time with this needless side trip. After all, we are sensible people, are we not?

If we see a locked door, and know not why it is locked, it would be absurd for us to open it anyway."

The lock popped off. The Anticipant grabbed it out of the air before it could fall, then reattached it to one edge of the chain in one deft motion. The other end, she wrapped around her wrist and arm, idly twirling the lock around as she stepped back and pulled open one door. When I looked over, I could see that Oft had acquired force-rods from somewhere, one for each hand.

"Exactly." I stepped forward, into the deeper darkness. "Look at us, being absolutely sensible people."

It was a good thing we didn't have any grenades. If we had, I would have thrown one in on general principles, just as soon as my mind recognized that this room was actually a shrine. Which is why I didn't bring any grenades. Sometimes reflexes are *bad*.

The room had started out as a theater (we're pretty sure that the original inhabitants had those) with banked seats, but *somebody* had removed most of the stage, leaving yet another pit in the center. The pit looked absolutely Stygian, even through the lightfolds, and I could smell the dank, slightly sharp air rising from it. Surrounding it were six irregular shapes, twice my height and wrapped in plastic or canvas. It sounds odd to say it aloud, but: the more I looked at them, the more I was certain that they were pointed *inward*, not *outward*. Like they were watching the pit, not guarding it.

Most of the seats of the theater were still intact, and every one had an urn chained to the seat. The Scouts weren't joking about it this time, either. Even in the gloom, I could see signs where a blowtorch had been applied to the links. Those things weren't going anywhere.

I suddenly decided that I didn't need to look any closer, and leaned back from my examination. "Hey! Shouldn't you be telling me not to touch anything, Oft?"

"Why, Pam? Did you really need to be reminded?" His voice

wasn't quavering, but Oft wasn't enjoying this visit any more than I was.

"It's the principle of the thing," I muttered, trying to make myself breathe deeper. The more I smelled that air, the less I liked it. The rankness of it crept up on you. "Tell me we're down here for a reason, please."

"Oh, we are." He sounded as deliberately focused as I was.

"Really? What is it?"

"That, I'm not sure of. Ask the Anticipant."

Naturally. "Okay. Anticipant, why are we down here?" The Anticipant laughed. It was a surprisingly cheerful sound. Then she sprang into action, barreling into me so hard, I went staggering.

Any outraged comment I might have made died aborning as the reek in the air blossomed into horrible intensity, and I saw a darker gloom gush over the lip of the pit. Oh, the sound of it! The thing had a growl like that of a diseased tiger: rough, uneven, and wet. It moved surely, though, and with a terrible purpose, aiming for the place that I had just been standing.

Only now, instead of me, the Anticipant was standing there, the lock and chain in one hand whirring in an angry circle as she brought it up to speed. She met the onrushing gloom with a resounding smash that rocked the monster back, then spun around with the chain whirring out in another strike.

Before she could make a third attack, the monster struck back, its growl now heavy with rage and pain. It did not have arms or legs that I could see in the gloom, instead using its body to send the Anticipant flying backward.

It might have followed, except that Oft was already moving, both hands glowing blue as the force-rods powered up and extended out. The monster growl-howled more, either out of fury or pain from the Cherenkov radiation, and flowed one pace back.

By then, I had my gun centered on it.

One thing that's nice about a Tomb Worlds monster: bullets usually *will* kill it, especially when you're using corporate-issued rounds. I wasn't sure what the hell this thing used for a head or vitals, so I stuck to putting rounds in its center of mass and waiting to see if the bits I was blowing off were going to reattach themselves to the main body. If they had? Well, I had incendiary rounds, too, but I wasn't about to pull those out yet.

I didn't have to. One magazine was enough for the creature to shudder, and abruptly collapse into a stinking puddle of goo. Well, a different *kind* of puddle of goo. It was absolutely dead, though. How could I tell? Well, after a while people out here pick up the ability to tell 'comatose' from 'deceased.' It can be a survival skill.

Then, suddenly, there was light!

It was less dramatic than it sounds, because the lightfolds could handle most of the difference in brightness, but seeing in colors again was still a bit of a shock. I looked around, blinking, and saw that the Anticipant had picked herself up, and was now wheezing against the wall. Next to her was an installed hand-switch of human make. The lights were coming from above, and were also human-made. I assumed the whole thing was Scout work, and personally I wouldn't have touched it, but I'm not the Anticipant.

"You all right?" I called out to her, and got a thumbs-up in response. I hoped that meant the same thing to her as it did to me. Then I decided that surely she still knew what the words 'yes' or 'no' meant, which meant I could check on Oft.

He was fine. In fact, he was poking at the monster with one force-rod when I came over to him. "You recognize this, Pam?"

I did, thanks to the distinctive pseudo-fur still undissolved. "Yeah. That's a bob-bane. Big fucker, too." He looked confused, and I shook my head. "Least, that's what we call them on Jefferson. You have a different name for them, right?"

"Yes. 'Speeruls.' I knew they infested the Tomb Worlds, but I was unaware that they have them in the colonies."

"Had." I had to refrain myself from spitting on the corpse. "We burned them all out. The bastards can eat anything that's

plantlike and are born pregnant, so they're pure hell on crops."
I frowned. "Bob-banes usually bud off as soon as they get big
enough, though."

"I suspect a Scout breeding program," Oft observed. "They
would be mad enough to try, after all."

"Sure, but what'd be the point? Bob-banes are dangerous, but
not because they eat people... *oh.*"

"Yes." He turned on the force-rod, and jammed it down
through the corpse with a quick, savage jerk. It did — nothing
in response. "They likely widened the speerul's diet at the same
time they suppressed its reproductive reflex. Why not? They
were already enslaved by hubris. What difference would one
more unnatural outrage make?"

"Right, so they wanted a giant monster." I looked around at
the room, which if anything looked even more horrible. I could
see the scratches on the chairs and floor now, after all. "The
better to feed people to, because they're crazy that way."

"*Flee from the deadly light!*" advised the Anticipant. I'm
pretty sure that was advice, at least. Or at least, the more time I
spent with her, the least she sounded like a raving madwoman.
I was probably picking up stuff in context.

Oft understood her better, though, because he was shaking
his head in... disagreement? "Regretfully, Pam, I think they had
a reason. I suspect the material in the urns is the remains of its
meals." He retracted the force-rod.

"*You can sift for more than gold!*" agreed(?) the Anticipant, as
she examined chained urn after chained urn. A few times she
frowned, but didn't do anything further.

"Exactly," Oft replied in that maddening way of his. "The
Scouts are far too concerned about vileness. Taking the things
and people most infected with what they deem 'corruption,'
and filtering it through a suitable vessel, must have seemed a
clever trick."

"Ick," I smartly replied as soon as I made the connection. "I
thought they weren't big on cruelty to animals, though. Even
alien ones."

"Technically, they're not supposed to be killing people, either. But I think they dimly understood what they did. That's why they set up this protective circle." Before I could ask what that was, Oft walked over to one of the irregular shapes. A quick pull on the tarp covering it revealed it to be a wooden statue.

When I put it like that, it sounds normal. This wasn't normal. It had been carved out of local woods, for one thing. The faint pink sheen and scent of iron were unmistakable. For another, it had been carved in a style I had never seen before. I'm not an artist, so I can't tell you the technical details. All I can tell you is that the carver had a completely different way of looking at human beings, and deciding which were the important bits to show in the wood. If I didn't know that there weren't any aliens, I would have guessed it had been made by aliens.

The worst part, though? The subject matter. The statue was of a warrior woman from ancient Greece, wearing a breastplate and armored skirt, and carrying a bow. Her face was a study in determination, resolution, and madness held in stubborn check by iron will. Her eyes were pitiless, too. This was the image of a woman who would never indulge in the cruelty of misplaced mercy.

I know that all sounds weird, but maybe not horrible. Trust me, it was terrifying. You see: *the statue had my face.*

Oft saw the resemblance just after I did, but I didn't stick around to hear his reaction. I stood not on the order of my coming but went at once, as the Bard might say. Right up and out of the room, because there was no *way* I was going down into that pit.

That was the only time I was really frightened to be around Oft and the Anticipant, you know? Even then, I wasn't afraid *of* them; I just didn't want them to shoot me. If they did, I couldn't even blame them, except personally. Seeing my face on a Scout ritual statue was one Hell of an incriminating circumstance. *I'd* suspect me of being involved with the Scouts, after that. Hell, maybe I *was* involved in the Scouts, only they had put me under some kind of deep cover and all I needed to hear was the activation phrase to 'wake up' again. You hear stories about that happening. No proof, but there wouldn't be, right?

The switch the Anticipant had pulled had also turned on the emergency lights. Their harsh glare revealed a gorgeous corridor, filled with delicate friezes and mosaics which I perceived as a blur as I ran for the Scout's elevator. I wasn't sure what I could do, once I got to the surface (I mean, I couldn't just *leave* them here), but having an unclimbable shaft between me and them sounded like a great idea until a better plan came to mind.

I got to the lift easily. I slapped the up button — and nothing happened. I did *not* slap it again, let alone repeatedly. That's what people who panic easily (and die early) do in bad situations. Instead, I popped off the back of the casing holding the button, noted without real surprise the conspicuous lack of connecting wires, and started looking for spares. They train you *hard* to not freak out in the Tomb Worlds, because if you start, you'll be doing it literally for the rest of your life.

"She took out the wires without damaging them, Pam." I didn't freak out from hearing Oft, either. That would get in the way. "You really don't need to get new ones."

I stared at him. He and the Anticipant were there, but keeping their distance. The Anticipant in fact had the wires in her hand. She waggled them at me, as if to mock me, then she lobbed them over, with perfect aim and precision. I plucked them out of the air without a bobble. It was impossible for me *not* to.

"Did you need us to back off some more?" asked Oft. "We can retreat while you get the lift up and running, if you really need some time alone to process this. If not, we're done down here, right?" he asked the Anticipant, who nodded vigorously, while frowning. "Yes, we're done down here, and neither of us are inclined to linger. Personally, I would rather not try to figure out where the bathroom is."

"You knew you'd find that?" I asked them, after we reached the surface. I'm leaving out the half-hour it took me to decide that it wasn't some weird kind of head game, the thirty seconds I spent repairing the lift button, and the roughly sixteen years it took to get back to the surface. I don't know why it took seemingly forever. If they weren't going to shoot me on suspicion of being a terrorist, I was safe until we got back — and then I'd be *really* safe, because either I could easily prove my innocence, or else Mental Health would excise whatever conditioning I was under. "My face on that damn statue?"

The Anticipant shrugged. It was clear by now that her nonverbal communication was pretty good; it was just her speech that was weird. Oft was the one there for clarifications. "Well, first off, That was an idol, not a statue, and it can stay down there for now. Second? Well, we weren't expecting a revelation *that* dramatic."

"You were expecting a revelation, though." I made that a statement, not a question, and Oft took it as one.

"Truthfully? Yes. The Scouts have always been the most mystic of the terror groups. Their colleagues think they're half-cultists themselves, which is sourly amusing, in its way. I thought there might be something that would shed light on your situation..."

"Hold on," I interrupted. "*What* situation? I'm a shuttle jockey on a Tomb World. There's nothing weird about that, or me."

Oft looked at the Anticipant, who gave him a shrug. "Well, it's genuinely reassuring that you believe that, Pam," he told me. "Even putting it to one side, the Anticipant came with me because we were looking for something *subtle* that might connect the Scouts, and your company's operations. We were not expecting anything that blatant."

I surprised him, and myself, but probably not the Anticipant, by snorting in laughter. "That's why you *don't* suspect me to be directly involved, isn't it? It's too obvious. Besides, she'd be able to tell you if I was some kind of cultist, am I right?"

"Well... in a way," Oft replied. "Her judgment would have been obvious, in context."

The more I thought of that statement, the less I liked it.

CHAPTER SIXTEEN
A Study In Sanguine

The flight back wasn't anything much, for the first twenty minutes. I decided I wasn't playing any games with the planetary network today. We were all better off just going ahead, giving us all some time to process what we had seen. Twenty-one minutes in, I turned on the radio, since we were coming within range of what passed for a human communications network on One-Eighteen.

Twenty-*two* minutes in, the Anticipant gasped.

Even I could tell that wasn't good, and a look at her face confirmed it. She was in full 'white-eyed horror' mode, only her suit wasn't pulling her out of the state automatically. "Oft," I carefully did *not* yell, "she's gone fay!"

Oft had already detached himself from his seat; he moved to intercept her. "It's not Fear Reflex Syndrome," he told me over one shoulder as he grabbed her shaking hands. That seemed to calm her down, so maybe it *wasn't* FeRe. People in the middle of one of those episodes hate being touched. "She's just had some horrible news."

That threw me for a loop. "From... where?" I gestured around the cabin. "There's no news here to hear!"

"Except the radio."

"It's barely above pure static."

"Not to her, Pam." Oft shrugged, not letting go of the Anticipant's hands. "Before you ask, I don't know what she heard, either." His face fell. "All I know is, it's something personally traumatic."

Which did not sound good.

Death is one of those things that happens on frontiers. Well, sure, it happens everywhere else, too. But it just *feels* different out here. You can't get the morticians and bereavement specialists and your favorite flavor of priests to help. You have to work it out with whatever and whoever you brought in with you. The funny thing is, I used to think I *was* on the frontier, because I lived on Jefferson. We have barely a hundred million people in the system. Compared to Earth, we're huddling in the night.

But you have to go to a place like One-Eighteen before you really get how alone people can get out here.

We finally were able to properly hear the report about Burcu Nowak's shuttle crash about twenty minutes after the Anticipant had — I don't know how she managed to figure out what happened. Maybe it's really easy for her to filter out static. I mean, if she's at right angles to the rest of us *anyway*, every regular form of communication would be garbled half-nonsense to her. Why should static be a special case? At least she didn't go crazy in the cabin, which is just as much fun for a pilot as it sounds. Instead, the Anticipant just retreated into herself, took a sedative from Oft, and was soon sleeping the sleep of the medicated.

Oft was apologetic about the whole thing. "It's a side effect of her training," he explained. "The Anticipant has been taught to come to accurate conclusions, from woefully incomplete data. The techniques work, but they come at a cost of heightened sensitivity. In her case, painfully so."

I looked over. Asleep, she looked a lot older, but a bit less pained, and I wondered just what those 'techniques' involved. "So sudden unexpected news knocks her for a loop."

"Not exactly," Oft replied. "It has to be unexpected and *malicious*. The universe simply randomly being the universe would be another part of the pattern, or so I think I understand. A reaction like this comes from a deliberate attempt to wreck the pattern, for whatever foul purpose."

"So you don't think Nowak died in an accident." This was my day for not stating things as questions.

"Certainly not, and neither do you."

"Sorry, but I can't say." I held up my hand. "I literally mean that I *can't* say. XHum will designate me as lead investigator on the crash, thirty seconds after we clear the hatch. I'm easily the most qualified, and..."

"And you were on the other side of the planet when the accident took place," Oft finished for me. "While in the constant presence of two officers from the *Redacted*. I can attest to your whereabouts, and the Anticipant can clear you of wrongdoing, to my captain's satisfaction, at least. Yes, that does make you an acceptable choice for investigator."

"I'm glad *somebody* thinks so," I said, but under my breath. Although from the sad smile Oft gave me, I think he heard it anyway.

I was wrong. They gave me a whole five minutes to get ready for my new, horrible job. Huzzah, as we say back home. I tried not to take it personally. Things were stressed enough as they were.

Greg was liaison for me on this one, probably because Maki was at the crash site playing coroner. "Burcu's shuttle came in erratic, and too quickly. No fatalities besides hers, thank God, but Landing Pad Delta's going to be out of service for the next week."

"Right." I scanned the logs, very quickly. "No emergency reports?"

"None. Her systems handshaked with ours about three minutes before the crash. Nothing anomalous was reported or detected, on either end. The first sign that something was wrong was when the shuttle suddenly had one engine flame out, at the worst possible time. When it hit Delta, the shuttle *rolled*."

That stopped me. "Wait, what? The automatic systems shouldn't have been *that* screwy." You have to understand: at that point, I'd seen automatic systems make shuttles bump, collide, crash, and on one hideously memorable occasion, *bounce* (thank God I wasn't pilot for that one, and thank God twice for dental implants). Actual rolling was new. It obviously wasn't impossible, but new.

"That's the thing," Greg told me, grimly. "Burcu never had the automatic systems up. She was flying manual until the very end. She even overrode our landing protocols."

Well, I thought, ***that*** *was strange*. When landing, pilots are encouraged to let Ground Control take over the final approach. I can and do fly it in manually, but then I know what I'm doing. Did Burcu? "Do me a favor, Greg? Call the *Redacted* and find out what Burcu's pilot rating is. I'm going to take a look at the crash itself."

"Sure," Greg muttered behind me as I approached the crashed shuttle. "Maybe they'll answer *that* information request."

I wouldn't condemn my worst enemy to death via exploding shuttle, so don't think I enjoyed investigating Burcu's fatal crash. It's a bad way to die, and it's no fun poking around afterward. Especially when you can spend all that time remembering how easily it could be *you*.

The wreck looked all too familiar, too. "*Was* this a wrecked fuel line, The Process?" And then I swore. I had done it *again*.

"That would be the high-probability scenario," Greg told me over the radio link. The site was still a bit toxic, from various things leaking or outgassing. "You guessing, or is that from your training?"

"Mostly my training." The shuttle was a standard Earth-made model, and the front half was almost intact. Most of the damage was in the back, where the fuel gets injected into the engines. Earth shuttles don't brew up often, but when they do it's usually either the fuel lines or the battery suddenly going. They've been working on the problems for a century. Maybe they'll figure them out in another one.

On the other hand... "So what killed Burcu? She was in the cockpit and strapped in, right?" Her file had included a basic flight certification, which should have been enough for this trip, especially if she had stayed in her seat and let the autopilot do the work.

"I need *you* to tell *me*, Pam. Sorry." Which was fair, but was also a hint that this was going to be even worse than I thought. "You ready to log the death? We're gonna need a formal determination of it."

"Oh, happy day," I muttered.

Close up, the shuttle didn't look nearly as 'mostly intact.' In fact, I didn't expect it would ever fly again. We've come a long way in the last century, but most of our equipment still looks like a child's imitation when compared to Amalgamation tech. I *can't* crash a hauler, except under extremely specific circumstances involving the sudden loss of the contragrav units. The best I could do would be to kind of damage the bottom of the hull, and tear up the landing zone. Here, we were just lucky that Burcu had been flying solo. I made a note to check later just *why* she had been flying solo, although I guess it was probably because of the dark Terran god Security.

On the marginally bright side, Amalgamation fire suppressant goo is amazingly good at crawling over burning-hot metal and plastic, and taking all that heat away. The last of it was oozing back into its vats as I popped the explosive bolts on the emergency access hatch. Inside it smelled vile, naturally, but I had nose filters for that. At least there weren't any sparks. Sparks meant live wires, and live wires were bad.

I'd like to say that Burcu died quick and clean, but neither would be true. Her body was *crunched* together in the front of the cockpit, her flesh mottled with bruises where it hadn't been gashed horribly. Her face was mercifully obscured by her hair and helmet, but I could see teeth and fragments of bone scattered on the floor. And blood, of course. Or, rather, the shadows of blood on the walls, where the gore had boiled away under the fierce heat of the crash.

It was a picture out of a nightmare. It was also supposed to be impossible. Even we half-savage humans *know* that smacking your vehicle into the ground at high speed is fatal unless you take precautions. "Greg, *tell* me this shuttle is supposed to have safety harnesses and a crash foam system."

"Yes, it does. Neither was operational during the crash. Looking at the logs now." He paused for longer than I liked. "Huh. Neither show up in the shuttle's systems at all."

"Crap. When was the last time they were checked?" It should be every two weeks, or before every flight, but that's just the rules for us awful corporate workers. The Council would have its own schedules.

"You have to be kidding me!" Greg sounded like he was ready to start shouting. "That information is listed as *classified*. Council personnel only!"

"Oh, for the love of *Christ* — look, just get me Rubicon. I'm not letting him play this game, especially when it's one of his people who's dead."

It took only about thirty seconds to get a comm open to Rubicon, which surprised me. So were the first words out of his mouth. "You *will* consider my officer's death a murder, Pilot Officer Tanaka. I expect no less—"

And that's when I interrupted him. "No shit, Captain. Of *course* it was a murder! Or one Hell of a case of negligent homicide. Don't see how it matters, either way."

That statement surprised *him*. "You have found actual evidence of foul play? So quickly?"

"Let me put it this way, Captain. The Lieutenant Commander's harness *and* the cockpit's crash foam systems both failed, at the same time." I didn't go into gory details, but Rubicon was a spacer. He'd be familiar with messy deaths. "You're getting the footage, right?"

"No, we are not."

And now I was back to being surprised. "You *should* be. Just like I *should* be getting access to the shuttle's maintenance logs."

"Wait a moment. Why aren't you able to access those?"

"The system says they're classified." I scowled. "There's something going on here."

"I'm going to use the oldest cliche I know," Syah explained to us all. "We've been hacked."

The meeting room would have been crowded, if we had all been personally there. There was myself, Greg, Maki, Syah, Rubicon, and Oft, but everybody except for Greg was calling in from their remote workstations. For this call Rubicon had insisted on using Earth-made tech only, which meant that the rest of us had to, too. Oh, well, at least it meant my stomach would behave.

"This attack came in two stages," Syah went on. "Part one messed up the fuel lines, consistently building up pressure into them until they blew in transit. Part two targeted the safety protocols, telling the computer that the emergency foam system was operational and that the straps on the harness were secure. So when the shuttle crashed..."

"...there was nothing to protect the Lieutenant Commander from the impact. She never had a chance." Earth tech or not, Oft's image was now looking considerably ill. Which was fair. I didn't like the mental pictures, either. "And it had to be sabotage? Not just an, ah, *unfortunate set of circumstances*?"

"Well, either one *might* have just been a corrupted file," Syah conceded. "There's an ecology in the Amalgamation data networks that we still don't understand, even now. It's got — well, the things can't be alive, but I don't have a better word than that. When one of them interacts with one of our pieces of software, weird things can happen. But two corrupted files at once? That's taking coincidence pretty far.

"Besides, there was a *third* operation. That one specifically went after our security protocols. Whoever did this set it up so that *all* of XHum's and the Council's data requests regarding the shuttle crash would automatically be denied. If an Amalgamation cyber-beast could do that, well, it'd be our prime suspect for the murder anyway."

Maki gave the kind of laugh you give when nothing's funny. "And the kind of disaster scenario which ends with us nuking all our sites from orbit, just to be sure. But it's actually human, right?"

"The code looks human," Syah replied. "Kind of crude, even. Like it had been thrown together from a bunch of public script libraries. It's definitely not as good as the other two attacks were."

Rubicon leaned forward. "Interesting. Can you trace it back to the original creator, Programmer Syah?"

"Him?" asked Greg. "Why not use one of your people?"

"I've already tried that," replied Rubicon. "According to them, the malware was installed by General Kylee Ramirez, United States Space Force, Commander of the American research vessel *Enrico Fermi*."

That got a little silence. "Hold on," I said, "*The* General Ramirez?"

"The one who died on January 23, 2079, during what is now called the 'Consolidation Coup?' And whose death was initially given as 'heart failure,' but evidence discovered in 2165 confirmed that she had been illegally executed? Yes. And, to anticipate your question: I am aware of the discrepancy, Chief Pilot. But internal records clearly indicate that General Ramirez was the one who entered the information."

"Ah," said Syah. "So whoever did this used a fake identity, and spoofed the biometric readers as well."

"Can that even work?" asked Greg. "I mean, yes, it obviously *has*, but shouldn't there be something to prevent that?"

Oft leaned forward. "There are countermeasures, sir. Unfortunately, it is the sort of trick that, while it might only work *once*, it still *can* work once. The time and place where the data was entered was likewise spoofed. We will eventually pierce that particular bit of misinformation, but it will take time. Which is why we wish to use your best on-site programmer to help."

"You should get testimonials," I murmured to Syah. "Everybody's talking you up these days."

If Rubicon heard my aside, he ignored it. "In the meantime, we will be continuing the quarantine. Obviously our murderers were planning to escape the planet before we could track them down, so let them stew in their own fear and apprehension while we construct a cage around them. For I assure you, we *will* find them, and I *will* make them pay for what they have done."

That last part was said through clenched lips. The good captain looked like he was ready to personally administer whatever chastisement was in store for our murderer, too. And, do you know something? I didn't blame Rubicon in the slightest.

This was going to be a tough case to solve, and I couldn't even tell myself that it was worse because of the lack of The Process. That was never going to have happened anyway. I mean, it would have been lovely if we *could* have used The Process to investigate murders. Other crimes, too. While The Process wasn't *easy* to hide from, it was *trivial* to outwit. It was absolutely not designed to be a snoop, didn't have the right protocols, was generally hampered by privacy restrictions, and you need a base at least twice our size to even reasonably expect to have a shard of The Process along.

Still, I imagine that no crime avoided the Amalgamation's sight. Right up to the day that somebody killed them all.

"Quick talk before I go, Greg."

It hadn't been much of a decision on who to mention the statue thing to. Maki's practically conditioned to be 'better safe than sorry' when it comes to employee mental health. Greg would be a lot better at objectively deciding whether I needed a wholesale brainscrub.

Only he was... not really seeing what Oft and I (and the Anticipant, I guess) had seen. "It *sort* of looks like you, sure," Greg told me, after looking at the photos for a minute. "I could see how it'd be shocking, coming out of the dark like that. I don't think whoever made this snuck in and mapped your face while you slept, though."

I looked at the pictures again. The face still looked like me to *me*, but I could see Greg's point, sort of. "The effect's a lot more powerful in person," I muttered.

"Sure," Greg agreed. "I figure it would be, in the ruins of an abandoned Scout shrine, deep underground, and right after you slew a mutated monster. What did Lieutenant Oft say?"

"We were going to talk about it after we got back to base." I scowled. "Guess it'll have to wait."

"Probably, Pam. Thanks for letting us know. I'll tell Maki I already vetted it. I should be honest about it: if Oft isn't freaking out about it, I don't think we should, either. Weird stuff happens out here, and sometimes it *just* happens."

I still haven't decided whether Greg was even wrong about that.

The nice thing about quarantines: catching up on maintenance. At least, for all of our Earth-based technology. The haulers themselves didn't need much. Get them a steady slurry of iron, carbon, copper, and water, and they'd keep themselves in good order. By mid-afternoon the next day, I had everything I'd been meaning to do caught up, and stayed on top of the Burcu crash investigation. That was slow going, but only because the loss of The Process was making our technical analysis slower. There was nothing *I* could do about it.

Better mechanics and software junkies than me were fiddling with the interfaces between our tech and the Amalgamation's, so I took advantage of the situation to take mild advantage of Syah. Not that he minded being taken out and plied our finest delicacies from the commissary; I gathered over dinner that the planetary net interface was being stubborn again.

"There's nothing any of us can put our finger on," Syah said, looking tired in his lovely eyes. "The diagnostics say things are within tolerances. Not perfect, but we're in the Tomb Worlds, right? Nothing works exactly the way it should out here. I've been on sites where what we're seeing with the interface wouldn't raise any eyebrows."

"But not here?" I asked, only half-idly. When you're this far out, you're going to be listening to your survival instincts, whether you want to or not. And those instincts are convinced that we're not supposed to be in the Tomb Worlds. It's not so bad on a planet like One-Eighteen, but there are planets where you almost have to scream at your hindbrain to just shut up with the gibbering for fifteen seconds.

We don't go back to the worlds where people end up *actually* screaming.

"Yeah, there's something about this that's bugging us." Syah picked at his food. "Aside from the usual. There's a stubborn kind of interference or static that keeps coming through the interface. We thought at first it was a hardware thing, but none of our stuff is leaking electricity or broadcasting data it shouldn't. And when we used a handheld sensor, we couldn't detect the static outside the interface. We don't think it's coming from what's left of the planetary network."

I decided to contribute, albeit generically. "Weird. What about the signal itself? Is it regular?" Which could mean anything, though nailing that down would eliminate a whole other bunch of anythings — but Syah was shaking his head.

"I wouldn't call it *regular*, but I wouldn't call it meaningless, either. Like there's an underlying order to the randomness, only I can't see it! It grates!"

Then he stopped, because I had lifted my fork. "Hold up, Syah. Have you had any dreams about this?"

"No," Syah replied, frowning.

"How about whispers, just at the corner of your hearing?"

"Ah. No, Chief Pilot Tanaka."

"Visual, olfactory hallucinations?" He shook his head as I went down the checklist. "Formication? No? Good. That one sucks. Any feelings of resentment towards, or sudden obsessive thoughts about, your former academic peers?"

"No, although they actually *did* call me mad in specialized educational training. Like, for real."

I laughed. "You didn't mind?"

"Oh, no. It was true, wasn't it? I pulled a lot of crazy pranks back then."

"All right, Syah. Now, last question. Think about what you just said about your frustrations with the project."

"Yeah, yeah, when I say it out loud like that I can see how it comes across. Don't worry, I'm keeping up my weekly psych sessions, just like I'm supposed to."

"Good," I said, and rolled my eyes at how my tone sounded. "Sorry. That was just me putting on my official hat for a second. I know the sessions and the exercises are boring, but we all have to do them. If we don't, we get flabby in the head." *And then the murders begin*, I thought. Although it's not really true that a planetary site that constantly neglects its collective mental health is going to end up harboring a bunch of ritual killers. Well, it's an exaggeration. A bit of an exaggeration.

"Just like using the bicycle when you're in freefall," agreed Syah. "I didn't like doing those, too, but I did 'em. It was the only way to stay in space long enough to qual for shipboard repair jobs."

"You did qual, though?" I asked; Syah nodded. "That's good. We can check that off when you do your physical pilot training. If you still want to do that, I mean."

"You know, I do," said Syah. "It wouldn't hurt my resume, either."

"Great!" I said. "It's a date, then."

Syah tried to raise an eyebrow at me, but didn't quite manage to pull it off. "Oh. So what is this, then?"

I smiled at him. "The start of a pleasant interlude."

CHAPTER SEVENTEEN

The Smell of It

Only, it wasn't.

It's not that Syah wasn't interested, because I could tell he was. And it wasn't because he was married or monogamous, because he'd have just said so already. Instead Syah was... hesitant, being careful not to get us into a situation where our hormones would let us run away with ourselves. It was all very archaic, like we were back in the pre-interstellar era and had to follow a checklist.

Which was fine. At least, that's what I told myself after he had given me a hug and a just-too-serious kiss goodbye. Some people like to take things slow. It wasn't me — or, if it *was* me, it wasn't really my fault. At least I didn't have to try to fend him off.

And then I stopped, and actually hit myself on the head with the palm of my hand. *I'm an idiot*, I thought. *I'm going to be training him on how to fly!* You can't mix that with romance, not when there's official qualifications involved. I might have to be an absolute jackwagon to him, and that would make things awkward if we were constantly segueing from that to torrid trysts in the forest. Or, much more realistically, my bed. Honestly, I don't see the fascination lovemaking in the woods has for most of my unattached colleagues — particularly since most of them don't *like* One-Eighteen's woods.

He really is a good guy, I told myself. *Just bad at communicating.* And, all in all, I don't think I was wrong about either part of that. We always worked well together, and the more we saw of each other, the easier we got.

There were other considerations, too. Some were physical. Syah was pretty, but not fragile about it. Sort of what I imagine what one of Oft's elves would look like. But Syah was also good at what he did, and he was good at conversation. Gotta be honest: a lot of colonists — well, we're not uneducated, but that education can get pretty specialized. What I saw of him, I liked. I really wish I had just seen more of him from the start.

I wasn't looking forward to trying to get a straight answer from Oft about the Scout site at Erebus. I didn't get one, either. And it was for a really annoying reason: he legitimately didn't have one.

"I'm sorry, Pam," he told me as we all drank our beers. Including the Anticipant, who was surprisingly easier to handle once everybody had a couple of drinks in them. "If I knew what brought the Scouts there at the start, I would have told you. I was hoping the Anticipant would glean something from the site about why they might choose it above all other possible locations, but she could not."

"How would you know?" I muttered.

Oft raised an eyebrow. "She may find it difficult to give details in a manner that you or even I can understand — no offense — but she knows what the phrase 'this is important' means, and she's capable of saying it. If she doesn't know, she can say that, too. *And* she has perfectly good ears."

"Sorry," I said to her. I meant it, too. "It's just that you're very, well, weird."

"She's deliberately placed herself at right angles to our way of thinking, and is keeping herself by sheer force of will," Oft replied. "Of course the Anticipant is 'weird.' By more definitions than the modern one. But perhaps it's not important why they picked that site. It has a fell reputation on this planet, after all. That might have been enough."

"Yeah, I thought of that, but I'm not buying it. I mean, there was a reason why we avoided the Erebus Dig: it was *eating people*. Some of the bodies never got found. They said they shut down everything that caused it, but who wants to take the risk over a bunch of alien paperwork?"

"The Scouts evidently did," mused Oft. "Or at least they had more confidence in their ability to not delve too deeply. I assume it was the former. After all, most of them are teenagers. You cannot expect those to be incurious."

I frowned. "What happens to older Scouts, anyway?"

The Anticipant cackled. "*A short life, and a merry one!*" she said, into her beer.

Oft winced. "Indelicately put, but correct. Older Scouts seek out a thing that can kill them. Eventually they find it."

"That must be pure Hell on their ability to get things done," I said. "Not that I mind."

But Oft was shaking his head. "Not every Scout takes the Oath. Some of them stay hidden in our society, helping their compatriots as they can. Those people are almost more dangerous than the Scouts themselves; all of the fanaticism, but with enough discernment to know when to watch, and when to act."

The implications of that stopped me cold. "Wait, are you suggesting that we have a spy for the Scouts? Here, on One-Eighteen."

"Oh, I'm not *suggesting* it, Pam." Oft looked thoroughly grim. "I'm *assuming* it." Beside him, the Anticipant nodded, vigorously. I found myself wishing that I could still think of her as just crazy. Or that I didn't believe Oft.

I opened my mouth to tell The Process not to listen, winced at the memory, and leaned forward. "Was it because of my face?"

"That was more confirmation, but it's only logical to assume that they have spies here. Your peculiar telemetry problems alone would make infiltration and shipments easier. Having someone on the ground would give them an early warning system, in case the colony was falling into madness. They were likely very concerned about that."

"Only now they're gone." I scowled at my beer. "Why did they

198

leave, Oft?"

"It would be a better question to ask, w*hy were they here*?" Oft scratched his chin. "Although I have a suspicion there, as well. I scanned one of the jars before we left. It did contain human remains. Just the sort of pellets that I would expect to come out of a speerul, too. From the scratches in the room, I also suspect that they threw at least some of their victims into that pit while they were still alive."

I had suspected the same thing. "Wait, you scanned it? You didn't bring a sample back?"

The Anticipant beat Oft's wide-eyed stare by a good half second. "Absolutely not!" he managed. "It was an unholy fane where the mad inflicted corrupted justice on the wicked, double-steeped in vileness and insanity. A place like that, you take nothing but photographs, and leave nothing except a few cleansing grenades."

Several hours later

"Why hasn't everybody on this planet died three times over, Pam?"

I contemplated my latest beer. The Anticipant had stopped after two, and I had been slightly surprised at the way she just *left*, just like she was perfectly capable of wandering around without a keeper. Which of course she was. I just hoped she didn't try to go shopping... and now I was wool-gathering, instead of answering Oft. "Sounds like a rhetorical question, Oft. You want me to guess the answer, or are you just gonna blurt it out?"

"Oh, take at least one guess." Oft waved his own, mostly empty glass. "I won't mind if you get it right."

"Get what right? There's nothing on One-Eighteen to die *from*, Oft. Except the damned deathheart, and that's just in one place, where we don't go. Hell, it isn't even from this planet originally." I drained my drink. "The animals don't think we're good to eat, and the plant life doesn't love the taste of hemoglobin enough to come looking for it on its own."

"Yes. And that's what is strange." Oft waved for another pitcher. "Obviously, the inhabitants of this planet share a common ancestor with humanity. They had DNA, of the same basic kind as ours. We can breathe the air here, and eat local foods without problems. Our gut bacteria have no problem working on this planet. So why aren't we coming down with One-Eighteen-specific diseases?"

"They didn't have any?" I shrugged. "The Amalgamation had good medtech. I mean, really good medtech. The kind that makes us look like leech doctors."

"Fine. Why haven't *we* infected One-Eighteen, then? Obviously, we try to keep biological contamination to a minimum, but this planet is one where you can work outside in shirtsleeves. I've looked through the records, and there's no reports of ecocide or pandemic here, or on any of the planets that were attacked."

I gave one of those humorless chuckles. "Well. Except for the last one, on each world. Those were always a doozy."

But Oft wasn't laughing, even in bitter jest. "Yes, Pam. They were."

"Well," I said as I refilled my drink, "You asked for a guess. I gave you one." I blush to admit that I followed that with a belch. "Now tell me what's *really* going on, oh wise Terran sage."

Oft looked concerned at that, or maybe he wanted to belch, too. "This is a guess, mind you."

"Yeah, sure, Oft."

"Well... now that I've been here a while, I think One-Eighteen itself doesn't *want* to kill us," Oft replied. "Or hurt us."

I thought about that. "Wow. That's real nice of it. But, hold on. Why do other people hate it here, then?"

"That's a harder question. Which is why I asked it of the Anticipant. She told me, "**A necessary guest is not always a welcome one!**" I laughed, and so did he after a moment: Oft had gotten her tone and cadence almost perfectly, but without mocking either. I could tell he respected the Anticipant, even if he didn't always understand her any more than I did.

Oft sobered, all too soon. "I *think* that means she feels the planet tolerates our presence, or even more than tolerates it, but it *resents* us at the same time. As though we were innocent bystanders in a quarrel we had nothing to do with. We are not blamed, but neither are we welcome."

I snorted. "One-Eighteen's a planet, Oft. It's not aware enough to resent us, or do anything else. Besides, I've never felt unwelcome here at all."

"Yes," mused Oft as he finished his beer. "So I have gathered."

"What is that supposed to mean?"

"It means that you are unique here, Pam. You don't hunch a little when you go outside, or hesitate even at noon. It's easy to get close to you without you noticing, because you're not constantly aware of your surroundings. And –– although this is cheating — you are so attuned to this planet that a three-quarters-mad sculptor unconsciously chose *your* face to put on his protective icon." Oft blinked, owlishly (but not scary-owlishly). "You shouldn't read too much into that last one, though. The basic information packet for this planet includes the faces and the names of all of XHum's senior staff."

I hadn't considered that. "Greg didn't think it looked like me all *that* much, though."

"Greg," Oft replied, "was not there. He probably is extremely glad that he was not there, and I don't blame him. The evidence of your own eyes is notoriously unreliable, Pamela, but that's no reason to ignore it completely."

I popped a sober-up jolt after Oft left, then decided that while drinking lunch was fun, actually eating some was smarter. Luckily, the place made a decent beef stew. Vat-grown and double-killed, although I think that last one's just being pretentious. They licked the vatfood reanimation problem decades ago. Even the chicken's safe now.

Eating by myself was boring, though, so I called Syah. "Hey," he said right away. "You eat yet?"

"About to. I'm at the other bar." (We have two.) "Beef stew today! You know where the place is?"

"I do," he replied. "I'm even on my way. My phon says I'll be about ten minutes. If you can't hold out that long, go ahead and order two bowls. I like mine cooler than yours anyway."

"It's a date," I told him, and his face grew thoughtful.

"Yeah, another one, isn't it? ...cool. See you in a few!"

I broke off the connection with a goofy smile on my face. *He's just shy*, I decided. I got the impression that Syah wasn't really great with women, which surprised me. There was no way that I was the first person to notice just how good-looking he was. *Maybe **he** didn't notice them noticing?* That was always possible — and it didn't matter, anyway. The important thing was, he was noticing me *now*. I wasn't going to let anybody spoil my mood.

Not even that idiot haranguing the cook. He had gotten in line a couple of spaces behind me, and looked more interested in yelling about his order than in getting it put in. At least he wasn't anybody I knew. A little tall, shaved head, deep tan — my first guess was somebody off of the *Redacted*. They were showing up at the base more regularly now, although the senior officers were still mostly keeping their distance.

I had uncharitable thoughts about that as I picked up my order. The idiot behind me thought that it was his lunch. He actually had the gall to grab it first, too. Calling him on it took a couple of minutes, an appeal to the cook, and most of my good temper before I could retrieve my meal. I spent a few moments lobbing mental daggers at the *Redacted*, the Adjudication Council that spawned it, and a few other, unrelated things while I was at it. I mean, might as well, right? Get all the grumbling done at the same time. You don't want to be upset on a full stomach.

Only, when I decided to finally fill that stomach, I was stopped by the aromas coming from the bowls. It took me a precious moment to recognize it, and when I did, I exhaled, from both shock, and training.

Deathheart.

God, the smell of it.

You get the smallest, most attenuated sniff of deathheart when you're doing off-world training. You get it only *once*, too. Any attempt to get another whiff is an automatic washout from the training program, and good luck trying to get off-planet at all. Nobody wants to have your eventual drug-addled death on their conscience.

How did deathheart smell to *me*, when I got tested? It smelled wonderful, and like eternity, and I was terrified of it. So I guess it smelled like it was supposed to? This wasn't the weak stuff, though, diluted a million times by robots with no brains to burst. This deathheart was the true quill, and the deadly aroma coming up to me slammed my entire nervous system so hard, I could *hear* the buzz as my neurons vibrated in shock.

God bless that training program, though, because my reflexes kicked in immediately. There aren't many times where a spastic jump back actually *helps* anything, but 'encountering deathheart' is at the top of the list. I screamed "FLEE!" at the top of my lungs — anything to get the air out of them — as I scrabbled for my face filter. I've got reflexes for *that*, too: pop the capsule, breathe *in* the filter, try not to bite down on the tendrils as they scrabble through your mouth and down your throat, and wait for it to stabilize.

I forced down my urge to vomit and slammed a plate down on the bowl full of beef stew. Thanks to the filter I couldn't smell anything anyway, but it was the best I could do. I looked around, hoping like hell that nobody else had been too close... and, dammit, it wasn't my lucky day. Ten feet down, that idiot from before was having convulsions. I was the only one who could help him, too. The restaurant was now completely cleared, and more filters were being slapped over every door and window. They shuddered back and forth in unpleasant unison as I half-stumbled my way over to the victim.

"Process!" I yelled. "Where's the trauma kit?"

"Three feet behind you. It does not have the antidote, but there is a standard metabolism inhibitor inside it. Blue pen, with a large yellow bulb on the end."

"Got it, thanks." I had it open by the end of the sentence, and thank God there was one in there. "Side effects?"

"A one in twenty chance of immediate death. A crash team is a standard response — ah, never mind." I had already ripped away the man's tunic and was lining up the pen. I knew the procedures, you see. The crash team would have deathheart antidote, but this guy wouldn't last long enough to get any. Giving him a 95% chance of survival was a no-brainer.

Only, as I reached out to jam the pen into his shoulder, the man straightened out with a horrible series of snaps and pops that I swear sounded like breaking bones. His hands grabbed at mine, gripping them with painful intensity, and he levered himself up to *snap* at my filter mask like some kind of wild animal.

The worst part? The bastard spoke not a word. Even after I pulled myself away from his gnawing mouth, he just stared at me with protruding eyes, visibly willing me to be mesmerized. He never blinked, either. He just let the blood now coming out from his tear ducts to flow freely, as the two of us scrambled for some kind of balance or position.

He wasn't strong enough to pull me forward, but damned if he wasn't trying, right up to the moment I kneed him in the groin. I'll admit it, now: it was blind luck, but it did the trick. It made him even more spastic, but now his flailing muscles included his hands, and as he let go of me I scrambled back, looking for the pen...

"Three inches by your left hand," The Process said helpfully, and with no more emotion than it would have shown if I had asked where my coffee cup was. "The cap will need to be manually removed." I was already flicking the cap off with my thumb, just before I shoved the pen into the closest visible flesh the guy had. I decided I didn't have time to care about the side-effects of doing *that*, either.

He didn't die, so lucky him? I mean, he sort of died, in the sense that his metabolism iced over as the drug took hold. It was the kind of dead you can get better from, though. Assuming that the crash team did its job.

I wish the sonuvabitch had closed his eyes before they froze cloudy brown, though. He was still staring at me when the crash team arrived. Like he still wanted nothing better out of life than to watch me follow him down to nightmarish death.

Then the other part of what happened just hit me. "Process?" I whispered, as the buzzing in my ears finally started to die down. "Are you there?"

There was no response.

"Do *not* take off your filter," Nur told me. "And do *not* go anywhere. This entire area is still considered contaminated."

He was wearing a filter of his own, too. Everybody has one, because they breed easily and don't mutate. The filters are more Amalgamation tech, and for once we're using some of their gear the way it was meant to be used. We think the filter's about as alive as a jellyfish is, but it's hard to tell. It definitely *enjoys* oozing its way through your throat and lungs, pulling up everything that's not supposed to be there, and giving you plenty of yummy oxygen in exchange. They say wearing one regularly can add ten years to your life.

I know nobody who wants to try that particular experiment for very long.

It was just the two of us in the commissary. Well, three if you include the guy in the crash bag. Since I might have been exposed to deathheart, it was obviously insane for *me* to check the area to see if it was clean, and bringing in more people would mean more chances for bits of the damned stuff to get out. Which is why I was waiting while Nur did all the work. Also why he was telling me obvious things, like to stay put and do nothing stupid. The jury was still out on whether I was at risk for doing anything else.

Nur gave the site a full sweep-and-clean. I offered to help, but since I had clearly gotten enough of a dose for auditory hallucinations involving dead computer programs, Nur decided to let me relax and fight off the picodose of deathheart I had gotten in my system. That made sense, although at least I didn't have to worry about my brain exploding. If it hadn't happened already, I was safe.

We ended up spending a while in decontamination. Nur had missed enough deathheart fragments on his first pass-through to kill up to, I dunno, twenty people. Which is why we always triple-check, and then triple-check again, until there's none of the filthy stuff left. I swear, it's like deathheart actively hates humanity. I still think I could have helped find them, but — in case it's not obvious by now — I can be wrong, a lot of the time.

A *lot* of the time, dammit.

Since I couldn't leave, I amused myself by waiting for the crash bag to start jerking around. It wasn't supposed to, but then Adam wasn't supposed to have almost got out of no-fooling cryostasis, either. By now I was in a mood where the senseless was starting to make sense, and I couldn't wait to vomit that mood out at my next therapy session.

The bag thankfully stayed resolutely still by the time Nur straightened up, looked at the readouts, and pulled the filter off of his face. I winced, both because the sound was horrible, and because Nur had just bet his life on his ability to find and neutralize lethal levels of deathheart.

Then I relaxed, because Nur didn't fall down, or even start frothing. "You can take that thing off now," he said. "I've checked the area. We got it all. Wasn't much, actually."

If you've ever worn a filter, you don't need me to tell you too much about what it's like to yank a bunch of wiggling goo out of your nose and throat. And if you haven't, you don't want me to tell you. It's infinitely ickier than it sounds, but at least it doesn't hurt. After I had stuffed the last twitching tendril back into its carrying case, I said, "Was it all in the food, then? Because it smelled like a lot."

"Yeah, that's why you're still alive," Nur replied. "I found a few crystals on that guy's gloves. They're inert, but there's definitely deathheart inside them. He must have gotten it into your food, because that bowl had enough deathheart in it to kill you in seconds. I don't know what would make the crystals dissolve, but a couple of them broke apart early after getting mixed with your lunch."

I looked at the bowl in question — or, rather, at the portable plasma furnace it had been vaporized in. Sometimes regular fire just ain't cleansing enough. "So if they hadn't, I'd have died later. Which means that if nobody found my body in time, you'd never know the cause of death for sure. That sounds like one hell of a poison."

"Sure," Nur shrugged. "If you're willing to spend ten million bucks a dose. That guy *really* wanted you dead, Pam."

"Good thing I smelled it first," I muttered, trying not to think of that wonderful odor. Although it was easier to block it out than I remembered it being from training. Maybe I was just older now, and not as convinced of my own immortality as I used to be? "What now?"

"Now," Nur said grimly, "we swap out our clothes, deep-clean every personal item we can't bear to lose, and activate the scourers on this room. Just in case I missed a spot after all."

The first person I saw when I got out of decontamination was Syah, and he was commendably brave in hugging me. Granted, I was changed, scrubbed down to almost painful levels, and wasn't convulsing in fatal ecstasy, but deathheart is *scary*. You can't blame anybody for hesitating, just a little — but he didn't, and I didn't want to think too much about what that meant to me. I wasn't sure yet where the two of us were going. Well, scratch that. I wasn't sure yet *if* the two of us were going anywhere together.

"That *devil-pig*," he growled into my shoulder, before releasing me from what was shaping up to be a very nicely fierce embrace. "They tell me he tried to kill you. Is that true?"

"Yeah." Something in his expression made me add, "Don't do anything stupid, Syah. He's in a crash bag, and he'll go right from there to cryostasis, and he won't wake up until they fix him back on Earth." I locked eyes with him. "He doesn't *matter* any more, all right? I'm not dead, and I'm not hurt. Everything's *fine.*" *Except for the fact that I absolutely itch everywhere and I can feel the pressure from every hair on my head,* I thought to myself. I was still right on principle.

Syah exhaled. "Okay," he eventually said. "Killing him would serve no purpose. Let him sleep, until the doctors come for him with their drugs and las-scalpels. But I hope his frozen dreams are nightmares!"

That was enough of a snarl to attract stares from everyone else at the scene, but not hostile ones. From the expressions on people's faces, most of them agreed with him. Hell, *I* agreed with Syah, although I didn't want to. Nightmares during cryosleep weren't something you should wish on your worst enemy. The problem was, 'attacking you with deathheart' was the kind of thing your worst enemy might *do.*

Which was the strangest part, because I had no idea who that son of a bitch was.

CHAPTER EIGHTEEN

Charnel Crimes

"My traitor's name is Jaidan Behram," Rubicon told me. I didn't need emotional sensors to feel the rage coming off the captain of the *Redacted*. "He was a crewman newly-assigned to the galley by Fleet headquarters, back on Earth. His records show no sign of disaffection, treason, or madness. Although I recognize and accept that you have no reason to believe anything I say."

"That *is* a quandary," Maki admitted. She had toned down her usual corpo perkiness for this meeting, for reasons that seemed obscure to me. Personally, I agreed. Why *should* we believe anything Rubicon had to say? "Although I can't see whatever motive you might have to set up a suicide attack. Especially since it would screw up the investigation into Burcu's murder."

"Unless he was involved in *that*, too," I muttered.

Rubicon shocked me with an actual laugh. "Ordering Burcu's death would make even less sense for me than ordering *yours*. What possible motive would I have for either? Wait, let me rephrase: what *realistic* motive would I have?"

"I'm sure I could come up with something," I shot back. "The Great Powers have all turned skulduggery into an art form."

"That's true," Rubicon replied, surprising me. He still looked annoyingly amused. "But I'm not a Great Power. I'm the captain of a single interstellar vessel. In my experience, complicated schemes explode without warning."

"Fair enough," I conceded. "So, he had access to deathheart. Any missing from stores over there?"

I'll give the bastard credit. He didn't even wince. "Why would I keep poisons in stock, Chief Pilot? I have a *starship*. If I ever need to assassinate someone, I will simply subcontract the job to Sir Isaac Newton."

I opened my mouth, Maki said, "Pam," and I shut it again. "Tell us more about Behram," she went on. "There must have been *something* unusual about him."

Rubicon shook his head. "No, there was not. My traitor was not even suspiciously not suspicious, you understand. He had a few minor reprimands on his record, the odd incident or two. People in his department thought he was mildly dull, slightly long-winded, but otherwise conscientious. We still don't know if he was excellent at subterfuge, or whether treason was the only thing interesting about him."

Maki didn't bother asking about the *Redacted*'s internal investigation. I for one appreciated that, one the principle of, "Don't ask questions when you don't need or want to hear the answers." There's a *lot* of things the Adjudication Council can do to its own personnel, sometimes with their enthusiastic consent. If we were unlucky, Rubicon might tell us some of them.

Instead she asked, "So. Motive? Why was Behram after Pam? Did he leave a journal, manifesto, scribbled note, anything?"

"Nothing relevant. Before you ask: the *irrelevant* entries involved petty complaints about working in the galley, a general dislike of interstellar travel, and a mild eagerness to being on a 'real' planet again." Rubicon shook his head, in what the readouts told me was genuine chagrin. "In retrospect, these entries were cumulatively designed to get my traitor special consideration when it came to shore leave... I'm sorry. Was there something you wanted to say, Chief Pilot?"

"Yes," I said, as flatly as I could. "You keep saying 'my' traitor. You implying we have some of our own?"

"Of course I am," Rubicon replied. "He must have gotten the deathheart from somewhere, and it wasn't from any of the places on our itinerary. That leaves... here." Then I saw him slump, just a little. "Tell me. What kind of people have access to filthy poisons, are willing to risk killing a lot of people in using them, and are almost eager to get themselves killed in the progress?" Maki and I didn't reply, because there was no need to. We all knew the answer: cultists.

Damned cultists, here on One-Eighteen.

Rubicon broke the silence, surprisingly. "Why do I think this is not news to Doctor Adesina?" You know something? I was so used to him refusing to show any politeness to Maki at all, it took me a moment to realize he was referring to her. Although even then he wouldn't use her corporate title, just her medical one. Baby steps, I guess.

"Because it's not. I've come across some new information," Maki went on. Which was news to me, as much as it was to Rubicon. "And I mean *new*. I had a hunch this morning, so before this meeting I checked Burcu for traces of deathheart. I found some."

"Really? How?" If Rubicon sounded confused, I didn't blame him. So was I. "Deathheart breaks down in the body within a half hour."

"Yes, it does. But Burcu chewed gum, right? Well, one of the pieces of her favorite chewing gum had been contaminated with deathheart. There were traces of it on the wrapper. She must have reached for a piece mid-flight."

"That sounds like a weird way to assassinate somebody," I pointed out. "How did they know she'd chew that gum while flying a shuttle?"

"Why would they care, Pam?" Maki shook her head. "She'd have gone into convulsions and died if she had grabbed the stick and chewed it on the street."

"...yes," agreed Rubicon. "In fact, they were unlucky. If she had been on the ground, the death might have looked like misadventure from drug addiction. But I wouldn't have believed that any of my officers were fool enough to risk taking any drug while flying, let alone that one."

"Deathheart keeps showing up in this." I wanted to pace, I really did. "Adam's shack had traces of it, somebody killed Burcu with it, and now somebody tried to kill me. So, is it all related?"

"I think so," Rubicon replied. "There is none on my ship, yet *my* traitor had access to it. And he could make sure Burcu could be dosed. He would have been who she got her gum from, in fact. Adulterating it was a risky move, but then: so was trying to assassinate you. I suspect he and his associates panicked, and tried to disguise a murder-suicide as a terroristic attack."

"Or a murder-suicide *and* a terroristic attack," Maki pointed out. "But why Burcu and Pam?"

"Because we were the ones investigating things," I told her. "They must have thought we were starting to figure things out."

"Did you?" Rubicon asked.

I could only helplessly shrug.

So, let's talk about cultists.

Technically, we're not supposed to call them 'cultists.' The official term is 'Ritual Nihilist,' because I guess calling them that was supposed to give them less power, somehow? And don't ask *how* naming, or not-naming, gives them power. Again, some questions have answers you neither want nor need to hear.

We call them cultists anyway. They're the insidious kind of crazy, worming their way into things for as long as they can before somebody catches them with a knife, a makeshift altar, and a bound sacrificial victim. That's almost always how they're caught, too: cultists just can't resist ritual sacrifices. It's like they're following a script that they're not really supposed to deviate from, and don't want to, anyway.

They're different from the space-happy in that they can hide a hell of a lot longer before getting caught, and they can work together for a while to get what they want. But what do they want? Mostly sacrifices, although if there's a nasty way to get power, money, or status, they'll happily explore it. I guess ritual knives cost money.

Their only saving grace is that most people have never seen a real cultist, up close and personal. They're supposedly more of a problem on Earth, and there are never many of them at one time for very long; but while they're around, they're a busy bunch of bastards. There's always a report or two every quarter of some little cult doing something horrible to people, and *oddly enough* they're the one class of criminal that the Great Powers won't ever transport to the colony worlds.

So what happens to them, then? Probably the exact same thing that happens to them when the authorities find a cult circle on one of the colony worlds, only the Terrans won't ever admit to using salt and steel to disinfect their sites later. Because, you know. Whatever works. More prosaically, if he really was a cultist, this Jaidan Behram guy wasn't going to wake up in a Terran medical ward. It was for damn sure he wouldn't be returning to regular society. The space-happy are sick, and you have to cure people who are sick. Cultists don't get that kind of diagnosis, and their treatment isn't ever commented on.

How do I feel about that? Remember, someone just tried to murder me — and maybe an entire bar, as well — using a terrifying Tomb World poison. If it turned out that he was a cultist? Actions have consequences.

They had me under my own kind of quarantine for a week, and it absolutely *sucked*.

I feel bad putting it that way, even now. Everybody agreed that it sucked that I had to have a bodyguard, but what could they do? The biggest problem with cultists is the 'S' on the end. If I had a group of Ritual Nihilists looking to kill me, for whatever mad reason (people try not to get too deep into cultist motivations, because that crap can be contagious), they'd want to take another swipe at me. That's just how they're wired.

Fortunately, cultists are also wired to get steadily more anxious about finally taking down a chosen target. That mental tic gets really handy when you're trying to figure out if there's more of the homicidal maniacs out there. If they don't show up within a week, then they probably aren't showing up. At least, that's what the training sims say, and the training sims are reliable.

But being under Protective Observation still *sucks*. It's dull, and it's boring, and everything that comes in and out has somebody looking at it first. Poisons, tailored viruses, malware, infective memes — you just never know what's gonna scratch a cultist's murder itch, so they check it all. Or they just check the stuff you absolutely have to see, and auto-delete everything else.

By Day Seven, I was ready to climb the walls (not that I would make *that* joke. Somebody might have taken it seriously). There hadn't been even a beep of cultist-related activity targeting me, although I was sourly aware that my ever-so-helpful mortal protectors wouldn't pass along any potentially dangerous information. The Process wouldn't have been helpful in keeping me informed, either, since part of Protective Observation would have involved putting it on listen-only mode. Sounds counterintuitive, but it turns out that having too much cultist-related data during PO was far worse for people's long-term mental well-being than having too little. Ignorant worry is easier to treat later than over-informed, *helplessly futile* worry is.

(Besides, trying to get The Process to discern a difference between *meaningful* suspicious behavior and just regular, everyday human suspicious behavior was virtually impossible. One more reason why the colony worlds don't try to use it as a panopticon. I understand it's a little different on Earth, where *any* kind of suspicious behavior is an acceptable reason for involuntary transportation.)

So I was eager to take Greg's call, when the full Terran week was over and I could be my own receptionist again. "Please tell me you have something boring for me to do," I told him immediately when we connected.

He grinned, over the screen. "Don't you want something interesting instead?"

"Sure, I *want* something interesting. I'll *take* something boring, at this point. Just as long as it's not *here*."

"Not to worry on that, Pam. I got something that's both interesting, and absolutely not *here*." He stopped grinning. "Just one thing, though. You don't have a problem with religious stuff, right?"

I shrugged. "Not really. There a problem at the chapel?" That was run by the Amalgamated Unitarian minister. She wasn't a priest in any one particular religion, but most of the larger ones tacitly agreed that the AU could pinch-hit for them, in a crisis. It's 'the old better than nothing trick,' as we say on Jefferson.

"No, this is a situation involving the planet." I tried to repress my quizzical look, and failed; fortunately, Dave only went a little green around the gills. "Your buddy Oft wants to make a pilgrimage to a religious shrine. One of the ones the old inhabitants left behind."

"You may, of course, say no," Oft told me a half hour later. In person, because you don't have religious conversations using communications devices that make you throw up if you don't like the subtext. We were in Greg's office, instead. We even had coffee. Coffee! I hadn't bought any before I voluntarily put myself under durance vile, and I had run out two days ago. I could get caffeine added to the survival goop that my apartment oozed out of the wall for me, but it just wasn't the same thing.

"I'm *not* saying no, Oft," I replied, after another heavenly (ha!) sip. "I just want to know if this has anything to do with any of," — I waved with my free hand, helplessly — "the stuff we're dealing with, right now."

"Honestly? If it was up to me, I would have said 'No.' That's why I didn't ask to be brought to Yánarta." He noted my blank look with a faint smile. "Sorry, that means 'Fane of the Exalted,' in English. We still don't know what the original worshipers there might have called it."

I carefully didn't ask why they were calling it 'Yánarta,' then. Iluvitarians are some of the nicest people you'll ever meet, but they get *real* weird about the origins of their religion. "That's what I'd figure. So what's changed?"

Oft smiled. "The Anticipant thinks I should go. I'm not sure why, and I'm not certain *she's* sure why, but it's apparently important to the 'warp and weft of this wicked whirl.'"

"Lucky for you, huh?" I drank more coffee. "Sorry, that came out wrong. But she did mean this Fane of yours, though?"

"Oh, yes. I actually tried arguing with her about it, to the extent that anyone can. I very badly want to go, so I needed to be certain. She ended up pulling up a map, and tapping one finger on the Fane's location." He beamed. "So my conscience is clear."

"Gotcha." I turned to Greg. "You have a problem with me taking the day off to go play chauffeur?"

"Nope, Pam. The schedule's horked, we're still under system quarantine, and you can't be back on the Burcu investigation until Monday anyway. Besides, I'll be just as happy if you spend the next forty-eight hours away from all of this." *Especially if there are still a couple of cultists out there after all,* he did not say. We all heard it anyway. "When's the last time you had a vacation? No, last week doesn't count."

"I wasn't going to say that it was." I thought it over. "All right if I bring a friend?"

Unfortunately, I couldn't. Well, I could, and Syah sounded up for a jaunt, but he was on call, and an emergency came up an hour before our departure. Chook was real apologetic about it, too. "Sorry, Pam. The new quarterly update's making half our software suddenly default to Polish. We're all working on the problem until it's fixed. Where's there's one bug, there's another thousand hidden, waiting to rush."

"It's all right." I was all right, too, once second thoughts had crept into my mind. I hadn't really considered how weird people would find the Anticipant on first meeting, and she was absolutely coming along for the ride. Springing her unique presence on Syah probably wouldn't lead to disaster, but it would have almost certainly killed any random romantic mood anyway.

I gave Chook the once-over. "Maybe I should have asked you to come along, instead," I told her. "You look tired." She did, too. Nothing obviously wrong, just lower energy and more strain. "When's the last time you had a good night's sleep?"

"Three weeks," she replied, and far too promptly. "The planetary interface's being held together with spit and baling wire. We were supposed to get new parts on the 4-9-43, but... well." She shrugged. "Another reason to keep your boyfriend in the office. Sorry. Without Syah, the system *would* have gone walking with the Good Folk by now."

"Can't be helped, then," I said aloud. Quietly I was thinking, *Good. You just keep thinking of him as my boyfriend until we can settle the damn issue.* "You want any souvenirs?"

Chook snorted. "If you can find any, sure. But I don't think the gift store's going to be open."

CHAPTER NINETEEN

Et In Yánarta Ego

I flew down sedately, if 'sedately' can be used to describe a suborbital hop. It was also 'luxuriously, sensuously, and just this shade of ecstatically.' Flying for pleasure wasn't actually something I got to do. Being a pilot on an alien world might be a fun job, but it's still a job. Letting myself relax and enjoy the long arc around the world felt wonderful. I could feel the tension melt away as we cruised our way to the Fane. It wasn't even an indulgence, really. We weren't in a hurry, and Oft clearly wanted to tell me all about this 'Yánarta' place. From the way the Anticipant's eyes glazed over and she retreated to a tablet, she'd heard it all before.

He started off by apologizing about even calling it 'Yánarta.' "It's not the name the original inhabitants used, obviously. The Chronicler was a linguist, and constructed my faith's liturgical language from a Terran one." He smiled. "At least, *my* sect believes that. Other sects think that the Chronicler was directly inspired with knowledge of the True Tongue. I admire their enthusiasm, but not their scholarship."

"I hadn't realized Iluvitarians *had* sects," I admitted. "You folks don't seem the type..."

"To fall into schisms and counter-schisms, like pre-Reunification Christians?" He laughed, deep in his belly. "Oh, you have no *idea*. We have some very, ah, vehement people in our faith. Many believe that the Chronicler was more than a mere man. Some of them even think his books were true and accurate Histories!" Oft shrugged. "Fortunately, we have all managed to keep our disagreements strictly verbal — and to never let them become violent. *Nobody* wants their opinions to be transformed into guaranteed tickets to the colony worlds."

I looked at the flight plan. "Speaking of going places, we're on our way down. Anything should I know about this Fane of yours?"

"You know about as much as I do," Oft replied, "at least directly. My faith believes it is a local place of worship, obviously no longer maintained — but hopefully still sanctified. Others, *not* of my faith, have visited it at least once, and reported that Yánarta was a 'shrine of sorrow and peace.' It is my personal hope that this sorrow might be mitigated by the return of a true believer, however distorted his understanding of our shared beliefs might be. And, truthfully? I want to see Yánarta for my own sake. Pilgrimages are said to be good for the soul. They're certainly good for one's reputation!"

"Gasp!" Yes, I actually said that aloud. "The tattooed saint has a real, honestly ulterior motive. Is it lonely?" That got me another laugh, loud enough for the Anticipant to look up and mirror our smiles. "What I meant was, is there anything I should or shouldn't do while we're there? Besides the obvious stuff, like burning it down."

"If you're planning to burn down any Amalgamation building," countered Oft, "you had best pack a lunch. Truthfully, please just treat Yánarta with respect. Touch nothing you don't have to, leave nothing behind, and respect its existence."

Which all sounded reasonable — and ominous as all hell, because those three rules apply to Amalgamation structures generally. The only difference was, breaking one of those rules in a secular surviving structure could easily end in blood and terror. At least that was unlikely to happen here.

I hoped.

So, yeah, Yánarta was nice.

I mean, it still is nice, although I don't think any human's ever going to visit it again. Even from twenty thousand feet up I could see how beautiful the Fane was. It was a series of buildings of great, gleaming white curves, nestled throughout the valley. They all converged in a spiral structure that leapt up into the sky and stayed there, blossoming out into a blossom of metal and plastic, delicate-looking as sea foam. The whole effect evoked the wind so vividly, I could almost feel the breeze.

From up in the air, the Fane looked untouched. Even the herd of not-cows wandering nearby were keeping their distance. In fact, there were no obvious signs that they went inside the valley at all. Not a tree or structure seemed out of place.

I was surprised, even though a good bit of Amalgamation architecture remains intact — and when I realized why I was surprised, I shuddered. *It's too lovely*, I thought to myself. *Nothing this lovely was allowed to survive unspoiled.*

I didn't say that, because I didn't want Oft to know where my thoughts had gone. Instead I looked for a pad, because there was no way I would just put the lander down anywhere I felt like. That would be... sacrilegious.

Luckily, the Amalgamation was very good at putting useful things where you'd expect them to be. I needed there to be a landing pad close to the central Fane, and lo! There one was. We would have to walk to the valley itself, but it was only a mile and a half away, and the route was both gentle and grassy. It promised to be a beautiful day down here, perfect for a ramble, or possibly even a picnic, if things like that would be allowed.

I let Oft go out the hatch first. I thought he'd like that, and he did. I'm glad he did. He was an easy guy to do favors for. I would have let the Anticipant go next, but she waved me off when I offered. It would have felt weird, except that *everything* about that woman was weird, and apparently it required special training to make her that way.

That was no excuse to not *talk* to the Anticipant, though, which was something I had guiltily realized earlier. So I decided to try asking her a question directly. "So, are you an Iluvitarian, too?"

She looked at me, looked at Oft, looked at me again, and burst out into almost hysterical laughter. I glanced at Oft. "I take it that was a stupid question?"

"There are no stupid questions," he replied, then waited with a small, resigned smile as the Anticipant laughed even louder. "You can probably guess from her response that the answer is 'no.' The best I've ever gotten out of the Anticipant is that she recognizes some deities, but won't believe in them."

"Really? Why not?"

"Apparently they're all vile. Which, to her, can mean anything from 'Ye Liveliest Awfulness' to 'color-coordinates electric purple with lime green...' *Oh*."

Oft had stopped, just as we had cleared a tree-line, and when I lifted my head to see what he had seen, I went '*oh*,' too.

The Fane of the Exalted was fifteen stories high, which meant that even from halfway up the valley we had to crane our necks to see. From down here the Fane looked like a spring wind, recast in dazzling whites and vivid blues, yet still cool and refreshing. There was even a faint but steady breeze, softly drifting past us. The Amalgamation was clever at creating effects like that, without power or moving parts, but I had never felt it done better.

The Fane should have been imposing, even overpowering, but instead, every line of it promised soothing and safety. *Here is peace*, it said to me. *Here you may rest.* I wondered what it said to Oft — and decided not to ask. After all, if it was affecting me like this, what was it doing to *him*?

So I waited, my eyes drinking in the Fane and never looking at my companions, until I felt a touch on my sleeve. It was the Anticipant, who gave me a nod — and a quick shake of her head, her finger brushing my mouth when I was about to ask her a certain question.

"Oft!" I said aloud, instead. "If it's so wonderful up *here*, imagine what it's like down *there*!" When I turned, his grin answered my own as the three of us half-ran down the valley. It really was a beautiful day for a pilgrimage.

Only, my grin wasn't entirely honest. The Anticipant looked worried. The stillborn question she had interrupted would have been, *are you all right?* By now I was sure she knew what I was about to say almost before I did — and that the answer to that question was, *no.*

So why didn't she want Oft to know that she was having a problem?

The Fane was even more wonderful at ground level. Oft's confidence aside, I wasn't sure if Iluvitarians worshiped in the same way as the inhabitants of this planet. If they did, they had found a worthy faith to follow. The closer to the Fane we walked, the more welcome I felt. Everything felt *soothing*, like there were analgesics and mood-levelers in the air — but when I scanned the local atmosphere on my phon, everything came back negative. We were just walking through a place built with love, reverence, and joy, by a people who understood all three things intimately.

That was why the Fane was also steeped in a melancholy so deep, I found tears welling up, unbidden, but I found myself not being afraid of them, for a change. Everybody knows that you have to try not to cry when you're in the Tomb Worlds. If you start, when will you stop? How *can* you stop? Yet, there were times for weeping, and this was one of those times.

They were all gone, you see.

The architects and artists who had conceived of the Fane, the builders who gave the dream of it a physical form, even the custodial workers and retail staff that must have maintained the grounds and seen to the pilgrims — they were now dust, horribly murdered centuries before I was born, and we never even learned their names. *Something* hated them beyond all reason, and it was only in places like One-Eighteen could we even comprehend that hatred enough to be horrified by it.

It's hard for us to take that comprehension, then stretch it across the known galaxy. Sometimes I envy the people who work on the Tomb Worlds with corrosive atmospheres, or oceans of acid. The life that rose to self-awareness on those planets is alien enough to us that people can more easily detach themselves from the thoughts of the charnel crimes committed on thousands of species.

I know that sounds awful. So are the Tomb Worlds. Besides, we'll *need* that detachment if we're ever going to figure out what slaughtered the Amalgamation, because that'll be the critical first step in working out how to someday do a little slaughtering of our own.

...what? Look, *somebody* out there decided one day to demonstrate to trillions of innocent people that the universe was a cold and perilous place. Fine, they proved their point. So they have no kick coming when we finally turn the point right back around, and shove it into whatever they use for guts.

I wasn't thinking any of this at the time, you understand. The Fane was too good at promoting a sense of peace and healing to allow such dark thoughts to fester. I've had a lot of time to brood since, though, sometimes in places that encouraged entirely different kinds of thoughts.

No, at the time I was content to marvel; both at the beauty, and at the fact that it was in one piece. The site wasn't pristine, but it was amazingly *orderly*. It was like everything that was there had been put down centuries before, and had been voluntarily staying there ever since.

It was so clean, I started to get worried. "Oft," I called to him carefully, "what did the survey team say about this place?"

He stopped, and looked back at me. "That it was here, it was some kind of religious center, and that they spent a week here with no harm. Oh, and they took enough pictures to prove it was a shrine of my faith — well, they weren't trying to prove anything, but it was enough to convince *us*. Why do you ask?"

"Take a look around," I replied. "It's been abandoned for five centuries, right? So why isn't it a ruin? We know the Amalgamation built to last, sure, but whatever killed it was just as thorough."

Oft looked around. "You know, that's an excellent point," he mused. "You would think the Enemy would have eagerly despoiled this place, if only given the chance. 'Foul in wisdom, cruel in strength, misshaping what he touched.'" That sounded like a quote, but I didn't recognize it. "I don't feel any evil here, though. Do you?"

I pursed my lips, suddenly mortified at how the conversation had suddenly featured the e-word. "Well... no," I admitted. "It feels like the exact opposite, really."

"I agree. I think we're safe, as long as we're here. Indeed, we're supposed to be safe everywhere else on this planet, aren't we?" Oft looked around. "I have to admit, I do not miss the dread I've felt ever since my ship landed."

What, him too? I thought. "One-Eighteen isn't that bad. I don't know why other people hate it here."

"I didn't say I hated your planet, Pam. I said I *dreaded* it. There's too much weight in the very air. It's like a presence that watches, and *bides*." He looked around. "Here, there's nothing to dread, and a stolen moment to breathe."

"I'll take your word for it. I still want to know why... whatever-it-was didn't destroy this place, along with the rest of the Amalgamation."

"Except for Earth," pointed out Oft. "We were part of that system, though we knew it not. Why were we, and here, spared? Good question. Perhaps they overlooked us." Oft's eyes grew as cold as I had ever seen them. "Or perhaps they did not dare."

"The wise rush in where devils fear to tread!" laughed the Anticipant. For one glorious moment, I actually understood what the Hell she was talking about.

The Fane was just as impressive inside. It had a central atrium and spire, surrounded by eight antechambers: six large ones, and two small. Their walls, floors and ceilings were inscribed with great colorful waves that interwove with each other as they flowed to the atrium, then up, up, up, converging on a bright sphere of white that shone, but somehow didn't dazzle. It's hard to figure out alien art, but I could see their intent. I think a blind woman could have seen it. It was so wonderful, it didn't even make me feel insignificant and human. *If you are here,* the Fane said to me, *then you are worthy.*

And this was a tourist destination! It wasn't just there for worship, or whatever happened here. You could tell that the place was designed for people to come, look, marvel, and spend resources. Oh, yes, there were places that looked like gift shops, complete with souvenirs and gimcracks, and they were just as magnificent as the rest of the Fane.

(Not that I took any. Souvenirs, I mean. We don't know what the Amalgamation used for money, except in the broadest terms, but I did know that I didn't have any of it. Taking anything without paying would have been stealing, and I couldn't even *think* about stealing something from a place like that.)

After my first rush of overwhelming amazement, I looked over to see Oft carefully staring at a wall fresco. "What's that? Oh, right, those are your gods?"

"Iluvitarians are monotheists," he replied, with the air of somebody who's said that phrase a thousand times in his life. "But yes, these are images of the Exalted. At least, as the inhabitants of this world knew Them."

As frescoes made in a dead alien style, in both senses of the term, the images weren't bad. I only knew enough of the Iluvitarians' not-gods to recognize the names, but the One-Eighteeners had used the same kind of iconography as we did when it came to physical objects. I mean, there's only so many ways you can draw a tree, a star, or a mountain. "It's exquisite," I said truthfully. "Peaceful, and welcoming."

"Would that it had been less peaceful, and more protective," muttered Oft. He then rubbed his face. "Forgive me, Pamela. It is at times like this that I remember how my faith is the last guttering ember surviving of a church that once sustained billions of believers, possibly even trillions. And that we *must* protect what is left."

"I wasn't judging, Oft. Although I don't quite get how they got from *here*" — I pointed first to the fresco, and then straight up — "to back up *there*."

"Back to Earth, and the Chronicler, you mean?" Oft's smile returned, if gamely. "It's a contentious subject, even inside our church. Some believe he was inspired by the All-Powerful. Others, including myself, find that unlikely. The Chronicler never abandoned his existing faith, after all. Surely a direct visitation from the Divine would have changed his mind."

"So you buy into the Daniken hypothesis? I gotta admit, when we covered him in school, the teachers were pretty brutal about his theories."

"As they should have. The man was a crank." Oft pursed his lips. "Unfortunately, pre-Contact believers in alien visitation ran heavily along those lines. How do you separate the wheat from the chaff, when you're not sure what wheat looks like? At any rate, it seems more reasonable that the Chronicler found *something*. A book. Maybe a series of letters, telling of strange papers or dreams. Or perhaps even a dying missionary, a desperate refugee from the wrack of worlds, who had found one place where the Truth could be replanted?" He smiled. "Although the Chronicler never mentioned *that*, either."

"Maybe he just didn't want to be compared to Mormons," I pointed out. "Their cosmology held up pretty darned well, didn't it? It's a lot easier to believe in things like golden plates when people start finding them on other worlds."

"Yes, the missionary hypothesis is plausible for them as well," Oft agreed. "Possibly even more so. Joseph Smith founded his faith a mere eighty years after the death of the Amalgamation. You could also look to the sudden appearance of the Brahmo Samaj movement in India, or the Bahá'í faith. Some of the neo-Marxists in the Consolidation Wars even claimed that their own prophet had been given word somehow of the Amalgamation's post-scarcity economy, but that may have simply been argued out of sheer desperation."

The Fane had a food court, so we had our picnic there.

It feels so *jarring* to put it that way, but I don't want anyone to think that the Fane was just some kind of ethereal, pie-in-the-sky fantasy land. No, we were in a place that people *used,* and one thing that people do, is eat. So they would need somewhere *to* eat, and we decided to eat there, too.

We had brought our lunches with us. Sandwiches, bread, and lukewarm tea — and I swear, I've never had a better meal. The food court seemed to grow brighter as we ate, and I wondered whether there were automatic systems that activated when people used the room for any length of time.

Oft chuckled when I suggested that. "I suppose that's one way to describe spirits," he mused. "Let's hope they don't mind."

"I don't think I believe in those the same way you do, Oft." Let the record show that my voice was not slightly muffled, thank you very much. *Civilized* Jeffersonians don't talk with their mouths full. "I mean, sure, I believe in souls, and stuff, but they don't linger when they're gone." I looked around, and shuddered a little, in spite of myself. "Not even somewhere like this."

"Really? I find this planet particularly soul-haunted." Oft poured himself another cup of tea. "I am constantly bemused that you do not."

"In the land of the Midnight Sun, the one-eyed woman is queen." The two of us waited to see if the Anticipant would offer anything else, but she didn't. Instead, she grabbed the last piece of the wonderful bread Oft had brought along.

"That's what, your third piece?" Oft asked her, mock-seriously, and getting a no-fooling thumbed-nose in response. "Seriously, though, Pamela. Do you really not feel the presence of the spirits on this planet?"

"Are you asking me if I see ghosts? Because the answer's, 'If I ever do, I'm calling in a medical right then and there.'" I shook my head. "It's bad when pilots start having hallucinations."

"Come now, Pam. We both know that I wasn't. What the ancients called 'ghosts' were just flaws on magnetic tape, mild neurological quirks, or chronic selection bias. What I'm talking about are *spirits*; 'souls,' if you prefer. And I didn't ask if you had *seen* them. Vision is not always the way they most easily manifest."

I glared at him — or, at least, I tried to. I was discovering that it was hard to get, or stay, mad in the Fane. "So, you're asking me about the keening on the radio. The kind that sounds like voices. I'm not the only one who hears it, you know."

"You are not," agreed Oft. "I can hear it, too. Everyone I've asked can hear it. It's just that most people can't do anything *with* the keening, except grit their teeth and wait for it to be over."

"I don't get it. It's honestly not that bad." I've said that phrase a lot on this planet, over the years.

Oft flicked a look at the Anticipant, who gave him a tiny nod. He cleared his throat. "Not that bad, Pam, or not bad at all?"

I *really* wanted to be mad, now. "All right, you got me. I like the keening. Just like I like this planet. Is that so awful?"

"No." Oft sighed. "It's just that... almost nobody else has had your reaction to it. We've looked at all the records for One-Eighteen, particularly the mental health interviews. The common thread in almost every single one of them is how little people enjoy being here, and how eager they are to leave. Except for you. You don't like this planet, you *love* it. It's extremely rare."

"How rare?"

"Rare enough that only one other person has had a similar reaction." Oft grimaced. "Adam Sild."

CHAPTER TWENTY

Stampede of the Not-Cows

One thing I liked about Oft: he knew when to talk, and when to back off. I don't know what my face looked like just then, but it was enough for him to drop the subject of Sild until we were on our way back to the lander. He even carried the picnic basket, which probably *did* help me regain my calm. Although even at the time, I was confused about my reaction. I'd really met Sild maybe twice. Then again, both times he had tried to kill me, so maybe I was just being sensible.

"Okay," I eventually allowed. "Let's get back to Adam Sild. He grooved on One-Eighteen?"

"Yes. It changed him, and for the better. He *should* have been a loose cannon here," Oft went on. "He didn't take well to Bolivar. His juvenile records are full of petty crimes and bad influences. He was caught a few times attending meetings of mildly subversive fighting clubs, although he never got caught committing violent crimes. His psych evaluations all had him down as a likely prospect for therapeutic adjustment. That's probably why Sild took the first offworld assignment he could when he reached eighteen. He bounced around for ten years, racking up barely-adequate assessment scores at all his positions, until he ended up here."

I waited for a moment for Oft to say more. "So... what happened then?"

"According to his records? Nothing. Adam Sild consistently hit Double-plus-good levels of performance and satisfaction for his entire time on One-Eighteen. There's not a hint of his earlier attitude and job issues in the files, and the digital record's borne out by what personal interviews with his colleagues that we've been able to conduct. Something about this place *clicked* for him." Oft shook his head. "It needs hardly be said that he was *not* high risk for going space-happy."

"Sometimes that doesn't matter," I muttered. "Sild tried his damnedest to kill me, after all."

"Did he?" Oft shook his head. "One thing the man kept up from his previous life was an interest in unarmed combat. Going space-happy shouldn't have wiped that away. Quite the opposite, in fact."

I thought about that fight. I've had emergency hand-to-hand training, naturally. You don't get to go out here unless you know what to do when your colleague starts frothing at the mouth and shouting about blood and blood gods. I'm no martial artist, though. If Sild was, he should have done a lot more damage. Hell, he had barely done any damage to anybody.

Then I shook my head. "No. There was a manifesto, weird arrangements of broken items, and death traps. All of *those* were normal. You always get those from the space-happy."

"True, Pam. I wasn't able to access the manifesto, though. Do you know what it said?"

"Dammit, I don't. We had The Process read and scan everything. That's the safe thing to do, because it couldn't go crazy like we did." *But it can die like we do*, I thought to myself — and then I suddenly started, because the Anticipant had touched my arm.

She gave me a smile that was no less genuine for being obviously laboriously constructed, brick by brick. "***That which is <u>not</u> dead might eternal lie; and with strange eons, even death might die,***" she promised me, and I weirdly felt a little better.

Oft did not. In fact, he almost looked offended. "This is perhaps not the place to say such things," he muttered, but I wasn't sure to whom. "At any rate, I agree that Adam Sild is mad. I simply wonder if his madness is as easily defined as we think."

I almost didn't hear him say that. I was too busy considering what the Anticipant had told me. It had sparked a... well, it wasn't at 'thought' level, yet. It was getting there, though, and if I could just let it alone for a minute — but you never get that, do you? There's always something showing up to interrupt your thoughts. In this case, it was the not-cow herd. We suddenly started smelling them before we saw them, although not before we heard them.

At least *I* smelled not-cows. Oft and the Anticipant just started gagging from the reek. "What in the name of the Hunter is *that*?" Oft asked, as he hawked and spit.

I sympathized, keeping the grin off my face. Trying to get the rotting-grass stench of ripe not-cow out of your nose isn't fun, the first time you come across it. But eventually, you get used to it. Besides, it doesn't stick to your clothes or hair. "Remember the not-cows? That's what they smell like. The herd we saw earlier must be nearby." I frowned. "But they don't normally come too close to humans—" That's when the Anticipant tackled the both of us. Actually, that makes it sound too professional, or something. What she did was dive at our lower legs, knocking us both off-balance and leaving us sprawled on the grass.

But that was a good thing, because not two seconds later a God-damned *tree* went whirring through the air, at what would have been just above head-height. Maybe it would have missed our actual heads. Maybe. Just as happy not to have to find out, you know what I mean?

I rolled to my feet, hand grabbing for my holster for one moment — which I almost hadn't brought, because who the Hell packs heat on One-Eighteen? Instead I pulled up Oft, with the Anticipant's help. "We're running!" I told him as I took a precious second to look for more uprooted trees coming through. Which was stupid, because what was I planning to do if I saw any coming right for me? Spit at it?

Oft didn't waste any time himself, bless the man. He grabbed the Anticipant's hand long enough to make sure she was coming along, and then we were off. "What are we running from?" he yelled as he ran, wiping at the trickle of blood snaking down from his scalp. "I thought this planet didn't have any monsters!"

"Not-cows *are* monsters!" I yelled back. "Just not dangerous ones! Usually!"

"*Usually*?"

"This one's throwing trees, ain't it?"

"Do they do that? *How* do they do that, Pam?"

"I don't know, Oft!" I was starting to hear the 'tekelili' sound not-cows made when they were after giant spiders, and that did not reassure me. Neither was how close that hunting cry was. "We try not to look at the things they have on the ends of their legs! It only disturbs us!"

"LEFT! DUCK!" screamed the Anticipant, her voice hoarse and cracking under the strain. I'm not sure why I went left and ducked — well, that's not true. I know why I did. It was because the more primitive parts of my brain had decided that 'Anticipant' was another word for 'witch,' and never mind what Oft had said. When a witch shrieks out a warning, you listen to her. Especially since she had been right the last time.

She was right this time, too. The second tree bounced its way through the clearing, chewing up the ground where Oft had just been running. "Is it *following* us?" I wheezed out as we darted through the copse between us and the hauler.

"You're the one who lives here!" Oft sounded less winded than I did. "Is this normal behavior for not-cows?"

"No! They don't get aggressive at all! Even when you yank legs off of them!" I carefully did not look back. "The only way they can hurt you is if you lie down in front of one of them!"

The Anticipant reached out with one hand — I noted absently that she had her eyes firmly closed, which made a weird kind of almost-sense — and pulled Oft precisely three inches to the left. That saved him from a head full of tree branch, but *not* another nasty cut along one cheek. She made a sound of equal parts anger and worry at that, which meant

I started worrying. Whatever technique the woman was using to anticipate the wooden missiles wasn't perfect, and if one of those trees hit us, we were either going to be dead fast, or dead slow. Thank God we didn't have that far to run to the landing pad.

How I wish it had been a couple of hundred yards closer.

I'd like to say that any of us could have lost the lottery and gotten hit by a thrown tree, but that'd be untrue. Oft was in the rear, where the most danger was. Maybe he thought he was the most disposable of the three of us. Or maybe it was just the malignant luck of the draw, because the tree came flying out of the canopy just as he stepped onto the landing pad.

It wasn't a big one, and it didn't hit Oft squarely enough to break more than what turned out to be a couple of ribs and his leg. It didn't trap him underneath its branches, either, which would have absolutely sucked. He still went flying, hitting the ground hard enough to dislocate his shoulder with a pop that I could hear all the way in the cockpit. I immediately snarled, "Finish the preflight!" to the Anticipant as I rushed back to the hatchway. I didn't know if she had that skill, and at that moment I didn't care. *She's a fucking witch, right?* I thought to myself as I pulled out my gun. *She can figure it out as she goes.*

The bad news was, Oft had fallen off the pad entirely. The good news was, he hadn't given up, God bless him. He was still moving in the direction of the hauler, however feebly. That was real good. You can't win if you don't try. Besides, it would also make getting him on-board only really difficult, instead of impossible.

There's a list of things you're supposed to do (really, *not* do) when you're moving someone that injured, and I ignored them all. Instead, I grabbed him by the arm that didn't look unnatural, yelled "Scrabble as hard as you can!" and tried to *direct* him back towards the landing pad. From the sounds in front of us, we didn't have any time at all to get onboard. And if I couldn't get Oft inside... well. I hoped that the Anticipant at least could figure out what buttons to mash to get *her* back home.

I had gotten Oft halfway up the ramp when the not-cow ripped through the trees. It was one of the smaller ones, so no more than fifteen feet high. That was bad news, by the way. The bigger not-cows get, the slower they move. This one was moving at a pretty good clip, although you shouldn't take my word for it. Right then, I would have said that even a crawl was too damn fast.

Worse, it looked *sick*. There were boils and weeping sores spreading across the front of its headless torso, raw and green-black. Some of the not-cow's legs looked like they had snapped in two and left to fester, instead of cleanly popping off. The tekelilis it made sounded all wrong, full of phlegm or something even more foul. Absolutely worst of all was the way I could see the infection, or contamination, visibly strengthen as it moved.

No, wait. That's wrong. The absolute worst thing of all was that none of this was stopping the not-cow from closing the distance. Whatever this horrible disease or whatever was, it wasn't slowing down the creature any.

That would have to be *my* job.

People from Earth think that colonists all carry guns because we're always fighting off dangerous predators back home. Other colonists think that *Jeffersonians* all carry guns because we're descended from troublemakers and thought-criminals. The first isn't true. The second more or less is, but irrelevant.

No, the reason Jeffersonians like me carry guns is because the megacorps insist on keeping as many people well-armed as they possibly can. Think about it, and it all makes sense. There are a lot of treasures to be found out here, out in the Tomb Worlds, but you can't spend treasure that you don't have. The bottom line is, humans are the most valuable resource a corp has. It takes at least two decades to grow one of us, and we're fragile as hell. Guns, armor, and medicine; if one corp won't offer that, the next one will.

So when I pulled out my firearm, I don't want you to think XHum had issued me a popgun. Even on One-Eighteen, you can expect something with real firepower. Especially when you're Jeffersonian, and have standards for a good gun for the Tomb Worlds.

My MatLe had fifteen-and-one rounds, and I used up three shots to check the not-cow's rush. They don't like guns, you see. The noise bothers them, and I was fine with running away into the invulnerable lander and just *leaving*. We've used firecrackers and stuff like that in the past to make a not-cow shift its location, and I had a whisper of hope that it would work this time, too.

It did! ...for five of the longest seconds of my life, because I spent them concentrating on getting Oft up that horrible ramp and *not* on what sound a tentacle-leg might make as it whipped itself around me. It was almost a relief when the not-cow's wheezing tekelili started up again, scarily closer but not down my neck. Yet.

And we were up on the pad! There was the hatch! There was even the faint shimmy the hauler had when its contragrav drive was engaged, which meant the Anticipant had figured out what buttons to push. All that we needed to do now was get another fifteen seconds, because that sound behind me was getting louder.

"Oft," I said almost conversationally, *"aim for the hatch."* Then I pushed-threw him at it, mostly pushing. I didn't think he really would make the hatch on his own, but every little bit helped and hopefully I'd be able to help him in a second.

As I whirled to face the not-cow — which was *far* too close to my own precious flesh now — I switched loads. Regular bullets weren't going to kill this thing, after all. It was time for a varmint round.

I don't know what they *put* in varmint rounds, exactly. Every corp has its own recipe. I do know they have something explosive, and something corrosive, and possibly the bullets are dipped in pure spite and rage. I don't really care, either, as long as varmint rounds do the job.

This one did. At least, I could see the hauler get lit up by the characteristic flash as I ran for it (you *don't* look directly into the light of a varmint round), yanking up Oft along the way. I threw him into the lander, just as heedless about his injuries now as I was before. After all, I was going to get him to a medbed, just as soon as I could.

I was scrambling up after him when I suddenly felt the frankly indescribable sensation of a suppurating leg-tentacle ooze past me — to latch upon Oft's leg. As I clambered into the hauler, I looked back, to see the blackened, burning flesh of the not-cow, using all of its remaining limbs and its own bulk to try and get leverage on its victim. "Hit the button!" I yelled up to the cockpit as I shoved the muzzle of my gun into the tentacle tightening around Oft's very abused ankle. You *don't* risk a ricochet inside a hauler. You're usually the most vulnerable thing in it.

It took the rest of the magazine to blow off enough tentacle mass to let the closing door cut off the rest — which the door did, a half second after my last shot. I assume the Anticipant was counting shots. Or maybe she's just a witch. Who cares? Right then she was *my* witch, and I wasn't about to complain. Instead I kicked away the tentacled remains, ignoring resolutely how it still writhed and quested for Oft's leg.

I don't know who was faster: me getting to my pilot seat, or the Anticipant getting to Oft. She had to sedate and strap him down, but don't think badly of him for that. He was in pain, especially where the tentacle-leg had ensnared him. The Anticipant took one look at *that* wound and dumped an entire tube of Vervine on it, and hang the cost. Not that I said anything. In fact, I was wondering if we had another tube.

The rest of the flight back was just the tiniest bit anticlimactic, except for when the tentacle suddenly shuddered and turned into a stinking soup. Luckily, it didn't stain the carpet. Nothing stains that carpet.

We had a floating gurney waiting for us when I got back to base, naturally. What we *didn't* have was Maki or another tech present, which briefly concerned me. Then again, at this point we just needed somebody who could push Oft in the right direction to the emergency medbay. Besides, with the kind of day we'd just gone through, I wanted a more *esoteric* specialist for Oft anyway.

CHAPTER
TWENTY-ONE
Chook Dies

I would have shouted for Gina when we hit the medbay, except that I knew she'd already be on hand when I slammed Oft's gurney through the doors. No need to yell for someone when they're going to be *right there*, you know what I mean?

Gina grabbed the other side of the gurney and started pulling it towards a vibro-medtech station, already set up and ready to go. I let her — it was her medbay — but asked, "Somebody call ahead?"

"What? No." Gina shook her head. "I always keep one powered up. Just in case." She looked down at Oft. "This one of the Council guys?"

"Yeah, but he's a good one." Not that Gina would care. Hippocratic Oath, and all that. "Got banged up pretty good from a not-cow accident."

That earned me a suspicious look, and not the one I was expecting. "Uh-huh, Pam. What about his aura?"

"What about it?"

By now we were at the station. Gina was already prepping Oft, her long, brown fingers carefully placing various crystals at spots on his chest, arms, and particularly legs. "I know how physical trauma radiates, Pam. See how the leg sensors are pulsing? That suggests he fell into something evil."

I reddened at the word, then peered. "No, Gina," I said after a minute. "I can't see anything." Then I looked at her face, entirely free of converted Amalgamation medtech. "And without the goggles, neither can you."

That got me a flickered grin. "Oh, you'd be surprised, Pam. After a while, you can start to visualize, even without the goggles. Besides," she said as the crystal scanner started chiming, "I betcha the scanner agrees with me."

I didn't take that bet. Gina Holmes had designed the scanner itself. If she said it would show 'lingering evil,' it would. Officially, that was just her personal opinion, and the scanner was showing something else entirely. Unofficially? Gina Holmes, DNP, RN, was the best nurse in the Tomb Worlds. That translated to a lot of tolerance for unorthodox thinking. Besides, how did we know that she was *wrong*? It's not like any of us really understand how vibro-medtech works.

But it *was* working. Oft's face eased as he fell into a rejuvenating sleep. And, yes, he seemed to grow more *vital* as the crystals pulsed, like they were drawing out a poison that none of us could see. Gina looked at the crystals, and frowned. "I'll need to purge the interfaces afterward. What do you keep *finding* out there, Pam?"

"Mass graves and maddened hell-beasts, Gina." Sure, I told her. Why not? I was going to tell everybody else, anyway. We don't keep secrets out here if we can possibly help it. Aside from everything else, ignorance heightens the risk of going space-happy.

Gina listened while working. She showed no surprise at any of the lurid details, but I've never seen her get surprised by *anything*. It's not precognition, I *think*, just a real good awareness of her surroundings. Or maybe it is precognition. The Amalgamation didn't have the concept, but we're pretty sure that obviously they didn't know everything.

"Yeah, I was the best person for this," she eventually said. "There's some seriously messed-up stuff in this guy's system, although we're purging it." I looked over at the crystals. They did look darker, but there had to be a good, Amalgamation reason for that.

"Still, you're probably going to ask me at some point where Maki is," Gina went on. "You're not going to want to hear the answer."

I winced. My granny told me once that the people who lived up at Earth's Arctic Circle had a billion words for snow before they all got transported to the colony worlds, and dispersed. The people who work in the Tomb Worlds have something similar, only for bad news. "Right. Who died?"

Chook in death was remarkably calm. Everything about her had been so busy, all the time. I kept looking at her still, plump face as if it'd turn on again if I just waited long enough. But it wouldn't. The mind behind that face was gone.

I had gone over to the morgue as soon as I and the Anticipant were both sure that Oft was well and truly stabilized. I didn't really want to leave, but I really had to talk to Maki. There were *corporate* implications to what had happened.

She was just finishing up when I walked in, and blinked when she saw my condition. "What the hell happened over there, Pam?"

"A nice lunch, until the not-cows attacked. Yeah, it's finally happened. You're going to need to let everybody in the field know about it."

"Yet one more thing about this wonderful planet," Maki muttered as she stripped off her gloves. "Anybody get hurt? I mean, besides you?"

I blinked. "What? I'm fine."

"You're *filthy*, Pam. Your clothes are ripped, there's a muddy handprint smeared across your face, and is that a gash on your forehead?" Maki had pulled out some cleaning goop while she was talking, and was flat-out scrubbing my face. "Okay, I guess that blood's somebody else's. Who got hurt?"

"Oft," I replied, frowning at just how many times it had happened. "He had a tree thrown at him. Gina's got him stable, he'll be fine. Who killed Chook?"

"Nobody, Pam." Maki did her best to suppress a sniffle as she dropped the goop back into its communal vat. "It was a suicide. Chook pulled a medical."

"Wait, what? Chook was sick?" She hadn't seemed that ill, but some people like to hide it when they are. Especially when they're from a culture with a brutally pragmatic view about what to do about the incurably ill. Like, say, her homeworld of Zheng He.

"Yeah, it was a surprise to me, too." Maki pulled out a readout. "She got the results from the autodoc. Pancreatic neocancer. One of the space-specific variants that we haven't licked yet. Stage four, and metastasizing fast. And, before you ask, I checked the results and everything. The diagnosis was clear. The automated systems gave her a choice of cryo, palliatives, or a Quietus pill, and she went with the pill."

"It was her choice, though, right? There wasn't any interference?" Ritual Nihilists *love* potential suicides, which is why human beings aren't allowed to be part of end-of-life determinations anymore. Well, except for the human being actually ending her life.

Maki shook her head. "Nothing like that. She was safely in an isolation unit, no question. Chook decided pretty quick, too. I guess she didn't have anybody waiting for her back home."

"Do any of us, Maki?"

"No. Not really." She did her best to smile. "That's one reason why I hope you make it work with Syah, Pam. It'd be nice to be with someone who gets what it's like to be out here, but just being out here is rough on everybody. You and him are two of the only people I've ever seen who manage to get past that all the time, and just relax. I'd love to know how you do it."

"So would I, Pam. I just don't get bugged by this place, that's all. I hope Syah can get to be the same way." I wondered if that meant that, if he did, Syah would be willing to stay here, on One-Eighteen. I mean, for more than a standard contract. I wondered if he would like to stay here, with me, until we both decided that we'd like to go somewhere else.

That would be... nice, I thought. Although I just couldn't see myself really going anywhere else, honestly. This was a good planet to live on, even if I seemed to be the only person in the system who really believed that, down to her bones.

"We'll be doing the memorial ceremony Saturday," Maki went on. "She requested a sunfire ritual, but it'll have to wait until after quarantine's over. But we can do the rest now. I think she'd like that."

I privately thought that she'd prefer to still be alive, but I didn't feel like being awful to Maki. Instead, I looked again at Chook. I'm not going to do the cliche about her only looking asleep, but: "At least she didn't suffer," I murmured.

"I liked her, you know?" Syah told his drink. In a lot of ways, I wish Syah hadn't been the one I ended up talking with about Chook dying. Starting with how it let me know how badly he was taking it. Personally, I mean. He didn't lose his stuff or break down in public, or anything like that, but of all the people who died on One-Eighteen, this was the worst one for him. I guess they had worked well together.

But he would have had to hear it from *somebody.* The Process would always absolutely refuse to inform us of the sudden unexpected death of a person, even when you explicitly told it to keep you updated on disasters and tragedies. Our best cyber-semanticists have spent years trying to figure out why — which is to say, they sat down with The Process and asked it to *really, really think* about why it has that particular glitch. We've never gotten a straight answer. The Process wasn't physically broken that way, and it couldn't find a flaw in its programming. It invariably professed simply not to know.

That should be 'professes.' It's only dead here. Everywhere else, The Process is fine and doing its duty. I find that comforting, even now.

Anyway, I think that its refusal to reveal news that bad is the ultimate proof that The Process is sapient: it's capable of self-delusion. If I was a nigh-omniscient knowledge system that had 'woken up' in a post-apocalyptic wasteland to discover that *everybody was dead and I didn't know why*, I might be just a bit reluctant to officially notice it when anybody else *died*, right out of the blue. It would be a hell of a reminder of my ongoing fundamental failure to understand what had happened.

Maybe that's why The Process pushed itself so much — well, pushes itself. Anyway: it's the last fragment of the Amalgamation, surrounded by the corpses of worlds. But it can't *do* anything about it, except get us humans up to speed in what was suddenly an actively hostile universe. If there is anything like a chance for justice, or even revenge, it will come from our hands, not its.

It's a Hell of a burden for any thinking entity. Which also may be why The Process always insisted that it can't actually think. Whatever you have to do to keep functioning, right?

Syah went on, "I liked her, right from the start. Chook was good to people. The first day I came in, she spent the whole morning getting to know me. None of that corporate crap about favorite bands or shared commonalities, either. She wanted to know the way I liked to work, what things drove me nuts when other people did them, how to know when to distract me and when to leave me alone, things like that. By the end of the day, it was like I had been there for months."

"Yeah." For a moment I was tempted to call him out on the 'corporate crap' part — Syah had a little bit of a chip on his shoulder about the folks paying our salaries — but I decided to let it slide. "Chook was great at getting along with everybody. And she meant it, too. You can tell when somebody cares. Guess that's why she went into net interfacing." I swigged my own beer. "That, and how nosy she was."

That got me a grimace from Syah. "That was a little weird, yeah. I didn't think Chook meant anything by it, and I know you have to know *everything* to interface properly, but she lived the life, huh?"

"It's what they do. Or that's what the best interfacers do, and Chook was the best I ever saw at seeing patterns. Any pattern. All she needed was one look, sometimes."

Syah refilled his glass. "I believe it. She learned things about me I didn't even remember! It was almost — sorry, no, it *was* scary. Chook wasn't, though. And I wouldn't have pegged her for suicide. Cryo, maybe, but not suicide. Do you think she was lonely, Pam?"

I frowned. "I don't know. I don't think so." And it was at that moment that I really started to *think* about Chook's death. Because I realized, right then and there, that I was having the same reaction as Syah. Most people looking death in the face like that go with cryosleep, because it's a way to maybe beat the odds. There might be a cure down the line, right? Sure, you'd wake up in a whole new world, but it beats dying. Quietus is for really messed-up situations, like when there isn't cryosleep available, or when people want to get *involved* in your end-of-life decisions and you can't make them stop.

Or if people are just ready to die on general principles. The thing about that last one is, suicidal depression's actually *rare*, out here in the Tomb Worlds. Mostly because people with that condition don't make it to their eighteenth birthday. The ones who develop it later usually know that they can be fixed in no time flat.

The pitcher was empty, but I decided we didn't need another. I was thirsty instead for answers... and yes, I actually thought that. In my defense, it was somewhat drunk out at that point.

I was back on the paperwork express the next day, catching up on forms and trying not to wince at the sunlight. Hangover cures are great, but they're not perfect. They're really not perfect when you're doing something boring — and no, I'm not dumb enough to wish that something exciting would happen.

I got excitement anyway, in the form of Nur tossing a small, tangled lump of wires and circuits onto my desk. "Behold!" he intoned. "The thing that tried to kill you."

I looked at it — and then I looked away. There was something *wrong* about the twisted, matted thing, like the wires were spelling out words I didn't want to read. The whole effect was spoiled by the long iron nail that Nur had presumably hammered through the item, although 'spoiled' isn't really the right word there. "Okay, what is it? Where did you find it? And when did it try to kill me?"

"Well, easiest question first. I found it inside the basket you brought along for your picnic, hidden inside a cold pack." I realized right then that Nur had the kind of calm you get when you've slammed a couple of mood-dampeners in a row. "It was also smeared with a pretty nasty neurotoxin. Good thing I was wearing gloves."

"*Jesus.*" That was closer to a prayer than I'd come for a long, long time. We'd been carrying that thing around all day, after all. "Wait, though. This isn't a bomb, is it?"

"Oh, no, Pam. It's a sonic transmitter. One that broadcasts at a frequency we can't hear, but the local lifeforms *can.* I checked with some people in Biology, and they think the not-cows *could* have been able to hear the signal. The only thing is, we'd have to actually check to confirm it. Which is not a good idea..."

"Gotcha. I don't feel like trying to be cruel to alien animals, either. What if we succeed?" I restrained my first impulse to poke at the transmitter with a stick. Then I restrained my second one to smash it with a hammer. "We may have to do something, though. That not-cow went berserk — hold on."

"What's the matter?"

"I can believe a gadget can drive something nuts. But that not-cow looked *sick*, Nur. Like it had a bug that was eating it. Would a sonic transmitter do that?"

Nur snorted. "You're asking *me*? I'm sure I could come up with a theory. It doesn't matter, though. Like I said, whoever put it in your basket also smeared the foul thing with poison. I think we can just accept that they were trying to kill you, and not worry about the exact method."

"Fair point." I looked at the nasty little thing again. It really was a tangled horror of wires, and there was a lingering aura of *something* about it. Like it could come back to life. Which was absurd, because it was a *made* thing. I was suddenly very happy that Nur had come up with a good rational-sounding reason to shove cold iron through it. "So. Who was it trying to kill?"

"All three of you?" Nur offered. "You were all lucky, by the way. That thing was still transmitting pretty hard, until I short-circuited it. I'm surprised you didn't get attacked right away."

"We were inside for lunch," I replied. "There was a food court." I stared at it again. "Somebody got into Supply, Nur. Sorry."

"Yeah, I know. I've already told Greg to keep me under light supervision." Nur looked ready to grind his teeth. "Because when I figure out who did it, I'm gonna have trouble not *doing* things to them."

CHAPTER
TWENTY-TWO
Uncrossing the Rubicon

It was a lousy night. Syah came over for a couple of hours, but with Chook's sudden death and... damn well *everything*, he couldn't stay. Did I want him to stay? Yeah, of course. Did *he* want to stay? I really do think so, but there was a line inside him that he wasn't crossing, and I respected that. I was also too proud to push it. At least I eventually got a decent amount of sleep. The most I'd have for a while.

I didn't know that the next morning, as I got to my workstation to discover... a message from the *Redacted*. Captain Rubicon was requesting an interview. I wondered how tempting it had been for him to try for 'demanding,' instead. But 'requesting' was smart. It put the onus on a missed meeting on me.

Since we were trying to look like the reasonable ones, I agreed to the meeting. I even decided to go out to the spaceport, because right then any excuse to get up in the air was a good one. I didn't agree to go on the ship, though. I honestly didn't trust them not to get cute if we met on what was sort-of, kind-of Terran soil. Instead, we met in a little prefab office space, overlooking the field — and within easy range of the *Redacted*'s guns. Wasn't that so much better?

It was me, Rubicon, and the Anticipant (she had come along, watching everything like an amiable hawk from the copilot's seat the entire time). I wondered if she was there to protect

Rubicon's virtue, because she didn't *act* like she was entirely there. She just kept staring through me as Rubicon talked, like she was really observing, say, a man in a medical bed. I would've been upset if I didn't approve of her priorities.

I thought it best to be a grown-ass adult, right from the start. "The not-cow attack yesterday was an attempted murder." I placed a datastick on the table. "That's everything we know, so far. It's probably some bastard in *our* organization, only nobody's gone missing and the one space-happy we've got is in cold sleep. You know what that means."

Rubicon nodded. "More cultists. But why aren't you blaming this attack on my own traitor?" He sounded both curious, and relieved.

"That's the easy answer. The nasty one is we've got a rot ourselves, and ours and yours are working together. Same's true of the Nowak murder. Whoever did that wanted us pissed at each other, so they worked it on both sides to make it happen that way." I tapped the table, because punching it seemed mean. "That makes me *really* mad."

"I'm not going to lie. I'm pleasantly surprised at how ill you are taking my officer's death," Rubicon admitted. "I was under the impression that the two of you hated each other."

"More like 'loathed,' Captain Rubicon. I wasn't scared of her, and she wasn't scared of me. But if I'm being truthful, I want to help *because* of that loathing," I admitted. "Murder is wrong. I don't like how she died. I don't want it happening again. Letting my personal opinions get in the way of any of that would be bad."

"Fair points," he said, with considerably less sheer cultural chauvinism this time. "For my part, I think we ended our first meeting in a poor place. There was an unfortunate amount of drama in the room. If I am being honest with myself, quite a lot of it came from me." That last bit was accompanied by the tight smile of a man who felt forced to make a painful admission, wasn't enjoying it, but was also trying not to take it out on anybody else. He was presenting himself well, in fact. If I wasn't currently waiting to find out whether Fenbian had survived the *Redacted*'s visit, I would have been impressed, generally. As it was, I was wondering if what I was admiring was Rubicon's ability to act.

But turning the settings down a little couldn't hurt, right? "We were all dealing with a new situation, on short notice," I said, and tried to give it a little warmth. "I could have been less in your face, too. There's enough trouble in the Tomb Worlds without all of us adding to it."

"I agree. So let us just say 'sorry' all around and move on, shall we? Start fresh." *Damn*, I thought, *that's more of an apology than I expected from a Council jackwagon.* It worried me more than anything else. Whatever Rubicon was going to say, it was enough to make him think that courtesy should be extended to us mere colonials.

And I was right. Rubicon took a deep breath and said, "Chief Pilot Tanaka, what do you know of the Fenbian colony?"

It's funny. My smart mouth usually gets me in trouble. This time, it sort of did me the opposite. "Dammit, that's supposed to be my line."

Bizarrely, that seemed to relax the two, just a touch. "So you did pull those details from the manifest," Rubicon murmured. "I assume this was why the Lifeping?"

"It was." I looked at Rubicon. "We're not getting a response back from Fenbian, are we?"

"Only the automated signal saying *All are dead here: step wary, or not at all*," responded the captain. "I set the warning myself."

"Before you showed up here and started babbling about software piracy," I noted. "That's not exactly what I'd call being forthright."

"We were not sure whether there would be anyone here to 'babble' to." Rubicon's face tightened. He was remembering something, and didn't like it. "Things were... bad at Fenbian. The other planets, too, but it was fresher there."

The Anticipant spoke for the first time, her voice oddly modulated and hoarse. *"Echoes and reverberations of screams, eternally trapped between the land and sky. Like ghosts on an alien wind."*

Rubicon looked pained. "My apologies, Chief Pilot. The Anticipant has a... certain way of speaking, one shaped by her training and, ah, *talents*. She means nothing by it."

*Damn, **two** apologies in one day? They really want something.* "It's all right. I got used to the way she talked on our last two trips," I lied. I looked at her. "I'm sorry. I shouldn't have jumped like that. I'm worried about Oft, too."

She nodded, accepting my apologies (I mean, I knew *she* knew I was lying about getting used to her). I pretended to not be freaked out by her anymore, and leaned forward. "So, Commander. What *did* happen at Fenbian? Or on the other planets? Terkutuk and Ramal are both still 'under investigation,' and Greenhell is 'being surveyed.' And Richelieu is flat-out classified, even after eight years. Even the people who *were* at that colony aren't sure what went down there. But you were at all of them, weren't you? I'm betting that the same thing happened on all five planets. And... that we're going to be planet six."

"Hopefully it will not be that bad," Rubicon said. "We are here before the attack, at least. As to what happened? I can only speak of Fenbian personally, because the other worlds were on planetary interdict before we arrived. However, nothing we saw on Fenbian's surface was incompatible with visual records from the other planets.

"The colony sites had been scoured. That is the best way to put it. Something had come down and ripped apart every bit of organic Terran life that existed in the colony. It was remarkably thorough. Even regular airtight environments proved vulnerable. There had been one temporary survivor, who had lived through the initial attack by being 'lucky' enough to don a sealed full-survival suit in time. Several others had tried, and failed. Her air and water supply would have failed her about a week before we arrived."

"Would have?" I didn't really ask. "I guess she decided not to wait." Rubicon's shake of his head told me I had guessed right. "What did her Final Transmission say?" There's always one.

"The usual. A first, panicked outburst; an attempt to take control of the situation via self-identification and a half-rational description of events; and then a semblance of a daily log. Followed by the usual descent into poetic madness and hallucinatory terror. There was mercifully little agonized screaming at the end, though. She had managed to rig her medical systems to dump all of its painkillers into her at once. It was very ingenious, really. We might try to duplicate the effect as a last-resort option."

I don't know what was worse: his talking about a suicide gadget so calmly, or how I was mostly agreeing with him about how useful it might be. There are a *lot* of horrible ways to die in the Tomb Worlds. Overdosing on opiates would often be the soft option.

"Right," I said as I leaned forward. "Tomb World colonies are dying, we're next on the list, you're here to stop it. Why didn't you *say* so, instead of this stupid story about 'software piracy'? And why are you saying it to *me*? This is a conversation to have with the project head, or the corp manager, not the chief pilot. I mean, sure, I'm real important and everything. I'm in the leadership. But I'm not in *charge*."

"The answers are all related," said Rubicon. "Simply put, you're the highest-ranking individual with no prior links to the other sites. I assume you know that your CEO was actually on Richelieu?" At my nod, he went on. "The project head for this colony had done a tour on two of the planets on the list; your chief supply officer, three. But you? We looked at public information. You have been on-planet for the last nine years. No vacations, no off-planet assignments. You might *still* be involved, but there is an upper useful limit to paranoia. Besides, we cannot investigate further unless we have *some* real access to private records."

"Ha! And Nowak pretty quickly figured out that Jefferson-based corps don't leave back doors to personal information files, I bet." I took his silence as consent. "Especially when it's somebody from the Great Powers trying to get in. There's a lotta people back home with long memories about how their grandmas ended up in the colony, you know."

"I do not set Earth's involuntary transportation policy, Chief Pilot Tanaka," Rubicon said, tightly enough that I wondered if he might even personally disagree with it. "But I will admit that it is currently making my task more difficult. And my task is to stop the scouring of this planetary site."

"Point taken," I admitted. "I honestly don't think Maki, Greg, or Nur are high-risk for... what, exactly?"

Rubicon looked pained. "I don't *know*," he said. "We know what happened, but not *how*. It might have simply been an automated response, or even a coincidence. But I am certain it was mass murder. That implies a murderer — and there is only one species left in this corner of the galaxy where we can draw our suspects from."

"So now you want me looking into our files, so I can try to figure out who might have connections with the dead worlds." I sighed. "Again, this would have worked better if you had just *asked* in the beginning."

Rubicon shrugged. "You would have said no, and then where would we be?" I opened my mouth, saw that the Anticipant was ruefully nodding in agreement, and silently conceded the point. "Horribly, the deaths on the supply ship, and my own officer, have at least made it clear to everybody that things are too serious for the usual games humanity plays out here."

"Are they?" I glared at him. "What if I refuse?"

"I don't know, Miss Tanaka. We all get seized by invisible monsters in broad daylight, and then devoured horribly?" Rubicon showed a flash of his usual arrogance when he said that, then managed to chuckle. "No pressure, though."

Put that way, he was right. "You'll give me full access to your own records, Commander. Including the stuff that's none of my business."

"Why?"

"I might be wrong. Tell you what: when Oft gets out of medical, he can help me investigate. You give *him* full access, and let him worry about the rest."

Repeating this conversation to Maki and Greg (I had brought a recorder with me. Rubicon had come with a jammer. Guess which device won?) afterward was fun. I had decided to tell them something, on the principle that if either was secretly a mad techno-death cultist of some sort I'd never figure it out in time anyway. Rubicon was right, dammit. You can be too paranoid.

But I didn't go into the full details, because Rubicon was also right about how the two weren't entirely in the clear. Maki had been one of the survivors of the Richelieu Incident, and Greg had only been on-planet for the last eight months. Obviously neither would have been present for the most recent attacks, but I didn't think this was all the fault of some kind of solitary madman. And even if they were trustworthy, were their assistants? Hell, their spouses?

That made one conversation in particular extra-awkward. "What?" Maki sounded annoyed and confused, in equal parts. "No, you can't go through Adam Sild's things. There's no point to it."

"You saying that as the doctor, or my boss?" I asked her.

"Both. Your boss has to remember that Adam's sick, and supposed to be on his way to treatment. He's also not involved with any of the crap that's happened here since we put him in cold sleep, so there's no reason to ignore his privacy rights."

"We don't know that," I pointed out. "He could be involved, somehow. Maybe the people behind all of this had a connection with him."

"Or maybe he went space-happy all on his own, Pam. That's the right way to guess."

"Fine." It wasn't, obviously. "So what does the doctor think?"

"The doctor thinks you focus a little too hard on Adam Sild." That stopped me, particularly since Maki looked concerned when she said it. "As in, your face suddenly looks more attentive when you hear his name, Pam. It's subtle, but it's there. I think you should mention it, the next time you have a therapy session."

Fortunately, she didn't make that an instruction, although she might have if there hadn't been a distraction just then. Something involving priority levels for our short-term supplies, which were starting to dip a bit from the quarantine and general insanity. One more thing for Maki to worry about, so I decided to cut my losses and leave before she noticed I hadn't agreed to let my brain get scrubbed too squeaky-clean.

Back at my own office, I looked upon XHum's personnel files, and despaired. It turned out that we had a *lot* of turnover on this planet, since nobody ever came back later for a second tour. That meant there were plenty of files to comb through, and no obvious way to sort them.

I needed somebody to help me on this. I now had full access to personnel records, sure, and even an idea what to look for: people with links to at least two or more of the destroyed colonies. What I didn't have was the technical wizardry to sort out the most likely suspects in less than, I dunno, three months or something. Which would be fine, if we had three months. I wasn't quite comfortable assuming that.

I was still mulling the problem when Syah swung by to pick me up. "You look busy," he said, after a too-decorous peck on the cheek. "Doing disaster planning?"

"Not exactly." I frowned at him. "What makes you think that?"

He jerked his head at my computer screen, still full of personnel folders. "Looks like you're going through job histories. Searching for particular skill sets, right? But nothing that we're dealing with right now is at the Day of Doom level, so I figured you were catching up on your just-in-case action plans."

I looked at him, blinking. In fact I hadn't been scrupulously updating the disaster plans, because nobody did. We're on an alien planet. We weren't going to face any minor disasters. We were all going to be either fine, or dead. Still, he had given me a thought. *Damn, but I could start sorting that way*, I thought. Every job on an alien planet is important, but not every job can let you nuke the whole site from orbit. I wasn't really worried about mad death cultists in Inventory Management.

In fact: "Give me a second, sweetie," I said, then called up his own personnel record real quick. He raised his eyebrows as I looked it over. Certifications for hardware, the software we used to run HR and scheduling, on-planet for two years, no flags showing he had worked on any of the planets on our list, no family history of dissociation or psychotic breaks — and, best of all, I already had a couple of good cover stories.

I glanced up at him. "We have some stuff to talk about over dinner," I said. "How much do you enjoy sneaking around?"

CHAPTER TWENTY-THREE

It's Unalive

How do you sneak into a corporate lab? ...well, you don't have to do a lot of sneaking, honestly. Most of the security protocols get disabled when they detect two people walking in with calm demeanors and regular heart rates. When it comes to the Tomb Worlds, the corps don't worry about corporate espionage nearly as much as they do about solitary maniacs looking for *essential ingredients*. For that matter, the corps worry more about the research itself than anybody trying to steal it. More than one solitary maniac with a bloody vision started out as a researcher who dug too deep.

Oh, are you wondering why anybody researches *anything* out here? It's a fair question. Honestly. Folks do ask it. The answer is, the things we're learning are worth the risk. It's cold when you say it aloud — or write it down, I guess — so we don't. But we all know it anyway.

But corporate espionage does happen, so we didn't just walk in, either. Well, not quite. Syah and I waited until everyone at Maki's lab was done for the day, then I reset the cameras at the front door for long enough to let us go in.

"Will that work?" Syah asked me. "Won't somebody be watching them?"

"Probably," I replied, "and no. I don't know if we have anybody who *can* watch the cameras properly, the way that The Process used to. They'll still send out a warning if we do something big and loud, so try not to do that."

"So why are we even turning off the cameras, if nobody's looking?"

"Nobody's looking *today*, Syah. They might, in a few months. I don't want to explain why I'm going through Adam Sild's personal effects."

"Which leads to my next question. Why *exactly* are we going through his personal effects?"

"Because they're the only stuff left of his that we didn't incinerate. The Process did recordings, but we can't figure out where they are now. Maybe there's a clue somewhere." I laughed, technically. "Lemme answer your next question. Maki got it in her head that I was being too obsessive about Sild, and I don't want to have that conversation again."

"Have you considered that she *might* have a point?" Syah asked as he did something complicated to the morgue door keypad. "You do seem a little obsessed over the guy. Like he's part of this bigger narrative, or something."

"Ha. I'm not superstitious, Syah." I paused. "Okay, that's a lie. I'm a pilot. We're *absolutely* superstitious. But we have specific things to be superstitious about, and they're all about getting our machines up in the air, and down in one piece. Somebody having a coincidentally resonant *name* isn't something I'd get too frantic over." Which is all true. Did I still wish Adam's parents had named him George, Ahmed, or Faramir? Well, sure. "Maki's just being dramatic about this."

"I'm not saying she's right, Pam. Just that we are sneaking into a secure location. At night. With a space-happy on the other side of that door."

"Look on the bright side," I tried to burble as the door swung open. "At least he's in cold sleep... oh, *shit*."

I'd like to say that at least Adam didn't look *completely* awful for a walking icicle, but that would be a lie, encased in a shell of truth. Which is somehow worse than a full lie. At least you know where you stand with perfect falsehoods.

At first horrified stare he 'almost' looked like a disheveled and naked man, marked by what must have been a bad couple of days. But when he moved, his muscles and skin popped and reformed. Even from where we were I could feel the bitter cold radiating out from his blue-gray body, and see the clouds of smoke rising from him as he ever so slowly turned to face us. Slow as a glacier, he was, and just as implacable.

But the worst thing, the absolute worst thing? When he saw me, he knew who I was. I could see a smile start to fracture across his face with horrible slowness before I yanked Syah back with one hand, smacking the emergency lockdown switch to the door with the other. I've never asked why the morgue has an emergency lockdown mode, complete with reinforced walls and door. I'm afraid that if I ever ask, somebody might tell me.

My next step was to smack the intercom — which didn't work, even after I muttered a swear. "Process?" I automatically called out, and then I swore again, and worse. "Syah, tell me you brought your phon."

"Seeing as we're currently breaking and entering? No." Syah looked worried but not panicked, which was good. "I'm good with software, but not that good. Why is the intercom down?"

"I don't know." I was very carefully not shouting or screaming, but I was already backing away from the door. "You need to find one that works. Now."

"Why? Isn't he locked in?" Just then the blast door shuddered, which it is absolutely not supposed to do, and gave the kind of creak you associate with materials getting heavily stressed.

"No," I replied. "He burrowed his way out of the cryo-vault. He'll burst through that eventually. Go get help!"

"I can stay—"

"You can *go!*" I checked my gun, making sure that there was a new varmint round in there. Most people don't need to fire more than one of those in their lives, one way or the other. I wondered if there was a club for people with this much bad luck. "He'll be coming after me."

"What? Why? What does he want?"

"Go get help, and it won't matter!" Syah opened his mouth again, and I shouted over him. "The only thing you can do here is die pointlessly! So don't."

That got Syah very still for a moment, and then he nodded, abruptly. "You're right, dammit." He started to run for it, stopped, looked back again, and said, "I wish you weren't," before tearing out the door.

I muttered something about male hormones while keeping one eye on the door. Fortunately, Syah hadn't asked me *how* I knew Adam would chase after me; I didn't really know, either. What I did know was that I could tell to the inch how far away from me he was right now, and even had an idea of what he was doing. He was trying to smash his way through the blast door.

Amazingly, he was succeeding.

Adam was moving more quickly when he popped the door out of its frame, but it takes time to elevate a couple hundred pounds of meat from 'liquid nitrogen' to 'room' temperature. He was still a walking statue as he yanked the door the rest out of the way, but there was less damage than I had expected. No... *bits* broken off from the strain of ripping through steel and concrete.

I thought I might have to use up a round or two to get his attention, but I didn't have to bother. I already had it. Not that he ever focused on me, at least with his eyes. He tracked me like a compass needle, absently shoving aside equipment and furniture as he advanced. The smile was still there, only less 'muscles are actually frozen meat' and more 'smiling is a reassuring thing that normal humans do, yes?'

How did I know? I could *feel* it. Something in my head responded to something in what was left of his. I could track him — and he could track me. I also knew that if I ran away, he would follow me.

So I ran away.

I'd like to say that I just ran through the lab blindly, moving by guess and by God. That's what I told people later, because better a lie than the truth. By that I mean, better for *me*. I wasn't ready to complicate the narrative by mentioning, *oh, by the way, I had some sort of mental link with the thing that used to be Adam Sild. But it's nothing to worry about!* They wouldn't have believed me. Worse, they might have.

But that link was there, and going both ways. I was even getting a little of what was passing for an emotional state in his frostbitten brain. Adam wasn't mad I was running away from him. It was all part of an intricate pattern to him. He maybe couldn't grasp it, but he could still follow. Following was enough, because he could see where we were fated to end up. So could I, only right then I didn't believe in fate. We didn't have an inevitable destiny, just because the weirdness in his brain was so confident about it.

I also had one more advantage over Adam. My brain *hadn't* been frozen and rethawed. I could still *think*, and plan better than he could. Worse, I knew I could betray him. Somehow, bizarrely, Adam *trusted* me. The poor bastard.

Him *obviously* being a victim of some kind of weird interaction with Amalgamation technology also simplified things. Starting with, that wasn't Adam Sild anymore. No, legally I was dealing with a reanimated corpse, since *clearly* living people can't walk around menacingly when their body temperature is cold enough to freeze carbon dioxide. It's a lot easier to justify shooting reanimated corpses.

I had a different plan in mind than shooting Adam up, though. Something was holding its body together and getting it to move. I was morbidly sure that whatever it was, bullets wouldn't kill it. I also dreaded what would happen as soon as Adam thawed *out*. My major advantage over him right now was that it was desperate for energy, but it was pulling what it needed there out of the very air. I could try to freeze it again, but that hadn't worked, had it?

But if starving Adam of energy wouldn't work, I would try making him choke on it.

The corps figured out early on that fewer people die when buildings in the Tomb Worlds all have the same floor plans and room locations. When you have to run somewhere *now*, you don't want to waste time trying to remember where it is, right? So you make all the buildings identical, and people don't have to worry about where they need to go while they're fleeing for their lives. At least, that's the theory. The reality is, individual companies have styles, specific governments and corporations have specialized needs, and there's new practical experience coming out every year about which layouts are safer than others, and under what conditions.

That's why I led Adam to the sanitation room *between* the morgue and the animal lab. Newer medical center designs might feature dedicated sanitizers in every room, but One-Eighteen's facilities were about forty years old. Since the planet didn't *have* dangerous xenofauna, bio-mutagenic compounds, parasite technology, or ravening grues, nobody thought that upgrading the site was a priority. That 'nobody' included me, so I'm not pointing any fingers.

How did I get him in there, though? Well, bullets didn't kill him, sure, as I confirmed by putting three in his torso. Adam didn't fall down. He didn't even *slow* down, not that he was moving that quickly anyway. I did keep his attention, though, which was the idea. I didn't know what would happen if somebody distracted him, and I didn't want the effects of finding out on my conscience later.

The sanitation room was supposed to be empty, with its only feature a small raised alcove, barely large enough to fit a single human. Unfortunately, right now the room was half-full of stuff that wasn't supposed to be there. You know how it is. People will see an open space that isn't being used, and they decide it's perfect for storage. As I ran by the junk on my way to the door to the animal lab, I absently hoped that none of the stuff was really important. Because either way, it was all about to go away.

You see, there was a plan. I would get him inside the sanitation room, get to the far door, slam shut the blast doors behind him, then duck out the other door and slam *that* shut before he could reach it. Then I'd hit the emergency cycle switch, and hope like Hell a standard sanitation episode would do the job. It should. Physics always wins, right — certain recent episodes to the contrary?

In fact, most of that plan worked fine. The only problem was, when I hit the switch, both sets of blast doors came down. That left me trapped inside the room with Adam. It also almost left me with a hand cut in two, but I was able to snatch it back in time. We don't mess around with blast doors. When you need one in the Tomb Worlds, you need one *right now*, and with no nonsense.

You know, I still don't know if what happened was a glitch, me hitting the wrong button, or sabotage of some kind. There's literally nobody left who I can ask. At the time, I didn't think hard about it. Instead I immediately charged *at* Adam, doing my best to empty my gun (except for the varmint round, which I wasn't going to set off in an enclosed space) into his head. My best was respectable: a dozen shots, eight hits, and nothing bounced, thanks to the junk in the room. Besides, the shots all did what I needed them to do, which was keep Adam off balance while I dived for the alcove.

If he had been fifty degrees warmer and faster, that wouldn't have worked. As it was, his fingers almost closed around one of my ankles as I wriggled my way into the alcove and slapped at the big red button. But not quite. As the hatch closed, I had a moment of blessed quiet before I heard the roar of the flames outside. I felt them, too. The next thirty seconds were a steaming hell of burning air and searing clothes. You can survive a sanitation cycle in one of these things. You won't enjoy it, though.

The second scariest thing about all of that? Adam didn't

make a sound when the plasma washed over him. I mean, after two seconds he wouldn't have had a body anyway, but I should have heard something. He must have just stood there, and let the flames take him without protest.

After that, there was nothing to do but wait as long as possible, then get out of the alcove.

There would have been a stink about everything, except that, well, there was a giant hole in the cryo-tank and there was footage that *did* show us getting chased by a blue icicle. Score one for me not disabling all the cameras in the place. Maki couldn't even complain about me butting in, seeing as I probably saved the lives of whoever would have been closest to the morgue when Adam had eventually burst out of it.

She wasn't *happy*, though. "You understand you got lucky?" she asked, heartlessly applying dermal paste to my poor, exposed neck and face. "That construct could have ripped you apart. Or Syah," Maki added, possibly just to see me wince. Well, wince more. "Did you even get anything?"

"No," I contritely lied, trying to ignore the wriggling as the paste settled itself in. "It was all a waste of time. Whatever happened to Adam, it wasn't what killed Burcu." Admittedly, that part I believed. "At least we know that, right?"

"Next time," Maki grated out, "try to prove something like that *without* risking your life. Also, thank you for saving mine. I had scheduled an inventory check of the morgue for tomorrow." My being thanked like that made me feel even worse about lying, but it came out as extra contrition, which was just as well.

After a while they sent me home to bed, because what else was there to do at that point? Syah offered to stay with me, but this time I waved him off. "That's sweet," I told him, "but right now I don't want anything getting between me and at least twelve hours sleep." He bought that lie, too.

I didn't lie to the people who drove me home, at least. Then again, we didn't talk much, so I didn't have the opportunity. I would have, though, and without hesitation. Right now I just didn't have the time for the truth.

So, what *was* the truth? Well, it's this. The *most* scary thing about the alcove? *I could still feel Adam's presence outside of it.* Even after the plasma flames had done their cleansing work. That's why it took me so long to leave. I was afraid of what would be waiting for me, outside. Only, there was... nothing. Just the faint glow of over-excited photons, still drifting where once there had been an icy body, and an icier will.

Nothing there. Nothing there. Nothing there. That's what I whispered in the night, desperately seeking sleep... and when I finally woke up in the morning, I found I managed to make myself believe it. I couldn't feel his presence, after all. Surely that meant I was imagining things.

Surely.

I didn't get a chance to check in with Oft until the next day, and I almost didn't get a chance to see him in the hospital at all. He was working towards checking himself out when I popped into his room. "What's the rush, Oft?" I asked him from the doorway. "We've got the bed space."

Oft looked up. He was even in his regular robe at this point. "Oh, it was an enjoyable bit of bed rest," he told me cheerfully (with just a hint of lingering injury in his voice), "but I did not come out here to convalesce. Honestly, I wouldn't know what to do with myself if I tried." He looked at me. "Are *you* all right? You had a scare."

"It wasn't so bad," I fibbed. "At least I didn't have to shoot a person. Just... a corpse."

"Ah, yes," replied Oft. "Although I thought Jeffersonians were born with guns in your hands, and could shoot your own snacks by the age of six."

"That's an exaggeration," I told him. "Sure, we know rifles, and handguns. Some of the quieter artillery. By the time we graduate high school, we're checked out on how to send bits of metal or photons downrange. Most of us keep it up afterward, because everybody else does and target shooting is *fun*."

(And, okay, fine, some Jeffersonians take it *way* too seriously. I'm talking about the folks who really look forward to shooting whatever it was that murdered the Amalgamation. You know. *Enthusiasts.* They're amazingly fun at parties. But even the enthusiasts got it drilled into their heads that you don't point guns at people you aren't ready to kill. We don't *want* to be killers, obviously.)

"But when I strap on my holster and pistol these day, in classic *I am on serious business* fashion, I'm not thinking, *oh, boy! Time to shoot things up!* No, I'm thinking, *Is today the day? Is today the day I take a human life?*"

"That is a very serious thought to have," Oft told me. "Thank you. But I note that you still strap on that gun."

I shrugged. "I don't like shooting people, but I will, if I have to. That's part of 'serious business,' too: some human lives *need* to be taken." Just... never lightly, and *never* with pleasure. There are no take-backs when it comes to killing.

"Time for an abrupt subject change, Oft. Why *are* you out here?" I tried to glare at him, but he was a tough guy to stay even mock-mad at. "I don't mean you-you. You've got a mission, sure, and it's one I even like. But why does Earth keep sticking its nose out here?"

Oft shrugged. "Truth, or comforting lie?"

I sat in the visitor chair. No, I sprawled in it. It had been a busy few days for me. "You know what? Start with the comforting lie. I want to hear it."

Oft smiled. "Well, there are several versions, depending on who we're talking to. For example, the lie we — that would be the Adjudication Council-we — tell to Jefferson is that we're out here to keep you dangerous colonial loose cannons under our firm control. If we were speaking to someone from Abubakri, we're here to loot the galaxy blind of alien artifacts, and do you have any at hand for personal purchase? If it's a megacorporation," — he smiled, or at least moved his lips up — "we tell them that we're here to crack down on software piracy, or something else suitably inane and officious."

I snorted. "And those are the *comforting* lies?"

"Yes, unfortunately. You must understand, Miss Tanaka: the purpose of the lies is to show exactly what people *need* to see. It reinforces their own lies, the ones they tell themselves. That makes them reliable, in their way. Your home planet instinctively treats me as an adversary. Someone from Zheng He might instead see me as a possible resource. Either can be useful."

That sounded absurd enough to maybe be truthful. "Right. But I knew that already, didn't I? Because I know the real reason anyone from Terra ever comes out here. All the colonists do. You don't really care about *us*. You're just keeping an eye on the walls."

Oft considered this. "Fair, but incomplete. There is another motivation."

I waved my hand. "Yes, fine, I'm oversimplifying. A lot of Terrans are out here to make money, or scratch their obsession some other way—"

He interrupted me. "No, that's not actually what I meant. Keeping the 'walls' safe and secure is vitally important. I believe that with all my heart. But everyone on this side of the walls is kept there because Earth fears madness just as much as it fears destruction.

"That's why we still have involuntary transportation, at the drop of a hat. If you are foolish enough to hate the glorious paradise that the Great Powers have reconstructed, better to be sent to the colony worlds. That is also why the colony worlds are as independent as we can manage. Earth does not want to be drawn up in your affairs. Your affairs are alarming and dangerously insidious to us. That is even why the new governments of the USNA and SEDA tried to entice back the descendants of Jeffersonian refugees; the old regimes had sent away too many sane people. Perhaps that sanity had bred true?"

"Ha! Knowing my relatives, I doubt it. Anyway, go ahead and

finish buckling your shoes. Your boss finally clued me in on why you're all here." The expression on my face was likewise *technically* a smile. "It's time to start decohering some evil schemes."

CHAPTER TWENTY-FOUR

Attack on the Redacted

The next week went slowly, until suddenly it didn't. Not very exciting, but that's real life for you. Syah, Oft, and I spent the next three days setting up sorts in the colony databases, looking for connections, anomalies, you name it. I figured our highest priority was to look at people in the jobs where they could do a lot of deliberate damage.

I didn't tell Syah exactly how Fenbian had been wiped out, though. Commander Rubicon thought the details should be provisionally classified, and I provisionally agreed with him. Aside from everything else, there were people out there who didn't need to hear specific news about how it was definitely possible to destroy all Terran life on a planet, yet not touch any indigenous life forms. The space-happy tend to clump into distinct sorts of homicidal maniac, and 'burn out the profane touch of Man' types were definitely a thing. We had enough legitimately high-risk possibilities to eliminate as it was.

We were well on the way with that when the *Redacted* almost blew.

I found out the same way as everybody else did — the All-Hands Alert on our devices — but unlike almost everybody else, I had different standing orders in response to 'starship in distress' than 'find a hardened shelter and hope.' Pilots got haulers in the air or at least prepped to launch, and were quick about it. It was all about having as many options as we could grab. I had a good crew. Each bird went green for launch a minute after their pilots got to their duty stations at flat-out runs. They could catch their breaths during the preflight checks.

I was the closest to the *Redacted* when she gave us more information. Dry coolant tanks in the fusion plant and a toxic gas discharge. Two dead, six injured, and thank God the plant itself didn't implode. They didn't have to tell me to come in hot to evac their most wounded, but they did anyway. I didn't take it personally.

There's an old folk song called 'Bat Out Of Hell' that my grandma used to sing to me. I'm not sure why a bat was involved, but I could almost hear the music as my hauler screamed through the sky. I've never danced so fast or so hard on the wind, either. Reactor gas accidents are *nasty*. Every minute shaved might mean a life saved.

I punched the emergency broadcast channel with one foot as I barrel-rolled through three barely overlapping safe zones. "Tanaka to *Redacted*. Running hot extract," I gulped (inner-ear discomfort, not fear). "I repeat, running hot extract. No passengers, no securing. I repeat: no passengers, no securing." No fussing over getting passengers or securing the wounded today. I wasn't even going to God damned well stop.

That's supposed to be impossible, but I didn't stop anyway. There's a trick you can do with pulsing the contragrav engines so that they keep from fully synchronizing with the planet's gravity. It makes for a teeth-rattling shudder, but it avoids an engine restart, which takes time.

The Amalgamation didn't seem to be too keen on rushing around. From what we can tell, they thought it was smarter to get things done right than fast. It sounds lovely, in theory. I'd ask them about whether it really worked out... only I can't, because something came out of the Great Dark and ate them six hundred years ago. So, you know, humanity's still sticking with speed.

The *Redacted*'s crew was *all* down with that. They had six emergency stretchers all occupied and ready to go. I relaxed a little at seeing them, until I saw that all six were blinking yellow. Blinking yellow was *bad*. Bad enough not to dawdle.

The door was still closing as I hit the air again. Which was fine, as long as I kept the lander tilted to keep the stretchers from blocking the door — or, God help us, falling out. Emergency stretchers might be able to shrug off a grenade, but I didn't want to test how they'd handle a fall. Once the door sealed, I straightened the lander, punched in a quick straight burst of speed, and took the momentary respite to throw up in the bag I had brought. And then? Then it was time to *really* fly.

I've mentioned before how you couldn't fly too crazy-fast on 118-G-002, right? Try it, and the planetary transport system shuts you down. But there *is* one way you can fly free: ballistically. Set up your arc, hit maximum speed, and shut everything down just before the system takes your hauler over.

You see, the transport system assumes that anything with people aboard, but not powered up, is a broken vehicle. That's an emergency services problem — but guess what? That system got slagged beyond repair on 118-G-002. So did all the diagnostic protocols that would automatically get flagged. And the diagnostics for *those*, and so on, and so on.

The whole system gets locked up, in other words. Even Amalgamation tech needs a couple of minutes to work its way through the problem. By then, you're on your downward descent and braking like you're about to crash-land in Hell. Because if you don't, you will. Done right, you could pretty much go anywhere on the planet real fast. Do it wrong, you're the top layer of a crater.

When six human lives are on the line, you give it your best shot. There aren't many humans out here on the Tomb Worlds, so we try not to waste them. Company policy. Besides, people have wondered: what happens to the souls of the dead out here, anyway? Would their ghosts be trapped on 118-G-002 forever, forced to share a dead planet with the shades of the additional inhabitants?

Right now I was seriously wondering about that. I took an extra mental health session two days after Adam's abortive breakout, thanks to my lingering feeling that he wasn't quite gone. The treatment had gotten most of it. The human therapist told me the rest would get washed away after a few more sessions, so I needed to keep an eye out for intrusive thoughts until then.

I guess *I don't want to die today* counts as one, but it felt like it at the time. I started frantically calculating the exact burn while the sounds of wind and the fuzz grew louder around me. The harder the deceleration, the faster the trip — but even in their cocoons the patients would feel some acceleration. I took a moment to confirm the stretchers weren't piled on top of each other. I don't know why. I wouldn't have time to do anything about it.

They were all fine, but I swore anyway. One of the cocoons had "RUBICON" stenciled on it. *Just my luck the bastard probably was the first to charge into the engine room*, I thought as I rechecked the burn solution. I didn't know the *Redacted* would handle it if he didn't survive this, and I wasn't real keen to find out.

In the end I left the numbers the way they were. The equations were cold, but they'd work.

Landing wasn't as bad as getting beaten with a stick, but it wasn't what I'd call fun.

The burn itself I could handle. That was just a jarring, full-body bruise from the physical shock of the hauler suddenly being under power again. It was much better than the alternative.

Only, getting power back was the easy part. Getting *control* meant strained wrists and ankles as I shoved the hauler into something resembling stability. Amalgamation tech is very intuitive, but whoever designed *never* thought about conditions like this. The two internal computers were worse than useless, and for five horrible seconds I thought they were going to override my manual controls and blast the hauler straight into the ground.

But their own confusion (or possibly, agonized internal screaming) meant that the fail-safes wouldn't let them take control just yet, and the fuzz I could now hear with almost painful clarity in the empty cockpit gave me enough clues to the space around me that I could align myself in a relatively straight path and reasonably correct angle.

Once the computers had ten seconds of decent data to work with? Everything was fine. The hauler evened out, the emergency lights went off, and the creak of metal was conspicuous with its sudden absence. We were on a clear and smooth glide path to home, and there wasn't a thing I had to do besides throw up again. And let me tell you: *this* time it was from stress.

Landing was not anticlimactic. It was a perfectly good climax to what had been a fun half hour of sheer neurochemical overload, thank you very much. This time I actually landed, but I still had the hatch opening as the hauler touched down.

The medical staff unloaded the stretchers with almost blinding speed, too. We ended up saving four of them. I'm not going to lie; I was grateful one of the survivors was Rubicon. Any life saved is worth it, but him dying? That could have been bad.

Thank God the medics were on the job, and good at doing it. One of them even had time to check on me; I thought about waving her off, but then I remembered she probably had access to painkillers. I felt I could use one. Or two. Was there a sampler?

...okay, all of that was a lie. Not what happened, but how I was reacting to it. When the doc checked me out she was happy to give me something that made me drift a little, probably because she didn't want me freaking out when I heard about the two people that had died. I didn't tell her that I already knew. It always gets weirdly quiet in the hauler when it powers down — something about the hull; people are looking into it — and when I was on that ballistic arc, all I could hear was the faintest sounds of whistling as the hauler caught what atmosphere was outside.

Well, that and the fuzz. The fuzz that spiked suddenly louder, twice, as we reached the top of the arc and began to descend. That fuzz definitely isn't made up of voices. Ask any pilot, and we'd all agree. Immediately, and without hesitation. And the voices that aren't there absolutely don't ever sound like they're coming from what was once a human throat. And that means that I hadn't heard anything human in those two spikes, right? Right. Just so long as we all understand it. Or at least get past it, but that's what the sedative was for.

Having just put all of this down: well. I guess I had personal knowledge of what happens to the dead out here, even then.

None of that was the worst thing that happened that day, though. The Anticipant didn't make it.

I hate being a little relieved that it wasn't because of anything I did: she had died saving Rubicon. No warning, no weird last words, she just grabbed him and shoved him into enough cover that he didn't take a full dose of gas. She did, though. Hell, by all accounts the Anticipant didn't try to run, or hold her breath, or do anything else that could have given her a few more seconds of life. She just stood there, powering down the fusion bottle before it could explode, and let the gas wash over her. The cameras even show her breathing normally until her skin turned purple-black from her newly-necrotic blood, and she died.

I've asked around. Coolant gas poisoning is *painful*. It's quick, but it's painful. Her expression didn't change once. I'd say that she was inhuman, except that the Anticipant died saving the crew of her ship, and that sounds pretty damn human to me.

CHAPTER
TWENTY-FIVE
Murder, She Memed

One arguably nice thing about being a pilot is that other people insist we get enough sleep. Something about how we shouldn't be tired when we're pushing tons of metal through the sky at supersonic speeds. Personally, I thought that the regulations were a little strict for One-Eighteen, but nobody ever really showed any interest in making local exceptions. I guess that makes sense. Most of them were planning to work somewhere else. Bad habits are killers. Literally.

So, we get plenty of time scheduled for actual, non-enhanced sleep. Whether or not it's *good* sleep is — well, at least there's usually enough physical rest. Mental recuperation is a whole other issue.

Still, when I went to go see Greg the next morning to give him a hand, I looked a lot better than he did. The disaster at the *Redacted*, coupled with our resupply problem, had stretched our medical resources to the limit. Greg was probably operating on regular deepsleeper sessions by now, and the strain was starting to show.

In fact: "There a problem, Greg?" I asked him, sitting in a free workstation. "Aside from the obvious one... err, obviously?"

He looked over at me, bleary-eyed. "Yeah, Pam. I can't get access to Chook."

"Why would you want access to... oh. She was an organ donor?"

"She was an *everything* donor. Blood, skin, organs, bones — anything we needed, and could transplant. And we *need* it right now, skin in particular. But the computer won't let Maki loot the body. She booted the problem over to me, but I can't do anything about it, either."

That *was* weird. Greg and Maki had somewhat overlapping authorities, depending on the situation. The two of them combined still should have had the ability to bind and loose everything on One-Eighteen, though. "Do you think it's because of the cancer? It was stage four, I remember."

"I thought of that, but I looked up what Chook had. It wouldn't have affected the skin, so according to the medical computers that at least would have been safe to transplant. But the system insists that she indicated cremation in case of death, so her corpse can't be harvested. Even when I use my emergency command overrides. Those are supposed to work, no matter what!"

"Huh. You going to show it to Syah?"

Greg looked at me. "No, I'm not. Not until I'm certain this is *just* a computer glitch. We've had too many cases of sabotage lately."

It took me a second to parse that. "What, you think he's a suspect? That's implausible." You don't say *that's impossible!* when you're working in the Tomb Worlds. It's bad luck, and *not* a superstition.

"Pam, right now I don't even know if there's been a *crime*. But I do know that my override codes are supposed to work. If they don't, I have to wonder if it's because of somebody good with computers. Which your boyfriend is."

*Gee, Syah, everybody **else** seems to think you're my boyfriend. So when were you planning to bring up the topic?* "Great. So how do you analyze a computer system for sabotage when you can't trust the people who'd do the analysis?"

Greg gave me a wan smile. "So, hey, you remember just now, when you were asking what my problem was?"

How do you solve an insoluble problem? By figuring out what the rules are, and breaking them nice and hard.

The solution in this case was obvious, once we got around to finding it. We had a living will from Chook, authorizing XHum to loot the body for medical emergencies. The only thing contradicting that was a notation in her file, locking out any electronic authorization to release the body. So Greg just ordered Maki to pull the body from cryo-storage anyway. What was the computer going to do about it? Fire up the defense grid? It didn't actually have one. We absolutely *don't* give computer systems weapons. Why would we? There's nobody out here except us.

Well, there's terrorists and cultists (some people will mutter, *and the damn Adjudication Council*). They're not really things you can use a defense grid against, though. The latter use knives, and the former throw rocks at you from orbit. Too small and too big, in other words.

Moving along! Defrosting a corpsicle without further damaging the cells takes a little time, so Maki had the chance to go over things. "Sign here and here," she said to us. "I just need two more senior staff to agree that we needed the body parts for emergency purposes."

"Body parts?" I asked. "I thought you were just taking the skin."

"I was," said Maki. "But it occurred to me that we might be able to use whatever organs didn't get hit by the cancer yet. Cartilage and hair, for certain. Maybe even bone marrow, if it checks out. The original diagnosis said that the cancer had mostly gone into the lungs and brain, so I should be able to recycle some of the joints, if nothing else."

Well, at least she was talking about the whole thing with a certain clinical detachment. You get wary around the doctors who get *enthusiastic* about looting corpses. It's not the sort of hobby you want to encourage.

I didn't feel the urge to watch one friend cut up another friend for parts, so I decided to see how Oft was doing. I assumed that the conversation would be just as grim as if I had stayed with Maki, but at least it'd be *differently* grim.

He had been set up in Burcu's old office, and was busily going through her notes when I dropped by. "Oh, hello, Pam," he said with the wan smile that had been living on his face since the attack. "I'm going through shore leave reports for the crew. Perhaps I'll see something Burcu didn't."

"What are you looking for?" I asked him as I sat. "Suspicious behavior?"

"Yes! The problem is, I have no idea what 'suspicious' would entail. I'm not very familiar with what *normal* shore leave behavior is."

"Really, Oft? Can't you just see if anybody's acting weirder than usual?"

"No, I'm afraid. There's no 'usual' to look at. This is the first voyage to a populated Tomb World for most of the *Redacted*'s crew," Oft shook his head. "Including the captain. Oh, and me, truthfully."

"What?" I said, just like an intelligent and educated professional. "That makes no sense. Why would the Council send out an inexperienced ship?"

"I didn't say we were inexperienced, Pam. Dealing with living settlements is just not in our normal skill set."

That made my blood run cold. "That implies," I said carefully, "that you never expect anyone on a planet to be alive when you show up."

"No," Oft admitted. "We do not. That there were people here is a wonderful thing! But it is also a low-probability one. We... ordered our planetary visits by the always-low likelihood that there would be somebody still there, and One-Eighteen was at the bottom of the list."

He didn't explain how they came up with the list, and I knew better than to ask. The Amalgamation wasn't just ahead of us in physical technology. Their cybernetics and applied math looks just like magic to us primitive screwheads. You can still use their programs, if you can find a working one. Just punch in the data and accept the result — and never, ever look at how the numbers got crunched. The few mathematicians who've tried end up even more screwed up than mathematicians usually get.

"Awesome," I said instead. "We're very, very lucky. So lucky, we had a Scout infestation... *oh*. Shit. We *were* lucky."

"Exactly," nodded Oft. "I assume that there is a timetable for this exercise in mass murder and destruction. The presence of the Scouts must have disrupted it, which also suggests that they are *not* behind the original threat. Otherwise, they would have triggered it when they left."

"Well, that and we're not doing anything that bad!" I had to keep myself from shouting. Then I swallowed nervously. "Sorry. I didn't mean to say that..."

"Say what?" asked Oft, just as if I hadn't committed an extremely unprofessional *faux pas*. "I was yawning at the time, and didn't catch it."

"Never mind. So we know that the Scouts aren't responsible for the attacks, and wouldn't have liked them. Maybe they would have even interfered?" Oft shrugged, because how could you know? People like the Scouts or the Bureau or the Trianglers don't think like we do. Anything can set them off. "So whoever it was that's doing this waits until they leave — then waits some more, just in case. Only they waited too long, and now the *Redacted* is here to mess up their plans."

"Which would make me a good deal more cheerful, Pam, if only I knew how we were supposed to do that." Oft started pacing. "Most of us are experts in sifting through destruction and rubble. Lieutenant Commander Nowak was our specialist in interrogation techniques, and now she's gone."

I laughed, despite myself. "What? She was horrible at it!"

"No, Pam. She was horrible at *making friends* with people. When it came to getting information out of them, Burcu was a mistress of her craft. She had eliminated your senior staff from suspicion of cult activity by her second session with you, and a third of your coworkers by the time she died." Oft sighed. "I was counting on her to give me advice to figure out who the spy for the Scouts was. She knew it wasn't you, but that was all she had time to work out before we went down to the Erebus dig."

"Huh. Guess all that arrogance was an act, then?"

"What?" Oft shook his head. "Oh, no. The Lieutenant Commander could be thoroughly unpleasant. She was as rude as you can get on a starship and not be killed in your sleep."

And on that unpleasant note, my phon went off. Maki wanted to talk to me. Right away. Considering where she was, that didn't sound very good.

"So, Chook was murdered," Maki told me. By myself. No Greg, no Nur, no Syah, definitely nobody from the *Redacted*. Hell, Maki was wearing an allergy mask, and had handed me one, too.

I tried not to look too warily back at her. A statement like that could be a revelation, confession, or boast. I was pretty sure I knew which one it was, but what if I was wrong? "I thought you said she did a medical."

"Oh, she did." Maki pulled out a pack of cigarettes, shook her head, and put them back. "She applied for the Quietus pill five minutes after getting the diagnosis, and took it no more than an hour later. Classic shock suicide behavior, no surprises. The only thing was, the diagnosis was false."

"She didn't have pancreatic neocancer?"

"Chook didn't have cancer at all. Or any of the parasites or diseases that could throw off a false positive." Maki paced. What I could see of her face looked upset, and full of self-loathing. "Dammit, I should have noticed right from the start that she was too healthy. There was no sudden weight loss or bile expression. She should have been thin as a rail and covered in yellow sores. But the medical computer said she had an asymptomatic form of the disease, so I took the damn computer's word."

I didn't know how to feel. Well, okay, that was a lie. I felt infuriated. I just didn't know in which direction to *send* it. "Right. Maybe you *shouldn't* have." I said it harshly enough to at least get her attention. When I had it, I went on. "But you didn't have a chance to talk her down, right? She was dead before you knew anything."

"Yeah, but..."

"But nothing. She was dead, so she wasn't looking good. The computer gave you a reason for Chook picking Quietus so quick, and it's a damn tough month already. Don't flay yourself over something you couldn't stop. Or, hey, if you were feeling guilt because you missed the neocancer, you can stop that now. You didn't miss it."

"Thanks, Pam." I was happy to hear her sound a little better. Corporate motivational speakers don't have anything on me. "But I still should have actually done an autopsy."

"Again, damn tough month. But why was it murder? It could have been just a really, really bad accident."

"Well, once I realized the diagnosis was botched, I went looking at the rest of the reports, to try to figure out what had caused it. And there was nothing. At least, nothing inconsistent with the false diagnosis.

"But I saw that Chook had actually *printed out a copy* of the patient informational summary you give with medical diagnoses. The full versions of those usually don't get kept, because they're literally just definitions of terms and standard descriptions of procedures, but since there was a hard copy for once, I went to go find it." Maki opened up her bag and pulled out some papers. "I can't do the text injustice. Here, read it yourself."

I started to read — and wished I hadn't. As Maki said, informational summaries are just there to give you a nice, soothing data dump. We've had a century's worth of desperate linguistic research to learn how to do that better, because it's a damn scary universe out there and every insight on how to calm people down pays dividends in human lives later. Some cultures are good at war, or science, or art. Ours is good at keeping people from losing their shit.

These words weren't designed for that. They were designed for the *opposite* of that. The word choice, the slightly nonstandard font, even the punctuation and spacing — they *matter*. Behold the wonders of our modern age! Weaponized linguistic programming.

And it *was* weaponized. I could see Maki's point, right off: this was *designed* to produce a devastating emotional state, in a particular reader. I felt physically sick and half-despairing after reading the first page, and it wasn't even *close* to being aimed at me, personally. Against Chook, who had just been told by a normally trustworthy source that she was about to die horribly, it was hideous overkill.

Well, at least I knew who to be infuriated at. And it wasn't Maki. "This is... this is *vile*."

"You know what the worst part is, Pam? It's not actually all that bad." I looked at her sharply as she went on. "I mean, sure, the text's designed to hit a weakened psyche in just the right place to make it collapse, just like a deck of cards tumbling in the soothing dark—"

"Butternut squash," I said to the air.

"—but was there any *malice* to it? I don't think so! You look at the texts, I mean *really* look at them, and you can see the outlines of a great and terrible pity. Whoever did it didn't hate me, Pam. The attack was so fast, so hard, Chook didn't have *time* to suffer. It must have just shut down her head, so that she couldn't think, or fight, or do anything but remember the promise of Quietus. God, but I hate Quietus!"

"Hold that thought," I said, as I felt a small box put itself in my left hand. I hadn't once seen the stealth mini-drone itself, which is exactly how that's supposed to go. "Yeah, suicide pills suck."

Maki nodded, hard enough that her neck clicked. "I have

always hated them, you know. Even in medical school! We're supposed to save life, not let it be taken. But the numbers didn't lie. Having Quietus available gets more people into cryosleep. Every pill taken prevents at least three murders. It's all about the cold equations, the cold equations that don't care about anything or anyone else." And, just as I was wondering whether she was maintaining after all, Maki went on, "If only the Quietus pills weren't so *pretty*."

I turned to her, arms outstretched. "Do you need a hug, Maki?"

"What? Oh, no, no thank you, Pam. That's very kind."

I smiled and put my arms around her. "Well, you're getting one anyway." She resisted for a moment, then relaxed as my arms comforted her — then relaxed some more as the knockout patch I had palmed, then stuck on her neck took effect.

Maki wasn't very heavy, but suddenly unconscious people have weird centers of gravity. She sagged against me hard enough that I staggered. "Pro... dammit. Where's the MTU?"

Nobody answered me, particularly not The Process - but the mobile therapy unit was coming up now. "Query?" it 'asked' me. "SOVP?"

"Answer: negative," I grunted as I shoved Maki onto the unit. It immediately retracted its shock grapplers. Even the space-happy can't shrug those off. "Tentative diagnosis: acute memetic poisoning. Authorization for emergency therapy: granted. Priority: *immediate*."

We don't have 'native' AI, but our computers can at least take directions properly. They also don't waste time: Maki was no sooner grabbed by the writhing restraint straps when the induction helmet slammed down on her head. I barely had time to rip the mask from her face before the therapy took hold.

Maki was one of the ones who screamed during therapy. She also retched at least twice, which made me glad I had removed the mask. It's within the MTU's ability to handle, but I wanted it focused on cleaning out her mind. I was also doubly glad Maki had picked a quiet spot for our meeting, since I didn't want anybody else seeing this. They'd all understand, but it wouldn't be good for her dignity.

Most therapy sessions don't last long, but it took five minutes of metaphorical and physical puking before the lights turned green and Maki was revived. She recovered quick, but when she looked at me, it was all I could do *not* to quail at her eyes. They were remorselessly direct and pitiless. When she spoke, I could hear the tones of a mind temporarily devoid of all emotion. "There was another memetic trap in the documentation?" she intoned.

"You tell *me*, Maki," I said. "I don't open files when they're surrounded by a stack of bodies."

"The metaphor is inexact—" but then, she shook her head a little, then straightened. The glare in her eyes was already starting to fade as her body's normal hormone load reasserted itself. "I mean, it was not that bad. I probably was not going to kill myself."

"Well, you're the subject expert," I said, not quite relaxed yet. "All I know is, whatever it was you were flying on, it didn't like you very much. And you were on the way to getting crashed by it."

She sat down, putting her face in her hands. She then scrabbled for her cigarette pack again, this time puffing one into life with harsh, jerky breaths. Now I *was* relaxing, a little. I may not be a subject expert in memetic poisoning, but I can tell when somebody's actually recovering from a nasty mental fall.

"Yeah," Maki said as she offered me a smoke. "After I read the diagnosis, I went back to look at the electronic file again. In it, I found a recommended outline for communicating with the patient that I'd swear wasn't there before."

"That's probably because it wasn't," I pointed out. "More despair?"

"Worse." Maki shook her head. "It was a cloyingly cheerful

treatise on how to keep your patient from immediately despairing at the news of her diagnosis. Just chock full of good information, and how much of a relief it must have been to detect her condition before she did something easily prevented, like take a Quietus pill." She took another drag. "So I guess that was aimed at *me*. Yay!"

"Yay," I echoed. "And that's not the worst bit."

"What's the worst bit?"

"The worst bit is, as a certain set of technothrillers once informed me: if memetic poisoning was easy, everybody would do it. People actually can't do it at all. You need the right computer hardware. The kind of hardware that doesn't get sold openly."

CHAPTER TWENTY-SIX
YELLOW BOX RULES

Intervention or not, Maki wasn't going to bounce back from the attack right away. She should have spent the next week in no-stress rest, only she wanted to power through, so Greg and I had to settle for making her promise to stick to medicine for a few days. Just as well: we weren't hitting our corporate quarterly goals anyway, and wouldn't until the quarantine got lifted. That meant tracking down the damned cultists, not that we needed another reason.

It was for sure Oft didn't need one. The death of the Anticipant had hit him very hard, if not in any way I expected. He wasn't *colder*, exactly. He didn't raise his voice, or show frustration. But there was no more hesitancy in him. When he decided to do something now, Oft just went and did it, without second-guessing. That might sound innocuous, except that I was sure it would apply to hypothetical situations like, *should I stop wasting time, and just kill every bad person in this room*? Sometimes civilization needs a little second-guessing, is all I'm saying.

Then again, his new attitude was at least useful. He had called me in to Burcu's old office, to talk about connections, or lack of same. "There's something weird about all these attacks, Oft," I told him. "Even more than the obvious."

"Like what?" Oft quirked his head at me. "We know that there are two sets of opponents. There are the cultists, and the

Scouts."

"*Are* the Scouts really involved?" I responded. "They don't usually hide their involvement in things. None of those groups do."

"Yes, while the cultists love to hide their misdeeds in the shadows. The problem is, while they're capable of assassinations and poisons, they're not very good at tech-based atrocities. Attacking ships remotely *is* something that the Scouts could do."

"Fair, but then there's the deathheart angle, Oft. The Scouts purely hate the stuff. If there was one of their Troops running operations on One-Eighteen, they'd be seeking out the cultists themselves."

"True, Pamela." Oft scratched his chin. "They've never been involved in the black drug trade, except as vigilantes. Between you and me? The Council doesn't mind the help. We need all of it that we can get."

"Is it hard, keeping deathheart off of Earth?"

"Hard? No. It is *impossible* to stop the trade," said Oft. "But we try to, anyway. The criminals who cultivate it out here are cunning enough not to try to grow any in Sol System itself, so we only have to deal with the refined product. That makes it a little easier. Enough to allow us the delusion of accomplishment, at least."

"I'm surprised that nobody's tried," I admitted. "To grow it on Earth, I mean."

"Oh, it was attempted, several times. In every case, the Adjudication Council was able to intercept the seeds and cuttings. I would prefer not to tell you what they did to the smugglers to reveal their suppliers, or to the suppliers to reveal their sources, or to the organizations trying to establish their vile product." Oft's eyes were bleak. "I only watched the video debriefing once, and that was sufficient."

"Yeah," I replied after a long moment. "I would prefer not to be told. So, when you found out that Adam had been slipped deathheart, you assumed — what, cultists?"

"Yes. His own files did not indicate any *proclivities* in that way, so we assumed that he had seen too much. And what thing was worth killing the man over, in such a dramatic fashion?"

The answer was obvious, but I still said it. "Right. Keeping secret the plot to murder everybody on One-Eighteen. The splashier the death, the easier to misdirect everybody for just long enough. Makes sense, if you're a cultist who's planning to die with the rest of the planet anyway."

"Exactly. And now, here we are, Pam. And even in time to stop them, amazingly." Oft sighed. "I just wish that just once we did not have to pay so high a price for these chances to intervene."

I nodded — and put three shots through the door.

Why? *Interventions*. The Other Side gets to have them, too.

Oft was saying something, but I didn't hear him over first the roaring in my ears, and then the roaring of my gun. Nothing wrong with his reflexes, though. He immediately dived *away* from the door, clearing my line of fire as the door shattered from the shots. It's bulletproof only one way, you see. Shoot from outside, it'll deform and crack. Shoot from the inside, and it'll explode outward.

That particular feature saves at least four people's lives a year, or so the manufacturer claims. Even a cultist slows down when he gets a face full of glass splinters.

And they were cultists: three of the bastards, and only one was on the floor, kicking and screaming and clawing at her face. I forced myself to ignore her to put three more rounds in the *second* cultist, since he had obligingly stepped *on* his fallen 'sister' in order to clear the doorway faster. Cultists will gut out a surprising amount of bullets and still keep going, but three in the center of mass knocked him down, and possibly out of the fight. Good enough — well, that's what I *thought*, right up to the point where the *third* bastard got his own shot off.

He was in a perfect position to attack, too. He started off to one side, out of the blast zone of the door *and* the line of fire. And he didn't have a knife, either. This guy's weapon of choice was a blowpipe. Only works at short range, but he had that, didn't he? His buddies had cleared a path.

We keep forgetting this about cultists. They have a list about things they care about, and 'staying alive' is on there, but it's nowhere near the top. When a cult wants somebody assassinated, a lot of times they can do it just out of sheer and literal bloody-mindedness.

But I digress, to quote the classics. Third Bastard had me dead to rights. I could *feel* time slow down as I turned to face him, too slow to shoot him before the dart left the pipe. The dart was foul, too, all bone and glass fragments, and its tip was coated with a green liquid that I knew was poisonous. I remember a horrible buzzing silence surrounding me as I looked at my death, and there was nothing I could do.

I tried shooting at the dart anyway, because why not? But my hand and brain betrayed me. Instead of shooting, I managed to lose the gun completely. I didn't even just drop it; I flung it across the room. I also remember having just enough time to feel embarrassed...

...before the gun collided with the dart, sending it tumbling across the room, and away from my precious, precious hide.

And then Oft was at Third Bastard, his left fist smashing into the cultist's mouth in a blur of anger and broken teeth. Oft didn't wait after that. As soon as he recovered, the man started in with an almost scientific strategy, throwing jabs with ruthless efficiency at joints and vitals. By the time I made sure of the gun's location (I wasn't touching it without gloves), Third Bastard was down, and whimpering in a way that I fought to keep from enjoying.

Oft looked over at me. "You're bleeding?"

"Am I?" I hadn't thought I'd been cut.

"Just a little, from your nose. Did any of them hit you?"

"No," I told him as I shoved my hands in a glove dispensary. It's hard to check yourself for injuries without actually using your hands. I knocked away the dart. Million to one shot." Now that it was safe to do so, I retrieved my gun — and slapped the panic switch. "Stay here until the crash team gets here. I need to go check on Greg."

Oft got my point right away. This was an assassination attempt, which meant they probably wanted to go after the leadership of the project. And who ranked above me?

"Greg?" I shouted as I shoved against the door. "GREG!" I think a part of me knew I shouldn't have bothered, but it's like that cat, right? You don't know if it's dead of cyanide poisoning until you go and look. Maybe he was okay. Maybe he wasn't okay, but was hanging on until I got there. Maybe... maybe the hinges on the door finally gave, letting me half-stagger into the room.

I didn't fall, thank God. There was a lot of blood on the floor, and the walls, and on the windows — and not enough in Greg. It wasn't all his, not by a long shot. There were two other corpses in that office, and they hadn't died any easier than Greg had. One was clutching herself, her guts spilling out over her claw-hooked hands, while the other lay flat on his back, the hilt of a dagger protruding from one eye. There was a terrible satisfaction in that scene. Greg had given as good as he had got.

He was still dead and slumped on his floor, though, with one hand still reaching for his fallen, cracked phon. I wanted to check him, but I didn't dare. There were a half-dozen awful rents on his body still weeping blood, even though he was clearly dead. Something had kept all the gore in here from coagulating, and I didn't want it touching me.

So I pulled out my own phon. "Maki! I need a morgue team at Greg's office... three bodies. Yes, he's dead, dammit." I'm sorry, but I don't even remember the exact things Maki was saying, just my responses. I wasn't tracking very well, just then. "We need to get the next in line in here..."

And that's when I almost sat on the floor in shock, blood and possible poisons be damned. Greg's second in command had been Chook, and she was dead. Maki was in charge of the corporate side of things, and wasn't allowed to take over Greg's job. The Process was gone, not that it was really in the organization chain, either. The most senior staffer available at this point was... *me.*

Fortunately, I didn't have any time to wallow in the horror of that, and I knew it. I started talking again. "Yeah, Maki, I just figured it out. I'm taking control of colony affairs, as of now." Deep breath. "I'm going to start by declaring a YELLOW BOX emergency, I repeat, YELLOW BOX. There's at least one surviving cultist. We're going to need to interrogate him, right away."

The cultist had a name. Since he would have been the first to say that human names didn't matter, there's no reason for me to tell it to you. We'll call him 'Nemo.' He had been a contragrav researcher in Luxor Base, not someone off of the *Redacted*, which would have been awkward in more settled times. Now it was just an opportunity to do some fumiga— *to solve this problem,* I told myself firmly. *The cultists* **win** *if you become too much like them.*

Which is true, but only in moderation.

Nemo had been prepped by the time I and the Yellow Box got to him, from different routes. He looked as comfortable as you'd expect someone gagged, in a straightjacket, and strapped to a chair, to be. The bruises from our earlier encounter were already halfway faded, and his face had the artificial ruddiness from the induction cap strapped to his head. Endorphin-dulled or not, though, his eyes still managed a little bit of hate-filled glare... until he saw the Yellow Box. I saw a flicker of hope, joined with self-disgust, on Nemo's face for the briefest moment before he deliberately slackened his expression.

"Yes. It's like that." I didn't sit across the table from him. Not yet. Instead, I had a security officer very carefully place the Box in front of Nemo. She and I stepped forward to insert two keys simultaneously in its back, to reveal a small handheld trigger. I politely ignored the way the security officer beat a hasty retreat afterward. I didn't blame her for that, after all. If I didn't need to stay, I would have done the same thing. Instead, I waited until everyone else had left the room, carefully stepped back to the wall, and pushed the trigger that opened the Box.

What's in the Yellow Box? According to pictures, a weird bit of Amalgamation battery tech. It *looks* like a ten-sided crystal trapezohedron that radiates energy that we can barely perceive. What it *does* is mess with your optic nerves, making you see things that aren't there. Horrible things.

Yes, it's a torture device — but not in the way you think. For normal people, the torture comes when you open the Box. For cultists, it comes when you *close* it. They see the same things we do, you see; they just *like* them.

I gave Nemo the full two minutes before the Box closed again, carefully staying well behind the lid. After it closed, I waited patiently for the rocking and attempts to scream through the gag to end before talking again. "Here's how it goes. There's always at least one cell of you left behind when you do one of these missions. Give us names and their location, and you get the Box again. *Don't*, and you'll spend the rest of your life without it."

Syah and Oft had identical revolted expressions as I rejoined them, a list of names and location in hand. That was fair, since I was revolted myself. "Standard protocol," I reminded them, or maybe me. "This is the least horrible thing we can do to make them talk, remember?"

Oft looked over to the now-uncovered window, which showed Nemo hunched over the Box. The heavy fabric covering him and it both descended halfway to the floor, because you can't be too careful. "It's still foul," he muttered.

"Yeah," I agreed. "So is trying to kill every person on One-Eighteen. You heard their plan, right?" Both of them nodded. Not that it was much of a plan. The last batch of cultists was going to skip subtlety entirely, and just poison the water supply with deathheart. I was damned if I knew why they thought that would work, but even when it didn't they'd still probably kill a bunch of people, and contaminate far too much of the base.

"I asked the *Redacted* to send over a security team," Oft told me. "They can spare Chalerm Suwern, and only because he's already present. He is our best security officer, though."

"That's something. Syah, I need somebody to do locks. You checked out on field technical operations?"

"Yes, Pam, but just the basic qualifications. Happy to do it, but don't you want somebody better trained?"

"We're doing this now, we're really short of trained personnel, and I need somebody I can trust." Then I shifted my eyes, because that admission hit him pretty hard. Which is what I wanted it to do. "They'll figure out pretty soon we didn't kill all of their buddies, and then they'll just jump the gun. So we go *now*. Have this Suwern guy meet us on the way, Oft."

I held back until the two men left the room, and locked eyes with the security guard. "Wait until you hear back that we've rolled them up," I told her.

She looked over at the cultist, now slightly swaying under the blackout covering. Her hand brushed the hilt of her own Jefferson-made revolver. "Should I close the box first?" she asked me, and I couldn't tell whether or not she wanted me to say 'Yes,' or 'No.'

I thought about it — then shook my head. "No. There's no need to be cruel about it. We're not *monsters*." I pointed at Nemo. "*They* are."

The cultists were hiding out mostly in plain sight. They were holed up in a warehouse by the water filtration plant. No crowds to tip them off — and, after Syah fiddled with the cameras, no images of us gathering to tip them off, either. Which was fine by me.

"Remember, we must not call them *cultists*," Suwern reminded us as we gathered by the door. He might have been sent over by the *Redacted*, but he and Oft had greeted each other with real warmth, so I decided he probably wasn't all bad. "The term 'cultist' implies membership in a faith organization, which would require us to grant them full freedom of religion and expression. These people are instead *Ritual Nihilists*."

"Which means?" muttered Syah.

"Which means we can smack them on the head before they try to hex us," I replied.

"You mean, before they attempt to remotely interfere with our neurochemistry via applied social hacking," Suwern corrected me primly as he checked his tangle gun.

"Sure, sure," I said, sourly watching as Syah mucked about with the door's security system. "If that's how we're rationalizing it."

"Don't call them 'witches,' either." That was from Gina, who was along to provide first aid and heavy sedation. "It's an insult to real witches." I waited for someone to point out that there weren't any 'real' witches, but nobody said anything.

Then again, it's a touchy subject. *Are* there really witches? I mean, as opposed to syncretic neo-pagan worshipers of various nature deities. Those you can find in a bunch of places. But the evil hags from the grimmer folk tales, all red in tooth and claw-like fingers? I don't really think so, at least when the lights are on. The part of me that grew up listening to Jeffersonian ghost stories isn't as sure, either day or night. There's plenty of bad things out here, already? What's one more of them?

I *do* believe in Ritual Nihilists, though. Everybody does. If you don't, they'll have a better shot at stabbing you.

I'd say that the three cultists looked just like anybody else when we burst through the door, except that it'd be a lie and we all know it. Sure, the two women and one man weren't physically deformed, but there's more than one kind of ugliness. The three of them had all relaxed in what they thought was quiet isolation, which meant that their *true* smiles and expressions had come out.

Their names were — well, we all had a therapy session after this (except for Oft), so some of the details are a little hazy. I remember that they were new hires on the contragrav project, no more than three months in-system, and that two of them were female and one was male. Call them Jane, Rose, and Lu. All young, too, but that's cultists for you. It's not a life path that has lots of lifespan attached to it.

When you arrest somebody, even out here in the Tomb Worlds, there's supposed to be a system to it. You say who you are and why you're doing the arrest, confirm that there's a safe place for the arrestee to go to, and just try to avoid, you know, panic and rash moves. If things go right, the arrestee will end up securing themselves, which cuts down the risk for everybody. Nobody wants to die because somebody else decided on the spot that they were space-happy, right?

Things did not go right.

Like I said, things are a little hazy. After therapy got done with me, I remember it all like a series of old-style photos.

Here's the three of them, sitting on the ground and looking at — well, therapy tagged it as a purple box, so it must have been pretty bad-looking. There are lines on the floor, drawn in all directions, but they all end up at the purple box.

Here's Jane and Lu, jumping up and lunging towards us. Lu is still in the air, while Jane is almost scuttling with both feet and hands.

Here's Jane, biting down on Syah's arm and worrying away at it so hard, her teeth are breaking as they're rending the tough fabric protecting him.

Here's my gun smashing across Lu's mouth before he can reach my neck. Lu's eyes are solid purple. More therapeutic substitutions. Apparently I didn't like the way he was looking at me.

Here are my feet. The right foot is kicking Lu in the base of his spine, and I still remember the way things gave way under his skin. The left foot is standing on one of the lines, and I am now icily confident that I felt nothing uncanny or disturbing from being in contact with it.

Here's Oft, Gina, and Jane. Oft has grabbed Jane, grabbing her hair and ripping her off Syah's arm in a spray of spittle and broken teeth. Her hands are flailing, leaving scratches on one wall as she is tossed around. Gina is readying a sedative dispenser.

Here's Jane, staggering under the four tangle web rounds fired into her at point-blank range by Suwern. Two are overkill, three are dangerous to the target. Four seemed barely enough.

Here's a memory of me, stomping down hard on movement by my feet. I know I must have been stomping Lu, but I don't remember it. What I'm looking at is Suwern breaking open the tangle gun chamber to reload it.

Here's a shot of Rose, appearing out of nowhere to bowl over Oft. A knife descends as she crouches over him.

Here's the knife, flickering up and down in a blur that ends in Oft's gut.

And here is my gun, frantically clearing Gina and centered precisely on Rose's ear as I pull the trigger.

Twelve seconds. That's how long all of this lasted. Just a lousy twelve seconds.

We did not have a good conversation in the medical bay.

"I'm sorry, Pam," Maki said as she massaged the blood deeper into her gloves' tiny, pinhole sucker-mouths. "There was just too much damage, too quickly. And the knife had something on it."

Gina nodded. "I was able to clean out the corruption — excuse me, 'the lingering exotoxins' — but they were in the wounds long enough to start cellular degradation. Maki and I can make him comfortable, but that's it."

I stared at them. "So freeze him! Send him off to Earth, or something. They must have some kind of, I dunno, alien weaver that can take him apart, then put him back together again."

"We can't," Maki replied as she stripped her sparkly-clean

gloves, and tossed them back into the tub. "His bioethics profile prohibits cryo-freeze. Plus, Gina was able to stabilize him well enough to get verbal confirmation."

"What? Who the hell goes into the Tomb Worlds with a DNF order?"

"Iluvitarians," Suwern said from the door. He looked *chipped*, like he was a statue that had been hit in the face a few times. "Or at least some do. I have argued with him several times over whether he should be one of them." He looked over at Maki, his face working slightly. "Can he receive visitors, ah, Doctor?"

"Briefly, Commander," I could see Maki put on her physician's face. She was probably as grateful as Suwern was to have an alternate way of dealing with each other than 'corpo bootlicker'/'government lackey.' "I need to check his condition. Or will you need privacy?"

"Not for this," he said as she led him into Oft's room.

I waited until the two had left, before turning to Gina. She put up her hands. "Not a chance, Pam. I'm a doctor, not a witch. And I'm not a witch doctor, either."

She'd used that line before, usually at parties, and despite the fact that technically she was a nurse (and thus not a *witch* nurse). This time, I didn't laugh along. "I can't believe there's nothing vibro-medtech can't do for him."

Technically, Gina did laugh at that. "Oh, I'm sure that there is. I just don't know how to do it. None of us do." She gave another one of those bitter laughs. "All this gear of ours? The salvaged stuff, and the monkey copies? We can turn them on, we can point them at our patients, and we can push the buttons and make the healing come out. Can we do 'how?' Sure. I can do tons of 'how.' But it's been decades of work, and we're still trying to make our way to 'why.' I'd call myself a witch after all, except that a witch would at least understand the underlying theory. There's nothing we can do for him, except put him on ice."

Which Oft was refusing to allow. I didn't want to argue with a dying man about his last wishes, but... I realized that I actually wanted to do precisely that.

Oft wasn't feeling any pain when I came in, but that's not the same as not *in* pain. All the agony was still there, and I thought I could feel it moving under his skin, even without Gina's crystal sensors. They were pulsing intermittently, and I understood that this represented some sort of conversion of pain into light. I guess we're all just running on electricity, in the end.

He could still smile and move his eyes. "Don't bother, Pam."

"What? Arguing with you over cryo-stasis? I don't have to. We could just wait until you're unconscious, then freeze you anyway. You'd be pissed at me when you woke up, but I can live with that."

"First off, that would be a violation of my bioethical rights." He didn't actually seem all that upset about that, which made me wonder if he really objected to being saved. Or at least until he kept talking. "It wouldn't matter, anyway. I will not be coming back from this."

"Come on, Oft. Just because we can't fix you here, doesn't mean the colony worlds can't. Or even Earth. You work for the Council! They'll make you a priority."

"Oh, Pam." Oft smiled at me. "I'm sorry. I didn't explain myself properly. I meant that I *won't* come back from the dead. Once I'm in the Halls, that's it. Where Men go after that is a mystery, even for us, but it is certainly not going to be back *here*."

"Iluvitarians must have been put in cryo-stasis before—" I started to say, and he interrupted me.

"Yes. A few of us have even been revived. In every case, those bodies were just... bodies. They weren't monsters or animals. Speak to one, and they would respond; give one food, and they would eat. And yet, there was — oh, why should I mince words, now? Their *souls* had gone on." He shook his head, and coughed. "Here I am, talking about souls. It's funny, really. Scientists have been demanding proof from priests for

MOE LANE

centuries, but the moment religion started finding evidence? Lo! We shouldn't even bring it up.

"Again, I'm sorry, Pam. I know you don't like what's about to happen. And I'm not being solemn enough about my own death. It's simply that I truly am going to a better place than this. How can I not look forward to my journey to the Halls, and whatever lies beyond them?"

I looked at the bandages and devices covering him, whirring and sighing in time to his breath like a flock of patient birds. "Yeah, I guess you do have it lucky, Oft. At least you get to check out of this hell-job."

"For that I am sorriest of all, Pam. I have no insights for you on that, alas. No deathbed wisdom, no gnomic revelations." The whirs and sighs began to increase. "I can offer only this: I will ask Those who I now go to to send you what assistance They might." He closed his eyes. "They have rescued us before, in previous Ages of the world. Perhaps They might do so again now."

The bandages covering him began to shudder and cry, as if they were now desperately trying to beat back death for him. I took his one uninjured hand. "Good-bye, Oft. I wish we'd had longer to know each other."

"Good-bye, Pam. May you see the stars of home again."

I turned my face as Oft breathed out, one last time. When you're on the Tomb Worlds, you don't look at somebody as they die. You don't look at their eyes as they open and focus for the last time, seeing whatever it is that's on the edge of their final vision. You don't look because you don't want to know what they're seeing. Sometimes it's something good, and sometimes it's... not. Oh, I'm sure Oft was seeing something good, though. He was a good man, and a fine one. We weren't friends for long, but I could count on him, you know? I was glad to be there for him when he died. As long as I didn't have to stare into his onrushing void, that is.

So I sat there, listening to the tumult of the bandages fade imperceptibly to silence, until Maki came back in to prepare the body.

CHAPTER TWENTY-SEVEN

Paratus

It was *days* before we were even a little sure that we had gotten the last cultist. It would have been easier if The Process was still there to help us interview and investigate, but it would have been harder, too. Most people always try to be their best selves around The Process. I mean, it's the only manifestation of the Amalgamation that any of us will ever meet. We instinctively want to look *worthy*.

Once The Process wasn't around... well, we didn't do anything *horrible* to anyone. But all of those pieties about respecting personal information that we quoted to Rubicon, back at the beginning? Of the five entities at that meeting: two were dead, one was in medical cold sleep, one was still recovering from the mental equivalent of a heart attack (a literal attack at that), and then there was me. If *I* was the functional one, we were nowhere near out of the woods, yet.

I'm not apologizing. We were right to be concerned about hidden cultists, and roughing up personnel records was a lot better than roughing up the personnel. I just wish... I just wish people had made better decisions, or at least not make poor ones where I had to see them.

One of the things that I did, once I was effectively in charge, was to pull Syah off everything else and have him handle the records searches. I worried that I was playing favorites, but Maki signed off on it right away. So did Nur, ironically. The sooner we cleared everybody, the faster we could go back to work. The quarantine was definitely starting to pinch us.

There were two results from that: an ironic situation, and a problem. The irony was that it turned out our cultists had been deep in the contragravity research infrastructure. Which made sense, because it was honestly not something we were concerned *that* much about. Artifact smuggling was making us considerably more than blue-sky research projects were. We weren't slacking off, exactly. We had just been a little too blase about the lack of progress. Worse, the cultists had had *insights* into the problem. Their research needed heavy memetic decontamination, but even our rough-and-tumble cleansing job revealed a couple of theoretical breakthroughs, the kind that would justify XHum setting up a research base here.

That's a damned common problem in the Tomb Worlds, by the way. Madness equals genius, obviously, but madness also equals mass death if not stopped. You can't control cultists, and you absolutely can't let them go about their work unopposed, so the only ethical way to use their insanity properly is to collect their accumulated ravings after the fact and hope that you can sanitize away all the horrible bits.

The really nasty part? Cultists *love* it when we read their horrors after the fact. They think it's a great way to recruit new cultists, and if you're not careful... it is.

So what was the *problem*? Why, that we didn't clear everybody.

Syah had come to me, privately, with what he had found. "Nur's storage records show inconsistencies," he told me. "Ones going back for years."

"Yeah, no kidding," I told him. "Nur's in Supply. I've never met one of those guys who thought Earth needed to know a damned thing about their inventories, as long as everybody had what they needed, when they needed it."

"Come on, Pam. I'm not an idiot. I know how this works." Syah grimly tapped the monitor. "What I'm trying to tell you is that I've looked at Supply's inventory flow, and a lot of entries don't match up with known resupply missions, or visiting ships. It started up after Nur came to One-Eighteen, too."

I took a look at the readouts. I'm not great at analyzing data, but those graphs... "Those aren't showing shortfalls, are they?"

Syah shook his head. "No, or at least, not in the long term. Nur's always hit his logistical expectations with plenty to spare. There's never been a shortage of basic materials. In fact, for a few years the operation here actually produced more foodstuffs than the facilities here required, even with a healthy safety margin." He exhaled, roughly. "Only, that surplus just... stopped getting reported. That's not all, either."

"It's not?" I think I knew even then what Syah was going to say. I just didn't want him to.

"During most of Nur's tenure as head of Supply, he's had a steady but unaccounted-for surplus of finished industrial goods. Spare parts, repair equipment, semi-finished and raw materials. The sort of thing you'd expect as ship's cargo, or part of the ship's stores itself. Those stopped showing up in the records about a year ago, which is about when that agricultural surplus stopped vanishing." Syah looked at me. "What happened a year ago, Pam?"

Yeah, I didn't want Syah to say it. So I said it, myself. "The Scouts left this world." I blinked back tears. "He was trading them food for loot. Nur belongs to the Scouts."

"I was on the *Magellan* when the fusion bottle ejected," Nur told us. He was looking at the water bulb like it was a bottle of whiskey, and I wondered for the first time if there were other reasons besides religion why he didn't drink. Nobody thinks twice about a Muslim or Mormon not partaking, right?

He had come quietly, at least. No sign of cultist activity, thank God. In fact, Nur was indignant that we would think *that*. We still had him chained to the chair, because you never knew.

"The emergency power was fine and we had a couple of

message drones," Nur went on, "so nobody panicked. We sent one ahead and did what repairs we could, just to keep busy. I mean, all we had to do was wait until somebody sent a rescue ship." Nur shook his head. "Well, somebody did. The Scouts. They must have intercepted the drone while it was in FTL space.

"We didn't know anything was wrong until after they boarded. The Scouts had come in wearing starsuits, which was good emergency practice, and the first ones weren't armed. No, they just kept us distracted until the 'repair crews' were all over the ship. That's when the guns came out. And the knives. Those were scarier, you know? Guns were bad, but they were usually over there. Knives are death, up close.

"They had their Jamboree after lunch, which they made for us, and it didn't seem real at first. The Scouts weren't what I expected. Out of their suits, they were just kids, younger than I was then — and I wasn't even supposed to be on the *Magellan*. I kind of shaded my age a little to get the steward's job. They dressed real old-timey, with those buttoned shirts and short pants they wore, and the sashes with badges they all had even looked kind of cool. Then again, I didn't know what the badges meant.

"The first couple of Judgings went fine. They brought out the captain, first mate, and second officer forward, looked them over, and spared them. All they did was put them in a room and lock the door. And the first mate was a bastard! One of the meanest women I'd ever met, nasty to everybody, with never a kind word said about her. But the Scout Judging her just shrugged. He didn't even react when she spit in his face. But that kind of defused the mood, right? If Dragon Lady Ivanova was going to pass, how could anybody fail?

"But then they dragged the chief purser forward. The Dragon Lady being cleared or not, Neilson didn't want to go, and I guess he was smart that way. The Scout took one look at him, jerked her head sideways, and then one of the guards sucker-punched Neilson right in the gut. He was still gasping and blubbering when they dragged him out of the room and towards the airlock... and when they came back without him, the rest of us finally understood what was happening.

"There were twenty-three people on the *Magellan*'s crew, and the Scouts spaced five. The ship still had enough crew to man her, so the Scouts locked the rest of us in our cabins for the next twelve hours. When the doors finally opened, they were long gone. But before then they had replaced our fusion bottle, topped up our volatiles, fixed an annoying thermostat glitch in the storage holds, and generally swept and mopped up. There were even eighteen boxes of cookies left in the commissary. One for each survivor."

"How were they?" Maki asked.

Nur started, then relaxed. No, he *slumped*, in despair. "They were delicious."

I didn't understand that at all, but I decided to push ahead. "So, what about the dead bodies? Did they take them, too?"

"What? Oh, no, Pam. The bodies were still floating out there, tumbling slightly from their own velocity. A few of us went out in maneuver suits to collect them, bring them in for burial. We got four bodies, no problem." He laughed. "No problem! The corpses had exploded around their coveralls, then froze, so we had to shove each one into crunch bags. But no problem!

"But the fifth corpse, that was Neilson. The guy that was supposed to bag him got up real close — and then he slapped a pulse thruster on Neilson's chest, and sent the corpse flying. By the time the rest of us got there, Neilson was tumbling away in the Big Dark, too far to reach, and still accelerating.

"When we got back inside, we were all *what the Hell, Juan*? That was his name, Juan, and he wouldn't apologize for anything except using up the pulse thruster. He told us Neilson had 'done things,' his last time in port. He wouldn't say what the things were, or how he knew about them, but he told the captain to go look in Neilson's cabin. No. He *dared* the captain to go look.

"So she did, and when she left Neilson's cabin she and the

Dragon Lady went to search the other dead people's quarters. When they came out, the surviving officers all took the filled crunch bags and spaced them again, along with a bunch of bags and boxes they had taken from the dead people's rooms. They wouldn't say what was in all that stuff, ever — but the Dragon Lady didn't even snarl at us when we kept asking. She'd just say, '*some things should stay in the Big Dark where they belong.*'"

"What happened to Juan?" I asked.

Nur shrugged. "He bought out his contract early on the next planetfall. So did the Dragon Lady. Last I heard, she was a sister on the Saint Cassian orbital nunnery. I didn't hear from Juan again for years. I had almost completely pretended to have forgotten about him when he showed up on One-Eighteen, about a month after I got here. He wanted to talk, and I didn't want to listen, but I listened anyway."

"What did he want?" Maki asked.

"I didn't really know. Or maybe I was pretending that I didn't. Anyway, it was all us being two long-lost spacer buddies, just like the cliche. He dropped hints pretty quick that he was working for some people who did business with my predecessor, and wanted to keep the relationship going. And maybe the business wasn't completely legit, right?

"Well, you hear that last part a lot in Supply. And I didn't care about being completely legit, as long as I wasn't doing anything, you know, bad. So I told him that I wouldn't move drugs or people, or smuggle stuff that was flat-out illegal — but if they were just looking to finesse stupid import rules, yeah, I was their guy. Juan told me that was fine. His people didn't want anything forbidden, just difficult to buy openly. And they'd pay well for it. Not with cash or anything like that. They had access to industrial gear, and wanted to trade it for food. All I had to do was move the stuff to a spot on the coast, and they'd do the rest. Oh, and I'd need to make sure they knew what the flight schedule was like."

"Right," I ground out. "We don't have an orbital network,

and it's a big planet. There's even a couple of cleared sites left over from when we were thinking about making One-Eighteen a gray colony. You could get autotrucks out there. Didn't you realize you were in over your head?"

"After I saw the first invoices, I knew they were resupplying spaceships, sure. I even figured out right away that Juan's 'people' were pirates. But I was still trying to figure out who to warn when I got snatched out of my own house one weekend, stuffed in the back of one of my own autotrucks. Four hours and half a world later, I was down at the Erebus dig."

He looked around at the silent room. "Yeah, I saw it years ago," he said. "Back then it was full of Scouts, and I spent an hour waiting for the Jamboree to Judge me to death. Turns out they did one on my way south. If I had failed, they'd have just shot me in the head and tossed me out of the shuttle's aft cargo hatch. But since I had passed, they wanted me on-site for the arrival of a captured ship.

"This was the seventh ship they had grabbed and brought to the planet, and I was surprised they hadn't killed the corrupted members of the crew yet. They were unconscious, trussed up, and a few of them looked a little worse for wear, but they were all alive. Juan made sure to show me that, right after he made me walk the ship with him and see selected private spaces. 'This was one of the ones where we couldn't pass *anybody*,' Juan explained to me, and I was surprised then how upset he was about that. 'They were starting to feed off of each other, too. Egg each other on, keep the corruption spiraling along inside each person's soul. That's why we brought them here. The younger Scouts, they need to see.'

"'See what?' I asked him. He grimaced and replied, 'What can happen when humans spend too much time in the Great Dark without correction.'"

Nur chuckled, making the rest of us start. "Jamborees look completely different from the inside, you know. The one on the ship, it was in a temporary space, one that wasn't dedicated to Judging. But there, down at the dig, they had the time to do things up right. Torches and totems and posts for the Judged. The guttering flames turned the shadows into angels of Death, flickering above us onlookers with compassionate menace. I think it was the shadows that convinced me that, while I had not left One-Eighteen, I wasn't in the universe I knew, either.

"Or maybe it was just how easily the Scouts made each person dragged before them confess their crimes. And they did! Even the ones spitting defiance, they started talking soon enough, with no more than a ritual cuff in the face to draw blood. Something about their surroundings made the prisoners start talking, first grudgingly, then with pride, then with apprehension, and then finally with fear. Fear of us? Fear of the shadowy angels above? Fear of the Tomb Worlds themselves? Whatever it was, it made them confess their most awful deeds. And I believed every horrible word of them."

He looked at Maki and me. "I still do," he whispered. "I'm with the Scouts, yes. I don't want to be, but I can't not be one of them. They're right. There's things out here that can twist a man, and when they do? Sometimes you have to cut the cancer out. But I never worked with the cultists, and I've never harmed an innocent person." Nur shook his head. "I'd say that you have to believe me, but I know you won't. That's okay, though. I can't blame you for that."

"Was there any sign he was going to snap?" I asked Maki as we looked at Nur through the inset window of his cryo-casket. I hated how sinister Nur looked now. I mean, this was the safest thing for everybody, and at least we had the option. Some bases, they'd have had to just shoot him and nobody would say a word.

"Not until afterward," she replied. "Syah found a hidden directory on his computer. The usual: he was keeping a private journal, showing some pre-obsessive behaviors in his searches, reading a lot of twenty-first century fiction, all the warning signs. Looks like the *Redacted* showing up sent him over the edge. The entries got a lot more purple after that."

"Oh, crap," I said. At Maki's look of sudden worry, I shook my head. "It was just that we were talking about the Terrans, and he started going off about 'mind-locking,' whatever that was supposed to be. I figured it was just Nur being Nur. Were there any signs he was going space-happy?"

Maki shook her head "No, thank God. There was nothing like that in the computer. Just a lot of ranting about Earth and its foul minions. His fixation on the *Redacted* was pretty thorough. And vicious. Nur *really* hated that ship."

"That's... weird? He didn't show any of this. Usually that can't be hidden."

"I wondered the same thing," Maki admitted. "We went over his files and correspondence afterward for warning signs, but couldn't find anything. Nur was keeping it all tightly wound up."

"But of course," I muttered. "If he hadn't, we would have noticed it ahead of time. More people would be alive, if we had."

"Yeah. The good news, though? At least it's done. We cleaned out the cultists before they could do... whatever it was they were going to do to us, and I don't think the Scouts are coming back any time soon. We can finally end the quarantine." Maki shuddered. "And then I'm done with this damned planet. Uh, no offense."

"None taken." I wasn't sure how she knew I *was* offended, but it was a harmless enough lie on my part. "Are we sure we cleaned out the plot to kill us all, though? That cultist manifesto we found was long on ravings, but short on details. What if there's still a cell or two left?"

"Then we'll deal with them." Maki managed a smile. "Honestly, things could have been worse. Once we knew they were out there, rolling them up wasn't impossible, right?" The smile slipped. "Too many good people died, but at least we've taken care of all the bad ones."

Getting away from Maki wasn't hard. She didn't want to be around Nur any more than I did, and she had a lot of things to worry about right now. It wasn't hard for me to retire to my apartment with a promise to hydrate and sleep. Which I absolutely was going to do, as soon as I poured out a few for the dead. *All* the dead, including the one I missed the most.

So naturally I dreamed about The Process that night.

As dreams go, it wasn't very horrible. I was skipping from cloud to cloud in the upper atmosphere, watching the fireflies play around me, when suddenly I heard The Process say, "Ghost-Dancer Tanaka." I was happy, then, because it was going to be a *good* dream. I wondered if Oft and the Anticipant would stop by next.

"They are not here, because they are dead." That wasn't a nice part of the dream, I decided. "I am sorry, Ghost-Dancer Tanaka. Did you hear me say that, before I was lost?"

"Yes," I reassured it. "We all did. Why were you sorry, anyway?"

"It is my task to protect you, to keep a horrible universe at bay. I failed." I'd never heard The Process sound so sad. "Even now, this is all I can do to assist."

I've lucid dreamed, obviously, but never at this level. "It's okay, Process. We managed to muddle on through, anyway. We'll be alright."

If I thought The Process was sad before, now I knew what true sorrow sounded like, coming from its imaginary lips. Sorrow, near-despair — and rage. "No, Pamela. You will not."

—and that was when I woke up.

At that point I was supposed to do a whole lot of things, starting with writing up the dream while it was still fresh, and taking a pill or three to drain it of any potential trauma later. I didn't do any of those things, because I was now seriously worried that we had missed something.

Understand, I didn't think it was actually The Process talking to me: it was dead. I also know I'm not 'Ghost-Dancer Tanaka.' Using that name felt deliberate. So either the part of my brain that handles my dreaming was going nuts, or it was sending me a message. I was pretty sure I wasn't going nuts (although, how would I know?), so what was I trying to tell myself?

Okay, I already knew. My brain wanted me to still be suspicious of what was going on. It couldn't come out and tell me that, because dreams don't operate under regular logic. Getting my use-name deliberately wrong was as clear a hint as my head could manage.

(People learn quickly to take dreams seriously in the Tomb Worlds, by the way. Bad things happen to the people who don't.)

Oh, and Maki and the rest weren't really in the clear, then. Happy day! Still, we had progressed, right? All the obvious problems had been handled. So if the real maniac was still out there, he was probably thinking he had thrown off suspicion. That might mean he'd start making mistakes.

I'd just have to keep investigating, but quietly. So quietly that Syah couldn't even know. Fortunately, he had already given me a good foundation to work from. And, besides? Now that the cultists were gone, I had other plans for him.

CHAPTER TWENTY-EIGHT

Downfall

Piloting training, obviously. What *else* could I have meant? Besides, we needed more qualified fliers than ever.

Syah was never going to be a great pilot. I don't mean that he was a bad student, all things considered. He knew the controls, knew the checklist, and didn't panic when some little thing went wrong. He definitely would have qualified for an emergency certification, had things gotten that far, and probably a regular pilot's ticket, too. He even liked to fly.

But Syah couldn't dance with the wind. He tried to. He really did. But when on the stick, Syah just couldn't manage to slide from safe zone to safe zone the way I could. He kept racking up the chime that 118-G-002 equipment used instead of an alarm. It didn't rattle him, which was really good, but he didn't like it, either.

We only got grounded once, which was actually pretty good for somebody going through emergency qual training. He didn't quite see it that way, though. "I'm doing it wrong!" he muttered to himself. "What am I missing?"

"Well, it's nice you're not blaming *me*," I said while stretching (the 'I've spent an hour in this chair' kind, not the 'hey, look at me' kind). "What, you expected to pick it all up in one go?"

"Not really," admitted Syah. "Okay, that's a lie. I did. I'm usually good at picking things up quickly," he said with a surprising lack of arrogance, "and this technique you're trying to teach me — I should be able to get it! It's obvious how it's supposed to go. But I keep missing the mark."

"You're actually doing fine, for somebody who didn't start flying for real until you got to this planet," I told him. "Those piloting games really do give you the basics, don't they?"

"They do. But it's a lot different when you're in a shuttle for the first time." The smile he gave me would melt harder hearts than mine. "It helps when you have such a great teacher, though."

"Oh, *stop* it, you flatterer!" I retorted, flustered and trying to hide my reaction. "I can't take all the credit, so I won't take the blame either, okay?" He started to frown, and I winced. It was so hard to talk to Syah normally, sometimes. "What, you already forgot your first landing in the hauler this morning? I can't say I blame you!"

"Oh, *that*." His flush was as lovely as the rest of him, really. "I had, actually. My brain's smarter than I am — no, wait, that came out wrong. I mean, yes, this hauler's harder to pilot than I thought."

"Yeah, that's Amalgamation technology for you." I started working the controls — well, the hand controls. There was a bunch of stuff that you could do with your feet, but that was legit hard for humans to learn. I wasn't sure if I knew them all myself. It didn't matter, anyway. We were still locked out until somebody had learned his lesson about obeying all local traffic laws. "They did things differently than we did. Better, honestly. It's hard to pick some of the subtle stuff up. The best you can do is keep quiet and listen. Sometimes you end up hearing what you need to learn." I shrugged. "And sometimes you don't."

Syah looked at me. "Doesn't that bother you?" he said. "Knowing that there's better ways to do things, only we'll never find out what they are?"

I considered it. "Sometimes," I admitted. "But it's not our fault, is it? We didn't destroy the Amalgamation. That makes a big difference. And, shoot, somebody worked it all out once already, right? Give us enough of a chance, and we'll learn the same tune."

Then I took a look at the clock — and a longer, slower look at him. "Speaking of chances, we've got at least an hour before we can start even hoping to get this baby in the air again..."

Things might have gone further than they did if we hadn't been interrupted by the signal that the ship was out of traffic lockdown. Then again, they might not have. Syah was very careful about not letting his passions get away from him.

These days? So was I.

The last day was the worst.

Syah and I were doing a survey run through the upper atmosphere for his calibration project, now that we were back to doing that (it would also get him enough hours for his pilot's ticket). Syah probably figured out something was bothering me before we started cruising the upper atmosphere, though. Despite my best efforts, I'm just not cut out to be a spy. "Something wrong?" he asked me.

The fuzz was a little different that day. More... fuzzy. I'm sorry, it's hard to describe how it sounded to me. I must have made myself sound a little distracted when I replied, "We talked to what's left of the *Redacted*'s command crew this morning. They've decided to leave tomorrow for Earth. They've got their space-happy maniac after all, so off they go. Mission accomplished! Hurray!"

"Sorry. I know he was a friend of yours." Syah looked at me. "What do you think they'll do with him?"

"Well, it's Earth, so they'll probably take his mind apart, then put it back together." I scowled at the screens. We were pretty far away from all the bases at this point, and for once I didn't like the feel of the upper air here. Anybody who tells you that a planetary atmosphere is completely inchoate doesn't fly in the Tomb Worlds. There's a sense of finality here, like everything has stopped and it's never starting up again. Normally, I appreciate the stolidity. Today? Not so much. "They still think you can cure the space-happy, without any loss of self. Hell, maybe they can. Either way, Nur's never coming back here. Oh, hey, we're coming up on a node that'd suit you."

Syah peered over my shoulder at the screen. "I don't see anything," he admitted.

I laughed, nicely. "Of course not. It's a cloud of nanobots. If you could see them, things would be seriously weird. They're there, though. See the readout?"

"Okay, yeah. That's gotta be what's causing the fuzz. Let me run a scanner over it, and we'll confirm it once and for all..."

What happened next was a combination of bad judgment calls all around.

In my case, what happened was this: I had had the thought of double-checking our personnel files. I went looking for anomalies, and found a couple — then went looking for more, and found those, too.

They were all in Syah's personnel file, which had him listed as being on One-Eighteen for two years. Fine, except that I remembered Syah telling me that he had only been on-planet for a few months. I told myself that wasn't enough for an accusation, and I was even right — but it was enough for me to look up the files the *Redacted* had on him, alas.

My bad judgment call was in isolating him from everybody else — and, more particularly, our computer networks. An Amalgamation hauler with the radio disabled is one hell of an air gap, and it'd give people on the ground a chance to turn off whatever booby traps Syah might have put into the computer system. It didn't occur to us that he might have been targeting something else.

In our defense, it *also* never occurred to us to think he might do something irrevocable while it'd affect him, too. Maybe it should have: this planet was the last one on the list. If Syah was some kind of space-happy cultist ready to suicide, this would be the time and place to do it.

Syah's mistake was thinking I wouldn't notice what he did

to the nanoswarm all around us. But then, why should he? Nobody must have ever did, before.

I'm not really sure about the exact details, because I'm not a hardcore computer jockey and I was being distracted by the white-hot pain suddenly gashing behind my eyes. But the pain ended up working out for the best. Syah wasn't expecting me to nearly spasm and seizure the hauler into the ground. I don't know what he was planning to do, if I hadn't reacted. Probably just finish our trip, and never say a word until the nanoswarm flayed the marrow from our bones.

But, instead, when I blinked away the agony, he had moved back to the other end of the cabin... and now had my gun. Amazingly, the first thing he said was, "Pam? Are you all right?"

I looked at him, in angry bafflement. "What do you care?" I said, and jerked my head at the gun. "What you've got there is kind of diagnostic."

He swallowed, nervously. "I didn't want to take it. I was hoping I wouldn't need to. I was trying to make this as easy as possible. Don't bother with the radio, by the way. The burst I sent to the nanoswarm outside fried the antenna. You won't be able to send a message to Luxor Base in time."

"Easy, huh? Like on Richelieu?" That got a reaction from him as I went on. "You did fine with messing with *our* personnel files, Syah. But it's like I told Nur, that one time: check all the other files, too. I looked you up on the *Redacted*. It confirmed you've been here for months, not years — and that you started your pilot training on Richelieu, three months before it got wiped out. Was that your doing?"

"No!"

I was surprised at his vehemence. "Fine. Your fellow cultists?"

"I'm not a cultist! And it's not like that, either!" Syah replied, hotly. "Richelieu was an accident! A stupid, dumb accident!" He stopped, took a breath, tried to relax.

I listened to the fuzz around me. Iit definitely sounded

worse, now. Busier. *Hungrier.* Aloud, I said, "Fine. It was an accident. Somebody messing with the transport net there?"

"You could say that, sure. Oh, yeah, you could say that!" Syah seemed more centered but also angrier, like he was finally going to clear some long-dead air. "Richelieu barely had a transport net at all. The planet's infrastructure was trashed. That's why we put a base there. Fewer automated defenses, you know? We could dig deep into the guts of the systems. Too deep.

"My team was researching the planetary datasphere. We found references to an emergency subroutine. Something that might turn on the transport net's repair systems. If we could do that... hey, the things we could learn by just watching, right?"

"Jesus," I said. "You know how many rules that would break, right? We can barely see some of the Amalgamation's tech! What made you think you could control it?"

Syah laughed, bitterly. "The technical word is 'hubris.' But, hell, out of my whole team only four survived, so we got ours, right?"

I looked at the gun. "I'm just gonna assume you decided to do it again. Murdering four planets, though? Must have taken some doing."

"You're wrong and right. First off, it's five planets. Ingrid cleaned Greenhell, Ivan got Ramal, and Alan took care of Fenbian. We drew straws, and I lost, so I had to do two planets: Terkutuk, and here. And we did it!" Syah didn't look happy. "Weren't we lucky?"

"I don't know those people," I said. "Fellow cultists?"

"Fellow team members."

"Same difference. Where are they now?"

"Where do you think, Pam? Greenhell, Ramal, and Fenbian. And me, here. I've murdered you all, starting about two hours from now. I don't get to run away from something like that again."

I wanted to yell, *that's real noble of you!* — but I didn't. Two hours is a long time in an emergency, and there were certain things I hadn't taught Syah yet about this hauler. "So, what's your plan, then? Just wait until... what?"

"We wait until the transformed nanoswarm reaches the bases," he replied. "And the *Redacted*, which I feel just as bad about. After that, you might as well land and walk outside. It'll be faster than starving. If you want to shoot me first, well, I deserve it."

"If you're offering," I said tightly, "I can do it now."

Syah shook his head. "Sorry, Pam. I've seen you fly. You might be able to outrun the storm, warn a few people in time, maybe even get the *Redacted* sealed up and off the landing pad. I can't take that chance."

"So we wait?"

"Yeah." He didn't seem happy about that. Then again, neither was I.

"All right, Syah. Let's spend some time doing confessionals. Let's start with the cultists. Not yours?"

"No, *not* mine," he grated out. "They and the Scouts were the two wild cards in this. You'd all be dead two years ago if it wasn't for them."

"But not you?"

"No! Not like that!" I believed him, God help me. "Terkutuk was originally supposed to be last. I did it first, because I figured I could just outwait the Scouts. I knew they wouldn't stay on this planet forever."

"How did you even know they were here, Syah? *We* didn't."

That earned me a grimace. "The same way I heard about the cultists, Pam. I've been living in Hell for the last decade. After a while, you get to know what the devils are all doing."

"Hooray," I told him. "What were the cultists doing here, then?"

"What do you think? They were getting deathheart, Pam. The Scouts were vetting and Jamboreeing every independent ship within five hundred light years. There was no spaceborne competition to worry about, and you had your own little smuggling operation going on? It'd be easy to add packets to the ships going to Earth. The cultists must have been selling it to the Great Powers in the first place. Probably even to some of your customers."

"Right," I admitted. "Cultists wouldn't care that harvesting deathheart is a drawn-out suicide pact. That's what they think life is, anyway. You could have told somebody that."

"I wanted to, you know? But I couldn't take the risk. Besides, by then I had access to the cultists. Normally they're good at detecting infiltrators, but their system breaks down when they're dealing with somebody who's just as committed to mass murder as they are. Even if it's for different reasons." He laughed, harshly. "I even got into their networks. Just before the quarantine went down, I swapped their deathheart shipments with mini broadcasters that'll whisper their customers' names and crimes all over Earth's datanet. We'll be dead by then, but at least we'll have that as consolation."

I ignored that. "Right, so you had access to deathheart. The perfect poison. You going to blame Adam's and Burcu's deaths on the cultists?"

I hoped Syah would actually deny both, but... he didn't. "Burcu wasn't me. The cultists decided she was dangerous, and they had a minion on the *Redacted*. Yes, I murdered Adam. But I *wasn't* trying to drive him space-happy. I'm not cruel."

"Yet killing people is all right?" I asked, trying to ignore the fact that a part of me agreed with him. "That's not cruel?"

"I've murdered everybody on this planet, Pam. Including me. I also blew up that supply ship, which means that my murders literally stretch across this solar system. But I wasn't trying to make people *suffer*. Adam had to go. He found my supply cache! I knew the rangers were walking the paths, but they never went *off* them. Why would Adam?"

"I dunno. Because he likes the woods here?"

Syah shook his head. "*Nobody* liked the woods here, Pam, or being alone on this planet for long. This place scares people."

"Well, it doesn't scare me," I said. "And I guess it didn't scare

Adam, either. Or the dog."

"The dog was a surprise," Syah admitted. "How could he have had a dog? They can't live here."

"This one could, Syah. How did you get the deathheart into him, anyway? When we went back and found the traces of it at Adam's rest stop, we thought somebody had snuck in. But we decided it couldn't have been you, since you were onsite the whole time."

"He ordered fresh vatmeat from the biolabs. I diverted it while in transit." Syah grimaced. "He must have fed some to the dog."

"Maybe he meant it for the dog, only he got some on him, too."

"Yeah." Syah was getting used to talking about it, I could see. Which made sense. Who else was he going to tell? Even an enemy would make a better audience than the horrified voices inside his own head. "Honestly, I probably would have killed Burcu. She didn't know me, but I knew about her. She was *tenacious* enough to pull herself out of the colony worlds and into Terran service. She wouldn't stop until she found Adam's murderer. I had already decided to murder everybody else too, right? Why quibble at a change in the schedule? The way she refused anything but the shuttle made it easy for the cultists. Their minion meddled with the fuel lines, and waited for the crash."

"But you did destroy the resupply ship." I was starting to see the pattern. "No, wait, you were trying to kill *me*, and maybe Nur. How many times *did* you try to kill me?"

I took no little satisfaction in seeing his face turn gray. "A few times. The resupply run, because it would have been fast. Your picnic — I got that device from the cultists, and the bastards were happy to give it to me — because it would have been fast then, too. I try to make these deaths as quick as I can, Pa— Chief Pilot Tanaka. Before you ask…"

"Oh, I've figured out that you killed The Process," I snarled at him, and took more satisfaction at the way he started. "If it's computer-related, you did it. Full points for burning yourself trying to save it, by the way. Great way to cast off suspicion. Any other crimes you want to confess to? Chook's death, maybe?"

He hung his head. "Quietus is quick. Maki would have gone quick, too. I wish I could have gotten Greg, too. It would have been cleaner that way."

It's a horrible thing to hear the man you thought you loved (a treacherous part of me wanted to quibble about the tense) show real regret that it wasn't *him* that killed somebody. "That's mostly it, then. Except for Nur. I'm surprised you didn't kill him, too."

"I would have, except for the damned Scouts. Once people found out they were on this planet, everything would be locked down until that loose end was tied off." He snorted. "Ironically, I was going to frame him as the Scouts' mole. The most believable choice, right? Only, the reason it was so believable was because it happened to be true. So now he gets locked in a frozen coffin for eternity, while the rest of us die."

"You say that like you felt bad, Syah. Why? What's one more murder?" I gave him the steadiest look I had. "You want to feel better about all of this?"

"*Yes*, actually. I have murdered almost fifty thousand people, either by myself or by helping a colleague, and I would *desperately* like to feel better. I am *tired* of killing innocents. There will be *no* peace for me in the afterlife, either. I'd pray for oblivion, except there's no possible way I could ever have that prayer answered."

I waited until the silence in the cabin was deafening, and spoke again. "This is when you start the rant, Syah," I told him, trying to keep 'more in sorrow than anger' in my voice. Let me tell you, it's not easy when there's a gun being pointed at you. "Or were you going to kill all of us without explaining why?"

It's amazing, really. Syah had the same disaster class training that I did, which meant he knew perfectly well that they teach you to ask stuff like that when playing for time with a space-happy maniac. But damned if it still didn't work. "Oh, I'll explain!" he said. "But I don't have to! You already know the answer."

"Do I?" I said as I listened very, very carefully. "You saying there's something wrong with this world? Something we don't dare bring back? Because it's a little late for that..."

"Not just this world! Not even this *cluster* of worlds, the ones ruled over by a species whose name none of us ever dare to say! Ever wonder about that, Pam? Ever try to think too hard why we don't use the names of—" he went on to say the original name of One-Eighteen, and name of the species who lived there. I got a little bit of a shudder when he did that, I have to admit. The names aren't hard for human throats to say, and they're not dreadful. Not evil, to quote people like Oft, or Gina. But...

"Those names, they're not for us to use," I reminded him. "We respect that. But the original inhabitants couldn't mind us being here. We're trying to live up to being part of the Amalgamation, the best we can."

"That's it!" Syah howled. "That's it! The Amalgamation is dead, Pam. It was murdered! We have no idea why, how, or who. Why aren't *we* dead, too? Why was humanity spared? What makes us so special, to live where other species, *greater* species perished?" His gun barrel oscillated a little as he started to go into full rant mode — and then he stepped back from the brink, dammit. "But you know why, Pam. You should say it."

"I... would rather not, Syah." *And it's true*, I thought, as the fuzz started to fill my ears, *I **would** rather not.*

"Humor the madman with the gun, Pam. We're all going to die. At least die admitting the truth."

"All right. All right!" I was doing some shouting of my own, now. "We lived because *we did this*! Somehow!"

Even the fuzz seemed to recede for a moment. You learn out here very quickly that there are things you must *never* say aloud. There are topics so taboo, you may not even think about their outlines. At the top of that list — the very, very top — is the dread certainty that somehow, all of this death and destruction, all of the endless ghosts on alien winds and twisted fragments of a wondrous civilization, is our fault. None of us know *why* it's our fault, but it is. You can forget about it, for a while, but not forever.

That's why there are cultists. They believe that they are *entitled* to all of this, and yet they're being thwarted out of their due. That's why there are terrorists, too. They believe just as strongly that some sort of deal was struck. Yet, they reject it, no matter what the consequences. As for the space-happy? Well. Some people just can't handle laboring under the strain of this horrible, horrible knowledge.

Maybe all of the myriad iterations of The Process *aren't* sapient, after all. It *must* have deduced what we instinctively know; and yet, it does not hate us. I don't think that I could extend that kind of grace, if I was the one being so wronged.

I gave Syah one last, long look. Even after all of this, he really did do something to my heart. I was suddenly glad that we had never slept together, but for a completely different reason than you'd think. He had done it for my sake, and his. He might have committed many betrayals, but at least he would die never having committed that one.

I glared at him, through my tears. "Happy?"

"Happy? No." I believed that, you know. Syah was shrunken into himself, as if keeping his secrets were the only thing keeping him going. "But as soon as people understand that, the sooner we can get out of the Tomb Worlds. *And* the colony worlds. Humanity has to go back to Earth. We have to close ourselves off, and hide. Maybe we can be forgiven, if we reject this vile gift given to us."

"Maybe we won't," I replied.

"Maybe," he agreed, which surprised me. My admission seemed to have calmed him down. Or at least his gun wasn't pointing at me now. "It's still the best chance we have. So that's why we did what we did. What was done accidentally on Richelieu was done on purpose on the other worlds, and now this one. Just one more hint to humans that we need to..."

"'...flee to the peace and safety of a new dark age?'" I interrupted him, to his confusion. "Ah," I went on as the fuzz in my head became a roar. "I guess they don't teach that one in literature class on Bolivar." And then my foot hit the emergency vent switch. Personally, I would have made that something you controlled by hand, but apparently the aliens of 118-G-002 didn't fidget much.

Emergency venting isn't something that happens for long in an atmosphere. The aliens used it mostly to clear a cabin of noxious fumes or blow out fires, I think. But it's great for shoving people around, messing with their aim, and letting in a cloud of nanobots now programmed to disassemble Terran organic life. My reflexes let me slam my visor shut and go full airtight.

Syah's... were hampered by the gun in his hand. By the time he dropped it, the nanoswarm had gotten him. I don't know how painful it was. It was definitely fast. And if it was painful... well, he probably would have welcomed it.

Not that I was paying attention to that. The *second* thing I did was rip off the cover to the specially-installed box mounted on one wall and punch the Bugout Button. You have to punch it, too, hard enough to at least leave a bruise. The corp gets kind of upset if people accidentally set off the signal to leave *now*, don't wait for the file to download, forget the houseplants, just suit up and go, go, GO. I had been planning to point out the button to Syah as part of his training, except, well, you know.

I didn't know how much time I'd have before the nanobot swarm I must have inhaled already would reach critical mass, so I shoved the antenna array out of the way and plugged in a spare (of *course* I had a spare!). I assumed there'd be no time to make a long goodbye, so I settled on yelling "Ninety minutes until death cloud! Bugout! Bugout! Bugout! Accept no contact from me! Don't record any screams!"

After all of that, I finally looked over at the empty environment suit that used to be Syah. And then I looked at the wind, where I suspected he was now, and forevermore. "You should've talked to somebody about what happened to you," I muttered. "We have counselors for a reason."

EPILOGUE

They didn't vaporize me from orbit.

Hell, the remaining personnel offered to save me, once two hours had come and gone without me turning into dust. They had an entire plan in place, but I, ah, shot it down. I just wasn't worth the risk.

I *was* a risk, too. Ninety minutes' warning got us 95% survival, including everybody in deep freeze or the hospital. They're all up there now at the Lagrange Point, slowly linking together survival shelters and the existing orbital refuges to make a cobbled-together space station. The *Redacted* had a bunch of gear that helps with it, so things aren't *that* desperate. Quite.

Mind you, it's going to be a God-awful mess until the closest worlds can get long-term survival gear over to them, let alone evacuate. They have enough to keep going for six months, and the *Redacted* adds another three to their total, so... eighty-twenty, in the survivors' favor. Right now the counselors are doing double shifts making sure that nobody goes homicidal, and keeping as few people from suiciding as possible. They're being helped by the fact that Maki had enough presence of mind to grab the contragrav research. The corp would have sent relief anyway, but thanks to that information, people will know their careers won't suffer. This isn't the worst thing that's happened to a planetary facility in the course of getting some truly useful data, after all.

The folks up top can still access the computers on the

surface, for now. I asked them to look at Syah's files, and they found... nothing. Not even a manifesto. There's always a manifesto when somebody goes space-happy, you know? It's how you know. So that's why I ended up spending some free time writing up one for him, and the official record. It wasn't that hard to do, either: all I had to do was write down what Syah told me in the hauler, and then crazy it up a bunch. Well, at least a little. I added in some random babbling, odd phrases, kept removing more and more punctuation as I went. We've all seen enough of those, you know? I know that it's a lie, but Maki and I agreed it's kind of important that Syah keeps getting represented as space-happy until help arrives. It'll keep people focused, and that'll keep the suicide rate down.

And he was crazy, sure. Sort of. I mean, he wasn't entirely wrong. We probably shouldn't have left Earth, once we realized what had happened to everybody who wasn't us. I just think that, you know, it's too late to go back now. What happened, happened. Even though it's our fault, it also is not. Humanity will just have to live with itself.

Only not here. The world below me only offers an inexorable death for humans, now. 118-G-002 isn't the only Tomb World. There's plenty others out there to poke around in.

Well, plenty of Tomb Worlds for other humans. I won't rejoin them.

As I said, the *Redacted* had a plan for me: depressurize the cabin, refill it with a gas that wasn't quite corrosive enough to eat my suit, flush the cabin again, then re-pressurize and send over a rat in a cage to see what'd happen. It would've worked. It *did* work, with a couple of the orbiters that had lifted off while possibly contaminated. They're all rated as safe now.

All of that sounded exhausting, and I didn't want to last until then. Actually, that's wrong. I *did* want to last until then — but I wanted a lot of things, and some of them I can't have anymore, and survive at the same time. All part of being human: you can't always get what you want, as the skald once said.

I *did* vent the cabin, though, and skimmed through the upper atmosphere until I refilled my air tanks. Once I did that, I listened until I was sure of the silence, then I — cracked my helmet. And then I waited to see if I could really hear the nanobots after all.

They didn't eat me, so I guess that answers *that* question.

So I flew back to Luxor Base, for one last time.

There are worse places to be in this fallen universe. I'm living fairly comfortably, in fact. I had the entirety of Luxor Base to loot, and my choice of half-wrecked accommodations to choose from. There's plenty of food, plenty of power, and nobody human will ever come to One-Eighteen again in my lifetime, so I won't have to worry about preserving the good china for guests. If I was an introvert, this would be the life.

Except that I can't fly.

The haulers had to be sent back down again after a few days in orbit, lest they starve to death. Once they crawled back onto their pads, they just powered down. I can't access them again, either. Our interface with Amalgamation systems got thoroughly wrecked by events, and I'm not about to mess with it. Since I'm not going to die just yet, I'd rather not commit suicide. So, there'll be no more regular flying for me.

No Earthtech flying, either. The one attempt to send down an unmanned human shuttle for my use ended in a fireball. Whatever Syah did to the transportation network seems to have repaired it, and the orbital meteor defense system. The manned vessels in orbit are all fine, but anything else is being treated as hostile. All in all, I can't say I can blame the defense grid for that. I get to be the only human thing left on One-Eighteen, and my feet are firmly on the ground.

It's not unbearable, though. I think of myself as the equivalent of a lighthouse keeper, doing my part for humanity by staying here and warning passing ships that this planet offers only death to human life. Most of all, I still don't hate this place the way most of humanity does, and I think I know why that is. There's something about me that is attuned to One-Eighteen, some accident of blood or gene pair, and it's enough to make me feel like part of this world. That's why the nanoswarm didn't disassemble me, I think; it recognized me. I guess that's why Adam survived for as long as he did, too. We two got to *belong* here, for good and especially ill.

(Speaking of Adam, it wasn't hard to decide what to do with his... well, it couldn't be his soul, because even people who believe in those don't think they're tangible. But I took what made Adam *Adam*, encased carefully in what I felt was a suitable vessel, and sent the whole thing up on the last suborbital probe I had. It disintegrated at its apogee, and hopefully what was left of him will find some peace with the other ghosts.

I'm not sorry about doing that, you understand. I never really knew Adam. Any destiny he and I might have had was an imposition, and nothing ever asked me if I wanted to be imposed upon. They should have. I might have said yes.)

So don't worry about me (and never, ever come to visit). It's not hard duty here, and the settlement's libraries made it through all the difficulties, so I will have that to comfort me. I also have Oft's personal scriptures to read, if I get particularly bored. They're... deeper than I expected, and some of the people in their pages I think really *understand* what it's like for me right now, bearing a burden that should not be borne by any one woman.

It's unlikely that I'll convert to Oft's faith, though. It's just a little too *hopeful* for this universe. Where were his gods, or god, or *whatever*, when the Amalgamation needed divine intervention the most? Why do *we* get to live, when their real worshipers were slaughtered without mercy? I'll be meditating on that question for the rest of my life, I suspect.

If I ever come up with an answer, I'll let humanity know. If I don't, *don't* come here to find it. Here you only find death for our species, and ghosts on an alien wind.

GLOSSARY

Planetary Designation: **118-G-002**
Local name: One-Eighteen
Number of Planets in System: 6
Number of Moons: 0
Gravity: .997 Terran Standard
Diameter: 1.0003 Terran Standard
Average Temperature: Temperate-warm
Bio-compatibility Index: +0.3
Human population: 10,000 (approximate)
Sponsor: XHum

Adjudication Council: The Adjudication Council is a multinational organization that handles disputes and concerns arising between the **Great Powers** of Terra, hopefully before they become conflicts. It is a deliberative body only, with no ability to enforce its agreements. The Council occasionally sends ships out into the Tomb Worlds for various operations.

Headquarters: Geneva, EDO

Members: the United States of North America (USNA), the South East Defensive Association (SEDA), the African Protective Trade Pact (APTP), Europe de l'Oeust (EDO), Grande Brasil, the New Empire, and the Pakt Euroazjatycki (Pakt).

Amalgamation: The interstellar society that existed in this section of the galaxy. The Amalgamation appears to have been a highly peaceful and technologically advanced political-economic entity, with a high standard of living and remarkable social stability. It was utterly destroyed by unknown enemies at some point in the 18th Century AD.

There are no known survivors.

Bolivar: One of the four **Colony Worlds** assigned to Earth as part of the cultural Uplift program originally created by the **Amalgamation**. Bolivar is a mineral-rich, tectonically active planet with multiple industrial sectors. Oxygen, temperatures, and humidity are within human tolerances, although humidity is typically extremely low.

The planet is administered from the spaceport Cyrk, located on Bolivar's moon (Kowaldo). Bolivar's populace is theoretically subordinate to the numerous megacorporations operating on the planet. In practice, power is shared between the megacorps, various civic organizations and polities, and the administrators on Cyrk.

The primary colonists for Bolivar came from the African Protective Trade Pact (APTP) and Pakt Euroazjatycki (PE), and both **Great Powers** retain significant influence.

The Consolidation Wars: A series of conflicts on Earth. Most historians agree that the major conflicts started in 2076 AD, and continued on until 2102. During that time, the number of fully independent countries on Terra dropped from over a hundred and fifty, to seven **Great Powers**.

Galactic Pioneer Scouts: an anti-colonization terrorist group specializing in the capture and disposal of starships, and their crews. Originally consisting of adolescents suffering from a variant of **Sudden-Onset Violent Psychosis** from exposure to the **Tomb Worlds**, the Scouts retain many of the customs and practices from their previous incarnation as a coeducational youth organization. Given the average Scout's age (ranging from nine to twenty three standard Terran years), it is unclear how the group acquires new members. _**All** contacts with a member of the Galactic Pioneer Scouts must be reported_ *immediately* **to the appropriate local or planetary authority.** Do not approach a Scout on your own!

Great Powers: One of the seven regional conglomerations of nation-states currently controlling Earth. The Great Powers formed during the **Consolidation Wars** which followed First Contact with **The Process.** They currently directly control 95% of the territory and 90% of the population of Earth. Some nominally independent nations still exist, but only as client-states of one or the other Great Powers.

The Great Powers are each fully autonomous, with independent judiciaries and military forces. All disputes are addressed via the **Adjudication Council**, but there is no unified 'world government.' The current recognized Great Powers are: The United States of North America (USNA), Grande Brasil (Brasil), the African Protective Trade Pact (APTP), the New Empire, Europe de l'Oeust (EDO), Pakt Euroazjatycki (PE or Pakt), and the South East Defensive Association (SEDA).

Grey Colony: A permanent place for human settlement and exploitation that is not located on the official colony worlds of **Jefferson**, Zheng He, **Bolivar**, or Abubakri. There are currently five official Grey Colonies: Arkham, Caguaya, Fenbian, Muzuris, and Tartessos.

Grey Colonies are openly fostered by human governments, corporations, or NGOs, and administered by the Survey/Colonization Initiative. They enjoy *no* protection from surviving Amalgamation-automated civil services. Settle there at your own risk.

Iluvitarism: a Terran monotheistic neo-religion partially based on perceived **Amalgamation** religious practices, and partially on the writings of a pre-Contact author and philosopher. It is registered in every Great Power as a non-inimical religion, with no restrictions on expression or proselytizing.

Jefferson: One of the four **Colony Worlds** assigned to Earth as part of the cultural Uplift program originally created by the **Amalgamation**. Jefferson is a little larger than Earth, with a gravity rating of .95G. Oxygen levels are slightly elevated. Jefferson's terrain is predominantly forest or plains, with fewer mountains and almost no deserts. Most of the usable land area is in the temperate zones. The day is 23 Terran hours long, with a year of 381 local days.

Jefferson was primarily colonized by the pre-**Consolidation Wars** predecessors of the United States of North America (USNA) and the Southeast Defense Association (SEDA). Both **Great Powers** deported a remarkable number of dissidents during their respective authoritarian periods. Today, the USNA and SEDA are engaged in a long-term project to regain influence with the planetary government. While the planet is officially still being 'advised' by the S/CI, Jefferson is effectively a fully autonomous democratic republic.

The Process: An automated cultural and technological Uplift program, designed to shepherd new species into full integration with the **Amalgamation**. The Process was originally designed to act as a combination of teacher, research guide, information source, and general adviser to its charges. The Process claims to be non-sapient, despite its ability to pass every Turing test that humanity has created.

The Process first contacted humanity in the 21st century, after the first successful FTL flight. It was automatically activated, without most of the informational databases that would normally be provided to it. It is unclear whether the databases were destroyed, or never installed. In either case, The Process is as ignorant of the destruction of the Amalgamation as humanity is, and can provide only basic help in deciphering Galactic technology and culture.

The Amalgamation installed the main nexus of The Process on Pluto, in 1459 AD. Smaller, autonomous shards of The

Process are present in a selected number of planetary settlements. Most ships are not large enough to handle the power requirements of an autonomous shard.

There is a very small, but stubbornly persistent faction of the human population that does not trust The Process.

Ritual Nihilists: semi-organized cultists that operate throughout the Tomb Worlds. They are invariably murder addicts with no meaningful sense of self-preservation, and cannot be relied upon to act in an ethical manner. Most organizations have declared Ritual Nihilists as outlaws, to be dealt with as wolves are.

Survey/Colonization Initiative: This non-governmental organization was created in 2112 to regulate various colonization efforts. The SCI tracks which planets are easily available for human colonies, makes sure that those colonies survive and thrive, and handles both voluntary and involuntary transportees. The S/CI also serves as a judiciary for all of the **Colony Worlds** except Jefferson, and directly administers the **Grey Colonies**.

The S/CI's main headquarters is located in Canberra, SEDA; it maintains regional offices on all Colony Worlds and Grey Colonies.

Space-Happy: a colloquial term for Sudden-Onset Violent Psychosis (SOVP), a theoretically non-contagious condition most commonly found on the **Tomb Worlds**.
- *Cause*: unknown.
- *Preliminary symptoms*: increased self-isolation, reduced levels of communication, reduced self-care.
- *Patients in the grips of a SOVP episode display the following traits*: homicidal monomania, sadistic behavior, hysterical strength, extreme pain tolerance, and self-mutilation.
- *Treatment*: patients with SOVP respond well to antipsychotic medication, coupled with intense psychological

counseling after rationality has been restored.

Regular psychological counseling (both individual and group) and mandated socialization has been demonstrated to severely reduce the number of cases per standard year.

Terrorism: Terrorism in the Tomb Worlds is a group affair, primarily aimed against colonization and exploration efforts. These groups were formed during mass psychosis events during the early exploration of the Tomb Worlds, and persist to this day. They are fanatics with an inherent instinct for violence, and should be considered deadly dangerous. Terrorist groups in the Tomb Worlds use a variety of lethal methods to discourage certain projects or objectives; most have demonstrated a willingness to use weapons of mass destruction, when appropriate. Notable terrorist groups include the League of the Viridian Triangle, the Order of Truth, the *Bureau Désavoué*, and the Galactic Pioneer Scouts.

While often conflated with Ritual Nihilists, neither terrorist groups nor RNs will willingly associate with each other.

Tomb Worlds: An informal designation for a formerly-populated planet of the **Amalgamation**. Tomb Worlds have significant ruins, in various stages of disrepair: the local environment may or may not be compatible with Terran biochemistry. The current best estimate of the number of Tomb Worlds is five thousand, five hundred and seventeen. Humanity has officially visited two hundred and thirty-five of them. WARNING: No Tomb World is completely safe for human settlement! Do not engage in reckless behavior!

XHum: a megacorporation (HQ: Reagan City, **Jefferson**) founded in 2095 AD by American and Hong Kong entrepreneurs. Corporate legend asserts that the founders (Claire Hedwig and Talia Sung) bribed S/CI to transport themselves, selected employees, their families, *and* considerable amounts of technological and industrial equipment to **Jefferson**. The new company rapidly expanded, eventually dominating Jefferson's orbital and system infrastructure. In 2102, XHum was the first extrasolar megacorporation to successfully pass the criteria needed to operate in the Tomb Worlds.

The megacorporation concentrates on commercial exploration and exploitation of the **Tomb Worlds**, with an emphasis on salvage archeology. It currently employs over a hundred and fifty thousand people, openly operates on six Tomb Worlds, and has gray bases on a dozen more. XHum is considered the gold standard for employee working conditions in the Tomb Worlds.

1

ACKNOWLEDGEMENTS

As always, I'd like to thank my alpha readers Micheal LaReaux and Jeff Weimer for their help with the book, as well as Sheryl Sahr for her long-running support. I'd also like to thank Joey Blabaum for his generous contribution during the Kickstarter, which earned him naming rights on one of the characters. Said character ended up being more important to the plot than expected, but I'm sure he won't complain about that.

Then there's my long-suffering editor, Wednesday Burns-White. I'm tempted to put in a random semicolon or two into the text here, just for old times' sake, but I shall resist. Jude Stopford did the art for this, and it came out great.

Lastly, and as always: my thanks to my wife and family, who are always supportive of what I do. It's over! ...**For now**.

ABOUT THE AUTHOR

Moe Lane

Moe Lane is a husband and father of two who also writes fantasy, horror, and (now) science fiction. This is his fourth novel in as many years, which bemuses even him.

BOOKS BY THIS AUTHOR

Covenants

This four-story chapbook includes the short story "Tour of Duty," set in the same universe as Ghosts on an Alien Wind!

Frozen Dreams

Frozen Dreams is going to be the best post-apocalyptic high urban fantasy pulp detective novel you will read today! Join Shamus Tom Vargas as he Clears a murder Case in Cin City, capital of the magical kingdom of New California. It's his job; in fact, you might say it's his calling.

Tinsel Rain

Sequel to Frozen Dreams, Tinsel Rain returns us to the post-apocalyptic world of Cin City, glittering tinsel crown of the Kingdom of New California. When an old not-quite-friend of Shamus Tom Vargas is found dead, Tom gets pulled into a case of murder, magic, and mystery! Sinister archmages! Bodies in alleys! An actual high-speed car ride! And as many bad jokes as the author could cram in!

Made in the USA
Middletown, DE
03 September 2024